SHADOW AGENDA

IAN LOOME

DEDICATION

To the survivors out there.

INDEX
Chapter 1 …7
Chapter 2 …13
Chapter 3 …20
Chapter 4 …31
Chapter 5 …45
Chapter 6 …62
Chapter 7 …67
Chapter 8 …73
Chapter 9 …81
Chapter 10…100
Chapter 11…102
Chapter 12…108
Chapter 13…116
Chapter 14…121
Chapter 15…129
Chapter 16…144
Chapter 17…153
Chapter 18...160
Chapter 19...164
Chapter 20...166
Chapter 21...169
Chapter 22...185
Chapter 23...189
Chapter 24...201
Chapter 25...209
Chapter 26...213
Chapter 27...221
Chapter 28...228
Chapter 29...232
Chapter 30...247
Chapter 31...266
Chapter 32...274
Chapter 33...284
Chapter 34...296
Chapter 35...315

Chapter 36...328
Chapter 37...337
Chapter 38...344
Chapter 39...350
Chapter 40...357
Chapter 41...362
Chapter 42...370
Chapter 43...379
Chapter 44...389
Chapter 45...395
Chapter 46...402
Chapter 47...410
Chapter 48...418
Chapter 49...424
Chapter 50...432
Chapter 51...437
Chapter 52...441
Epilogue...447

SEPT. 18, 2009 LIMA, PERU

The familiar-looking man seemed nervous, fidgety.

He was in his thirties, with short black hair and a wide, angular face, his cheekbones pronounced, his nose thin and his eyes dark. He was dressed unstylishly in black sweatpants, white Nikes, and a denim jean jacket, and he had a small purple-and-black carry-on bag on his lap that said "Puma" down one side in white vinyl lettering.

He sat with his knees close together and his hands on the bag, alone in a row of five red plastic chairs, each attached to another by a long black metal bar that ran across the backs of the seats. The bus depot was expansive, maybe fifty yards from one end to the other, and lit to tolerable levels, neither bright nor dark.

It was nearly seven o'clock at night, and most of the seats were empty, because most of the long-distance buses were done for the day. The handful of people in the waiting room kept to themselves. A few people shuffled by the small kiosk in the center of the station, glancing over as if a fervent desire for coffee and a quick read might prompt its operator to reopen.

It was a typical night but the man with the Puma bag was nervous nonetheless, and sat worrying about what might lie ahead once the long coach-style bus was rolling along coastal and mountain roads, lanes seemingly too narrow for two vehicles and dropping off into impenetrable brush hundreds of feet below.

He knew he had a role to fulfill, a purpose. The familiar-looking man fixated on the idea; it gave him a sense of reassurance he needed to go through with his task. His family had been part of the cause for as long as he could remember, and the cause would always provide a role. But he did not know exactly what that role would be. They'd made it clear that he couldn't know, that there might be consequences and his bravery might be pushed beyond normal human limits. That he might fail.

And so he sat, thousands of miles from home, surrounded by people he did not know, heading towards a destiny shrouded in fear and uncertainty.

But he was resigned to it. The dream of freedom for his homeland was one he shared with everyone he knew: his family and friends; his mother Khoka, elderly before her time, stooped, her heavy features always a little sadder than they should be; his fiancée Ekaterina, so serious and political, her dark hair pulled back tightly against her pale white skin and narrow face, her eyes grey-blue pools.

The overhead lights were several dozen feet above him and the station was air conditioned to room temperature, maybe even a bit chilly for most people. But he was sweating. The beads clung to his hairline. He briefly raised a denim-clad arm from his lap to wipe them away. Seconds later, new beads replaced them.

In the plastic row of seats opposite his, a little girl of five sat watching him. She was in her Sunday best, a red dress and pinafore over a white blouse and white stockings. Her shoes were shiny patent leather, and they dangled a half-foot above the ground. She watched him sweat for a few minutes, her young mind trying to assess why he looked different from other people; then she tugged on her mother's shirtsleeve, to her right. Her mother was in her early forties, a serious-looking woman with a pinched face and straw blonde hair. She wore a sensible grey dress and white blouse and she was reading a nearly day-old edition of El Comercio, newspaper pages spread wide in her hands.

The familiar man watched the little girl lean over to ask her mother a question, whispering loudly; not loudly enough for him to hear, but accompanied by a little sideways glance that told him he was the subject.

"Be quiet, Pili," the woman said softly in Spanish. "It's not polite to stare, little one." And then, perhaps with motherly concern or perhaps just plain curiosity, the serious woman stole a quick look herself, and saw a pasty-looking young man with a carry-on bag. *Probably gets sick on long bus rides*, she thought. Then she went back to her newspaper, and Pili went back to staring at the familiar man.

She didn't know why he was familiar. She was too young to understand a memory from a day earlier of his face, from when she walked through the living room to get her dolly, past the television and his oversized image on the news. He had a beard in the television picture and had been wearing an olive-colored military style cap. But there was enough of him in front of her for Pili to know he seemed familiar and, by default, interesting.

3.

A passenger about the same age as the familiar-looking man came over to sit with the woman and little girl. Her father, probably. He was thin and his jeans had been ironed; they had stiff creases down the front of each leg. His cream-colored buttoned-down shirt had a faint line pattern to it and his light blue jacket was collarless, a nineteen eighties style. He had a trio of paper cups in a cardboard tray and handed one to his wife and another to his daughter.

"Make sure she goes before she gets onboard," the woman told him. She made no other comment and did not thank him, the familiar man noticed, but instead merely sipped her coffee. Pili held her smaller cup of hot chocolate between her tiny two hands, her eyes wide as she slurped at the sugary cocoa beverage. The father sat down next to them in the last seat in the row, the little girl between them but hardly the only reason they were separate. The mother read her paper, and he stared ahead, and the familiar man wondered for a moment what fate lay in store for them.

Further along to their right, across from the next set of five red plastic chairs, a couple in their seventies was watching as Pili's mother ordered a bathroom run. The couple chuckled and stared at the little girl through squinting smiles; the elderly woman had blue-rinsed white hair, pushed up in a bun, and gold-rimmed glasses; her husband was heavyset, balding, with a moustache and spectacles that had square brown metal frames. The little girl frowned, embarrassed. She tried to tuck her head behind her mother's left arm, behind the newspaper and away from prying eyes.

The familiar-looking man watched the elderly couple for a moment. But once they'd finished observing the girl, they sat in an uncomfortable silence for a full minute, before the woman finally said, in a strangely thick accent, 'It will be so nice to get back home to Ayacucho, see if my plants are still alive." She spoke like a rural peasant to the ear of the average Lima resident; but that mattered little to the familiar looking Chechen, who spoke halting Spanish at best.

2.

The old man fished a piece of gum from the pocket of his green coat. He unwrapped it unsteadily, his hands shaking about as much as anyone would expect after a long life. Then he looked around for a garbage can to put the wrapper in. The nearest was next to two women, standing at a bar-height grey laminate shelf. It ran along the tinted floor-to-ceiling windows, overlooking the line of buses. The woman nearest to him was in her twenties, black, with red tints in her long, curly hair braids. She was tall, like a model, dressed in business attire; her friend was shorter, blonde haired despite her dark skin tone, wearing a blouse and skirt. They saw him approach and stepped away, and the old man threw the gum wrapper into the bin. The tall black girl smiled at him, and he smiled back, secretly proud of the attention, even if, at his age, it was for different reasons. The old man had observed long before then that, as he'd gotten older, young women tended, once again, to treat him as if he were a cute kid.

"I understand the gum thing," the tall businesswoman said. "My ears plug up when we get into the mountains."

"Not mine," the old man said with entirely false bravado. "I just like gum." There. That sounded pretty suave, the old man thought. He tried to smile rakishly as he said it. They giggled a little at the comment, although he knew deep down that once again it was because he was the wrong type of cute.

The perspiring, nervous man from the television watched the old man walk back to his wife and sit down sullenly next to her. "Well, I still find you quite manly, Jorge," the woman said quietly, in a tone that was more like a clinical assessment than a joke or a supportive gesture. A few minutes earlier, they'd shared a humorous moment at the little girl's expense, so the familiar man knew the elderly couple had that special connection, that connection he had with Ekaterina.

His jaw hurt. The swelling had gone down as the anaesthetic had worn off. But it still felt like he'd been punched by a brick. He kept his hands on the carry-on.

Across from him, little Pili stared at the bag. Then she stared at him. Then at the bag. Then she tugged on her mother's sleeve again, her feet kicking slightly, the overhead lights glinting brightly off her shoe tips. She just wanted to tell her that the man with the bag looked sick; but her mother wasn't interested.

Above, a tinny speaker announced the bus was ready for boarding.

3.

The familiar-looking Chechen man found a seat near the back, as instructed, and sat down. He placed the purple-and-black carry-on under the seat ahead of him. It was late, and the bus was two-thirds empty.

The old couple was seated across the aisle. The driver, a large man, looked tired, half leaning on the gigantic steering wheel. He couldn't restrain a yawn as the people filed by. The familiar young man could see the creases around the older man's eyes, the tell-tale signs of a different kind of fatigue, the weight of life experience.

The Chechen was nervous, frightened of the gravity placed upon his assignment.

He was frightened too by the amount of money they'd promised his family. It made him wonder what was in the bag. He knew well enough not to try and find out. But that just made him want to try even more. He knew what his rebel compatriots were capable of in their bid for world attention. He wondered whether he'd ever see Ekaterina again, or whether…

He looked at the bag under the chair again. Perhaps it was nothing nefarious, just something highly secret, a basic courier job. But he didn't think so. He'd waited in the safe house for three days, as they'd instructed. He'd huddled in the dark, with no television or radio or internet. By the third day he'd begun to feel ill, nearly constantly nauseated. He'd taken to chewing car sickness pills like they were candies.

The little girl was in the seat behind him. Her mother had buckled her in already, so he didn't have to worry about her kicking the seat, assuming her tiny legs could reach. "Mommy," she said. "Mommy, mommy, mommy, mommy…"

Her mother was talking to her father but broke away. "What, honey?"

"When we get … when we get home…"

"Yes?"

"When we get home, can I meet a prince?" Pili asked earnestly.

"You never know dear," her mother said. "There aren't many princes around these days. They aren't seen in public very much."

"What's 'in public'?"

"That means outside, walking around with ordinary people."

The familiar-looking Chechen rebel couldn't help but smile. He thought about his niece Aybika, about the same age as the little girl. It was worth living for, that laugh; able to bring joy to people who saw nothing but hardness. His sister Polla, Aybika's mother, was the same way. When she laughed it had a chime to it, a crystal ring, bell-like and wonderfully pronounced.

The driver walked the aisle, ensuring everyone was ready and that no one was smoking, a rule they all knew would be ignored by someone on board within the first hour. He returned to his seat and shifted the double-clutch coach into reverse, slowly turning the wheel as it did so, then proceeding towards the main road.

In the seats just ahead, the two businesswomen were talking, trying to sound like old hands at traveling, though both were too young to qualify. "…just hate Lima. It's so crowded and expensive, and the people are always so cynical about everything," the black girl said.

"But it's a big market for us," her friend said. "If we lock this down, we could both be in management before we're thirty."

The Chechen tried to follow the conversation but it was difficult; he had to think of the phrase first in Spanish, then think of the version in his own language, and it still did not feel natural, despite months of practice. But it was obvious that they were not important; important people flew, and avoided multi-hour bus rides.

Soon the bus was rolling at highway speed, following the curvy road that ran out of the city and south along the coast. They would follow it for several hours before turning up into the mountains. The mountain passes were steep, narrow and slow-going, and the trip would take nearly seven hours all told.

The familiar-looking man tried to breathe deeply and slowly but his nerves were betraying him. He wanted to go to the bathroom and vomit. He didn't want to use the little paper sack they provided in the seat pocket. That was unseemly and embarrassing. But he feared that he would soon be left without a choice. He'd run out of the anti-nausea pills. He felt himself perspire heavily, but the droplets were cold, almost icy. The nausea hit him again and he fought it down, prayed for the strength to keep his dinner down.

"You okay sweetie?" the straw-haired mother asked little Pili.
"Yes, mama!" Pili volunteered.
"You want to listen to Doodlebugs?"
"Uh huh."

The Chechen smiled again, feeling a small sense of hope. A sense that maybe he had been paranoid, cynical. Perhaps he'd just caught a virus. That would explain the sweating, the difficulty keeping food down. He turned his head slightly to the right and watched the old couple, who were both trying already to go to sleep. The old man had a mask on and a blanket over his lap. He appeared about to fall asleep, the familiar-looking Chechen thought, when he quickly removed the gum from his mouth and placed it…somewhere. His hands went into the pocket of the seat ahead of him, and the on-looking Chechen assumed – hoped – there was a wrapper in there, too.

The little girl was laughing at the Doodlebugs' song, giggling the way only little kids can, with pure joy; he wondered whether she'd ever reach the same ripe old age as the old man with the gum and the bravado. For the first time in many months, the Chechen felt optimism.

The explosion ripped through the rear end of the bus, obliterating the back end in a second. The gigantic ball of flame ignited its fuel tanks, the air inside the passenger cabin instantly hot enough to cook the travellers where they sat, a column of flame descending on them before they even had time to scream.

The hot gases expanded rapidly outwards, ripping the bus to millions of pieces in violent combustion, scattering the remains like tin confetti, along with those of the little girl and her mother, and her father, and the two nicely dressed businesswomen, and the charming old couple, and the weary, overweight bus driver and the nervous, sweating Chechen. The blast flung the debris for a mile, most of it crashing over the edge of the roadway to the Pacific Ocean below, the carnage partially obscured by dense, black smoke.

2./

MEDELLIN, COLOMBIA, SEPTEMBER 16, 2012
THREE YEARS LATER

It had been over a hundred degrees since noon, and Walter Lang was sweating profusely as he sat on the café patio; it was filled with young businessmen and women eager to grab a salad or sandwich before returning to the office.

The armpits of his tan-colored short-sleeve dress shirt were quickly stained through; the odd rivulet of perspiration made its way from his hairline, down past his left ear and into his matted, sweaty chest hair. It had been years since he'd been to Medellin but the heat certainly hadn't gotten any easier to take. The city was charming, welcoming despite the nation's sometimes negative reputation for vice and violence. But he was thankful he'd gotten a hotel room with a near-industrial strength air conditioner.

He wore a pair of Ray Ban aviators with steel rims, to ward off the sun and maintain a low profile, just another Gringo businessman. At fifty-six, Lang knew he was too old to be called middle-aged and when he looked in the mirror, he saw a face creased by time, the skin taut; but he still had most of his hair and it was mostly still brown, a fact in which he took a degree of pride. It wasn't that he was normally a prideful man, quite the contrary; it was the very fact that Lang was so private that made him that little bit more self-conscious when someone actually checked him out.

Not that that had happened on the patio, where the local women all seemed to have walked off of a Vogue cover or out of a Bond movie, all curves and tans and perfect lips.

In movies, he thought, the spy always gets the girl. More typically, Lang knew, he just picked up the check.

3.

Lang looked at his aging steel-banded Seiko watch every few minutes, nervous as the locals hustled and bustled along the adjacent city street. It had been so long, he thought, so long away from this part of the game. The conventional wisdom was that once you were out of the field, you were out of the field. There had to be good reasons for that, Lang thought. It was a pragmatic industry. Maybe he was biting off more than he could chew; maybe it was a young man's game. Maybe, maybe, maybe…

He polished off most of another bottle of water, its blue plastic cold, flecked with drops of moisture. He scanned the adjacent street in both directions again, trying to spot someone out of place among the crowds of lunch-going workers, tourists, local young women out shopping. But it was bustling and busy, the roadway loud and congested with vehicles.

He didn't spot the man until he'd already entered the restaurant; he was short, with dark curly hair and a wispy beard, wearing a white summer shirt and tan trousers. He immediately approached Lang's table.

"Pardon," the man said in Spanish. "But would you happen to know when the weather will cool off?"

"Only in the northern hemisphere," Walter replied fluently. "I'm not from around here."

The man smiled at the confirmation code. He pulled out the plain wooden chair and took a seat across the small square table from the American. A middle-aged, balding waiter in a black vest and bow tie spotted them and came over to get the man's order before they could begin to talk, and the man asked for a bottle of Costena, a local beer. Once the waiter had left, the new arrival leaned forward, resting slightly on his forearms so that they could speak softly and still hear one another.

"You're late," Lang said.

"It's Medellin," the man said. "Nobody gets anywhere on time these days."

It was true, Lang thought; the city's rebirth in the wake of the suppression of the drug cartels had led to increased investment, increased visitors, increased traffic. Already a busy city of more than three million, the sidewalk and street congestion looked a lot like parts of D.C.

His new friend looked around the patio several times, nervously assessing whether he knew anyone there or even recognized any faces. A few glanced back; at least one or two young women looked stern, deliberately off-putting, just in case he had the wrong idea. "But you should be grateful: I'm taking a big enough risk just sitting here with you."

"We're paying you well every month, Enrique, and so far with little-to-no return on that investment." It wasn't a real issue, Lang knew. The few thousand the man received was nothing to the agency.

2.

"I know, I know," he said. "But let's be honest with each other: the cartels have ears everywhere here. They may be taking the brunt of the army and police efforts right now, but that does not mean they've lost their ability to deal with problems, yes?"

Walter leaned across the table slightly for emphasis. He wasn't a big man – maybe five-eleven and a hundred and sixty pounds – but he wanted his point understood the first time. "When you contacted us and told us you could provide information, we made it clear that the consequences of not doing so after taking our money would be difficult for you. Do you understand that? Do you know what I'm telling you?"

The contact leaned back slightly in his chair, looking either worried or like his ego was bruised; Lang wasn't sure which. It didn't really matter, as long as he understood the implied threat.

"That's very easy for you to say, my friend," Enrique said. "But you do not live here day in and out. The cartels' reign may be over for the most part..." He checked the room again, trying not to be obvious, "...but anyone who is not afraid nonetheless is a fool. The last time I checked, your people were not inclined to cut a man's ears and tongue off. Or worse."

Lang knew what to expect next; a veteran handler, he had volunteered for the assignment despite a decade away from field work. But some things didn't change; when a source was delaying, humming and hawing about the agreement, it was usually a pretence to ask for more money. They nearly always asked for more, eventually.

"You've brought what I need?" Lang demanded.

"No, not here. Too public," The man said. Lang gave him a stern, questioning look, but the smaller man motioned with both hands for patience. "Don't worry, don't worry, I have all of the material. But like I said..." Enrique glanced around the restaurant again, settling on the waiter near the bar as he glanced their way, "... eyes and ears everywhere."

"We had an agreement. Time, place, hand over, done."

"And this is fine for you, Señor," the contact said. "But Medellin is a lot more expensive these days. Rents are going up; food is expensive and I have a large family to feed..."

"Get to the point."

"I need another five thousand dollars." Enrique stared intently as he said it, trying to gauge how the request was being taken.

"Out of the question."

"Then three thousand. I have a little girl; she needs surgery on her foot to walk properly, so that the other children do not tease her. She is my world."

He was an amateur, Lang thought, revealing such a personal detail -- or a liar; given his family's money, probably the latter. There was no way David would authorize the spend in any case, and Lang couldn't contact him to try; he was there off the books, unofficial, deniable. The Colombians, usually eager to work with America on narcotics suppression, had been surprisingly uninterested in their potential source. The agency wasn't willing to give up an inroad quite so easily. Privately, a night earlier in his hotel room, he'd looked out over the city lights and wondered just which set of desk jockeys was making the wrong call; if it was the Colombians, then okay. If the Colombians had good reason to doubt Enrique? Then he had his own reasons to worry.

"Enrique, you push this and your little girl might find herself growing up without a father," he said. "That's not my call. But there are people above me who believe in enforcing obligations. And you owe us." He hoped it had a double meaning to the man, if he was setting Lang up; he hoped it sounded like they'd come looking for payback.

So long away from all of this. He was beginning to remember that anxious feeling, the feeling that had prompted him to get out of the field in the first place; it was a sensation of constant vulnerability, that no one could be trusted. He glanced over the short, stocky man's head at the other patrons, looking for anything out of place but seeing average customers, friendly exchanges.

"Okay. A thousand, then," Enrique said. "For one thousand more, we'll exchange, you go about your business; I fade away until you need me again."

Lang considered the request. It had taken two years to recruit Enrique, whose brother was a Barranquilla cartel insider, a former hit man and lieutenant fronting legitimate businesses to launder the Antonio Villanueva cartel's money. They chose the larger city of Medellin because the attention from authorities was lower after the enforcement successes of recent years.

Another chance at Villanueva wouldn't come again anytime soon, Lang thought, and the drug lord was, by all indications, the largest supplier of cocaine to the U.S. west and southwest. So an extra thousand he could handle; it was half his remaining petty cash for the op, but there wasn't much else to spend it on. He was scheduled to be on a plane home in less than twelve hours.

"Fine... but only because we appreciate the risk you've taken," Lang said. "Where and when?"

2.

"We go now," Enrique said, "while everyone is working in my community." He lived in a modest neighbourhood in Bello, just north of the city, called Quintas De La Cabanita. Lang had read his file, committed his home's location to memory, as well as that of his wife's workplace, his children's school. He hadn't seen anything in there about a daughter with a club foot.

"We can take my motorcycle," Enrique said, nodding across the street.

"No, I'll follow in my car," Lang said. He hadn't been on the ground in Colombia for twenty years, but he knew better than to go anywhere while on assignment without first having an exit plan. "Write down the address in case I lose you."

Enrique glanced furtively around the café one more time, just to ensure no one was paying more attention than seemed normal. Then he took the chrome ballpoint desk-set pen out of his top pocket and scribbled the address on a paper napkin, before sliding it across. "It is humble," he said, "but a proud neighbourhood."

Lang checked the address; it was the same as the one in the file. Again, he wondered why a cartel lieutenant's brother was living in a modest suburb. It was core training to trust the intel he was getting from Langley, but his personal experience told him that analysis from a distance wasn't always that reliable. He put the napkin in his breast pocket and nodded.

"Okay," Enrique said. "Let's go."

They left the café and crossed busy Calle 10A, to where both had parked; their spaces were about thirty yards apart. Enrique's motorcycle was an ancient Honda, perhaps a 250 cc; it had been fastidiously maintained, its black paint job gleaming as if it had just rolled off a 1968 showroom floor. "Stay right behind me," he told Lang as they crossed the street. "It's easy to get separated here."

"No," Lang said. "I'll follow but you won't see me. I'll be well back." As risky as taking Enrique's offer of a ride might have been, the most common trap laid for kidnap victims locally was to have them follow closely, then cut them off in both directions with vehicles at an appropriately quiet intersection, eliminate any chance of escape.

They reached his car. "Are you certain?" Enrique said. "It is a difficult route..."

"I'm sure," Walter said nodding towards the bike. "Get going."

The drive took a half-hour and traffic was heavy throughout, the roads meandering up and down the mountain city's undulating terrain. Instead of following the main highway that ran through the center of town, Enrique led Walter on a less-travelled route through older neighbourhoods to the northwest, then back northeast to Quintas de la Cabanita. They followed the two-lane Rua Echeverrí as it sloped down into a trendy neighbourhood of pastel-colored homes, past a monolithic multi-hued, gray-brick, architect-designed cathedral, its curved roof in old wood, like a miniature take on the Sydney Opera House. The road seemed crammed with yellow taxis, like Manhattan at rush hour, right up until it turned into Calle 58 and traffic thinned somewhat, merging onto the freeway "El Regional." Then they moved into a poorer neighbourhood and the cars were replaced by small motorcycles and scooters, many of the same vintage as Enrique's ride.

Lang stayed back as he'd promised he would do, judging the pace and flow of traffic, keeping an eye out for sudden movements, for people switching lanes around him or weapons being drawn by motorcycle passengers, anything that might indicate he'd been compromised. Enrique exited quickly from the left side of the freeway onto Calle 80, past the three-story red-brick morgue and adjoining cemetery to their right, then up a hill and back into the palm- and elm-tree-lined residential neighbourhoods. They zig-zagged through a series of industrial parks before turning back to the north, then the northeast, passing the Sena De Pedegral technology center, then up parallel to the highway into Bello. Lang glanced at the rearview mirror. He could see the far south extreme of the city as it sloped back up the mountainside, the view partially obscured by shadows from the clouds just above.

Quintas was the kind of old neighbourhood that in most U.S. cities would be gentrified, restored by people who liked old things and had lots of money to keep them from falling apart. The houses were smaller, older, mostly made of cinderblocks. Some portions of the area were rundown while others seemed middle-class, normal. As with much of the city, a long-term casualty of poverty was paint: many of the homes and businesses were simply cemented together in shades of brick red or gray, unadorned by anything except splatters of mortar. The houses were set close together, without yards, roadways in front and alleyways behind.

2.

Enrique turned left down a side street, between a small community store with a blue awning advertising meats and groceries, and a row of homes. Then he turned right, onto a long alleyway that ran off as far as Lang could see. There were trees and a mesh fence to the left, buildings to the right. Lang followed cautiously five cars behind, almost losing him on the quick alley turn, stepping on the brakes of the rented Toyota just before passing the entrance, seeing the motorcycle a hundred yards along. He turned the wheel and pointed the car down the alley.

He wasn't ten yards in when the truck screeched to a halt behind him, blocking the entrance. Another backed out of a space behind one of the houses, ten yards ahead, boxing him in exactly as he'd worried might happen if he followed too closely – and if Enrique had sold him out.

Lang reacted on instinct, getting out of the car quickly, not even bothering to close the door, sprinting towards a gap between the houses that backed onto the alley, recognizing his need to flee the trap before it closed all of the way. He looked back for a split second to see if anyone was pursuing him, just as a larger man in a red-and-white striped vest stepped out of the bush carrying an assault rifle, an AK-47 knockoff. The butt slammed into the side of Lang's head and he went down hard, his mind swimming.

He tried to stagger to his feet, blinking through the haze. He saw Enrique running towards him, the sky beyond a grey, cloudy smudge. "See!" Enrique yelled, looking past him to someone else. "I told you that you could trust me!" A pistol fired twice, the report just a few feet behind Lang and loud. The bullets' momentum stopped Enrique's progress, and he collapsed in a bundle. Walter tried to turn his head, to see where the sound had come from; his last glimpse was a dark shadow from the butt of the assault rifle as it came down hard one more time.

3./

OCTOBER 10, 2012, WASHINGTON, D.C,

The funeral parlour chapel was small and plain, a long aisle from the door separating the eighteen rows of nearly empty wooden pews; it had whitewashed walls and a terracotta tile floor, beams of light streaming in from a pair of stained glass windows on the west wall as the attendees listened to the pastor at the pulpit.

Two dozen people in mourning divided themselves between the first three rows on each side of the aisle, a mixture of men and women, one child, a boy of about ten.

Joe Brennan had been quiet throughout the short service, not meeting with the widow and son when he arrived or offering condolences; he knew they didn't want to hear from another former SEAL. He rocked on his heels slightly, hands held together uncomfortably in front of him as the pastor spoke.

If it hadn't been for his time in the service, they probably would state, Bobby would still be alive. It had been his widow Bea's mantra since Bobby's suicide ten days earlier, and it was probably true. Brennan turned his head perhaps five degrees, searching her out with his peripheral vision. She wasn't crying, but her bottom lip pouted out slightly and her eyes were dark bottomless wells of sorrow. He looked away quickly and took a sharp breath, surprised after so many years and so many missions at how upset he felt.

It wasn't that Brennan felt guilty; when they'd served together in Iraq, he recognized right away that there was something a little different about Bobby, that the stress of being over there longer than the rest had unhinged him a little. He took chances he shouldn't have, played the hero when it meant endangering others. He'd barely made it through the nerve-shattering Al Basra assignment. Bobby always had a look, too, a certain nervous tension, a clench-jawed attempt at looking gung ho that shouldn't have fooled anyone.

But it did.

2.

Brennan was never certain when it happened, or how a SEAL with a half-dozen years of experience suddenly lost his nerve. It was before Al Basra, he knew that. It had just been the straw that broke the camel's back. But while others had missed the signs and always put their confidence in their teammate, Brennan had spent many dangerous days in the Gulf watching Bobby out of the corner of his eye.

Knowing something was wrong and being able to do basically nothing to help had worn on him; so no amount of reminiscing could make Brennan feel any less remorseful, any less sad that a good man had died young, taken away by the impact of the Post-Traumatic Stress Disorder that had plagued him for the better part of a decade.

The priest was saying something about God's plan and how Bobby's decision was surely part of it that mere mortals just couldn't understand. Brennan tuned it out again and stared at his shoes for a few moments. It might have been comforting to his family, who were devout, but it wasn't what Brennan wanted to hear. God hadn't taken Bobby for any purpose; Bobby's death was a product of the selfish detachment that came with leadership, sent into places to see and do things no good man should ever see or do. Brennan clung to the knowledge that at least they'd made a difference; at least, he knew, Bobby's legacy wasn't lacking.

"You okay?"

He turned his head slightly and looked up. Callum McLean had spoken softly, tactfully. He was a large man with a blond crewcut. McLean was a good five inches taller than Brennan, six-five in his bare feet, a huge-chested, broad shouldered tank. They'd served together for nearly twenty years; McLean was the kind of team member who kept people alive with his mere presence. Brennan had always tried to tell himself that if Callum was the most talented and strongest guy he knew, he at least had the advantage of speed... but the truth was, Callum was faster than him, too.

"Yeah. Yeah, I'm okay," Brennan said.

"You don't sound it. Or look it. You know we couldn't have done anything about this, right?"

"Huh? Sure, yeah." But Brennan didn't know anything of the sort. Bobby had been along for Al Basra and Brennan had known he was close to cracking, and Brennan had said nothing. He didn't feel guilty, he told himself. Bobby's decision was Bobby's decision, not his.

"Chances are, even if Corcoran hadn't precipitated what went down, he still would've cracked eventually," McLean murmured. He'd known Joe since Great Mistakes, the affectionate name for their Recruit Training. They'd been best friends for nearly two decades, and he didn't deserve to be beating himself up. "Besides none of it was your call."

"The op was my design, my responsibility," Brennan whispered back. They'd been over this before, and the timing wasn't appropriate, he thought.

"But it was Corcoran's call, Corcoran's decision to go off plan. And Bobby's decision to pull the trigger."

Off plan? That was one way to describe it, Brennan thought. "Look, let's just drop this? Okay? We can talk about it later. You know we will anyway."

After the service, McLean waited outside on the broad marble steps that led from the funeral parlour to its parking lot. The attendees slowly filtered out and past him. It was a few more minutes before Brennan appeared, hands in his pockets, staring morosely at his shoes.

"I had to try and say something to them," he said softly. "They were very polite."

"You want to go get a drink?" McLean said. "Some of Bobby's friends from his first team are meeting up at the Old Ebbitt Oyster Bar."

Really? Brennan thought. *They picked a bar full of politicians?* He shook his head. "I don't think so, not today."

"Well… I'm going to head over there pretty much right away."

"Okay. Look, don't worry about me, all right? I'm good. I'm fine."

He didn't look fine, McLean thought. Joe looked like he'd just lost a family member. But he left it at that, knowing that, no matter how tough he felt about things inside, the one comrade he didn't really need to worry about was Joe Brennan. He'd figure things out.

Brennan took the expressway south, his driving automatic, his mind elsewhere as the traffic zipped by his sedan to the suburbs. His phone rang. He used the hands-free button on his wheel to answer.

"Brennan."

"Agent Brennan? It's Jonah Tarrant; David Fenton-Wright's assistant?" He phrased it like a question, unsure if a field agent would be familiar with him. Brennan wasn't exactly inclined to stop by Langley on a regular basis. "Are you busy?"

By busy, Brennan knew, he meant on assignment or working on something of national security interest… which also meant that he already knew the answer, as nobody went into the field anymore without Fenton-Wright's personal approval. The deputy director hadn't been in his post for long but had been with the agency for nearly twenty years all told, and had a fearsome reputation for keeping control over every detail.

"No, just driving home," Brennan said, hoping to cut Tarrant off before the inevitable occurred.

2.

No such luck. "We need you to head on in," Tarrant said. "We've had some difficult news." Once again, "we" meant Fenton-Wright. Brennan considered himself a nuts-and-bolts sort of guy, firm in his convictions and his sense of right and wrong. He wasn't so sure how Fenton-Wright self-assessed.

"Anything more specific?"

"Not on this line. Come on in, Joe, and we'll talk. It'll just be for an hour or so."

That was never good. If they couldn't talk on an unsecured line that meant it was either an assignment for him or bad news about someone else's. Either way, it wasn't the day for it, not after Bobby.

"Look... I'm ten days back from Sri Lanka," Brennan replied. "Do we really have to do this today? If it could wait until tomorrow..."

"It's about Walter Lang," Tarrant said.

He was about thirty miles out. "I'll be there in a half hour," he said, ending the call.

Walter was a staff operations officer, and Brennan had torn a strip off him when he'd said he was going back into the field, even though it seemed unlikely a year earlier that they'd take him up on the offer; he'd been a mentor for Brennan's nine years with the agency, a good man with a solid, sober sense of the importance of what they did for a living, the true value of national security. Beyond that, Brennan just plain liked him.

He stepped hard on the accelerator.

At the agency, he left his car in the guest parking area and walked the short distance to the narrow path that led into the courtyard, across the red brick patio to the glass doors, under the broad glass arch. He stopped at security and got a guest pass, having left his own at home in Annandale, miles away. He clipped it to the front pocket of his black suit, crossing the marble lobby floor with the giant agency seal, passing two sets of grey stone columns before reaching the elevators. It seemed quiet in mid-afternoon, and he shared the elevator car with just one other person, a smiling woman in her fifties with frayed honey-blonde ends and a thickly woven olive-green cotton pant suit; she got off on the second floor. He rode on to the fourth, to the offices of the multi-faceted National Clandestine Service.

Tarrant had been told by security that Brennan was heading up, and he waited at the elevators, a short, plump young man with curly light brown hair, his hands in his pockets out of slight nervousness. Well-regarded for his analytical abilities and grace under pressure, Tarrant nevertheless couldn't help but feel a little inadequate when he ran into guys like Joe Brennan, field agents with a strong track record and no small amount of minor celebrity at the office. He'd seen Brennan's mug in his field services file, but he still didn't have a sense of the man until he met him face to face.

Brennan shook the younger man's hand firmly. "Walter's spoken about you," he said. "It's good to finally meet you, Jonah."

"I wish it were better circumstances. Let's walk and talk." They headed towards the executive offices, through a small series of staffed cubicles, young analysts and officers on headset phones. "You couldn't have known this because it's officially off the books but Walter was on assignment in Colombia."

"Was?"

"He volunteered because of his fluency and because our official hand down there is tied up with bigger things. Walter said he was tired of being chained to a desk and that it was a good lead."

That sounded like Walter, thought Brennan. He'd been complaining for years, even though his retirement from field work was well-earned.

"Walter was never an agent," Brennan said. "He was an Ops officer, a handler."

"Yes," Tarrant said as they walked, choosing his words carefully. "David felt that there was considerable risk in this circumstance and wanted someone who could operate blind. His experience as a handler and later cultivating sources as an SSO ..."

Brennan stopped walking and cut him off. "As I said, Walter was a support player, not ParOps. Did he have any local backup?"

Tarrant shook his head as they began walking again, turning down a narrow corridor past a series of offices, the lights off in most, pressboard doors open but no one home. "The Colombians were... unenthused by the nature of the project." At the end of the hallway, he used his security card to swipe a keypad and the executive offices door unlocked with a quiet click. "But David felt the potential information was too valuable not to have a try. It was relatively low-risk, just a drop from an existing source."

Brennan had been around ambitious types like Tarrant and Fenton-Wright before; he knew better than to say what he was actually thinking… which was that describing a black book, one-man operation in a hostile environment as "relatively low-risk" might have been taking things too lightly from the start. *It certainly wouldn't have been the first time*, he thought; *probably not even the first time this month.*

Fenton-Wright's office was at the back of the section, down a non-descript uncarpeted corridor – something about static electricity and computers -- past a secretary and waiting area, and past two more nondescript offices including Jonah Tarrant's. The deputy director's was large, almost imperious by agency standard, with double doors, a huge copy of the agency's emblem emblazoned into the carpet ahead of his antique desk, a sitting area off to the left. Behind the desk, windows looked out onto the central yard, the day still bright and sunny in the room's muted atmosphere. The secretary ushered them in; Fenton-Wright was seated but rose quickly and walked around the desk to greet them each with a handshake. He had a gray suit on with a white shirt and yellow tie, but his jacket was slung over the back of his desk chair. "Gentlemen," he said. "Thank you for coming. This has been a difficult day for some of us and it isn't going to immediately get easier. Please… have a seat."

Brennan noticed his orange hair had thinned to almost nothing since the last time they'd met in person, three years earlier. Now it was just a neatly trimmed crown, flecked with white. Fenton-Wright had long, thin features, his skin always pink and slightly florid, as if waiting for a skin condition to break out. He'd always struck Brennan as something of a vulture, in both personality and mannerism, his neck slightly too thin for his head, which bobbed forward slightly as he spoke.

He motioned to the two chairs ahead of the desk and they sat. Tarrant crossed his legs uncomfortably, his body language tense. Brennan got the immediate sense Fenton-Wright's bad news went beyond Walter being in a small amount of trouble.

"Joe, I know you're on vacation and I do apologize for having to disturb that; but we felt it important that you hear the news from us first," Fenton-Wright said. "After all, we know you and Walter have been close friends for some time now."

Drop the other shoe already.

"More than that, however, we felt it prudent to remind you of how important it is to keep those with emotional investments away from an operation that has gone badly. We all know full well how emotional attachment can cloud a field agent's judgment, and that's the last thing Walter needs right now."

"What happened?" Brennan asked, trying to get to the point.

"We lost contact with Walter ten days ago in Colombia," Fenton-Wright said. His delivery was flat, emotionless, a pure statement of fact. "He'd agreed to meet with a highly placed source with information on the location and shipping routes of the Villanueva Drug Cartel, as well as the identity of a particularly dangerous forger."

Brennan's diplomacy momentarily went out the window. "You let Walter into the field in Colombia alone, on a narco case?" He didn't actually say 'are you nuts?', because he didn't have to. The tone was sufficient.

"Sometimes I have difficult decisions to make very quickly," Fenton-Wright said. "I won't apologize for that, Agent Brennan. Walter spent nine months in Colombia…"

"Twenty years ago."

"Yes, but that doesn't change the fact that he speaks Spanish like a local, knows the cities in question and knew the risks," Fenton-Wright insisted. "He's a fully trained operative…"

"Twenty years ago," Brennan repeated. "He's been on a desk for the last decade, you know that."

The deputy director had expected resistance. Brennan was the kind of troublemaking know-it-all who would interject with a problem whenever possible. "We're not here to discuss or argue my authority," Fenton-Wright said, his voice toughening. "We're here to ensure that you recognize your responsibilities as a clandestine operations officer, and to reassure that you will not become involved in this matter without my say so."

Tarrant spoke up for the first time. "Your psychological profile suggests you're likely to try and intervene personally on Walter's behalf, Joe," he said. "You know that's unacceptable."

Brennan ignored the implied threat. "Where is he and who has him?"

"Insufficient intel at this time," Fenton-Wright said.

"Do we have boots on the ground looking?"

"As I said, my inclination is for you to not be involved in this. It's too personal. But rest assured, we will do whatever we can within reason to ascertain his safety and see if we can arrange an expedient pull-out." His delivery remained flat, all business.

Brennan stared hard at the man for a moment; he hardly knew Fenton-Wright and had rarely ever dealt with him. His knowledge of office politics was limited to the odd conversation with an ops officer. But he recognized a weasel answer when he heard one. "So you're leaving him there to fend for himself? Is that it?"

"As I said, the details are need-to-know. But rest assured…"

"Sure," Brennan said. He got up to leave.

2.

"Agent Brennan," Fenton-Wright said as he made for the door, "Don't ignore my directive on this."

It wasn't a request, Brennan knew. As he walked out of the office he didn't reply, but he had the urge to tell Fenton-Wright where he could stuff it.

The drive home was uneventful and Brennan tried to keep his mind off the meeting by listening to National Public Radio, a show on the damage to wetlands in the counties bordering D.C. An avid angler, the subject should have been interesting; but he couldn't escape the mental image of Walter shackled in some armpit prison.

There were only two likely options: he'd either been caught by the government and was being worked over before doubtless disappearing into the Colombian penal system; or, he'd been caught by the Cartel, in which case he was being tortured for information or just shot and dumped in the jungle for the wildlife to finish off. An exchange seemed unlikely; U.S. policy didn't look kindly on swapping drug dealers for government employees who weren't supposed to be inside another nation's borders.

Brennan exited at Annandale, the road taking him past a series of new housing developments, six-foot-fenced-in family lots half the size of what they used to be, but with homes that seemed grand compared to those of his youth. It was a nice place to live, and he knew it. He turned onto their driveway, a short strip of asphalt with a car port, adjacent to their nineteen sixties three-bedroom bungalow. They'd been pragmatic about the place; the white siding was new and lifetime guaranteed, there was a big backyard for the kids compared to most new lots and a deck made of pretreated lumber. They planned on living there for a long time, so it had had to be right, with a sunken living room and a nice open plan kitchen adjacent to it, with white cabinets, steel pulls his wife had chosen and black granite countertops.

Carolyn left a note on the counter saying she'd taken the kids to play with Michael, Callum and Ellen McLean's son. Michael had Down syndrome but was such a happy and wonderful child, they'd had no problems convincing their own pre-teen son and daughter that he'd make a good playmate. The note also said Callum was on his way over.

The doorbell rang a few minutes later, just as Brennan uncapped his first beer. He carried the sweating bottle of Michelob to the front door with him.

McLean had brought his fishing rod with him. "Only a few more weeks until winter kicks in," he said, holding it up. "And you looked this morning like you needed a break."

3.

They drove out to Huntsman Lake, past innumerable subdivision crescents, privacy fences and roofs all one could see of them, set against backdrops of dark green trees.

The narrow, oval body of water was cut off from civilization by lines of trees along each side, with road access at each end; the trees gave it the illusion of being away from the rest of mankind. It was stocked, a dam lake that needed to be drained every few years to clean out sediment buildup. But the day was warm, just shy of seventy, and they knew that even if the bass weren't biting, they could still pick off a less-than-cautious catfish or two.

More than that, it would be quiet during the week. The lake was large, and still, and dark, with plenty of shoreline to afford them some privacy. They found a shaded spot under some trees and cast off the bank using night crawlers, the wriggling guaranteed to get the hungry fish interested.

Both men were silent for nearly the entire first hour, just enjoying the solitude, the company, the taste of a cold beer and the slow ripple of the water as it lapped against the shore.

"You know, you look like hell," McLean finally said.

Brennan frowned. Why did Callum pull the big brother routine every time he sensed tension? "I'm fine. Just forget it."

McLean propped his rod against the forked stick he'd buried in the mud for just that purpose. "Bud, how long have we been friends again?"

"Nineteen years, I think. Something like that."

"Yeah... well in nineteen years, the only time I've seen you with that crappy look constantly was when we lost someone in Iraq. And this morning. Like I said..."

"I know," Brennan said. "This isn't about Bobby. Not really, anyway."

"What then?"

"Work."

"Ah." McLean knew he wasn't supposed to ask. They hadn't technically been teammates in years, and he'd only just received his own honorable discharge. But he'd looked on Joe as a "brother from another mother" for so long, he couldn't really help it. "Serious?"

"Deadly. A friend of mine is in trouble."

"In the field?"

"Yeah. Look, it doesn't really matter because I've been warned off. I'm not allowed to get involved."

"Huh," McLean said.

"What?"

"It just reminded me of back in the day." He almost smiled a little when he said it. "You know..."

2.

28

"And… we're back to Bobby," Brennan said. "This isn't like that. Al Basra was a shit-storm. In this case, my friend went into something knowing it was deniable."

McLean watched a hawk circling, looking down on them from hundreds of feet above, no doubt searching for the smallest movements, the instant of a prey's weakness. "The brass won't help the guy?"

"Something like that, although the official word is they're doing all they can."

McLean guffawed at that. "That's a crock of shit line if ever there was one."

"Yeah."

They fished some more, McLean certain for about two exciting minutes that he'd landed a huge one, only to break his line on a tree snag. "Goddamn," he said. "That was ten-pound test."

"Don't yank it so hard when you set the hook and that won't happen," Brennan said. "You just need a quick, sharp pull, just once. They grab the bait and you're good to go."

"I know, I know. Geez, I taught you, not the other way around. I've forgotten more about this lake than a landlubber like you would…"

"I want to go get Walter," Brennan said, interrupting the thought.

McLean let it hang there for a minute. "Okay. Do you have any idea where…"

"No. But I still have some friends in the agency, people who can get me the latest intel."

"Have you talked to Carolyn about this?" Both had been married for almost a decade. Both knew the expectation once they were off the military's clock and calendar, and that their wives were tired of them being gone.

"No, she doesn't know yet."

"Are you going to tell her?" It wasn't because he expected Joe to deceive his spouse; but Carolyn also worked at the agency and had a bright career ahead of her. As a senior analyst she'd be obliged to tell her bosses anything she knew, if he shared details.

"Not the details, just that I'll be gone for a while. She knows what that usually means."

"So she'll assume it's a legitimate operation…"

"And won't worry as much, assuming I have logistical support, yeah."

McLean nodded, but he was thinking down the line. "If she finds out later on at work, she's going to be incredibly pissed."

"Another hill for another day," Brennan said. "Can you help me out with some equipment?"

3.   29

McLean's personal arsenal had grown over the years. He had military spec gear and a few toys beyond, and it didn't require a sign-out or a requisition form. There wouldn't be a paper trail.

"What are you looking for?"

"I'll get you a list when we get back."

McLean's line began to jiggle, shaking the small forked branch. He took control of the rod, waiting a few seconds until he felt a pull, then jerked on the line gently, setting the hook in the fish's mouth. It was fighting hard, for a catfish, squirming and wiggling to free itself, the tip of the rod jerking to each side as the fish tired itself out with the force of its struggle. He let the line slack and let the fish run a bit then cranked the line closed again and halted it sharply before reeling it back. After a couple of more runs, he slowly hauled the exhausted catfish to shore.

It was big, perhaps fourteen or fifteen pounds, maybe thirty inches long. "He's old," Brennan said as they netted it at shore and brought it in. "He looks good."

"He's going to look even better in buttermilk batter, frying in a pan," McLean said, his smile showing the catfish no mercy whatsoever.

2.

4./

OCTOBER 22, 2012, NEAR LOS CEBONES, RURAL COLOMBIA

Brennan lay on his chest. The soil was hard on top of the hill and nearby irrigation diversion kept the grass from growing much. It made it a good spot for reconnaissance. He was propped up on his elbows, paying keen attention through a set of night vision binoculars, the dark plastic against his blacked-over face and hands. The valley was spread out before him, including the compound. It was almost eight o'clock.

The guards were predictable. They followed the same basic movement patterns, from a, to b, to c, back to a. It was natural to them and it had doubtless been a long time since the motions were prescribed, given a real purpose.

The compound was hell-and-gone from anywhere; there were a few other farms around, and a few other compounds. But even the nearest village could only charitably be called occupied.

And the jungle? The jungle was dense and tangled, thick green branches knotted together, an unforgiving mass of perils that required a machete just to gain entry. It was easy, Brennan figured, for a guy making grunt pay to let his guard down a little.

Brennan's eyes tracked the movements. The mansion was at the back of the compound. In front of it was a huge parking area. A barracks – big enough for perhaps twenty men – sat along the left fence, and a pair of thatched huts along the right. One guard stood in front of each hut. There were two more guards at the main gate, another in front of the barracks, two in front of the mansion. Brennan waited patiently. Eventually, a dog and handler circled from behind the barracks, following their usual route. On the other side of the compound, by the huts, another did the same.

He swung the binoculars back to the left; a small whitewashed building made of cinder blocks and a corrugated tin roof sat just outside the left fence, within twenty yards of the jungle tree line.

3.   31

There were no power lines running to the property, isolated as it was, and the handful of solar panels on the mansion roof couldn't supply enough juice for the whole compound, Brennan thought. But diesel generators made noise, the kind of low rumble crooked bastards like Antonio LaJoya Villanueva wouldn't tolerate. Villanueva was worth several fortunes, so he could afford alternatives. They'd built the small concrete building just off the property, where it could annoy as few people as possible.

But it also created a hole in their security.

Brennan crept slowly backwards on his hands and knees until he was part-way down the hill and out of the compound's line of sight. He hadn't seen an exterior perimeter guard or anyone else keeping eyes outside the electric fence, another mistake. He circled slowly around the base of the hill to the thick foliage of the tree line, following it, just out of reach of the thin white glow of the compound's bright lights. The jungle was loud, alive with the hum of cicadas and the odd calls from tropical birds. He moved slowly; the trees were full of potential noisemakers, and a fleeing flock would be like a smoke signal to the guards, so hacking through troublesome vines and branches was out of the question. It was laborious, taking a step, then pushing aside foliage, then extracting his boots from the tangled grass and roots, then repeating the process. It slowed him to a few yards every thirty seconds to a minute, and made the trip of three hundred yards seem like miles.

By the time he checked his watch, twenty-six minutes had passed. It was ten-thirty at night. Brennan crouched low and checked his sight lines.

He checked the roving dog handlers with his binoculars, waiting until their view was obstructed by the barracks. He knew he could come in from the left side of the outbuilding and it would prevent them from getting an open look at him; but the whitewashed concrete accentuated the lighting from the compound, meaning he would have to get inside quickly or risk exposure.

He scoped the lock on the outbuilding door; it looked like a standard padlock, easily defeated with his combination bolt/wire cutters. He took them out of a pocket in his web belt and quickly covered the ground between the trees and the outbuilding wall. Brennan peeked around the corner, ensuring the patrol wasn't near enough to spot him or downwind of his scent. Then he quickly reached around and snipped the padlock, discarding it into the grass.

2.

He opened the door slowly, just wide enough to squeeze inside, then closed it behind him and traded the bolt cutters for his pen light. He had to crouch. The shack was empty save for the generator, a four-feet-by-two-feet metal beast that shuddered and vibrated as it kicked into life. He was relieved nothing had made the shack home; tiny, hot enclosures in the jungle were prime real estate for snakes and spiders. A bite would complicate an already complicated night.

Disabling the generator was necessary because of the lighting in the compound. But doing it loudly would also serve as a fine distraction. The heat inside the shack was extreme and he sweated heavily. He took his pack off his shoulders and withdrew the timed charge, a wad of C-4 hooked up to a small digital clock, a battery and a pair of contact leads. He studied the generator for a moment, looking for the fuel tank. Brennan shuffled around to the back side of the big engine, placing the mouldable explosive on the tank but out of the line of sight of the door, in case the snipped padlock was discovered prematurely.

He moved back to the door and switched off the penlight, then listened for a few moments, shrouded in darkness, trying to ensure there was no one directly outside the cinderblock shed, or perhaps a perimeter patrol that he'd missed. Then he slowly pushed the door open again, just enough to squeeze through, closing the door as he slid back around the corner, out of sight. After another quick, cursory check, he crouched low and headed for the tree line, nerves half expecting the hot sting of a bullet in the back, until he was safely under cover again.

Near the top of the hill, he went back into a prone position, keeping his profile low, until he could safely watch the compound. Brennan swung the binoculars towards the two shacks. They seemed more likely to be holding his target than the barracks building. He zoomed in tight on the first shack's guard, who was sitting on its steps, smoking a cigarette, an AK-47 clone leaning against his right side. The lights were out inside, and even at full magnification, Brennan couldn't see any movement.

The second shack was another matter. The guard there was attentive, at the ready, on his feet and holding his weapon in front of him, scanning the proximity constantly. The light was on inside, and Brennan waited for a sign of life. He was patient, and it took several minutes. But eventually, he saw what looked like a man's head pass from one side to the other of the long, slotted window in the shack's south wall.

Bingo.

3.

He scanned the tree line on the right side. It was slightly closer to the fence but lit up more brightly, partially caught by spotlights on top of the mansion. He backed out of sight again then removed a small case from his pack. He opened it, and took out the three component pieces of the folding sniper's rifle: the barrel with silencer, the breach, and the stock, assembling them quickly and methodically. Then he mounted the rifle onto the small bipod legs to stabilize it. He affixed the powerful scope, checking its range settings against those of his night vision binoculars. He lined the crosshairs up, tracking the attentive guard, keeping the base of his skull in focus. Brennan then swept his field of view slowly across the camp. Near the barracks, a couple of guards were sitting by a camp fire, and Brennan watched the smoke curl and shift and bend, trying to judge its speed and direction, to get a guesstimate within five miles per hour of actual.

He wasn't sure from the smoke, so he traced his perspective back to the jungle, looking for the bend of branches that would indicate a fifteen mile per hour gust. Then he adjusted the scope again to compensate, before swinging his aim back to the guard and refocusing. He removed the detonator from his belt and waited until the roving dog handler was as near to the generator shed end of the barracks as possible. The blast would be too far away to hurt the animal; but its hearing and sense of smell would be almost instantly shot in the rush of noise and column of smoke.

Brennan waited until both guards were facing due north; he kept his right index finger on the trigger, eye to the scope. The tripod allowed him to keep his left hand free and he used it to slowly depress the detonator trigger. He took his time with everything; it had been a difficult few days, and things had to go right.

TWO DAYS EARLIER, BOGOTA

"Let me guess: you were expecting someone with a more... how would you say, 'nefarious' appearance, no?"

Enrique Obregon had agreed to meet Brennan at the airport. He'd been the initial contact on Walter Lang's situation. They'd emailed him after Walter failed to make it home and he'd finally replied, just a day before Brennan's arrival, to say that Walter had never shown up for the meeting.

He'd offered himself as an impromptu guide and advisor when Brennan called him from the arrivals terminal. The agent browsed around the massive duty free store as he waited for Enrique to arrive, settling on a small bar of white chocolate and a copy of Time, paying for both with local pesos. Then Brennan sat back, with his small soft-sided suitcase on the hard moulded-plastic chair next to him, and watched the doors to the road outside.

Twenty minutes later, Obregon had shown up driving an old 1990s model BMW, boxy in chocolate brown. Brennan knew next-to-nothing about him. He'd tapped a few contacts at the agency before leaving and been told Obregon's identity, and that he was a Fenton-Wright golden boy, a local who really wanted to actively work for the agency fulltime and therefore was willing to give them just about anything they asked for.

In Walter's case, it had apparently been his brother, and his brother's employer, a cartel boss named Antonio Villanueva. At the airport, Enrique made straight for Brennan, smiling. He was a tall, thin man, with a wispy moustache, dark hair and dark eyes.

Brennan still had his tan from Sri Lanka, but apparently that wasn't enough to prevent him from standing out from the locals, as his host had no problem picking him out.

The man nodded as he approached, one hand outstretched. "I hear it's windy in Los Angeles these days," he said.

"Give or take the Canadian airflow," Brennan said.

"I'm sorry about your friend," Enrique said genuinely. "Did you know him well?"

"Well enough," Brennan said. "Work is work, though. Am I right?"

"Of course."

"Doesn't pay to make things personal."

"A very healthy perspective, señor," he said. "One I support wholeheartedly; I'm sure you're aware of my circumstances?"

"Sure; you were supposed to meet him at a café downtown and he didn't show," Brennan said. "You bring a car?"

"Yes, a BMW with air conditioning," he said. "Can I take your bag?"

"No, that's fine. I need the exercise."

They began to walk towards the airport doors, the passenger traffic light on a Saturday morning, business commuters mixing with passionate student couples, hitchhiker types with jean shorts and backpacks.

The car was parked illegally at the curb, the platform overhang shading them from the worst of the rising sun.

"Don't you worry about tickets?" Brennan said. His host grinned brightly at him but didn't reply, instead using the car key to open the BMW's trunk. Brennan shook his head. "That's okay. The roads here can be sort of bumpy. I'll just hang onto it."

"Suit yourself," Enrique said. Brennan couldn't tell whether there was a hint of distaste at the decision, but it didn't really matter. Enrique was just a means to an end. The escort walked around to the driver's door and opened it; Brennan opened the opposite back door and got in the backseat. It was brown leather, bucket style.

"What, you're not going to ride upfront, get the lay of the land?" Enrique asked.

"No."

If the local contact expected any more of an explanation, it wasn't forthcoming.

While Enrique started the car and did a shoulder check before pulling out, Brennan quickly went through the bag and unzipped the special liner that disguised its actual content from airport screening; inside, a handful of Callum's weapons were strapped in, each broken into component parts. There was also a small set of thermal imaging binoculars, a digital detonator and two ounces of C-4, enrobed in coffee and dark chocolate then wrapped in thick orange plastic to defeat the explosives sniffer at Dulles.

He withdrew the barrel, slide mechanism and pistol grip for the specially designed Sig Sauer nine-millimeter. Once he'd assembled it he took out the thin nine-shot clip and snapped it into the handle; then he chambered a bullet. Then he unstrapped the small cigar-tube-sized suppressor and screwed it onto the barrel tip.

"I hope that's not for me," Enrique joked nervously, glancing furtively over his shoulder at the operation as he guided the car in and out of traffic.

Brennan said nothing, slipping the pistol into the back of his waist band under his shirt and putting a second clip in his pocket. Then he zipped up the case again. He glanced around at the other traffic, self-conscious in the moment, seeing if anyone else was paying attention. But half the cars were some form or another of cab, in bright yellow, mostly unlicensed he guessed, and the drivers so familiar with the daily grind that they didn't pay much attention to anything anymore, including other cars.

"Did you find me a room? Like I said, I didn't get a chance..."

"I've got you booked in at El Nacional. You'll like it; it's in the tourist part of the city, so there are lots of restaurants and amenities and things."

"I'm not here for a vacation. I'm here to find my friend."

2.

"Si, si, es verdad," the tall man said. "I did not mean anything by it."

The hotel was a functional cement block from the nineteen seventies, maybe fourteens stories, no balconies, each room cooled by old-school window air conditioner units. Unlike hotels back home where suicidal occupants were a worry, the windows obviously opened as more than a few were cracked so that the occupant could lean out and smoke a cigarette.

They parked by the front doors at the curb, ignoring the offer from the doorman to take Brennan's bag. Inside, the double glass doors opened to a white-and-grey-specked marble floor, with large pots containing palms beside the doorway. Past them, a long grey carpet had been rolled out over the marble, no doubt to lessen the damage from years of tourism traffic on the approach to the front desk. The lobby ceiling towered thirty feet above, a glass skylight letting the brightness of day inside.

Enrique nodded at the concierge and led Brennan towards the elevators. "It's an old hand-crank but they had it converted to electric several years back," he said. "Charming, no?"

Brennan remained mute, the elevator creaking as it slowly rose, floor by floor, Enrique smiling and nodding his head, the American's silence unnerving him somewhat. "It is a shame about your friend, but maybe the news will turn out to be okay. Perhaps he simply met one of our lovely young Colombian women…"

The elevator creaked past the ninth floor, then the tenth, Brennan silent, alert and focused on doors. They were old, double sliders with a cage on the inside that had to be opened manually by the passengers. The carriage creaked to a halt on the twelfth floor.

Brennan nodded towards the gate. "After you," he said.

Enrique opened the gate, the cage folding inwards with a squeak; he stepped into the corridor, Brennan right behind him. It smelled musty, like the humidity had gathered in the smoke-riddled blue-flowered carpet. The walls were covered in dusty rose wallpaper and the hallway led to a T-junction, where the rooms began. "You're in 1215," Enrique said, taking an old-fashioned key on a plastic room tag from his pocket. He stopped at a door halfway up the corridor, checking both ways before reaching for the doorknob.

And then he stopped, his arm still outstretched halfway to the door.

Brennan had pressed the tip of the silenced Sig to the back of the man's head. "That answers a question," he said quietly.

"My friend, I don't think…"

3.   37

"Shhh…" Brennan said. "You talk too much. Here's what's going to happen: you're going to open the door and walk into the room just as you were supposed to. But you're not going to warn your friend in the bathroom."

It had to be why the 'contact' hadn't just given Brennan the key; he knew he could expect a trap, that a nervous cartel insider wouldn't take ten days to explain what was going on or get back to them. Whoever had answered that email wasn't the real Enrique, of that he was certain.

But if they hadn't planned to ambush him at the door, whoever took him by surprise had to be in the only place he could hide and still have the advantage, the room everyone walks by when they first enter a hotel room. 'Enrique' opened the door nervously; Brennan followed him, his bag in his left hand, dropping the pistol to his side, so that his right arm hung down out of sight, the gun by his thigh, as they walked past the bathroom.

Then he pivoted and turned in a single motion, tossing his heavy carry-on bag backwards toward 'Enrique' as he raised the gun; the assassin stepped out of the bathroom, his own pistol in hand. The man's eyes registered a moment of stunned surprise that his target was facing him before the bullet struck him in the forehead, the momentum snapping his body backwards slightly before he crashed to the carpet.

Brennan pivoted and dropped low, in case his guide had avoided the bag and was in a position to counterattack; but 'Enrique' had caught the case, then staggered backwards to lean against the far wall, by the windows. His mouth was agape at how quickly everything had gone wrong. Brennan took two quick strides forward then shoved the gun barrel into the man's wide-open maw, feeling the suppressor scrape past teeth. The man made a gagging motion but did not resist, his eyes filled with terror at the imminent prospect of death.

"I could have killed you eight different ways already at ten different occasions; but you're still alive. Nod if you'd like to know why."

The man nodded, the barrel bobbing up and down.

"I need to know where your friends are holding my colleague. You're not the real Enrique, so I have to assume he's dead. Nod slowly again if that's true."

The man did as he was told.

"Good. There's a chance you might even walk out of here. But for that to happen you have to show me on a map where I can find him." He began to look the man up and down. "If you refuse to give me what I want, I'll take something else. Something permanent, so that you know I'm serious. Let's see, I could cut off a testicle…"

"Hmmm!" the man said. "Nhhh!"

2.   38

"Or, maybe just the big toes on both your feet. You don't technically need them for balance, as you can walk on the side of each foot..." He slowly withdrew the gunmetal suppressor until it was just an inch in front of the man's face.

"Please..." the man said, his voice weak, plaintive. "Señor, I can show you where he is. The fact that we did not succeed means I am dead already to my employer; but if you cut my toes off, I cannot even flee..."

"Did you kill Enrique Obregon personally?"

He shook his head. "I believe that was Francesco, the man you shot."

Brennan grabbed the tall, thin man by the lapels and turned him around before pushing him down onto the cheap loveseat, next to the obligatory hotel desk. He kept the gun on his hostage while he reached into the overnight bag and retrieved a map. He tossed it, folded, to the would-be assassin. "Write down the address, circle it, do what's needed to identify it. But understand me when I say my people have a reach even the cartel can only dream of. If you cross me, we will find you, and you will truly regret every having been born before we kill you. Am I clear?

"Si, crystal clear," he said. "Your friend is being held at a ranch owned by the Villanueva family." He circled a spot just outside Barranquilla. "This doesn't show up on most maps as having anything nearby, but it is a big jungle, Señor, and if you can find a satellite image, you will find the ranch."

"So how come you're less afraid of Villanueva than me?" Brennan said.

"It is a matter of circumstance," the frightened man said, shrugging. "I am afraid of both; but you are the one here, with a gun."

"True." Brennan raised it and shot the man once, through the head, a small amount of spatter spraying the back of the loveseat. The thin man slumped onto it on his side, spasmodic; Brennan shot him once more through the head, picked up the map and his bag, and walked quickly out of the hotel room.

TWO DAYS LATER, 8:28 P.M., NEAR LOS CEBONES, RURAL COLOMBIA

3.

Brennan depressed the switch; he closed his eyes and missed the initial blast, not wanting to affect his night vision when the electricity was cut to the bulk of the compound. The C-4 explosion levelled the little cinder block shed, showering the area with chunks of debris and flaming diesel fuel, the tree line nearby quickly catching fire. The lower part of the compound was pitched into darkness save for the campfire, a chorus of confused and anxious voices chattering in Spanish, noisy enough to be heard from four hundred yards away.

He opened his right eye again and found the guard in his scope. As he'd expected, he was staying at his post, near invisible, even as his associate at the second shack rushed out of the front gate and around to the other side of the compound, along with the second dog and handler. The lights in the house, powered by solar and a separate generator, had stayed on. But the glare barely made it to within ten feet of the remaining guard, who was shrouded in shadows.

Brennan took a deep breath and held it, then slowly squeezed the trigger, allowing the shot to surprise him, so that he wouldn't subconsciously try to avoid the kick and move off target. His wind adjustment was perfect. The bullet went through the guard's neck, destroying the basal ganglia, the group of essential nerves at the base of the brain that connect it to the spine. The man slumped to his knees before pitching face first to the ground.

Across the compound, the fire had caught the longer grass between the fence and jungle, and most of the guards had rushed beyond the perimeter and around to the left side of the property to fight the flames. Brennan knew that if he was lucky, the immediate assumption would be that the generator had just blown, although there was every chance they were expecting company after the aborted hit in Medellin; his target had been held captive for twenty-two days, at least, and Villanueva was a cautious man.

He made his way quickly down the hill in the dark, ignoring the anonymity of the tree line. He followed the electric fence along the right side of the property. It had stopped humming, a clear sign that the generator was its power source, as Brennan had suspected.

Walter Lang was exhausted.

2.

His captors had fed him a diet of weevil-riddled cornmeal gruel, bread and water; he'd only just taken to ignoring the tiny black bugs as they wiggled through his food; for the first ten days he'd stuck to bread and water, but the ongoing lack of nutrients and protein had taken a physical toll. He'd lost fifteen pounds and his face was gaunt; his eye sockets were sunken and sallow, his cheekbones prominent. They'd taken his Ray Bans, which were prescription, limiting his vision to ten feet ahead of him. His hair was matted with sweat and his beard had grown scraggly. They'd taken his clothing when he was captured, and he wore just a stained set of cargo-pants, cut off at the knee to make impromptu shorts, along with plain sandals.

He held no illusion that rescue was imminent. His mission had been covert and deniable. Villanueva was believed to be supplying a third of the cocaine in the western U.S., but the agency had only a cursory interest in his shipping routes and main business, or that of his U.S. gangster contact, Paul Parker.

Villanueva's people, on the other hand, had found a lucrative and accurate supplier of fake passports, social security numbers and stolen credit cards, and rather than just use the paper for smuggling had begun selling it to other criminals, including three suspected extremists picked up a few months earlier on their way to 'jihad' overseas. They were caught due to a tiny mistake, with one forgetting to sign his passport, then doing so at the airline departure counter in halting English script, despite an Anglicized false identity. Lang's job was to find the forger; the fakes had used real passport blanks, which meant the forger had a contact from the State Department supplying him, probably someone clerical and low-level enough to go undetected. But that would include thousands of employees. A sweep was out of the question; Lang needed the forger to give him a name.

Villanueva's associates had pegged him as DEA almost as soon as he'd arrived in Colombia, which wasn't far off, but also meant they were sure he could offer more valuable information. So they'd interrogated him and, when that failed to work, tortured him. First, he'd been water boarded: drowned and then resuscitated repeatedly, the pain and fear almost unbearable. When that failed, they moved onto electro-shock and applications of nerve pain.

After two weeks of it, Lang had been left a shuddering mess, unsure of whether he'd said anything but believing he'd remained unbroken. Eight more days had passed without incident, other than the occasional visit from a guard with food. Lang defecated in a pot in the corner that they emptied every few days, leading to a terrible smell and swarms of flies drawn by the heat. He'd passed the time as taught, by creating memory and counting games that could take his mind off the heat, pain and loneliness. First, he'd tried counting flies and cockroaches, but had given up after a few days and a sense of futility in telling one fly from another. So he'd switched to recalling the plot lines from the British TV episodes of *Sherlock Holmes*, starring the late Jeremy Brett. When that became impossible, he'd moved on to trying to find a mathematical relationship between the number of syllables in various nursery rhymes, and when he ran out of nurseries, he moved onto regular songs by genre.

Were they even trying? Did the agency give a damn, or had he been written off, abandoned off the books? Walter had developed a degree of world-weary cynicism about his role in service of the American people over his decades with the agency. What would he do himself if he was in David Fenton-Wright's position? Save the money, time and embarrassment by just leaving him there? He liked to think not.

He was counting the syllables in Bob Dylan's "Like a Rolling Stone" when the blast happened, the shockwave shaking the shack's walls.

For a moment, Lang's hope returned.

Across the compound, the figures of the guards fighting the flames were backlit by the burning grass and foliage, dark smoke obscuring the stars above. Brennan kneeled and took out his cutters, quickly snipping through several connected segments of the lower right-side fence and leaving a small curtain of wire to pull aside. He put the tool away then crawled through the hole, coming out behind the shack. He moved cautiously around the due-north side, aware that someone from the mansion could be paying attention. The guards were occupied with the fire, and had managed to set up a hose, to start spraying down the burning area with water.

Brennan quickly moved up the shack's steps and knocked a pattern on the door. "Walter!" he hissed.

In the shack, Lang heard the knock and the sound of a muted voice. He couldn't tell who it was. "Hello?" he replied. He raised his voice slightly. "Hello?!?" He put his ear to the door and heard "stand back," so he quickly moved to one side. The door exploded inwards with the force of Brennan's kick, slamming against the interior wall of the shack.

2.

Lang wasn't sure what he was seeing was real. He'd hallucinated before, but the images had been surreal and warped. "Joe?" he asked, his voice halting and weak.

"Come on, we're getting you out of here," Brennan said. His friend looked haggard, skin and bones. "Can you walk?"

"Yeah. I mean, I think so. I'm weak and have dysentery. Need some real food and clean water."

Brennan moved back to the doorway and looked around. At the mansion, someone had figured out that the generator might be a diversion and had the sense to assign two guards to the roof, to use the spotlights more efficiently. One light was trained on the area around the destroyed generator, while the other was sweeping the yard, ensuring the compound wasn't under attack. The flames had either been beaten down, watered out or were smoldering, and guards were beginning to re-enter through the main gate.

"We need to go, now," Brennan said.

Lang looked glassy-eyed and confused. "My assignment... we need to find the forger," he said, dazed, his eyes dancing around as if he'd lost track of where he was.

Brennan threw an arm over Lang's shoulder. "Lean on me," he said. "Watch yourself as we go down the steps." Brennan had prepared for a quick exit; beyond the tree line on their side of the compound, a small path ran down into the neighboring valley, where a de Havilland Beaver float plane was tied up and waiting. "We've got to move quickly beyond the tree line, okay? You're going to have to be able to run on your own."

"Okay," Lang said. He didn't ask what the alternative was; both knew they'd only have minutes before Villanueva's men caught up to them. The pair staggered down the steps; Lang stumbled and fell, then regained his feet; a moment later they were crawling through the hole in the fence.

They were at the tree line when the spotlight caught up to them, the light blinding for a split second; voices were raised, calling after them, yelling. Brennan pulled the machete from his pack and started to quickly hack a path into the overgrowth. Walter followed closely, squinting to keep view of his friend, bullets zipping through the leaves around them, crisp, green, disintegrating flotsam drifting freely, shouts becoming louder, frantic voices in Spanish. At the fence, the guards had discovered the clipped hole and were inspecting it; a trio climbed through the hole to follow immediately.

The machete was taking too long and Brennan gave it up, tossing it aside and pulling his way through the overgrowth. He looked back; Walter was barely keeping up, stumbling just to stay standing. "About two hundred yards," Brennan said, anticipating the question that Walter was too tired to ask. A few moments later Brennan pushed the foliage aside, revealing a steep hill down to the stream, a hundred and twenty degree drop off. It was checkered with rocks, scrub brush and thorny bushes. Another bullet whizzed by and a leaf by Lang's head disappeared. "This is going to really suck, so make sure you bundle yourself up in a tight ball…" Brennan said. He took his jacket off and put it over his friend's shoulders. "Wear this. It might help."

Lang looked down the hill, to where he could just make out the moon glinting off the plane's white wings. It looked about a half-mile away. Then he heard the voices, almost on top of them. "We're out of options, I guess," he said.

"Yeah," said Brennan, taking off his pack and discarding it. "After you."

Lang closed his eyes and dove down the hill. He did as suggested, tucking himself into a ball, but it didn't help either man avoid the rocks, logs and brush, and they bounced painfully throughout the trip. At the bottom, Lang uncurled himself, feeling every jab and stone, lying on his back to get his wind.

A hand reached down and grabbed his. "We have to keep moving," Brennan said, hauling Lang to his feet. Above them the guards were trying to clamber slowly down the hill; it was too steep to stay upright and fire accurately at them, but the odd shell whistled in from nearby and thunked into the muddy bank by the stream. The plane was only twenty yards away now, the engine firing, spitting gasoline and spluttering for air, prop beginning to rotate, pistons whining. The pilot, Eddie, was an agency freelancer, a veteran hired hand. He climbed out of the cockpit and stood on the pontoon to hold open the passenger door as they clambered first onto the float and then up and inside.

"Get us out of here, Ed!" Brennan yelled over the prop noise.

Their exit ticket jumped back into the cockpit and into the pilot's chair. The plane taxied ahead on the water, the grizzled pilot pushing the engine to its limit. Bullets skipped through the water as the guards tried to bring the plane down, and one ricocheted through one side of the hull and out of the other, just as Eddie managed to pull the yolk back fully.

The plane shuddered as its pontoons escaped the surface tension of the river in a shower of water; it began to gain altitude, a chorus of tracer bullets accompanying it into the night sky.

5./

WASHINGTON, D.C. JUNE 17, 2014

The senator poured himself a glass of cold water from the pitcher that sat just ahead of him on the semi-circular chamber table and flicked through the multi-page list of notes and questions again. His square-framed glasses glinted under the room lights. He took another sip of water. Then he played with his pen, tapping it on the long, smooth desk, which was shared by the committee members. Then he cleared his throat, his aged, wrinkled and baggy face betraying no hint of emotional investment.

The committee desk was elevated, seating for a dozen politicians set in front of the back wall of the chamber, a pair of tables ahead of it for witnesses and their legal representatives, each featuring a pair of microphones and a similar pitcher of water. His colleagues waited patiently for the senator to collect his thoughts.

Walter Lang sat alone facing them at the table to the right; the table to the left was empty. The gallery, too. The hearing was official, but the contents were publicly sealed for what the agency cryptically deemed "reasons of national security." Lang just wanted them to get on with it; the decrepit specimen ahead of him, the senior Republican senator from Alabama, had taken an hour already and had yet to ask a question Walter felt he could answer openly, without compromising someone's role.

The senator moistened his lips briefly with the tip of his tongue and tapped his pen again. He leaned towards the microphone as if about to say something… then leaned back again and reconsidered the question. Lang watched him with a sense of loathing. Men like the senator were always interfering, always getting in the way of the agency's ability to protect national interests; and it was always a matter of self-interest, or political expediency. No one on the select committee on foreign intelligence gathering was sitting there because of their constituents' demands for more agency oversight, of that he was sure.

After a few more moments and some clearing of throats from his colleagues, the senator leaned in to the microphone once more.

3.

"Mr. Lang, I feel we've been talking for a while now, with this the third day of this hearing. And yet I have yet to hear, sir, any sense of contrition on your part for your role in this incident, an international embarrassment in which your agency used in excess of ..." he checked his notes, ".... one-hundred-and-seventy thousand dollars' worth of money and equipment paid for by the U.S. taxpayer. Or, for that matter..."

"Senator Morris," Lang said, interrupting him, "I've indicated already that my superiors are best suited to decide the nature of any penalty I may face with respect to internal agency discipline. I've acknowledged the incident."

"Or, for that matter," the senator continued, as if Lang hadn't even spoken, "any explanation of how you managed to marshal the resources that went into your extraction in Colombia. According to your version of events, we are expected to believe that a single agent extracted you without a scratch from a compound full of highly-armed drug cartel members, with no outside support, and of his own initiative. And somehow, your expenses in being there in the first place showed up as a line item in your budget, albeit one without any explanation or context. Can you not see, sir, how my colleagues and I might be somewhat skeptical that such a miraculous mission – two men against several dozen armed criminals – could have taken place?"

Lang knew what they wanted: a confession that the mission had been a black op, official but off the books. After twenty years with the agency, the chance of him giving that up was non-existent, particularly to a political blowhard like Morris. But Morris was a Republican and with the President in his second term, there would be a shit storm if the Colombia op was made public, one that might make the Democrats more vulnerable in the next election. An admission that it was official would give the senators grounds to move to open hearings, which was doubtless Morris' other angle, and provide fodder for months of bad press. Lang didn't really care about the politics; but in bureaucracy, he knew, you didn't publicly bite whichever hand was currently feeding you.

A few chairs down, the committee chairman leaned in. "Senator Morris, while I understand your zeal with respect to this line of questioning, Mr. Lang has indicated the same version of events on at least four occasions now. Perhaps we can move on to a line of questions that is more likely to be lucrative."

Lang saw the intervention through the filter of two cynical decades in the business. The chairman, Addison March, was also Republican and from the south, and even more ambitious than his rapidly aging peer. Doubtless, March had angles to pursue to hold the government to task.

"Hmmph," the senator from Alabama replied. "The chair may wish to remind Mr. Lang that even though this is a closed session, he is testifying under oath."

"No," March said, "no, I don't think that's necessary right now, senator. If you're finished with your questions perhaps we can move…"

"No, I still have several," the elderly politician said. "Mr. Lang has yet to indicate who this agent was, which agency employed him or how the individual might have been disciplined beyond his initial suspension."

That, Walter thought, *is because it's classified, you vulture.* "As I've indicated before, Senator, revealing that information could put other members of the security establishment at risk."

"And yet you claim the agent is inactive. How can people be at risk if the individual in question is not on active duty?"

"I'm sorry Senator," Lang said, leaning close to the microphone and not remotely sorry, "but that information is classified for reasons of national security."

March interjected. "If I might suggest, senator, it seems clear Mr. Lang will not disclose the agent's identity and I'm sure he feels he has good reason. Perhaps he could share with the committee the identity of the agency responsible for the mission?"

It was a clever, political question, Lang thought. If he claimed it was a classified matter, it would be tantamount to an admission that the operation had been covert. If he said that no agency was responsible, he'd be lying under oath. But he'd been around for far too long to walk into an obvious trap.

"As I indicated to the senator previously, I was not sanctioned in any manner when I attempted to infiltrate the Villanueva Cartel," he said.

The balding-and-bony March smiled thinly, his undersized teeth barely showing, the sneer a mixture of contempt for the answer and appreciation for its political correctness. "Yes, I believe you have mentioned that several times. My colleague seems to find it amazing that you got out alive. I, on the other hand, find it somewhat unbelievable that a man of your pedigree in the intelligence community would go out into the field for something as banal as intel on a drug trafficker in the first place, let alone do so without sanction."

Maybe the fact that March was trying to force the line of questioning away from his doddering associate was a sign that they were running out of inane requests, Lang thought. "If it will make the chairman feel better, I'll apologize for the fact that he finds drug trafficking banal," he said.

3.

A murmur went around the committee table, which March ignored. "Perhaps," the chairman said, "we'll go back to Senator Morris, then, and see if he has any more questions in his lengthy, lengthy list." He smiled at Lang again, only this time with his mouth open a little, like an alligator trying to lull a bird into a false sense of security. "I'm sure he does."

It took another two hours before the senators finally decided they'd had enough for the day and went into recess – although not before ordering Lang back for another session the following week. He left the chambers then closed the double doors behind him, letting out a lungful of stress and leaning against the now-closed entry. In the eighteen months that had passed since his rescue, he'd gained back the weight and been taken off the agency caution list, able technically to be field assigned again. He knew it wouldn't happen; when you blow a black bag job, you either wind up dead or grounded, tied to a desk as a controller or adviser, or if you were lucky enough, section chief in some backwater town.

But technically, his job was back to its old self.

It was exceedingly rare for David Fenton-Wright to be nervous. His career had been one of caution, pragmatic political association and careful assessment of his exposure to criticism. But the Director of National Intelligence had never summoned Fenton-Wright through his secretary before; it had always been a personal call, convivial and supportive. This time it was different, an appointment set up a week earlier. It felt like a court date.

There was only one approach, of course, which was to hang Joe Brennan out to dry once more. No matter what the director thought from the hearing scuttlebutt, the official version wasn't going to change.

It was technically true, although a quick look at Brennan's psych profile in the days leading up to the fateful rescue mission had convinced him that the best way to get the agent to take on the task himself – and the fallout either way – was to tell him he was barred from involvement. Brennan's profile suggested he'd always stood up to authority, even when it wasn't the most astute move.

Fenton-Wright wished they were meeting at Langley, where he felt in control. The director, Nicholas Wilkie, spent most of his time on Capitol Hill these days, keeping the president and the National Security Council happy. It was a purely political job, Fenton-Wright felt, a liaison role between Langley and the political talking heads. It wasn't that he didn't admire Wilkie, who'd made it to the most important position in the intelligence community despite not having a background in the field. That spoke to his political prowess and his ability to manipulate consensus in his own direction, Fenton-Wright knew, all valuable tools. But Wilkie was aging, becoming less and less involved in the hard decisions, deferring more and more to Fenton-Wright and his opposite number at the NSA, Mark Fitzpatrick.

Wilkie was leaning back in his desk chair when Fenton-Wright knocked. He was in his early seventies and had avoided both agencies' mandatory retirement ages by presidential veto. But he still had a full head of white hair and a quick mind.

The director had a sheath of printouts in one hand that he was studying, reading glasses halfway. "Ah David! Good to see you. Come in, come in." He swung out of his office chair and walked over to shake Fenton-Wright's hand. "I've just been reviewing a transcript of Walter Lang's first-day committee testimony. He did a fine job."

Fenton-Wright suppressed his urge to scoff. "Well, the jury's out of course, until we go through the other three days' of transcripts, but I would tend to agree," he said instead. "Of course, had he been more careful in Colombia, we wouldn't have been in this mess to begin with. Now I have a top field agent suspended and Lang on a desk; so we're effectively down two, with nothing to show from his efforts." He was careful not to call it an operation; it was going to remain unofficial.

"Now, David, be nice," Wilkie said. "Walter volunteered to go into a difficult situation. Let's not be too harsh with him, all right?"

"Of course," Fenton-Wright said. "Joe Brennan, however, is another matter. He was directly ordered to stay out of this."

"He got our man back," Wilkie noted. "He may not be reliable, but he is effective. We have that at least."

The director had always been an optimist; it was part of his nature, part of the reason he could build bridges between parties, find consensus. Fenton-Wright considered him weak for it but knew eventually he'd get his chance. Wilkie couldn't hang on forever.

"Yes, well, that doesn't change the fact that he undermined the authority of everyone in a senior position within the agency," Fenton-Wright said. "I don't want him back any time soon."

"If we let him go…"

3.   49

"We'll have an association grievance to deal with; and he's popular with some. There's always a chance that cutting him loose could jeopardize the situation's deniability. But if we just leave him on indefinite leave and he collects his paycheck, there is that much more pressure on him to honour his national security obligation."

Wilkie thought about it. There were worse fates, he supposed, than being on permanent vacation. And Brennan had a reputation for being honorable. "If we must, it should suffice. What about the other matter I forwarded -- the European file?"

Fenton-Wright nodded as if familiar. In truth, he'd barely glanced at the details. A U.S. agent under deep cover on an ally's turf codenamed Fawkes had made a rare information drop; it was the first time he'd even been heard from in sixteen years. But despite the agent's profile and track record, the details seemed out-of-the-blue at best, Wilkie had said, allegations that a respected business group based in France had a hand in an African insurgency a few years earlier. Given Fawkes' importance long ago, when the Cold War was at its peak, it had to be treated seriously, even if the few who knew of him doubted he was still reliable.

"It's under review," he replied tactfully. "Our man is attempting to gain access to more information via those same connections. If there's any more to it, he'll attempt to offer himself up as a valuable political commodity, see how the business cabal reacts. His understanding is that it just lost a member."

Wilkie frowned. "Are you sure that's the best approach, David? We're talking about someone who has been in deep sleep; the embarrassment if he was exposed, both to him and to our British colleagues…"

"I realize that, director," Fenton-Wright said. "But we have little choice. And we have the added benefit of his social stature; were he caught, he could always claim he was acting on behalf of Queen and country, independent of their security services."

"Aren't we risking the possibility that he's working with MI6, trying to embarrass us, compromise us and put us in a position where we owe them a rather larger favor? He's been ingrained into high society there for decades. He hasn't been a regular contributor since the Seventies. It seems exceptionally strange that he'd come out of the woodwork now; he must be nearly eighty."

Fenton-Wright smiled ruefully. "Seventy-seven. With respect, director, it won't be that long for either of us…"

"Yes," Wilkie said, "but I don't expect either of us will still be here. Keep a lid on him, David. Make sure this doesn't blow up in our faces."

2.

Brennan had agreed to meet Walter at a small bar off Eighteenth Street, a brew pub run by Czech immigrants who made Lang's favorite draft. Brennan hated driving into D.C., leaving Carolyn and the kids alone in Annandale for the afternoon just so that Walter could tell him what he already knew or suspected: that he wasn't going back to work any time soon.

The pub was near-empty, the lunch crowd having already left. The U-shaped wooden bar was next to the entrance as Brennan walked in. There were a couple of regulars still hanging around; a weathered looking man in a flat cap was chewing a toothpick; a younger guy with dark mutton chops sat talking to the barkeep; the sturdy-looking employee had short blond hair and his sleeves rolled up. He was cleaning pint glasses.

Brennan automatically assessed the room for threats, eyes flitting between the tables and the booths along the back and side walls; he scanned each person in turn quickly, looking for facial hints, small ticks or changes that indicated they were paying too much attention, or any at all. He noted the second exit at the back. He liked the place: quiet, unassuming, private.

Lang was waiting in the back corner booth, one of three along the rear wall; he was rubbing his hands together slowly under the bare wooden table, hunched forward a little and looking nervous, as ever.

Flat cap's eyes followed Brennan has he crossed the room, cutting between a few four-person tables. Brennan slid into the booth opposite his friend, vaguely annoyed that he had taken the seat with his back to a corner and the best view of the room.

Lang shook his hand. "Thanks for driving in. I know Carolyn's on vacation right now so I appreciate…"

"Skip the playbook sentiment, Walter, it's me," Brennan said. "I don't need the caring boss speech."

"I know. It's just…"

"Get over it. None of this is your fault. Sending you down there was foolhardy to begin with." He didn't tell Walter what he really thought: that leaving a senior agent to die for the sole reason of covering up a bad decision was a betrayal in itself, one that he pinned squarely on Walter's boss, deputy director David Fenton-Wright. "So how did it go?"

"It's still going. They want me back in for another go on Monday; I think the chairman sees me as fodder for his next campaign slogan. And that ass Morris asked me the same question in a different form at least nine times over the four hours."

"What are they hoping to get out of this?"

3.

"Ammunition. The GOP dominates the committee. When word got out …"

"You mean when someone leaked it to the press."

"Sure. Anyway, when word got out the Dems went into such a frenzy of denial in the first three days that they might as well have been hanging a sign over the President in neon saying 'he ordered it'. So they're going to spend probably a whole week testing the limits of human boredom in closed session, trying to get me to admit it."

"Have you…" Brennan was hesitant.

"What? Named anyone? Of course not." Even in the relative anonymity of a near-empty pub he was cautious.

"Who's the committee chair?"

"Junior senator out of Tennessee named Addison March. Have you followed what's going on these days?"

"Not so much."

"He's the new GOP golden boy. Young, ambitious, on point. Well… young compared to the rest of those skeletons, anyway. He's charming in public and a piranha in the House. I think he scares the liberal elite to death. Hey... when's Carolyn coming back, anyway?"

Brennan said, "That's up to her. We've got plenty of help with the kids; not that we really need it right now. I'm home all day." He couldn't hide the bitterness.

They were dancing around the issue of his suspension, neither man wanting to get to the moment, like a convict who knows he has no chance at his parole hearing. It was difficult for both; Lang's guilt at Brennan paying the price for Colombia was considerable. But he was a good soldier. Even though Lang's move to management gave him the authority to bring Brennan back in, the chain of command meant that he needed Fenton-Wright's permission to do so.

"So," Brennan said.

"Yeah. Look…"

"It's a 'no', right?"

"Yeah. I'm sorry buddy," Lang said. "Shot down again. Pretty strongly this time, too."

Neither wanted to consider the other possibility: that at the highest level he'd been blacklisted, burned. The agency had an inglorious history of paying former operatives not to work. Their pay never went up beyond prescribed increases, it never went down, and they were never called in again.

"They're putting me out to pasture, aren't they?" Brennan said. "Walter, I'm thirty-nine years old. I can't become a house husband at thirty nine. I can't walk away ... it's just wrong."

2.

Lang had mentored Brennan for seven years and his soft spot for the former Navy SEAL was considerable. But he wasn't going to try and soften the blow, or infuse him with false hope. "I'll keep fighting for you, you know that. But it doesn't look good, Joe. It's the timing, that's all. If we weren't going into a new election cycle…"

"We're always in an election cycle in this country," Brennan snapped. "They run for office permanently when they should be running the country." Then he regretted the tone. Walter wasn't the enemy. "I'm sorry, Walter, I didn't mean to bark at you. You know what I mean."

"I know. It drives us all crazy, watching a country run on three- and four-year plans instead of looking long-term, just because some narcissistic jerk who managed to raise a few bucks wants a title and a free ride. But that's not going to change any time soon, and they're not going to change their minds. You're a cliché to them, Brennan, a relic of a different era. These are pen pushers, guys who have two-hour country club lunches. They don't want anyone drawing attention to how little they actually do. It's got nothing to do with the op, or the purpose, or the public. It never has. It's about their townhouse in Georgetown and their McFuck You Mansion in Jackson Hole. They have to keep the politicians happy. They don't give a shit about the public, and they sure don't give a shit about you. Or what you can offer."

"That's…"

"Bureaucracy," Lang said grimly.

"I was going to say it's all kinds of bull. But we both knew that, too. I'm going to have to resign, you realize that, right?"

Lang frowned. "I'm not even sure they'd accept it right now. They want you under wraps."

"They know I can't talk publicly."

"It's not publicly they're worried about. Besides, think of Carolyn."

"What about her?"

"If you walk away against their wishes, she's left working at the agency. She's on a career track, Joe. She'll be in executive before long. You really want to ruin that?"

For a second, Brennan wanted to ask Walter whose side he was on -- and who saved who; but he did as taught in leadership training and reframed it dispassionately; he knew Walter was just being bluntly honest.

"Yeah, I guess," he said. "She's worked so hard in the last year. I was pretty bad to be around for the first few months after I was suspended and she hung in there for me."

"It can't have been easy for either of you," Lang said. "Again, you know how sorry…"

3.   53

Brennan shook his head vehemently. "No, cut that stuff out right now. You'd have done the same for me."

It was probably true, Lang thought. Probably. He wondered whether he'd have had the courage. It was one thing to work undercover. If you were doing it right, conflict was usually off the table. He'd blown it, and he knew it, and Joe Brennan had paid for it. But would he go into a heavily armed compound for Joe? He wasn't sure he had the guts.

"What are you doing for the rest of the summer?" he asked, changing the subject.

"Carolyn's rented a place in the Napa Valley for the next four weeks; then we're going to play it by ear. She might come back to work at that point."

"Napa?"

"Wine tours. She figures we can get zonked while the kids go horseback riding, or something."

"And when you get back?"

He shrugged. "Like you said, it's probably not up to me."

"You could always work freelance. They've never cared much what work agents did in their own time, as long as it didn't lead back anywhere and isn't intelligence related. And there's a lot of work out there for a good contractor. There's no shame in security consulting, for example."

Brennan gave an affirmative but he kept what he was really thinking to himself. Walter had a guilty enough conscience already. "Sure. Did you manage to figure out the press leak?"

"No. But I've got a few ideas."

"NSA?"

"Possibly. More likely one of ours. There are a lot of different interests on this one trying to massage it for leverage, progress on some angle or project of their own." The distaste on Walter's face was obvious, Brennan thought; for a second, he considered the year past and wondered again why they both did it, why it was still important to them.

The thought was interrupted by a new arrival. Even with the door in his left rear periphery, Brennan spotted her the moment she walked in, her cream-colored overcoat sticking out like a neon light in the dingy surroundings. He turned his head quickly, knowing everyone at the bar would be doing the same.

"You know her?" he said quietly to Lang.

"Familiar. Can't place her." They both knew that could be good or bad, and it merely heightened the tension. Brennan got up. "I'm out of here. Call me." He moved towards the back door.

2.

Lang nodded in return. Brennan didn't need to explain; Walter was an old hand. When someone suddenly appears who's out of place, it's better for an agent keeping a low profile to play the short odds and get out. Otherwise, questions might ensue, or conflict, or both.

The woman approached Lang's table, watching Brennan for a moment as he disappeared through the pub's back door. She was young, Lang thought, maybe twenty-seven or twenty-eight, five-seven, fit but not muscular, short brown hair, wearing heels, which aren't conducive to a foot chase. If she was an operative, she was playing a cover. In fact, she reminded him of his ex-wife, Vicki, at the same age.

"Mr. Lang?"

Lang took a casual sip of his pint of draft. Then he leaned back against the booth. "I'm sorry; I don't believe we've had the pleasure…" *If her hand goes into her purse too quickly*, he thought, *it's a quick downward heel strike to her ankle bone. In those stilettos, it'll break like a twig.*

She held out a hand to shake. "Alex, Alex Malone." She glanced at the back door. "I think I scared your friend off. Sorry about that."

Walter waved a hand at the door. "It's nothing. He had to run, get back to work. You'd like him."

"Yeah?"

"Yeah, architect from Michigan, in town for a lecture at George Washington."

She nodded and smiled. "Do you have a few minutes to talk?"

"That depends what you'd like to talk about, miss."

"May I sit?"

He gestured to the opposing bench. "Please."

She sat down, placing her purse on the seat next to her. "A friend of mine at State suggested you'd be the person to talk to. I'm working on a story about…"

He stood up and cut her off. "Good day, Miss Malone. I don't talk to the press."

She stood up with him. "Please! Mr. Lang, my pieces have wide readership, and I really think we can help each other…"

Lang paused for a second and studied her. She had an earnest face, an expression of hope and nervousness. He'd seen it before on young reporters; he hadn't talked to them, either. "Not interested, miss." He headed for the back door.

"I'd like to talk about David Fenton-Wright," she said.

He stopped in his tracks again. That was a surprise, which was probably why she'd thrown it out, a last gambit to keep him interested. But Lang had been around too long. "No one's stopping you," he said, before pushing the back door open and stepping outside into the bright sun.

3.   **55**

As he made his way to his car, Lang made a mental note to run a check on Alex Malone. Anyone who knew his habits well enough to find him at the Czech pub was someone he needed to worry about.

When Brennan got home, Carolyn considered not asking him what had happened.

She was in the kitchen, cutting vegetables for the casserole she'd planned to make for dinner, her pale golden hair pulled back, cheeks flushed from the heat. The cutting board was covered in tiny pieces of celery, onion and carrot; occasionally, as she chopped, she'd push a piece towards the pile too firmly and have to scoop it up off the cheap yellow-and-white tile floor.

She'd known the answer before he left, but was forbidden from telling him. They knew it would happen when they got together, that sharing careers in intelligence would be difficult. Careers full of secrets, twists and turns that married couples weren't supposed to take, worse by far than the secrets couples normally keep.

She had plenty of other things to worry about, too. She worried that she'd never look again like she did before she'd had kids, or whether she'd even find enough time to get back into shape. And she worried about her husband, who had come and gone throughout their marriage, disappearing for weeks at a time on national security issues.

It wasn't getting any easier, she told herself. Maybe if they could just find more time for each other, they'd stop feeling tense, resentful. The trip could give them that, time to just spend with each other, no expectations. Lately, everything had been an argument; the simplest things seemed to prompt harsh words, like they'd lost patience with one another after years of diplomacy.

"Babe," he said perfunctorily as he closed the front door behind him and hung his coat up. He didn't sound down or up, but it was obvious he wasn't going back to work. Not that she needed any sort of explanation; David had made it clear to her that Joe was persona non grata at the agency as long as he was deputy director.

She watched him out of the corner of her eye as she kept chopping; he retrieved a can of beer from the fridge nearby. "Are the kids excited about the trip?" he asked.

"I suspect the fact that we're going to be within a couple of hours of a certain theme park is why they've been such little angels all week. I take it the answer was no."

2.

"You take it correctly," he said. He popped the beer can open, slurping away the froth that rose quickly. He stared at the can for a moment, obviously more satisfied with it than with the rest of his day. "They let Walter give me the news in person, which is a typically cowardly David Fenton-Wright move, trying to make Walter feel guilty for the deputy director's failed mission."

The one advantage to a wife with Top Secret security clearance was that Brennan could talk about work. Sometimes. Sometimes, she really didn't need to know the details. In this case, he knew, she was probably fully versed in what was going on; she was probably bursting to talk to him about it even before he got home. He'd stopped being delicate about her boss in front of her. A year off the job did that to a guy.

She paused in her chopping, tense at the return of the push-and-pull between her career at the agency and Joe. She didn't want to talk about that stuff.

He looked annoyed, standing there in a sweater and jeans, beer can in hand. She just wanted it to go away. "Well, for four weeks we get to put all that stuff to one side, right?"

"That's the general idea," he said. "A little sun, a little fun, a little vino…" For professional reasons, Brennan rarely drank. He was planning on putting his normal routines to one side for the duration. "This was a really good idea, I have to admit."

She reached over and grasped his right hand in her left, then squeezed it. It was quick, but it said a lot, he thought. She knew how isolated he felt, how cut adrift. And she was trying to be there for him, even though he seemed to make her uncomfortable these days, as often as not.

Brennan said, "Where are the kids? I don't get the big 'daddy, daddy!' greeting anymore."

Carolyn turned back to her work. She picked up her knife and scraped the diced vegetables off of the cutting board and into a bowl. "They're six and seven, now, hon; they're getting less clingy as they get older."

It was stunning to Brennan to contemplate how quickly they'd grown. Josh was becoming a little version of his father, only instead of intelligence work he was the foreman of the world's least-efficient Tonka construction company. Jessica was so smart, always head of her class, always the playground mediator, getting along with everybody. He was amazed, when he truly thought about it, at the job Carolyn had done; he was away too much to take any credit. He worried sometimes that his relationship with them would fall by the wayside, as it had with his own father, who had spent twenty years in the military, often posted overseas and on occasion without his family, only to die in a car accident two years after returning home.

3.

He moved over to her and put his arms around her waist. "Do they have their mother's wisdom?"

"They do, I think."

"And do they have their father's good looks?"

She slapped him with a tea towel. "That's a terrifying thought. Especially Jessica. Let's just hope they avoid your lactose intolerance and the subsequent wind damage."

He let go of her waist, and she laughed. "Hey!" he said. "No fair!" They caught the moment, the look in each other's eyes of happiness and comfort, exactly as it had been when they were younger and delirious with each other.

And then it faded, and they let it go, smiles slowly disappearing, both acutely aware that the tension in their lives was pulling them further apart.

Carolyn turned back to her vegetables.

She said, "It'll be good, you know? It'll be good to get away for a while, leave the Beltway behind."

"And when we get back?" he said. They knew eventually she'd have to make a decision; he didn't want her to return to work. It wasn't as if they were hurting for money and they were both skilled, able. But he couldn't ask her to stay away.

She stopped chopping again and gave him a strained smile. "Let's worry about that when we get to it, okay babe?" Then she changed the subject as adroitly as possible. "How was Walter?"

"Tense; which is to say, he was Walter. He's still chewing antacids like candy and blaming himself for everything. He thinks the NSA has a mole in the agency feeding it budget damage."

"He always thinks there are moles in the agency," Carolyn said, walking over to the refrigerator. She opened it and retrieved the stewing beef she'd bought that morning. She took it back to the cutting board. "And he's probably right. I'm sure we've probably got people looking in on a few of our colleagues as well. Some things never change."

Brennan looked around for toys or other signs of play. "Where are the kids, anyway?"

"Backyard."

He walked to the window over the kitchen sink. Jessica had Josh down on the ground. She had him pinned, her knees on his arms. She was growing faster than her brother and was several inches taller, her long blonde hair hanging down over his face.

"Hey!" Brennan called. Then he opened the window, a turning handle swinging it outward. "Hey! Jessie, get off your brother!"

"He tried to stick gum in my hair!"

"Let him up! Josh, leave your sister alone!"

2.

They got up reluctantly, dusting themselves off. Brennan contemplated how surreal it was, to be surrounded by so many normalcies; how stark the contrast was with Barranquilla, or Fallujah, or Sri Lanka. He'd always told himself that, for all his sense of duty, he preferred home. Watching his kids, his wife a few feet away supporting him, it was the first time he was certain of it. Maybe…

He shook the thought off. He'd never been one to settle, to lose focus or give up early. He loved his job, believed in it. His kids gave him joy, but the work gave him purpose. Brennan took his beer into the living room, grabbing the remote control from its familiar spot on the arm of the old tan leather couch and turning on the six-year-old TV. She'd left it on CSPAN, and a press conference was about to start. The anchor was talking about the committee hearing earlier that day.

"And that was Sen. David Morris, the veteran Republican from Alabama, on his disappointment in today's testimony. Again, hearings into the recent CIA Colombian operation scandal are closed to the public for reasons of national security, a fact that opposition politicians have called deplorable. And with that, we take you now to the press availability at the government services building with Sen. John Younger, the President's economic security advisor and a National Security Council member. Our correspondent, Tom Barr, has been there waiting for his speech. Tom?"

Brennan turned the volume down then changed the channel completely. He'd had enough of that world for one day.

Senator Younger watched the television on the corner of his desk with growing amusement. The senator was medium height, stocky, with a crown of greying hair and strong features, eyebrows too bushy for their own good. He was leaning back in the antique typing chair that sat behind his desk. The TV feed was a recording of the earlier press conference by Senator Morris. Younger chuckled heartily and shook his head; Morris looked a hundred and twenty years old. Addison March must have cringed watching it, imagining the puzzled looks on the faces of a key demographic.

Younger's own presser had been smooth by comparison, a few quick jokes, some pithy quotes for the reporters he knew fairly well. His phone intercom sounded. "Sir, Mark Fitzpatrick from the National Security Agency is here to see you."

"Send him in, Alice," Younger said, his eyes still on the now-mute press conference. He couldn't help but beam a smile as Fitzpatrick joined him.

3.

"Senator. You look like you just won a new car." The NSA man liked the senator. In another life, Fitzpatrick figured, he'd have been a longshoreman or a shop teacher.

"Mark, my boy. Good to see you."

"You must be watching Morris."

"He's like a wrecked steamship about to crash into port. He wrangled his way onto the select committee without March having much to say in it, and now it's costing him. He looks like another old, white Republican beating up on POTUS."

"Don't these people watch the numbers? The public loves this stuff; rogue agents on unauthorized rescue missions, undercover operations taking on nefarious drug dealers. If we could figure out the name of the nut who went in and grabbed Lang, we could run him for VP. If they keep this up," Fitzpatrick suggested, "you'll be in an ideal position to announce…"

Younger cut him off. "Now, let's not go there quite yet, Mark. There's still the matter of the president's endorsement. I'd much rather know for certain… I'm sure you understand that POTUS' backing means a lot right now. His numbers are finally tracking north again, we're out of the worst of our overseas adventures, and the donation base is building."

It wasn't that Younger distrusted the president; he just wanted everything locked into place before any of their policy differences intruded, or one of the 'also rans' began to raise offense. His relationship with the man had been tenuous until the last year, when both started to become nervous about leaving a legacy.

"You know you've got my support, John."

Younger got up from his desk chair and pushed it in, then walked around his desk and offered Fitzpatrick a hand to shake. "You've been loyal and I won't forget it; just know that."

"I know, I know. And I'd like to think that if anyone in House has a respect for the long tradition of naming new directors for a new administration, it would be you. That's why you can be sure I'll be there for you when you need me. "

"You're still clear of any agency grief?"

"Sure," Fitzpatrick said. "Your NSC role gives me a plausible rationale for our visits."

Younger patted him twice on the shoulder. Fitzpatrick was nothing if not straight about his ambitions; he wanted the director's spot when Wilkie retired; judging from appearances, it could come any day.

"Better days ahead, my friend. Better days ahead. Did we get any word on what the final disposition was?"

"The agent who went rogue is suspended. Walter Lang is back in a purely admin role, though Fenton-Wright taps him for a lot of advice."

2.

"Suspended? Unfortunate," Younger said. "Is there anything we can do about that?"

"Uncertain. I'll keep my ears open." The trick, Fitzpatrick knew, was talking to the right folks; nothing slipped out of the agency without someone having an axe to grind. But there were plenty of those.

Younger was sure he would. Fitzpatrick had become a dependable asset, able to get things done, willing to roll the dice on the senator before a nomination was tied down.

Fitzpatrick wanted passage to the corridors of power, and he knew the price was unswerving loyalty.

3.   61

6./
SEPT. 4, 2015 PARIS, FRANCE

The asset arrived at Paris Charles De Gaulle Airport at just after nine o'clock in the morning, a man with dirty blond hair cut short under a black baseball cap, a quilted navy blue vest jacket, a tan turtleneck sweater, jeans, dark blue hikers. He was tall and had a blue-and-white carry-on bag over his shoulder and was about as anonymous as any of the million or so blond westerners who'd pass through the airport on any given day; and he looked younger than his actual age, which accentuated the effect.

Not that it mattered. He was trained to move with a natural gait, deliberate, head down, uninterested in those around him and uninteresting in return. He blended into the crowd effortlessly despite his height. If he did catch an eye, his facial mimicry would convey a perfect expression of ambivalence or fatigue.

No one paid attention as he passed between the glass-case walls of the duty free area, where he managed to turn his head the seventy degrees required to obscure his face from each security camera in turn; nor as he stopped and bought a small decaf coffee; nor at Passport Control, where his thoroughly forged documents were stamped and passed through without so much as a question by the bored-looking officer in the booth.

The inside of the airport was the closest he'd seen to a 1960s science fiction set, like they'd decided to design it using cast-off props from Barbarella; the escalators were inclined planes: sliding, stepless walkways at acute angles, enshrouded in Perspex bubbles. Some passengers looked around with an obvious mixture of puzzlement, amusement and admiration, but the asset remained nonplussed and completely uninteresting to anyone.

The baggage carousel was mercifully quick. The case was the fourth item offloaded, and it circled its way around to him inconspicuously, looking every bit the hard-sided electric guitar protector it appeared to be when run through the airport's supposedly infallible scanners. He picked it up, slung his carry-on back over his shoulder, and headed for the sliding doors that led outside, to the taxi stands and pick-up zone.

He flagged the next cab in line.

"Où voulez-vous aller?" the driver said in African-accented French.

The asset gave him an address in Clichy-Sous-Bois, a nearby suburb, and the driver made a disappointed noise. The thirty-minute ride would have few opportunities to stretch the trip for additional fare and the neighbourhood in question was not good; the driver knew – he lived there himself.

"Voulez-vous prendre le 'D40' ou l'N370'?" the driver asked.

"D40, d'accord?" The asset said it forcefully to make it clear he didn't want the driver messing around.

The trip took ten minutes longer than expected, even with the driver cutting in and out of traffic so quickly the asset found it difficult to sit up straight in the back seat. He was at least twenty over the speed limit most of the way, the asset noted, but the road congestion was significant, and every so often they would grind to a halt for a few minutes.

The contact's apartment was in a ten-story block just off Av. Paul Cezanne. It was early evening and getting dark, and it was wet and drab, with numerous street lights either broken or burned out. The apartments were built with white concrete-and-rebar blocks; the building's non-descript exterior was long mottled and stained by dirt and water, just one in a long line. Across the street, a building was broken down completely, the two remaining exterior walls covered with elaborate graffiti. It was the last in a row and had fared worst; most of the apartments lacked balconies, making the surrounding buildings hard to tell apart from offices. Even the inhabited blocks had been scrawled upon with spray paint, though mostly by untalented taggers, the signatures woeful attempts at artistic style, slashing black scribbles that did little but accentuate the grime.

Six wide concrete steps ran up to the front doors of his destination. The asset scanned the street; cars were crammed end-to-end on both sides but it seemed quiet otherwise. Housing in the neighbourhood was cheap, and along with the poor it drew the unfortunate and those who preyed upon them. He wasn't surprised the contact lived here; the contact was considered unreliable and untrustworthy, a backup plan, to be used only in the most necessary of circumstances due to inherent risks. But the asset was working without a net; no handler, no support. He had limited assets and fewer options. Anyone more reliable might check back on him, as well; the last thing he needed was outside static.

The front security door's lock was broken and it swung open freely. The building's lobby was near featureless, a plain linoleum floor, the tiles dirty and torn, with the right-hand wall covered in tiny metal mailboxes. At the end of the lobby was the elevator. To its left was an office, and to its right, the stairs.

The elevator car smelled of urine. The asset took it to the fourth floor, the doors beginning to open before it had actually settled and was level with the hallway.

Only one hallway light bulb still functioned, along with an exit light at the very end of the corridor that cast a red shadow. The contact was in Apartment 4D and was expecting him. The door wasn't the standard issue, but rather a steel reinforced barrier, painted off-white, with a spy hole and a camera above it. He knocked three times, the metal echoing deeply. After a pause, a panel slid back near the top of the door.

"Yeah?" The voice was deep.

"I'm here to see Petr," the asset said in French.

The panel slid shut. Twenty seconds later, he heard the bolt being drawn back. The door swung open. The man guarding it was large, well-built in overalls and a t-shirt, toting a Mac-Ten machine pistol. Inside, the main hallway opened into a bachelor apartment, with everything but the bathroom contained in an open floor space. The walls were empty, painted a drab green and the floorboards were scuffed and dull. At the back of the room, a dark brown wooden desk sat before the windows, and behind it was the contact, Petr. He was short, with a mop of blond hair that went to just below his collar and green eyes hiding behind undersized glasses. He had a guard on each side, both muscular again, both standing with their hands politely in front of them. The asset didn't see any weapons, which he assumed meant they were concealed, probably just tucked into waistbands. The one to the asset's right had a bulge by his ankle suggesting a backup piece. Both seemed focused.

"Come in my friend, come in," Petr said. "So I'm told through a mutual acquaintance that you require some special paper."

"You got my specifications?" The asset had forwarded them before leaving the U.S. If he'd had his preference he would have used someone back home for the detailed work; but his mission was off the books, strictly unofficial. Anyone working with spooks was out of the question. So he had gone to Petr, who had a reputation as a ruthless gangster but a superb forger.

"Sure, of course," the man said, his accent eastern European. "It wasn't easy, pulling that many identities together that quickly. Why you want this, anyway?"

That made the asset anxious. Solid suppliers knew not to ask those sorts of questions. "I like to travel a lot," he said. "And I'm collecting airline points."

Petr laughed at that and his boys quickly joined in. "Funny guy, eh? I like funny. You got the money?"

The asset took a wad of crumpled euros from his inside pocket and threw it onto the desk. "That's five thousand."

Petr nodded. "That is what we agreed. I tell you, Mr. American, you have some balls to come see me, eh? I mean, we don't know each other, you just get my name from some contact I haven't seen or heard from in two, three years. If I didn't know better," he grinned, "I would think you might be a cop. Or planning something illegal."

"Just give me my paper and I'll be on my way." Keep it cordial and professional, the asset told himself. No reason to suspect…

The wire looped around his neck swiftly and silently from behind, but the asset's training kicked in and he managed to get two fingers under it as the guard from the door tried to pull the garrote tight, to choke the life out of him. He dropped his case onto the ground, freeing up his other hand.

"Maybe since we don't know you," Petr said, "we take whole thing and keep paper, yes?"

The wire cut into his hand. The asset threw himself backward, the weight bowling the strangler over, the pressure released for a moment. The wire was still in place, and his attacker grabbed at each of the wooden handles on its either end, then wrapped his legs around the asset's waist, making him near impossible to pry loose.

"It is nothing personal," the forger said matter-of-factly, "just business."

The wire cut deep, blood beginning to drip in busy patterns all over the floor.

"Don't struggle," Petr said, "Victor is much too strong for you, my friend. It will all be over sooner if you just give in."

Both men lay on their side battling for control; the asset tried to kick backwards with his heels, to catch a shin or kneecap; but instead, the garrote got tighter as the attacker pulled with all of his might. He felt his air diminishing, face flushed from the artery that was being cut off in his neck. He pushed his left hand upwards, so that his arm was between the wire and his neck, knowing he'd only have one chance for the move to work. He thrust the arm through the loop, pulling it away from his skin, then flung his head backwards, smashing the man in the face with the back of his skull.

The tension in the wire temporarily slacked off and the asset pushed hard against it with his arm, the attacker letting go of one end of the noose. The asset threw a hard elbow backwards, catching the guard on the curve of his cheekbone right below his eye socket and sending him to the ground screaming, clutching the bone.

3.

Guards number two and three were coming for him now. The one on the left had already retrieved a pistol from the back of his waistband and tried to level it; but the asset was nimble, ignoring the pain in his hand and arm from the cuts, rolling sideways and coming to his feet, wrist-locking the gunman's arm, swinging it toward his colleague even as the guard opened fire, the three shots catching the second guard flush in the chest.

As his partner went down, the asset broke the first man's wrist with a hard twist, the crunch of the small bones audible, then drove the side of his hand into the man's larynx, crushing it and sending him to the ground, spluttering for air, his pistol bouncing loose and sliding a few feet. The first assailant was almost to his feet again, and the asset turned smoothly, grabbing the man by his hair and driving his knee into the man's face, the cheek damage compounded with a shattered eye socket. He repeated the action twice with furious strength, the guard dead before he hit the floor.

The asset picked up the pistol. Petr hadn't moved throughout, seemingly stunned by how efficiently his men had gone down, but now reached quickly for the gun that lay flat on his desktop. As he grabbed it, the asset used his free hand to grab the letter opener that lay next to it and drove it through the top of Petr's hand, pinning it to the desk top. The forger screamed.

The asset twisted the letter opener slightly and the man screamed again, this time ending it with a deep, woeful moan of pain.

"The paper: did you get it done or was rolling me the plan all along?"

The man looked at him blankly, sweating profusely, the shock of the moment paralyzing him. The asset twisted the opener blade again and the man moaned once more. "No! Please, no more! Top drawer, is in top drawer!"

A manila envelope sat on top of the other drawer contents and the asset grabbed it. Then he contemplated the forger. The man could identify him, and had proven completely unreliable; it was unfortunate, the asset thought, but the police would probably be there soon, drawn by the gunshots. Response times were likely as bad as any country, in the fifteen to twenty minute range. In any case, there was no point being quiet about things. He turned back to Petr who was wide-eyed with fear.

"No, please... I have family," the forger said.

The asset picked the wad of money back up off the desk then shot Petr once through the forehead; the gangster slumped forward on the desk, his life draining away like so much spilled ink, his eyes wide open but empty, his face displaying nothing less than a final moment of surprise.

2.

SEPT. 6, 2015, MONTPELLIER, FRANCE

The odd camera flash was still going off, though most of the press had gotten their shots at the beginning of her speech, thirty minutes earlier. The representative to the World Trade Council's Special Committee on Environmental Security took an extra-long pause.

Marie La Pierre wanted to frame her final words dramatically, to lend them some gravitas. The pause just fit. She'd learned early in her thirty years in politics that due to her short stature, she needed her diction and delivery to be perfect, to make up for any bias her audience might hold towards her size. Then she moved slightly closer to the podium again, brushing an errant brown hair away from her glasses before looking out over the roomful of delegates once more. "And that is why, ladies and gentlemen, we must be ever vigilant in an age where our planet is under assail daily; we must never shirk our duty to protect this planet from those who would care nothing for future generations but only for profit in the now, gain in the immediate, at the expense of our children, and our children's children.

"And so the Special Committee thanks the EU delegation today for its continued, unwavering financial and legislative support, for the working relationships we have forged, and for the efforts the committee has made around the world in ensuring nations, businesses and their leaders respect the environment, as well as the concerns and cultures of indigenous peoples."

She surveyed the room. Most of the delegates were elderly men, overweight, suit wearing, long accustomed to high pay for little work. A parade of grey-haired, aging policy addicts with too much ear hair and collections of warts. The speech was a prolonged handshake, a chance for the committee to ensure the delegates went back to Brussels with the right message; in truth, the conference had been one long government junket, a chance for the committee to host European movers and shakers for a weekend by the Mediterranean. The purpose was to send them home with a head full of happy memories and a nice gift bag. As pompous and self-important as most of them were, La Pierre knew, the committee's work was the focus of her public life these days. She considered it too important to fall victim to bureaucracy or politics, and that meant keeping everyone fat, happy and inattentive.

After the session had adjourned, she waited until most of the audience had shuffled out. Her assistant, Miriam, joined her as La Pierre descended the short flight of steps off of the stage.

"That went well," Miriam said. "They seemed very receptive."

La Pierre smiled politely. The girl was barely into her twenties and had only been working with her for a few months. She was six inches taller than the politician, pretty and slight of build, with narrow hips and a flat chest, the kind of figure that looked good on a runway in designer fashions. Secretly, La Pierre wondered if Miriam wasn't biting off too much, wading into the fray. She was a help -- but a naïve one, at that.

"They seemed ready for the roast beef lunch," La Pierre said. "Never mistake politeness for engagement. People in leadership are always polite, even when they're skinning you alive. Come on, let's go have a drink."

The university pub was typical, a bunch of cheap fake-wood tables, a line of high-backed bar stools, a few beer taps. It was nearly empty, just one couple on the patio sipping wine and eating salad for lunch. La Pierre ordered a double gin-and-tonic while her assistant, worried about her boss's perception of her, had a club soda. "Do you think there will be any trouble with this year's funding request?" Miriam asked, apprehensive to fill the air with something other than silence as they waited for their drinks.

They took a seat at one of the high tables, the politician's feet not even close to touching the floor while seated on the tall stool. But she didn't seem to mind. "Hmmm? Oh, I don't expect so," La Pierre said. "The committee has had such success going into places individual nations have traditionally tiptoed around that there's probably a certain sense of reliance there."

"Even after the incident in Dar Es Salaam?"

La Pierre hadn't thought about Dar Es Salaam in months, a failed UN attempt the year prior to rescue a group of western scientists, funded by the committee, from extremists. It had mostly passed from the public consciousness after the media lost interest; most of the extremists also died in the shootout. In fact, until the scientists' deaths, few in the public had ever heard of the committee.

"Politicians have expediently short memories," La Pierre cautioned her. "The public also forgets quickly and moves on when distracted. But Politicians do not even require the distraction; just a desire to leave difficulties in the past for expediency in the future."

Miriam admired her boss. Though La Pierre was only five-feet-two-inches tall, she projected magnetism and dynamism. She always seemed so focused, Miriam thought, so unflustered by outside interruptions. For a leading conservative politician, it was essential she always be cool, calm and collected – except when addressing her voters, of course. Then passion ruled the day.

And it worked. Though at least half the politicians in the assembly found her politics offensive, she still managed to get things done, to affect change, sometimes on a national level. There was no doubt that some of her sway came from her family's long history in politics; her father had been a mainstay of the far right for decades, following the end of the Second World War.

"And they seemed okay with the arrangement to stay in the city," Miriam said. "That must be good news."

There had been a small move afoot to have the committee relocate to Brussels, which La Pierre had no doubt would give member states the impression that it could be controlled more easily – exactly why they had agreed on Montpellier in the first place; it was large enough to suit the purpose, close to Nice and Italy, and there were no other major EU offices in the city. And it suited other political ends; La Pierre had other business in the small French city, though not of the type she would ever share with the impressionable young Miriam.

A serious and often dour woman with an easily repeated short haircut, La Pierre felt as though her time was being wasted when she had to sit through pointless conjecture or personal discussions. But Miriam was an efficient booker and manager of her schedule, so it was worth putting up with her.

"Will you stay here over your vacation, Madame?" Miriam asked. "The weather is still very nice…"

"I shall return to Paris for a few days then come back," La Pierre said. "Have you made plans?"

Miriam smiled. "My fiancée is coming to visit from La Rochelle."

"Ah hah! Young love," said La Pierre. "There is nothing that can compare. What does he do, this fiancé of yours?"

"He runs a restaurant; fresh seafood and soup every day, that sort of thing."

"Hmmph," said La Pierre. "The west coast is nice, but only if you can stand the English tourists."

"Of course, Madame." Like her employer, Miriam despised foreigners, particularly those from Africa and Asia. Her father had taught her many years earlier that they were parasites, ticks that sucked the lifeblood from France then hung onto her until she was immobilized by financial commitments. He was no fonder of British or American visitors, who typically hadn't learned the language and spoke loudly at all times, and with an insincere familiarity. "So far his experience has been a good one," she said. "But you never know with the English."

After the drink, they walked across campus to the parking area, which sat by Rue de Truel; it was sunny, and both enjoyed the chance to unwind. Students strolled along, books and laptops under arms. La Pierre's limousine driver had been instructed to meet them at the pickup zone in front of the lot, just a five-minute amble from the bar. As they approached, the limousine driver stood at the ready then quickly opened the back door so that they could climb inside.

La Pierre looked around, drinking in the city. Even though she was looking forward to Paris and seeing her husband Gerard, she had grown fond of Montpellier. It felt a little bit like home. It wasn't designed to impress, although much about it was impressive; if anything, it had become a college town, a center of education and commerce. So it didn't compare to Paris on a grand scale. But it had culture, and decent restaurants and, perhaps most importantly, plenty of places for quiet reflection.

She wondered if she was making a mistake, aligning with foreigners, working outside the auspices of her French political role. The Association Commercial Franco-Arabe was pragmatic, to be sure, a business cabal with undeniable influence via its well-connected board; but she secretly feared how her role within the group would be received by her supporter base, if they ever discovered her involvement. She had been re-elected repeatedly on promises of ridding French soil of its pervasive foreign influence, and yet she was spending her weekends immersed in an organization that was global in its reach as could be, exerting its influence in the domestic affairs of multiple nations.

But she did not dwell on it for long. Ultimately, La Pierre had decided, her goal of leading the Republic would be best served by using the ACF to manipulate public perception, to direct its formidable financial and political muscle towards her own ends and against opponents.

She missed Gerard whenever she had to stay in Montpellier. He was a realist, her sounding board. Perhaps it was old-fashioned these days to still love one's husband after twenty years; but La Pierre was no fashionista, and they had never been happier together.

2.

The asset knew he was running short of time. He'd found the building a day earlier, a five-story walkup along Av. Emile Diacon, less than six hundred yards from the location. It was a square brick building with black metal fire escapes up one side. He hadn't been sure of access, but it appeared under renovation. No one had been working there a day earlier, and the trend continued. The block around it seemed silent, a mash-up of small, older homes and government or education-type low-rise buildings. He scanned local roads in each direction; they were quiet, nearly devoid of cars. He carried the hard-sided guitar case from his rented car to the side of the walkup, then jumped up and grabbed the bottom rung of the collapsible fire escape ladder, pulling it down to just above ground level. He climbed the four flights to the highest wrought-iron balcony, then one additional ladder attached to the wall, snug to the brick, that led up to the roof. He pulled himself up and over the lip, the texture of the brick rough under his hands.

The roof was flat and empty, just a skylight midway, a one-foot concrete wall around the edge. He placed the case on the ground next to it, facing toward the target zone. He opened the case and took out the bipod first, then began to assemble the weapon.

The shot was long, but the wind was near still and the asset had hit numerous targets from a greater distance. He had no self-doubt. It had been a long wait, nearly six years; in the week prior he'd played through it multiple times in his head, running through scenarios, calculating methods of egress, escape routes and likely police intercept points, cross streets that law enforcement would close off in an attempt to bottle up and find their man. He had no choice but success; things were just getting started, and the asset was along for the ride.

He attached the sight and took wind judgments, adjusting in two-and-a-half mile-per-hour increments, to make up for the breeze being so slight. As with a day earlier, the location was busy, a steady stream of fat cats getting ready to go somewhere and get fatter, limousines and upscale sedans pulling out of the lot adjacent to the college. But as personal as the mission felt, the asset was a pro. There was no need for any collateral damage, and no great desire on his part to stretch the mission parameters.

The asset waited for five minutes, then ten. He was beginning to think he'd missed the window, although his advance scouting had suggested the lunch hour would be perfect. He swung the crosshairs along the row of parked cars.

There.

He spotted the pair when they were less than twenty yards away from their vehicle. He lined up his target, took a deep inhalation of breath and held it. His barrel tracked them to the car, moving in a smooth, deliberate motion to match their pace.

Then it stopped.

Then he slowly squeezed the trigger.

Six hundred yards away, Miriam watched her boss scan the area and wondered what she was looking for. She would never have a chance to ask.

The .338 caliber bullet passed cleanly through La Pierre's neck, severing her carotid artery. She collapsed to her knees, blood spraying from the wound, before tumbling forward onto the cement. Miriam screamed, then tried to help, trying to staunch the bleeding with her hand, but unable to stop it from gushing out onto the sidewalk. The limousine driver crouched beside her and tried also, the puddle of blood growing larger, soaking into his pant cuffs; La Pierre's eyes were empty, a light switched off inside; the nearby traffic continued to pass by, oblivious to what was happening, horns honking, lanes changed at a pace unsafe to all.

Six hundred yards away, the asset was already down the first ladder by the time Marie La Pierre breathed her last, her final look at the world just a vacant gaze towards the blue Mediterranean sky. By the time the ambulance arrived, he was halfway to the airport in the back of a cab. By the time police forensics had determined the possible origin point of the shot, he was in a different city altogether, leaving nothing behind.

2.

8. /

WASHINGTON, D.C.

Walter Lang hated being overnight duty officer. It was thankless, and it was rare that anything important or actionable happened. But for some reason, he always got called in nonetheless. Even then, protocol for a serious incident was to call in the deputy director, so in effect he was a message boy delivering an unwelcome message, waking someone up with very little helpful detail to offer.

The sniper report out of Europe wasn't an American security issue, but La Pierre was an important figure to the continent's far right, and that always came with implications, the possibility of more trouble in retaliation. It came in at just after six in the morning, as Lang prepared to end his shift and go home for a solid eight hours of sleep. He contemplated pretending not to see it and leaving it for the morning duty officer, but instead decided to call Jonah Tarrant for an assessment; as David's de facto right-hand man, he thought, Jonah would know whether it was worth hauling the deputy director out of bed and risking his wrath.

Tarrant answered right away and Lang explained what had happened. "There's no word yet on a suspect or motive," he concluded.

"The administration is a big fan of the environmental committee," Tarrant said. "We can't completely ignore it; at the very least, within a few hours, they'll want to know if it jeopardizes the committee's operations."

"Should I call David?"

"That's up to you," Jonah said, wanting deniability, realizing that Walter had called him for the same self-interested reason. "But we have a good working relationship with the French right now, and the Brits don't. We could offer assistance There are points to be scored."

But scoring points just required the work, not the oversight, and Lang had made the mistake when younger of waking up a superior unnecessarily. It was a fine line; it was also ridiculous and unprofessional to have to worry about calling him in the first place. But it was what it was. So instead, Lang roped in the analysts early and set them to work, six of his brightest young minds.

3.

When David Fenton-Wright finally arrived at the bullpen, the analysts had been pulling research and making calls for two hours. They were seated at a half-dozen terminals, the results displayed simultaneously on projections across one wall.

Fenton-Wright watched Lang overseeing it all for a handful of seconds then waded in. "Assessment report," he said.

"A delegate to the WTC enviro committee was assassinated four hours ago," Lang said. "Single shot, from distance. Real craftwork; locals are saying six hundred yards plus, so totally concealed."

"What about the victim? What can you tell me about him?"

"Her," Lang said. "Marie La Pierre, fifty-two. She's a former provincial politician from Limoges, southwest of Paris. Highly nationalistic, a conservative but not a traditionalist; she has won support in the weakened French economy for her stance against immigration and she has a fairly extensive list of enemies."

Fenton-Wright seemed deep in thought for a moment.

"Sir?" Lang said.

"La Pierre. La Pierre. That's interesting." But he didn't elaborate.

Lang couldn't stand the man. David struck him as a political predator, always on the lookout for the easy answer and the positive press clip.

"Is that meaningful to us in some way? The name of the victim?"

"Need-to-know," Fenton-Wright said. "It's related to Fawkes. I'll let you know what I can. Are we working on an enemies list?"

"Paris has already sent one out through Interpol. It's long." Lang recognized the codename for the agency's deep-cover man in Britain. He knew nothing about him other than his existence, a secret discussed only at the highest levels. "So it could be personal instead of political?"

"It's possible," Lang said. "At this point, it's too early to rule anything out."

"What do we have in France right now?"

"A handful of assets on standby and a team at the embassy in Paris. Not much."

"Get them into play," Fenton-Wright said. "Let's see if we can help our Euro friends narrow this down – with their permission, of course. Anything on the hitter?"

"Meticulous, professional. Picked up his shell casing and even brushed dirt over the spot on the building ledge where he set his rest. Likes a western weapon, doesn't mind an absurdly long shot. No prints, no fibers. As for matching a name to it? Your guess is as good as mine, David."

"Anyone else?" he called out loudly.

2.

A young analyst to his left spoke up. "Sir? We've got a full workup."

That was a neat trick, Lang thought, *given that we don't know detail one about the shooter yet.*

"Go ahead," said Fenton-Wright.

"White male, late thirties, about six-foot-tall, extensive military experience."

"Elaborate."

"According to French police, the furthest smudges from the wall were one and seven-eighths of a foot away on the rooftop, indicating his kneeling distance and putting him at a likely height between five-feet-eleven inches and six-feet-two inches. The bullet was a .338, suggesting a military shooter from a western nation, possibly American, British or Canadian."

It sounded fancy, but what it amounted to was nothing, Lang thought. The projects would be based on common variables from multiple cases; but commonalities were never guaranteed. All they needed, for example, was a suspect with arms two inches longer than the norm, and their height profile could be off substantially. "Why late thirties?" he asked.

"The profile suggests someone with recent activity, based on the availability of shorter kill shots. The shooter was very confident, sir," the analyst said. "Older snipers who've been out of the game for a while? I don't think they go over five hundred yards just to get a marginally better escape route. But this guy was supremely sure of himself."

Even though it was just a more formal repetition of what Lang had told him, Fenton-Wright nodded, hands on hips, pleased with himself, as if he were the one doing the actual work. "Have we contacted our European and British friends yet?"

"Yes sir," Lang said. "They're waiting for our queue. They're expecting us to contribute because the president has been the environmental committee's biggest fan, but they're going to want to sign off on anything we do and take a lead, of course."

"Would that it weren't so," Fenton-Wright said. "Okay, let's get to work people. Let's see how we can shake that shooter loose."

SEPT. 8, 2015, PARIS, FRANCE

Under a cool-but-sunny sky, the gray Rolls Royce Phantom sedan pulled up to the curb outside the stubby brown-glass building housing La Banque de Commerce Français on Rue Chabon, just a few blocks away from the Champs Elysees. The driver wore a matching gray uniform with a peaked hat. He got out quickly, his patent leather boots glinting as he avoided the oncoming traffic and moved around the back of the car to open the rear door.

Yoshi Funomora stepped gingerly out onto the near-vacant sidewalk, looking both ways as he did. The shooting two days earlier had made them all nervous, he supposed. Any one of them could have been in Montpellier giving that speech.

Funomora was a heavy man with typically thick, dark hair. The Japanese representative wore a three-piece suit and bowler hat with spat-style brogue shoes, and even though it was sunny, he carried an umbrella with him at all times, just in case. He covered the few feet to the bank's entrance without incident, scanning the street behind him one more time before heading inside.

The public portion of the business was immense. Along one wall were a dozen teller windows, all staffed and busy and with waiting lines. Along the other were a series of offices used to conduct loan business and interviews. Customers milled around the center of the room, waiting for a turn on either side. At the very back, under a porcelain wall-hanging depicting Charlemagne on horseback and adjacent to the vault, was the double-sized entrance to a large conference room. The doors were usually locked, as only one group was authorized to use it, a group that, as far as most of the world was concerned, did not exist.

The chamber was functional, a semi-circular table taking up most of the room. It faced a series of screens hosting newscasts and political channels from around the globe. The five others had already arrived, each with the table ahead of them lit, a small card featuring the name of their home nation in small black print but their faces shrouded in the adjacent shadow. The chairman turned in his seat slightly and watched Funomora as he made his way to the last seat, next to La Pierre's empty chair.

"Now that Japan has graced us with his presence," the chairman said, "he can perhaps fulfill his obligation as the ACF's security adviser and explain what happened to France."

Funomora understood the implication in the chairman's tone, that somehow he was responsible for what had taken place. Personally, he blamed La Pierre. She was continually inflaming domestic politics in her home country, paying more attention to her supporter base than her responsibilities. The ACF had become accustomed to her absence, despite her stated loyalty. She had spent increasing amounts of time working on environmental issues. Now, her life was under a microscope, which meant outside attention. Outside attention was never particularly welcome.

"I would have thought it obvious," Funomora said. "France was shot dead by an assassin."

The chairman leaned towards his microphone. "Perhaps instead of being glib, Japan can explain why this happened and why he did not predict it."

"My apologies, chairman," Funomora said. He recognized the chairman's power and had no desire to make an enemy of the man. Besides, it was counterproductive. The ACF existed to extend the power of its contributors, not to divide them in the same manner as the nations they purported to represent.

"It is my belief at this point that we are dealing with a disgruntled individual, mostly likely someone angry with La Pierre's domestic politics, and further to that, someone standing to profit from her environmental work being truncated. There is a fairly long list of suspects."

"Have we had an opportunity yet to confer with our international security partners?" The chairman knew that the ACF had a long reach, supporters and admirers recruited from the ranks of covert intelligence around the globe.

Funomora had spent the entire prior evening at a brothel, but had no intention of sharing that tidbit. "Not as of yet, although experience tells us that at this point those agencies will be modeling hypotheticals and trying to narrow down a list of assailants."

"Why should it be someone disgruntled?" another panel member asked, his British accent clipped and formal. "And who among them would have the resources and contacts to hire an accomplished assassin?"

Funomora had no idea, no answers. But he'd learned over his lengthy political career that saying something was usually better than saying nothing. He'd also come to understand the massive advantages to protecting the ACF: the members offered diplomatic access to national leaders and security services, and the chairman's vast family oil reserves could underwrite almost unlimited funding and manpower, the ability to drop into any part of the world and, though force or commerce, affect enough change to meet each member's requirements. In some cases, that may have simply meant a small change in government policy with great financial benefit down the road; in other, more lawless places, it had meant tactical intervention; and it was done with aplomb, never a hint that the ACF's efforts had been compromised by international authorities.

"The first part is easy," the Japanese diplomat said. "La Pierre's use of division to succeed domestically has united the political left against her. She incited hatred of immigrants, Anglophobia and held an elementally fascist/neo-conservative approach to her role."

"And the funding for this venture?" the chair asked. "Is there anyone on her enemies list well-heeled enough to put this all together?"

"A few," Funomora said. "It should not take us long to get an idea of where this originated and who may have made the call."

The chairman was skeptical. "Perhaps," he said. "We shall have to wait and see what the security establishment comes up with. For all of our sakes, Japan, we had better hope you are correct."

Britain spoke up, his tone clipped, upper class. "Is there any reason to believe the ACF's secrets have been compromised? Could someone be aware of La Pierre's clandestine activities on our behalf?"

Funomora had been suspicious of 'Britain's' motivations for six months, ever since his replacement of the now deceased 'America'. He ignored the source of the question. "No, chairman. The group is secure. Of that you can be assured."

The chairman nodded, but said nothing. He was far less confident in Japan's security efforts.

China spoke up. "Shall we replace her?"

The chairman shook his head gently. "Not immediately. Eventually, of course, we must grow stronger. But we must ensure, first and foremost, that we maintain secrecy. There are simply too many interested outside participants to make any sort of noise right now. To ongoing business. China…"

"Yes chairman?"

"Can you advise on the situation in Harbin?"

2.

"The suppression of the south city gangs has, as we predicted, been a massive boon to the narcotics sales of their rivals to the north. Along with our consulting fee, we have agreed to the gangs' request to pressure the regional assembly for a drug crackdown, in order to justify price increases."

"Excellent," Khalidi said. "Our Afghan operation are still producing a steady supply?"

"They are, despite competing with Tillo Bustamante's operations for the best prices on poppies by the ton," Russia said. "When we cut them off…"

"The blowback will start a war between the two sides that will decimate the Harbin underworld for years," China said. He leaned forward into the light, turning towards the chairman. "Once again, chairman, masterfully executed."

Khalidi ignored the compliment. "Britain, have you had any luck on the tobacco issue?"

"Not as yet," Britain said, his accent clipped, old school Eton or Harrow. "However, my discussions with the Health Minister and others continue. I think we'll get there."

"Good, good," the chairman said, satisfied. "Germany, how are we on the hydrogen fuel cell funding?"

"I continue to exert pressure on the chancellor, chairman," Germany said, his voice older, more hesitant. There was always something slightly tired about Herr Doktor, Funomora felt. "There is little opposition, in principle, to anything that will help the automotive sector, and the sector owns most of the research into Hydrogen systems. However, some sectors of the cabinet are leery of further inflaming the nation's relationship with France and Spain."

Khalidi nodded. "Fine, but don't let it get away from you, Germany. Gentlemen, we are on the precipice of our most productive year since the ACF's formation. Let us not let La Pierre's death deflect us from that fact. We still have much important work to do."

After the meeting had broken up and the ACF board members had gone their separate ways, the man designated as "Britain" took an older-model, boxy white Renault taxi to Rue Jacob, just a few blocks south of the River Seine in the city's sixth district. The area was, like most of Paris, flanked by six- and seven-story walkups in light grey concrete, the ground floors mostly devoted to shops, boutiques, cafes and wine bars. The area was also home to a series of chic hotels and the apartment prices were surprisingly affordable for Paris, as far as Sir Anthony Abbott, Lord Cumberland, was concerned.

3.

The Eurostar to Paris only took four hours from London these days, which also made the apartment sensible; it wasn't that Sir Anthony had tired of hotel rooms after years as a diplomat and bureaucrat. It was the mere fact that, despite the French tolerance for marital infidelity, Sir Anthony had no desire for his relationship with a local woman to become public.

He'd worked within the British intelligence community for decades, so he knew better, knew that Annalise was a weakness a man of his stature could ill afford. And yet, he loved her as much, in her own way, as he did his wife. It was selfish; she was thirty years his junior, just reaching middle-age and still extravagantly beautiful.

At the building's lobby front desk, he gestured a greeting to the doorman before taking the adjacent flight of marble stairs to the third floor. He was breathing heavily and cursing his age by the time he reached the apartment. He began to fumble with the lock but before he could insert his key, the door swung inwards.

"Anthony!" She was wearing a dinner gown, already made up for the evening, her honey blonde hair pushed up, eyes made up, lipstick fresh. "I wasn't expecting you for another half hour."

"My meeting ended early," he said, leaning in to kiss her on the cheek. "A spot of dinner up the street, then back here for dessert, hmm?"

"That sounds lovely," she said. "Did you bring me back anything nice from London?"

"As a matter of fact…" he said, producing the skinny jewellery box from his inside jacket pocket.

She chewed her lower lip nervously then pulled the little green bow, undoing its knot so that she could open the box. She lifted the lid. The locket was gold, small, wafer thin. Her eyes widened. "It's lovely," she said.

He took it from the box and helped her put it on, attaching the little clasp above the fine hairs of her lower neck. "To remind you of me when I can't be here," he said.

2.

OCT. 1, 2015, LAKE ACCOTINK, VIRGINIA

Brennan stared over the water, his line dipping just below the surface but immobile, the lake top almost still. He had hoped to land something he could take home to Carolyn for dinner but it had been a multi-hour exercise in frustration.

Callum McLean looked on, amused.

They'd been casting lines off of the bank on the tributary creek that led into Lake Accotink, south of Annandale; they sat on the mossy ground, under the overhanging tree branches, in an area where the grass had been trampled down by repeat visits. The weather was cool and the water was placid, dark green. They'd brought a whole cornucopia of live and artificial bait: crickets, worms, red jigglers; fuzzy leaders and purple divers; but nothing was biting. The lake had been drained a few years earlier but the trout stock was supposed to be getting healthy again.

Brennan checked his friend for a moment and received a placid smile back. Callum was the epitome of a services man; he still got up at dawn, still rolled his clothes to pack them, then rolled them out under the hotel mattress when he travelled to keep them pressed; and he was fitter now than Brennan had been during active duty.

He'd also warned Brennan the creek was so low these days that not much was biting. But he hadn't listened, figuring he knew the lay of the land better than his ex-SEAL buddy, who'd only moved to Annandale a year earlier. McLean set his rod against a fallen tree trunk but was watching the line, just in case. He'd cracked a ginger ale and was sitting back in a folding chair, watching Brennan cast and recast.

"You can drop bait as many times as you want," McLean said. "Ain't going to make the fish magically appear." McLean knew he could talk to Joe openly, without worrying about offending him. He had stayed in when Brennan discharged nine years earlier; but now his own time in the services had come to an end. They didn't talk about it much. Both realized how difficult it would be for the larger man. "Besides, it's too hot for trout now. We should have gotten here earlier in the day."

Brennan was unconvinced. "Look at all those reeds and rocks: if that's not trout country right there…"

"It's not," McLean said. "For someone trained to be a survival expert, you sure are one lousy fisherman, you know that? You might find a jackfish down there normally, maybe some rock bass. But not in this stream. You notice how few flies there are buzzing the surface? No organic matter to attract them. They may say they restocked this stretch of water, but it sure hasn't taken yet."

3.   81

"You could have told me two hours ago, before we got here."

"I tried, remember? But you were busy reminding me of how you were an old grizzled country hand who 'knew this creek backwards and forwards, doggone it'."

"Uh huh. You knew that was idiotic though, right?"

"Hey, if I stopped you every time you were about to do something dumb you'd never have learned anything in Iraq. Come to think of it, I did, which is why you're still here. I guess I just haven't learned yet, either."

Brennan reeled in, then cast out again, not even bothering to check the condition of his live bait. Both men fell silent for several minutes, the only sound the slight rippling of the water and the birds in the surrounding trees. "Felt weird, watching them burying Bobby," Brennan finally said. "After everything that went down at Al Basra, I'd figured we'd lost him a long time ago. But he almost made it; he almost got it together again."

McLean nodded but said nothing. He'd already brought up Chief Petty Officer Terry Corcoran's aborted mission once that week, and knew how difficult it was for Brennan.

His friend had had confidence in the chief, trust. He'd helped keep him alive, too, through a second tour in the Gulf. Then they'd been assigned to help take back an offshore pipeline control facility, one of two teams of SEALS who stole in under cover of darkness to 'liberate' the key facility from Saddam Hussein's forces.

They'd taken the control room within an hour, as ordered, and rounded up the Iraqis, locking them away in a storage room, unarmed and dressed only in their underwear, waiting for a larger force to arrive and secure the place long-term. But during the short gun battle, the second unit had disappeared into the bowels of the facility. When they didn't respond to radio hails, Brennan had volunteered to go find them.

What he'd discovered instead was a massive vault, filled with some of the late dictator's obscenely large collection of stolen art, jewels and gold – and Corcoran leading the second unit as it pillaged the place. He'd struck a deal with his friend, a warrant officer nicknamed Paddy, that they'd divide the spoils without reporting the find.

Brennan had played it by the book, threatening to report them, and things had come to a head quickly, weapons drawn, all pointed at one another. Then Bobby had gone looking for Brennan at McLean's request; he had almost reached the vault when a figure carrying a weapon had burst out of one of the offices. Bobby opened fire, centre mass, without thinking. The child, a son of one of the Iraqi officers who had been widowed during the U.S. bombing campaign, died instantly.

2.

Eventually, they'd diffused the situation in the vault and the find had been reported, though Corcoran had insisted Brennan would have a target on his back for life. The only real casualties had been the little boy and Bobby's mental health. He was never the same after that, McLean thought.

"He liked you a lot, you know," McLean said. "He admired you."

Brennan smiled at that. Bobby had been a great guy once, a long time ago. And Callum was the best friend he'd ever had, a brother, someone he could tell anything. He was surprised they'd been out for two whole hours, and his buddy hadn't raised his stalled agency career.

As if on cue, McLean used one of his giant hands to set the ginger ale can down. "You know, you could always re-enlist."

"If I wanted, I still couldn't," Brennan said. "One particular guy at the agency has me dangling; he's had me dangling for two years now. I get the pay check and I guess one day I'll get the pension, but I'm permanently inactive." He tried not to sound bitter. It was what it was, as Walter liked to say. "What about you? You figure out what you're going to do now that you're out?"

McLean told Brennan how tough it was to go back to civilian life. "I've been doing some consulting but it's tough, you know. I don't really have business contacts. There's just not a lot out there for me," he said. "I mean, I can kill a guy eight different ways before he looks at me funny, but that doesn't do you much good in the business world. I can field strip and reassemble an M60 in a minute, but I know jack shit about computers. I can survive for days with nothing, but I don't know how to get a bank to give me a business loan."

Brennan thought about it. What was he supposed to tell his friend? His own changeover had been problematic, at best. He'd found himself facing an uncertain future; the switch to the Agency had come three years before he met Carolyn, after it scouted and approached him, during a Thailand vacation that had devolved into a mess of its own.

Maybe Callum needed the same kind of offer.

"Not that I'd recommend it, given my situation, but you could always..."

"No," McLean said before he finished the thought. "Once I'm done, I'm done. I've found a few freelance security jobs so far; it's enough. It's not perfect, but it's enough. That's the deal. No more working for the commander-in-chief. I guess if things really go to shit I could always go back and teach. Annapolis is always looking for qualified instructors; I could go bust some midshipman ass for a while. Make me feel better, if nothing else."

"How is Ellen taking things?"

3.

McLean shrugged. "She's good, I guess. It's weird, and I almost don't want to admit this, but when I was in, all I could think about was getting out, getting home and spending time with her. Now that I've got an endless supply of it, I find myself trying to get away, taking any work I can find, anything involving security, the military, training; it's like I just can't relate to all the normal stuff she's talking about. Michael's troubles with his schoolwork, and her parents visiting, and the mortgage and… it just feels sort of like I'm stuck in someone's dream and around the next corner, it'll turn into a nightmare. Or worse, it won't change at all."

Brennan wanted to offer encouragement, but Callum's story was nothing new to other returning veterans, guys who'd seen sides of life – and death – that civilians could never imagine. It made a lot of day-to-day living seem rote, scheduled pointlessness. It had been easier for him because he'd always been a contrarian, the team's alternate voice. After so long taking orders, Brennan had wanted out of the navy. But to Callum, the SEALs had been like family. Brennan knew he'd lost his sister and his father within three years of each other, the former in a road accident and the latter from a long, painful decline due to cancer. And he knew Callum needed support, something to keep his mind off work, to stop him from being morose.

He didn't have any answers, at least not right away. Instead, he just said, "Don't worry, brother, it'll get better. It does get better."

"Yeah," McLean said. "Eventually, I guess."

Brennan got home shortly after lunch, fishless. His first thought was to tell Carolyn how he'd had a huge one jump the hook, making the whole trip seem kind of worth it; then he decided against lying, because she could read him like a book.

Then he remembered she wouldn't be home for four more hours, at the earliest.

It had been four weeks since they'd returned from California, and two since she'd gone back to the office. His only demand was that she wouldn't talk about the job when she got home at night; given his status as Carolyn's sounding board for pretty much everything in life, the idea had gone over like a lead blimp. But despite her protestations, so far it was working fairly well. Now he just had to get used to the idea of her bringing home the bacon while he sat on the shelf and grew stale.

2.

He came in through the back door, went to the fridge and grabbed a bottle of water, then flicked on the small kitchen countertop television. CNN was reporting from London, where the chairman of an environmental panel was addressing British security officials regarding the month-old shooting investigation. Brennan watched for a few minutes and turned it off in disgust. He'd never much liked the media, but he had even less time for bureaucrats and politicians.

The phone rang. He let it sit there for a couple of seconds before picking up, knowing it would just kick over to the answering machine if he didn't.

"Yeah."

"That's friendly," Carolyn said on the other end.

"Yeah, sorry." He absent-mindedly scratched the light beard he had coming in. "What's up?" She never called from work.

"Have you been watching the news today?"

"The shooting investigation? Not really. Callum and I were hanging out."

"So, fishing but not catching anything, then?"

"Something like that."

"Anyway," she said, "can you get dinner ready for the kids? I'm going to be held up here again."

Again? She'd hardly been home in the week, leaving before six thirty in the morning to beat the traffic rush and working overtime every night. "Is this going to be an ongoing issue?" he asked, even though he knew there wasn't much he could do about it.

"It's David. You know how gung-ho he can be. He's had me working on multiple files, and I'm a bit overwhelmed." The tone suggested she wanted support, but Brennan wasn't in a giving mood.

"Maybe you need to tell him that," he said, knowing she wouldn't. "Maybe you need to put your family first and come home for dinner occasionally." He regretted it instantly, felt like an ass. He knew none of it was her fault, but he resented her, resented that Carolyn was still valued by the agency.

"I'm trying honey," she said, "really I am. I know it's frustrating, but we've just had a run of crap here that has been never ending. Keep a plate for me, okay?"

After he got off the phone, Brennan thought about calling Callum, seeing if he had more detail on the Annapolis training positions. He worried about his friend's reintroduction to everyday life, setting his own schedules, making all of his own decisions. He was lucky he had Ellen, Brennan thought; no one seemed more of a lifer in the SEALs than McLean, and he seemed genuinely perplexed by a normal life. It didn't surprise Brennan, who'd known Callum when he was young, right after enlisting, still starry-eyed, undisciplined, yet to be moulded by the rigors of a tough, scheduled routine and an even tougher job.

He needed to get out of the house, to get back to work. He checked his watch; it was just after two-thirty in the afternoon, almost time to go pick up the kids. It felt like he'd just dropped them off, like the day's mundane chores were beginning to turn into a routine. That couldn't be good, he thought. It wasn't how he saw his life going after the agency; but then again, there was no 'after', as far as Brennan could tell. In a way, he and Callum were facing a similar problem. Brennan just decided he cared a whole lot less than he once had; a whole lot less than his friend still did.

That night, while Carolyn slept soundly on one side, her hand under the pillow and a serene look on her face, Brennan tossed and turned in his sleep, the return of an occasional nightmare waking him every so often. He replayed the Al Basra incident unwillingly, the images harshly sharp even after so many years; Corcoran swaggering down the hallway, convinced he was untouchable, then almost stumbling over Bobby; Bobby, on his knees, weeping over the body of a thirteen-year-old boy; Corcoran laughing it off, his friend Paddy smirking.

He'd had the dream before, but it never got easier to take.

DEC. 4, 2015, LONDON, ENGLAND

The parade of images on the projection screen was brutal, stark and clear in the darkened room, each shot a repeated theme of men in balaclavas and military fatigues knocking in front doors, young people being arrested, college students in t-shirts and pyjama pants shocked to the core to have their homes invaded, tossed to the ground, arms pulled behind them roughly as they were restrained. The special police units tossed smoke grenades, and flash-bangs, and on several occasions shot and killed fleeing suspects before they'd even been questioned. They hit targets in the cities of London, Barcelona, Paris, Montpellier, Rennes, Bordeaux and Pau, all of it being meticulously filmed for analysis by multiple EU intelligence services.

2.

Most of the film would never be seen publicly, but Sir Anthony, Abbott, Lord Cumberland was obliged to sit through the entirety, hours of video, thousands of pages of reports and briefings. The low light in the room made the whole thing seem that much grimmer.

As the Prime Minister's liaison to MI6, he'd been given the unenviable task of drafting the preliminary report outlining Britain's contribution to the sniper hunt. From a position of public perception, of course, Britain was not involved, merely advising their French colleagues. But there had been quiet consensus among EU partners that such a brazen attack on a politician in a non-leadership position represented a significant danger, a pervasive risk of further similar attacks, and an ensuing fear that could damage the operations of multiple governments.

Sir Anthony was old and wise enough to know that wasn't true, and he watched with increasing scepticism regarding the value of the raids; he leaned on his hand, elbow on the table, cynical bright blue eyes beneath his aquiline profile and dark silver-grey hair and moustache, barely illuminated by the projector. His body language was usually still young and spry – relatively -- even though he was in his early seventies. But as he watched, he folded one leg over the other's thigh, leaned on his elbow, his mood bordering on morose.

The images were ghastly, he thought, the worst excesses of authority.

He knew no matter how many politicians keeled over or were murdered, governments would just roll on. It was the reality of bureaucracy, the manner by which governments kept operating even after the oft-spectacular, seemingly important political defeats and ideological changes of major elections and minor coups. In reality, Sir Anthony knew, most of his colleagues could fall into a deep, dark hole and most of the public would be none the wiser – except, perhaps, that the cost of government would be cut in half and they'd probably save some money.

Nevertheless, he'd sworn an oath to fulfill his role in the public service to his utmost, and so he sat, for endless hour on hour, at a large, oval conference table at MI6 London headquarters, watching the films and listening to an exhausting review of enforcement efforts, narrated by a middle-aged service officer in a drab blue sweater as he droned on in a monotone. The operations had hit back alleys, back rooms, safe houses, private offices, college dormitories. Agents from a half-dozen countries – mostly working at cross-purposes – swept through the ranks of the European and western military/industrial complex looking for ties to the shooter, any inkling or word that someone might have expected it.

Marie La Pierre's political enemies were trotted out and publicly vilified, then quietly let go. Eco-terrorists were grilled under hot lights; and left-wingers, who had reviled her before the shooting, did so even more after a day or two of interrogation.

And after three months, more than a thousand interviews, dozens of interrogations and several million pounds in expenses ... they had nothing. Not a hint, not a print. There was a suspected forger murdered in Paris a few days before the shooting who was known to have worked with Islamic radical groups, and could have helped out the shooter in some way. But if he had, that piece of business had died with him.

Lord Cumberland had the unenviable task of explaining the lack of progress to a select committee of the House of Commons. He walked the marble hallway of the east wing with purpose in his stride, joined by the director of MI6 – dubbed 'C' – along with its director of foreign intelligence, as well as Sir Anthony's executive assistant. His mind was on the job at hand and he ignored the row of classic portraits, the antique wood benches that no one ever used. He'd already briefed the Prime Minister at Number 10 and was not looking forward to repeating the exercise two or three more times over the course of the next few days.

Such was the price of inclusion, he supposed. His role as MI6 liaison and chairman of the intelligence review board was to consider whether the activities of the WTC environmental committee prompted the assassination or whether La Pierre had been targeted by domestic malcontents. Elevated to the upper house twenty years earlier for helping to evacuate British and Commonwealth citizens trapped in war-torn Rwanda, Sir Anthony was respected enough on all political fronts to compel confidence that the investigation was being taken seriously. And even though his peerage was not hereditary, his family was old money, well-connected with anyone who was anyone in parliament or the business community.

Sir Patrick, as C was known in his social circles, had actually headed up Britain's contribution to the La Pierre investigation. But Sir Anthony recognized Sir Patrick's growing infirmity; he was eighty years old, a small, frail man. It left him a figurehead to a series of intelligence community bureaucrats and alpha dogs doing the heavy lifting.

He was strictly along for show; the foreign intelligence director, Peter Marsden, was there to make sure that, should someone ask Sir Patrick a question, he would know how to answer it. They couldn't very well let Sir Patrick figure it out for himself; making a knight of the realm look old and feeble in front of the media didn't serve anyone's purposes.

2.

The committee room was filling up, mostly men, mostly in suits, a parade of assistants and other bureaucrats ostensibly there to make life easier for the people making the decisions – though no one actually believed it worked that way.

Cameras weren't allowed but press were, although only a handful had bothered to attend, doubtless relying on the British Press Association for coverage, if they could even find a spot for it in the nightly newscasts or on the next day's front page. These days, Lord Cumberland thought, it would be more likely ignored in favour of the latest entertainment star shenanigans. He'd stopped reading everything except the Economist and The Times – as well as his own clippings from a service, of course.

He took a seat with his colleagues at the witness table. The committee chairman was sympathetic and friendly, an old party Conservative back to the Thatcher days. He came over and shook Sir Anthony's hand, making several comments the peer didn't really hear, as his mind was elsewhere.

The session lasted over an hour and Sir Anthony supposed it was tedious for most, as they had no more evidence three months later to go on than they'd had at the time of La Pierre's death. They knew nothing of La Pierre's extracurricular activities, or her membership in the ACF, and Sir Anthony had no inclination to tell them.

It was, after all, Lord Cumberland's real interest in her affairs. He had managed to manipulate his way into an invitation to join the group, proffered by the founder and chairman himself, the Jordanian industrialist Ahmed Khalidi. He had replaced the now-deceased American panelist, initiated into a group whose sole purpose seemed to be the acquisition and application of global power.

"And so in conclusion, ladies and gentlemen, every indication to date is that this was an isolated case, pointing to a single fanatic behind the trigger of a high-powered weapon, intent on causing misery and destruction. I should note that, from a personal perspective, Madame La Pierre's domestic politics raised concerns with many of her peers in government.

"Having said that, we cannot deny the dedication she brought to her pursuit of environmental criminals and protection of the planet. It is our hope that uncovering her assailant will put to rest any fears of a vendetta or issue with the environmental committee's work, which has received near universal praise from national leaders, and once again demonstrate, via prosecution and public censure, that civilized societies will not stand for this aggression.

3.

"To that end, Sir Patrick assures me that the intelligence community continues to pursue the assassin with zeal. With that, ladies and gentlemen, I would like to end my formal presentation and make myself available for questions."

An hour later, Lord Cumberland was ensconced in the back of his limousine, enjoying the drive home to Kingston-on-Thames, where his modest home and garden belied the image most have of the peerage and wretched excess – even if the location put it far beyond the financial reach of the average Londoner.

Along the route, he passed the small red mailbox, attached to a private home's black wrought-iron fence. He habitually glanced its way, even though he rarely stopped in front of it. He'd used it as a drop just once in six years. In fact, until The ACF had approached him, he thought his days of spying for the Americans were over.

They'd recruited him in the early seventies; he was a principled former Cambridge man, angered over a decade of espionage embarrassments at the hands of the communists. His family fortune dwindling in the era of increased Soviet influence, he accepted their generous contributions towards his anti-communist league; angered at the twice-elected Labour governments of Harold Wilson, he readily agreed when his American handler suggested ratcheting up their collaboration, accepting a post first with the civil service, then with MI6. For twenty years, he'd fed their allies every state secret he could get his hands on. Even after the Iron Lady, Margaret Thatcher, took over, he continued to spy for America, aware that he was too deeply immersed to ever get out.

But if catching a communist spy was a triumph, catching one working for one's allies, he presumed, was nothing short of humiliating. In a sense, he hoped it might eventually make his position untenable to the Yanks; he hoped they'd simply cut him loose.

The driver clicked a remote control to open the gates and turned the car up the short driveway. The house was whitewashed, with old, dark wooden joins and an A-frame roof. Half of the side wall was obscured by the vines that had grown over the years. In front of the house were flower beds filled with the fading remains of what had been colorful annuals, the weather no longer co-operating.

The maid, Julia, opened the door when he arrived and took his legal briefcase, then his coat and hat. "Lady Cumberland is out shopping, sir," she said as she hung his coat up in the closet at the foot of the stairs. "She'll be back in a few hours."

2.   90

"Thank you, dear," Sir Anthony said. Julia had been with them for more than a decade. "Pour me a Gin with Angostura, would you? I'll take it on the patio."

Several months before La Pierre's death, he had been brought back into the fold. The Americans understood his nervousness. They'd been trying to infiltrate Khalidi's group for several years, however, and the chance of losing his intelligence was unacceptable, they said. So cutting his losses and stepping aside was out of the question.

He retrieved the paper from the telephone table in the main hallway. It was his habit to decompress after work by trying to finish the crossword in The Times, and on occasion, he actually managed to get it done with reasonable haste. Sir Anthony walked to the far end of the corridor, where a glass door opened into the back garden. An old brick patio lay beyond, home to a wrought-iron table and chairs with a sun umbrella, though it was tied down for the winter. It was cool in the backyard but dry, and he settled in just as Julia arrived with his drink.

"Will sir be needing me any more today?" the maid asked. "I'd like to leave a little early if…"

"That's fine, just fine," he said. "We can fend for dinner."

"I took the liberty of preparing a chicken pie, sir, and it's still warm on the rack by the stove, should Lady Cumberland return in time for the meal."

"Lady Cumberland" was his wife, Gretchen. They'd been together for fifty years, but the last twenty had been somewhat distant, his career continually keeping them apart. He wondered if she knew about Annalise; he hoped not. He still loved his wife, even if she didn't feel the same way in return. And if she didn't, he knew that that was his fault as well.

"Thank you dear, that's very decent of you," Sir Anthony said. "Run along now! Go and have some young person fun."

She curtsied politely. "Yes sir."

He took a seat, the unstirred drink on a coaster, odd droplets of moisture surrounding it on the wrought-iron latticework tabletop. He looked through the glass, casting his mind back to his youth; he was filled with regret over his decision, but Sir Anthony supposed that being forced back into the spy trade was part of his penance, a reminder that he'd never be free of having betrayed his home country.

It was more complicated than that, of course; no nation was the epitome of its ideals, and there would always be justifications for working surreptitiously against the state. But in his heart, he would always be an Englishman, and one who had betrayed England, even as the country he admired so much, America, displayed chinks in its armor, mistakes that proved it just as imperfect as other democratic nations. Communism was dead, and even though it had been the driving force behind his passion to defend capitalist democracy, he found that without an opposing ideology, he'd not only lost a sense of purpose, but also his justifications for behaviour he now accepted had been deplorable. He thought about La Pierre; she was an unctuous, unpleasant woman, Sir Anthony thought. He was not sad that she was gone; but he did worry. Had someone targeted members of the ACF or was the shooting merely a result of her own divisive politics?

A breeze briefly swept across their small backyard, blowing leaves, a hiss and crinkle as they caught the updraft, flew upwards a few feet, then slowly settled down to the brick patio once more. Sir Anthony didn't mind the late-year weather. After a day of racing between meetings and hearings, it felt refreshing to be out in the damp, cool air. He missed Annalise already.

He flipped to the crossword, folded the paper over and then down the middle, giving him a good working surface. "A cheap wigwam is ominously bound to fail," he said aloud. "Ten letters."

He didn't have a chance to hear the 'thwip' sound the bullet made as it cut past the edge of the hedge, before it pierced his neck and eviscerated his basal ganglia, destroying the connecting nerves between his brain and his body, switching off Lord Cumberland's life like a cheap light bulb. He slumped over the table, his head thudding to the surface, lying flat on its right side, his eyes wide open, mouth agape, his gin and tonic still on the table in his right hand, the angostura bitters swirling an angry rust-red in the clear drink, as the pool of blood formed on the table behind his skull.

DEC. 5, 2015, WASHINGTON, D.C.

Jonah Tarrant was present, which was new. Perhaps that explained why everyone was so tense, Walter Lang thought. National Security Council sessions were never exactly lighthearted, with half of the dozen people around the table in business suits and the other in dark-olive military dress; but today seemed dourer than typical. Lang sat to one side, within leaning distance of Fenton-Wright, in case his boss needed his input. Increasingly, that seemed rare.

Any nervousness about Tarrant being in the room certainly wasn't warranted, either; for all his political calculations, most people seemed to think Fenton-Wright's confidante was a pretty nice young man. Nevertheless, the conversation had been heating up for several minutes, barbs flying around the long oval table almost as frequently as facts. That, in and of itself, was nothing new; in his two years of sitting through NSC meetings, Lang had had his share of pointed debates. But as was often the case, he felt like the politics of the La Pierre and Lord Cumberland investigations were outweighing practical considerations.

"It's out of the question," David Fenton-Wright said, after the secretary of defense raised the novel concept of ignoring European jurisdictions and sending a team after the shooter. "First, we'd be treading on the toes of important allies, and would be bound to offend. Second, there's still no indication this requires any kind of ramp up. Our sources in the EU say they're leaning strongly towards a single shooter in both cases, perhaps with an ecologically based ax to grind."

The secretary of defense sounded mildly offended. "I'm not sure I appreciate your tone, deputy director," he said. "We're just exploring all of the options, putting everything out there on the table. You suggested Lord Cumberland's diplomatic co-operation was vital to our interests. I responded in kind, sir."

"Well, I'm sorry Mr. Secretary," Fenton-Wright said, "but it's important that we realize we don't really have a ticket to this dance. They haven't set a place for us at the table. And I don't imagine the current crop of EU parliamentarians is inclined to change that. This is their baby."

At the head of the table, the President had listened quietly, interjecting only to ask for the odd clarification over the course of the hour. Finally, he raised the point no one else had. "John," he asked his economic security adviser, "is it possible this is retaliation for Dar Es Salaam?"

Though the President had long known the agency had a mole in the British government, he had been shocked to find out the late spy's identity, just ten minutes before the meeting started, during a brief meeting with Fenton-Wright and Lang. If Lord Cumberland's true nature as a double agent were discovered during the sniper investigation, the embarrassment and diplomatic damage could be incalculable, he knew. He was also aware that at least half the room was, at Fenton-Wright's request, still unaware that the late diplomat had been a U.S. agent for decades.

Instead, he was hoping it was somehow about Dar Es Salaam. The Dar Es Salaam operation had seemed like a scene from a SWAT team takedown, a UN task force storming the captured portion of the embassy and triggering the explosion that had killed fourteen people, including three U.S. foreign service staffers. If it was about Dar Es Salaam, he believed, they already had a head start on the investigation and could perhaps wrap things up before any details of Sir Anthony's duplicity came to light.

John Younger considered the question carefully; more and more often, the president had come to rely on him for information and direction outside of the scope of the economy, and Younger was taking full advantage of it. "It's possible, sir, but unlikely.'"

"Why?"

Younger had been fully briefed by both the agency and the NSA, where he'd once served. "First, the lead time. We're talking a year between that incident and the first shooting. Second, there's the deliberate nature of the targets, politicians from different nations with little, if any, interplay. We've managed to put La Pierre and Abbott in the same room together, but only three times in the last five years, all EU social functions."

The president said nothing. Younger did not need to know about Ahmed Khalidi's group, and had not been privy to the file. Fenton-Wright and Director Wilkie had convinced him that its existence should be denied until there was enough evidence that the conspirators could not wriggle away.

Younger continued. "It has never been the M.O. of radical Islamists to go after the decision makers, to hit them where they live. It could be a new approach, but on the balance of probabilities, it's not likely. They sow fear by going after the public; most members of the public dislike their own leaders, so politicians tend to make poor targets. As well, radicals would gladly claim responsibility in a case like this, for the notoriety alone. But no group has come forward. So this isn't a broader concern, it's something specific to the two individuals who were shot. On the whole, I'd have to agree with David; this is out of our hands right now, at least above board."

2.   94

The secretary of defense was often the cynic at the table, convinced he had the military strength of the nation at heart while his peers jockeyed for personal political gain. He'd listened to Fenton-Wright discuss the situation for nearly an hour; he'd never trusted the man. "What about below board?" he said. "I get the sense I should bring it up, in case the agency gets the interesting idea of going ahead with something without first having discussed it with the council."

Fenton-Wright resisted an urge to snap at the man, although Lang caught the flash of anger. "Perhaps this is a discussion we should have outside of the President's company," he said firmly. "There are implications…"

The President waved him off. "Thank you, David, but we're all big boys here; we all know there are good reasons for some operations to be off the books."

"Yes sir," Fenton-Wright replied. "But even if we have the discussion, my advice would be the same. I'm certain there are implications beyond the realm of mere success and failure that are play here, but…"

Mark Fitzpatrick, the National Security Agency representative, had been sitting at the far end of the table in silence throughout, deep in thought. The president looked down the table's shiny dark surface towards him. "Mark? Does the NSA have anything to add?"

He was a slight man with receding brown hair that curled slightly on top naturally. He took off his glasses with a flourish, which Fitzpatrick had learned at media training could add gravitas in front of a camera. "We'd concur with the deputy director," he said. "An off-the-books mission here could raise tensions with our European partners…"

"Which is still better than some madman on the loose shooting them," the President said. He knew what Fenton-Wright was really trying to tell him, which was that Fawkes' cover had to be maintained, even in death. They needed to be involved, but even at the NSC, there was risk in discussing the spy's identity.

"Perhaps true," Fitzpatrick said. "But the inherent risks are considerable, and it will be seen as arrogant if exposed, due to the assumption that our European partners can't handle it."

"They've had months and gotten nowhere," the President said.

"True," Younger said. "It would have to be someone off the grid, with complete deniability. This is David's area, really."

Fenton-Wright almost panicked; he'd expected the NSA to put up some resistance and at the very least try to get involved in some manner. He was accustomed to getting some consensus behind his ideas but not endorsements. Endorsements meant he'd be left with direct responsibilities, political risk.

Still, there was one safe option.

3.   95

He smiled at the assembled group and leaned forward on the table. "We do have an asset who could handle something like this. He's smart, a former SEAL and navy investigator, and an expert in covert operations. He can get the quick results we're hoping for; but he's been under wraps for a while."

The defence secretary's eyes narrowed. "Under wraps?"

"I believe that was your request, Mr. Secretary," Fenton-Wright said, "something about agency missteps not embarrassing the navy?"

The politician looked puzzled. "You've lost me, David."

"Cast your mind back a few years to Colombia, Mr. Secretary," Fenton-Wright said. "You recall an extraction that went poorly involving a former SEAL…"

The President interjected, "That was your man Walter, wasn't it? That was you, right, Walter?"

Fenton-Wright answered for him. "Walter was the agent extracted, yes. The man doing the extracting was there on his own initiative, and he's been out in the cold ever since. If the NSA has no objection, it might be the right time to give him some hope that he can resurrect his career."

Fitzpatrick shrugged. "He's your boy, David. We won't object to the scope if your guy is going to take any heat – which I assume would be the case."

"It will be strictly, as you put it Mr. Secretary, 'below board'."

The President turned to Younger. "John, what do you think?"

"I think we should be nervous," he said. "There are working relationships at stake here, and official "unofficial" status isn't going to help those situations."

The President considered it. He wondered if Younger's caution related to his upcoming campaign. "Point taken. But the political blowback would be minimal."

"Perhaps," Younger said. "As David indicated, deniability is a key to this working."

It wasn't the president's preferred approach, working off the books. But there was more involved than the Brits knew and reputations were at stake; so, potentially, was the nation's working relationship with one of its largest trading partners. Fawkes had to be protected.

"Do it," he said.

Fenton-Wright walked to the planning session with Walter Lang by his side. The deputy director looked annoyed as they strode the hallway to the elevators.

"How did we go from 'we don't do black bag jobs' to 'under the table' in all of three minutes?" he complained. "The secretary just threw us under the bus."

That's the key issue here, Lang thought sarcastically, *whether we're looking good.* "Everyone in that room has a long memory," he suggested. "However this turns out, the agency's not going to wear it, unless we do nothing and Fawkes is uncovered."

"Or unless John Younger gets his way," the deputy director says. "He's had it out for us for a while now."

"He's probably going to win the nomination, you realize that."

"Don't remind me," said Fenton-Wright. "The President seems genuinely enamoured of the guy. But you notice how he never puts his own ass on the line; he just adopts one of the existing positions in the room."

They were approaching the double elevators that would take them to the ops centre. Lang reached into his pocket to check his phone. "Go ahead without me," he said to his boss. "I just need to make a quick call."

Lang waited until Fenton-Wright had entered the elevator and the doors had closed. "Hey, Terry? Yeah, it's Walter. Look, do me a quiet favour, okay? See if you can drum up a list of realistic profiles of guys who could make a six-hundred-yard shot into the wind. Before anyone goes after another political target, let's see if we can't narrow our list of potential snipers down some."

Terry gave him an affirmative. Lang hung up and hit the elevator down button, then waited for the car. The analysts allegedly already had a potential suspect to discuss. He wasn't sure why, or even if they came up with the name themselves. And if the decision was purely political, it was bound to have lousy consequences.

The planning session had been convened hastily, the deputy director demanding the presence of his three assistant directors, along with several other senior staff. They sat around the map table at Langley against a backdrop of computers and analysts.

"Ladies and gentlemen," said Fenton-Wright, "we have our assignment, which is to root out, identify and arrest the sniper who has assassinated a pair of EU politicians. What we need now are suspects. NCS, what have you got?"

3.   97

The deputy director of the National Clandestine Service got up and moved to the overhead projector at the end of the table. He turned it on and immediately brought the contents of his laptop to life at the end of the room, on a drop-down screen. It was a headshot, a man with wavy dark hair and a moustache, a tan. "This man is Faustillo "Tillo" Bustamante. Some of you may be familiar with him, but to those who are not, Bustamante is one of the heaviest investors in the emerging wind energy field in his native Spain. He also has wind holdings across the remainder of Europe and plans to build more."

He hit a button on the projector remote and it slid to the next web page. "This is a clip from *Paris Match* magazine, last fall. The angry guy pointing the finger is, once again, Bustamante. What we can't see in this shot is who he is pointing at: the WTC environmental committee members. This was right before he was thrown out of an open session in Montpellier, France, for verbal harassment of La Pierre. Bustamante has been at odds with the committee for recommending a curtailment of national funding programs for wind power, a recommendation he claims has cost him tens of millions of dollars."

Fenton-Wright smiled. "So, his motive with respect to La Pierre is fairly clear."

"Less obvious," the deputy director said, "is why he would go after Lord Cumberland. We suspect it may be because of Sir Anthony's security ties and the fact that much of Senor Bustamante's wealth is derived from illicit activity, including the shipping of opium poppies through the ports of Marseille in France and Tarragona in Spain, in order to produce heroin for resale. Much of this product winds up in the U.K. He has the means, the motive and ample opportunity to have financed and planned both assassinations."

Lang had taken his customary seat to David's left, where his boss liked him. He suspected it was so that Fenton-Wright had a whipping boy in close proximity, to wear any bad decisions. But at least, he figured, he was still at the table. He wondered about the intel behind the clandestine service's choice.

"Do we have any actionable intelligence whatsoever that Bustamante was directly involved?" he interjected. "Or are we just blowing smoke with this one?"

2.

The analyst looked pained, but Fenton-Wright broke in before he could answer. "Let me worry about that for now, Walter," he said. "He has threatened committee members in the past, albeit obliquely, and at one point, Fawkes' initial contact suggested, he was being considered for a role in the Association Commercial Franco-Arabe, the front for a cabal bent on geopolitical control, a front our man eventually infiltrated. We know little about it, but that might also shake out if we put the asset into play; we see if there are things going on with Bustamante that we should know about. Then we pull him out. If things go well, it's no muss, no fuss. We can operationalize any evidence he finds after the fact."

Lang didn't say a word; but internally he was seething at yet another ad hoc approach by his boss. Fenton-Wright had never been in the field; he'd never even been a handler. Distance from the realities of undercover work must have made it easy to reach such decisions, Lang supposed. It was easy to tell someone else to take all the risks and put their life or career on the line. For Fenton-Wright, he thought, it seemed entirely too common.

"What are we looking for, specifically?"

"Two things," Fenton-Wright said. "First, we believe Fawkes may have tried to pass on some intel prior to being taken out but didn't recover anything from either of his drops or from his personal affects. If Bustamante was involved, he may have taken the information, either inadvertently or with some prior intel that Fawkes had compromised the group. Second, any evidence or actionable intel on the shootings."

At the other end of the table, Carolyn was carefully taking notes on a tablet, keeping track of how the assignment had unfurled to that point. "What about the asset?" she said. "I assume we're going with someone senior on this?"

Fenton-Wright smiled at her. "We'll talk about that after the meeting," he said. "I have some work I need you to do in that regard."

Carolyn seemed oblivious, but Lang had a sinking feeling in the pit of his stomach.

10./

ANNANDALE, VIRGINIA

Joe was in the back yard playing with the kids when Carolyn got home. She didn't disturb them at first; she snuck around the side of the house and found a perch on the deck stairs to watch them. He was pretending to be pinned, one kid on each arm. "Nooo!" he declared. "Caught by the terrible tickle monsters!"

The kids were laughing, and for just the barest moment, Carolyn was happy. Then she thought about David's request, and watched Joe with the children, and she felt emptiness deep down inside. It bordered on sadism, what David had asked her to do.

But she didn't have a choice. She tried to rationalize it to herself that Joe would understand because he knew what these people were like. After all, hadn't he wanted back in?

At one point, months earlier. Now, he just wanted out. And he wasn't going to get his wish. *I can't do this. I can't be the one who tells him.*

"Hey Hon," she said, alerting them to her presence. The kids ran over and hugged her. Brennan slowly followed them, leaning down to peck her on the cheek.

"You're home early. Or on time, by anyone else's schedule."

"Yeah," she said. "Listen, we need to talk."

"Uh oh. Sounds serious," he said.

"It is. It is sort of serious, Joe." She filled him in on Fenton-Wright's request. "He wants me to smooth the way and to let you know that all is forgiven."

"What's the catch?"

"You have to go undercover, see what you can shake loose on the Euro shootings. And you'd be flying blind, for jurisdictional reasons." She waited for an angry reaction, but instead he just seemed stunned. "You're not saying anything. That's kind of unnerving."

"What should I say?" He sat down on the step next to her. "I'm guessing this was David's idea?"

"I couldn't say for sure." It was kind of true; they hadn't discussed where David had gotten the idea. She just knew it came from his office. "But he wants you there, certainly." She waited for a few seconds, though it seemed like minutes. "Well? What do you think?"

"I think that three years ago these people just about crucified me for a deniable op. Now they want me to accept one on their behalf after being completely frozen out? That takes some balls."

She was worried he would refuse. He was still on the agency payroll but had been inactive for so long, she thought he might actually get away with it. That would end her career; David would see to that. She also knew what Joe had been through after Colombia, how isolated he had felt. Was it really fair to ask him to go through something potentially similar?

"You could say no," she said. "What are they going to do? You're not a SEAL anymore, just a government employee. Technically, as long as you don't break the Espionage Act and reveal secret information, all they could really do is fire you, right?"

They both knew that wasn't entirely true. A lot depended on who made the call. "There are things you do on the job unofficially," Brennan said. "Things they can hold against you later. Things they can get sealed by a Special Court, so the hearings aren't even public. Hell, they could probably wrap me in paper and I couldn't say a damn thing about it."

"But would they go to all that..."

"Yes," he said, cutting her off. "And you know that."

"I'm sorry," she said. And she meant it. "He didn't give me a choice but to ask you. He gave me this long harangue about remembering who I work for, and that my career was tied up in 'the kind of decisions you choose to make at this juncture', whatever the hell that's supposed to mean."

Brennan loved her, deeply and completely. And he did so knowing that Carolyn could be insincere; she could put herself ahead of him just a bit too easily. But maybe she was worried about the kids, about what losing her income could do to the family.

Maybe.

"When does he want me in?" Brennan said.

She shook her head. "He doesn't. A file will be mailed to you; that's all you get."

He got up and walked up the steps to the house, leaving her there.

3.

11./

DEC 9, 2015, BARCELONA, SPAIN

The Mediterranean city sprawled like a terracotta-tiled blanket over the hilly terrain that bordered the sea, a mix of modern glass and steel, perversely modernistic new architecture and traditional whitewashed concrete buildings, grouped closely to produce shadows that could help citizens stay cool in the midst of summer. It was a temperate sixty-eight degrees, but the sun hid behind a slate gray sky and the air seemed heavy with moisture, as if it were calling out for a flash of rain at any moment to wash away the last tourists of the season.

Outside the airport, Brennan caught an off-white cab downtown to the El Torero Hotel, a short trip through intense multi-lane traffic to an aging eight-story sandstone building that sat near the circular Placa de Catalunya park.

Like most of the neighbourhood the hotel was well-preserved and ornate, a monument to when architecture followed the whims of its creator and not mere functionality. Small carvings of cherubs surrounded a clock above the hotel's grand metal nameplate; the building featured decorative cornice and concrete mouldings, along with faux Juliet balconies outside each window, fronted by black iron railings.

It was a trendy area of the city. Brennan got out of the cab, a carry on over his shoulder. Pedestrians filled the street; many were young, hip, wealthy looking, brown leather jackets and designer purses. Others were old Spain, sports coats and flat caps adorning old men who leaned on canes. He was drawn back to his last visit, fifteen years earlier. The Spanish had eschewed strip mall culture, so the cobblestoned street was lined with stores, selling everything from travel insurance to diamonds. That drew people, filled the sidewalk, and imbued the city with vibrancy.

He paid the cabbie from a money clip loaded with Euros and looked up at the hotel. The file on Bustamante had been concise-but-meticulous, and Brennan sensed Walter had a hand in it. The drug lord and wind power mogul kept a suite on the top floor, and was usually surrounded by muscle.

Belying the exterior, the hotel lobby was modern, a mix of contemporary glass and wood with cool tile floors. He checked in at the long black marble reception desk, booking a room on the seventh floor under a long-standing clandestine cover, Roger Bates; his backstory was the he was a rubber products manufacturer from New Jersey and was in town for a quick vacation, but the clerk avoided any personal questions.

The room itself was uninspiring, featuring the typical firm mattress, sponged oil paintings and cheap furniture that he'd seen at a dozen other overnight rest stops. But it had a decent wireless connection and was dependable enough for his purposes. He kept his bag packed but hauled his laptop out and set it up on the desk, next to the television. He opened his overnight bag, removing black, form-fit clothing and a pair of crepe-souled shoes that would allow him to tread silently. He left the clothing and shoes on the dresser, then went out into the hallway.

He checked the stairwell at one end and found it unlocked and empty; then he did the same at the far end of the corridor.

Brennan took the elevator up to the top floor. Outside the doors, the corridor to his left ran east-west. To his right, a small window was set into the wall on the south side of the building.

He peered around the corner by the bank of elevators. There were only three rooms, each a grand suite. The largest, he suspected, was Bustamante's. At the end of the hall a security guard in a dark gray suit and tie sat on a stool next to the door. Based on his boss's paranoia and background, there were probably three or four more inside, at least.

Brennan's task was simple: he needed ears inside the suite. That meant either getting inside and bugging the place or finding an alternative, such as inserting a fibre optic line through the wall plaster. He'd considered the layout of each floor and the building in general when he'd arrived. But to be certain, he rode the elevators down to the main floor again; the lobby was busy; the guests were young professionals and older tourists, the hotel stylish but hardly full of family amenities.

He made his way back to the sidewalk outside. One side of the building was connected to its neighbour while the other side was the end of a block, open to the street. He walked around the base of the hotel, checking out the roof and where the ledges sat relative to one another. Then he went back inside and took the elevator back to his room, where he changed into his black clothing and slung the small overnight bag over his shoulder.

He took the elevator back up to the eighth floor, waiting for a few moments after getting out of the car and watching its indicator numbers to ensure both cars had gone down to lower levels. He popped open the window on the right-hand wall.

3.

As he'd noticed outside, the two-foot wide ledge ran right around the top floor. He climbed out into the dimness of the early evening, pulling the window all-but-closed behind him. Brennan shuffled his feet carefully, following the ledge around the building and keeping his back to the wall, pausing at each window to check and ensure no one was looking out before passing by. He didn't look down, but it wouldn't have mattered; after nearly two decades of training and operations, he'd learned to turn off any nervous sentiment, to take a cold and calculated approach. He climbed around the corner of the building to the street side and the wind momentarily buffeted him, a gust pulling him away from the ledge. He leaned in, using his body weight to resist the momentum until the wind died down again.

Brennan had calculated where Bustamante's multi-room suite would start but he checked each window in case, peeking around the corner of each deep well and getting a look inside. The first two were bedrooms, one larger with an attached bathroom but both plain and functional. The third window was to the living room, which seemed to occupy most of the building's north side; Bustamante was propped up on an antique-style sofa, watching a large television above the fireplace. He was heavyset, with black-and-gray curls and a thin black moustache above the kind of jowls a man gets when he lets himself go, later in life. Two guards patrolled the suite, each armed with a machine pistol slung over a shoulder. A third was standing just inside the front door and a fourth sat adjacent to Bustamante in a deep, short-backed armchair.

Brennan took the small carry-on bag and placed it on the ledge. For a split second, he caught sight of the adjacent square below, the trees and ant-sized people nearly one hundred feet down, the wind and the sounds of city life blending; he turned away from it, refusing to allow for distraction. He unzipped the bag and withdrew a hairpin-sized black microphone, attached to a small suction cup. He wet the cup quickly with his tongue and attached the microphone to the bottom corner of the window, where its sensitive ribbon condenser would pick up sound as vibrations through the glass, then broadcast it wirelessly back to Brennan's laptop. Then he pulled off two small strips of duct tape and used them to ensure the suction cup would stay attached. The window was a good fifteen feet from the sitting area, and it would take considerable bad luck, he thought, for someone to notice the tiny object.

He began to make his way back around the building, the wind picking up slightly and causing him to pause every few seconds, to wait for it to die down, the gusts strong and loud at the increased altitude. Brennan took his time, shuffling his feet along the ledge carefully and keeping his back to the wall, not looking down at the ant-filled street below. He rounded the corner … just as a guard opened the window to a bathroom, the frame of it catching Brennan flush.

2.   104

He half-stumbled backwards, his feet sliding off of the ledge, his weight carrying him over the edge.

He grasped outward at the last moment, catching the ledge with both hands, every muscle straining to keep his body momentum from swinging too far forward and causing him to lose his grip, his fingers rigid almost to the point of breaking, the street below a blur of bad intentions. His black gloves were deliberately tacky – a sticky polymer grip that helped him hold on as he swung suspended. He pulled himself back up until he could get his arms and chest to resting height against the narrow shelf, then swung the rest of his body up and back to safety.

He lay there for a few moments, panting, his arm muscles strained from a sudden onrush of fatigue.

He heard flushing from inside the room. The guard had evidently finished with the toilet; Brennan rose and carefully pushed the window closed, just far enough to get safely around it.

At the elevators, he climbed back through the small window and closed it firmly behind him. He took off his gloves, placing them in the carry bag, and rolled up his sleeves to reduce any suspicion generated by his clothing; then he took the elevators back down to the seventh floor.

Back in his room, he started his laptop, plugged in a USB range extender and ran the microphone's app, before putting on a pair of headphones with a long cord.

Bustamante's Spanish was flawless, but characterized by a slight lisp common to Catalans.

"… and don't bring me any more of that fucking lettuce," he was telling one of his flunkies. "I just want the sandwich and the fries, not all of the food for rabbits that they always use."

Like most in intelligence, Brennan hated stakeouts. It was one thing for an analyst to get excited about the contents of a tap, to generate something useful. It was another to be the person doing the tapping, sitting listening for hour upon hour for a grain of information.

"Juan, put on the recording of Aida," the tycoon said, about twenty minutes in. "I want to catch up."

An hour passed, then two, with Bustamante saying little. His food arrived and he ate it, complaining that the hotel had once again put lettuce on his sandwich. Someone got him a drink, then another, then later on some bottled water. Brennan listened implacably, his training preventing boredom or anxiety from intruding as he waited for a comment, a word, a slip – anything that might tie the wind magnate to the shootings.

Just before eleven o'clock, Bustamante went to bed. Brennan checked the timer on the audio recording so that he'd know where to cue it to the next day for checking. Then he went to bed himself, sleeping above the covers.

3.

Brennan rose early the next morning and substituted his smartphone for the laptop, taking his ear buds with him to the restaurant adjacent to the lobby, where he ordered breakfast, eating a plate of eggs and bacon slowly as he listened in. Bustamante wasn't up yet, so all that he heard was the occasional sound of a guard moving about the suite.

When the businessman finally rose at eight o'clock, he ordered breakfast from room service then discussed business matters on the phone for the better part of an hour. His tone was mercilessly superior as he reminded his staff how upset he was to be holed up in the hotel all of the time, with too many enemies to be a public figure any longer. He sounded intermittently paranoid and psychotic. Brennan wondered how Bustamante had managed to hold an organization together for so long without some sort of mutiny.

He went back to his room and switched back to the laptop, checking out the rest of Bustamante's file for the third and fourth time while he waited for something to happen.

There. The businessman was talking to someone about the Lord Cumberland shooting, the first actual mention he'd made of the sniper case. "What about his woman?" he told the lackey on the other end of the line.

"His wife?"

"Not his wife," Bustamante said, sounding slightly disgusted. "His mistress. The French woman."

"She has already spoken with the authorities."

"So? That does not mean she told them everything. If, as we suspected, he was working at cross purposes with the chairman, he might have passed something to her, something useful. Something that could incriminate the lot of them."

"Should we talk to her?"

"Do you think so?" Bustamante said sarcastically. "Get going! Get hold of our friend in Paris, get him to pick her up and have a chat."

The other man agreed and hung up.

It was early afternoon by the time the stakeout bore fruit again. Bustamante was talking to an assistant about checking something out, something about a shipment.

"What's the time of arrival by that route?" Bustamante asked.

"Several weeks. That is the reality no matter who they use," the assistant said.

2.

"Mother of God!" Bustamante sounded annoyed. "We're not talking about Christmas presents. He has doubtless gone to ground once again in the meantime. The question is whether he has kept the fissionable material."

"And if so?"

"Then he will sell it, not use it. If terrorism were the point of this, he would done so years ago. No, he wants money, and lots of it. And it is worth a lot to the right people," Bustamante said. "If not... well, then perhaps it is too late already. Either way, it is lost to us, and the prospective negotiating power that comes with it."

"Where did he get it from in the first place? The Russians?" the assistant asked.

"You don't worry about that stuff, okay? You just keep me updated on where things are at." There was silent for a moment before he elaborated. "It went missing twenty years ago in South Africa, after the end of Apartheid; I'm not even sure which stories about it are true."

"But Khalidi..."

"He has a lot to explain, my friend. They paint me as some villain in their grand drama, but we both know the truth. If I get hold of that device and the fool who stole it, I have all the leverage I will ever need."

Brennan frowned as he listened. Whatever Bustamante was talking about involved a nuclear weapon, which was about as grand-scale as the agent could imagine. Was he referring to the industrialist, Ahmed Khalidi? What was Bustamante getting at?

Once it was clear that Bustamante was done for a while, Brennan took off the headphones for a moment and left the audio track recording. It seemed bizarre to be sitting so far from home, so far from Carolyn and the kids, listening to a man talk casually about what sounded like a stolen or missing nuke, when just a few days earlier he'd been fishing with a buddy, wondering if he'd ever get back to work. It reminded him of when he'd first joined the agency, just out of the SEALS, and been immediately dumped into an undercover op in Thailand. He'd forgotten what it was like, trying to keep the nervous tension switched off.

Thinking about his family didn't help, so he shut it out, aware even as he did so that perhaps it was bad for the soul.

He needed more. More detail about the weapon, the shipment and Khalidi, as well as possibly Bustamante's involvement in the shootings and Lord Cumberland's mistress. There were two choices: running the stakeout indefinitely in the hopes of catching something, or going to the source.

3.

Brennan figured the path was clear. He'd been told not to engage, but the stakes had changed. He needed to interrogate Tillo Bustamante. He took out his phone and, after contemplating a few options, placed a call.

12./

DEC. 10, 2015, PARIS, FRANCE

Annalise Boudreau's fingers sought out the thin, smooth surface of the locket that hung from her neck, playing with it absent-mindedly as she looked out the window of her Paris flat.

The shoppers on Rue Jacob were bustling along the chilly street, bags in hand, the cafes still busy despite the turning season. She knew she'd miss this; the apartment's location was prime real estate, after all, and the weekly rates were far beyond what she could afford without Anthony's help.

And Anthony was dead.

She crossed her arms, feeling small, resisting the urge to chew on her knuckles out of sheer nervousness. Unaccustomed to supporting herself – she'd been somebody's mistress in one form or another for twenty years – Annalise wondered what would happen next. She turned her head ninety degrees to catch her reflection in the dressing mirror at the end of the room. She was still attractive, still fit even at forty-two years old. Someone would still...

She stopped the thought and felt tears coming on, but held them back. Her parents had always taught her to be proud, and although she had been a kept woman for two decades, Annalise had been with the English lord for most of that time, his secret love, away from the cloying, frigid professionalism of his society wife. She'd long stopped thinking of it as survival, or of him as just a meal ticket. She'd really come to love Anthony, his stiff awkwardness when affectionate, the strength of his hold. She certainly loved the lifestyle, as he'd long ago told her that money was no object. He'd known early, instinctively, that she was not inclined to waste.

Not that that would help when the landlord turned her out, she thought.

His death had caught her flatfooted. A day before he'd returned to London, they'd gone for brunch at Renoma, shared eggs benedict and bad jokes about English weather. He'd kissed her hand, and he'd reminded her of how much he loved her.

Less than forty-eight hours later, he was shot dead in the backyard of his family home in suburban London, and her world had been turned upside down.

Appealing for help to their friends was out of the question, and she wasn't sure how it would be received in any case. Most of them were society associates, no one she would ever spend private time with or share secrets; no one she could really trust.

There was a knock on her apartment door, three short, hard raps. Her head turned quickly, surprised by the sound. Normally people had to be buzzed in to the building, to register with the doorman in the lobby.

She crossed the living room, past the white-and-black-check retro Habitat furniture. She looked through the peephole; there were at least three men, all dressed in suits.

Perhaps this was it, she thought. Perhaps this was the landlord's lawyer, come to tell her that she was no longer welcome in her own home. She frowned; that didn't make sense; as far as she knew, Anthony had paid the rent for several months in advance.

She put the chain on and opened the door a crack. "Yes?"

"Madame Boudreau? We need you to accompany us, please."

"What's this about?"

"You are familiar with the late Lord Cumberland, yes?"

"Yes."

"This is regarding his assassination."

Official business, then. Annalise sighed. She had already talked to the Gendarmes and the English intelligence officials. They'd looked attentive and interested throughout and had taken copious notes, but at the end seemed unconcerned with anything she could tell them.

"Is this going to take long?" she said. "I'm meeting a friend this evening."

The shortest of the three men stood ahead of his two helpers. "Nothing to worry about," he said, smiling broadly. "We just need to go over a few things."

She did not ask the men for a badge, or an arrest warrant, or anything official to confirm their identities and task. It did not occur to her for a moment that anyone might make such a thing up. After all, Annalise had never found herself to be an interesting person, never had the confidence to feel needed by others, never been in trouble. "Let me get my coat," she said.

The man put a hand on the door. "May we come in?" he asked, taking a half-step forward before she'd answered. He pushed past her before she had a chance to answer, the two enormous helpers following him.

"Now excuse me, but I don't think I said 'enter'," she tried to say, backing into the room to get out of their way.

2.   110

The small man turned to face her. His gaze was nearly expressionless. He began to turn back the other way, away from her, but instead pivoted quickly on his heel, bringing a swift backhand around, slapping her hard across the cheek, knocking her down. "Shut up," he said. "Be quiet while we search and we may let you live."

Two of the men began to ransack the apartment, not paying attention to her sitting on the hardwood floor, a look of shock and fear written across her face. Very quickly, Annalise felt that fear grow.

BARCELONA

The package arrived at the hotel four hours later, wrapped in brown paper and tied with string, as if someone had sent cookies and a few changes of clothes to a kid at camp. The hotel called up to Brennan's room and he went downstairs to retrieve it. Once back in the room, he cut the string with the steak knife from his breakfast and unwrapped the paper.

It had cost five thousand dollars, which was highway robbery; but it was the agency's money. Like most agents, Brennan had access to emergency accounts when needed. The Glock 21 .45 pistol came modified and equipped with a suppressor, as requested, and the three vials of chemicals he would need were intact. There was no way to test them for validity or potency, but the supplier was a long-trusted agency source in the city.

While waiting for his wares, Brennan had checked back over his notes. Storming the door wasn't out of the question; if they were sloppy, the guard out front would have a key card on him to the room. Once past him, the element of surprise and the suppressor would probably have done the job. But his instructions were to not engage except when necessary and he knew there had to be an easier path to Bustamante than gunning down his thugs.

He considered their schedule again, the routine of the four guards inside. Then he put the headphones back on and waited for Bustamante's man to call room service, which seemed to be the source of all food that was brought to the suite.

Brennan went down the hall to the elevators and took them to the eighth floor, then waited with his back to the elevator buttons. It took about twenty-five minutes more before the doors slid open and the young waiter pushed the cart out of the car. He stepped behind the waiter and quickly wrapped him up in a choke hold, applying pressure with the crook of his elbow to the carotid artery until the decreased blood flow knocked the kid unconscious.

It took less than seven seconds. Brennan knew he only had a minute or two at most before the waiter would awaken and wonder what the hell had just happened to him. He took the kid's white jacket and put it on, noting it was too short on the sleeves and rolling them up to compensate. Then he used a fireman's lift to put the waiter over his shoulder, laying him back down on the floor of the elevator car and taking it down to his floor. The doors slid open and he checked the hallway before running as quickly as he could to his room door, the kid a dead weight over his shoulder. He dropped the kid onto the carpet beside the bed then taped his mouth shut and bound his hands and feet. Then he blindfolded the waiter, before heading back down the hallway to the elevators. He punched the button for the twelfth floor.

In front of the elevators, he removed the lids from the food trays on top of the cart. He withdrew the shortest of the three vials from his pocket. There were five plates, which meant either Bustamante or one of the guards wasn't eating with the rest. It made sense; at every prior meal for two days, they'd all eaten together, save for the man on front-door duty. He lifted the plate lids; club sandwiches, which was par for the course. Bustamante didn't exactly eat lightly. He sprinkled a small amount of the colourless, odorless liquid into the food, then re-covered each plate and wheeled the entire cart around the corner, down the hallway to the suite.

The guard at the door was as wide as the doorway, with slicked back hair in a ponytail, and a moustache. He held up a hand. "I don't know you," he said in Spanish. "Where's Jonathan?"

"Day off," Brennan said. "His father is quite ill."

The guard lifted the tray lids quickly but seemed satisfied there was nothing amiss.

Brennan stood and waited as the guard turned towards the door with the cart.

The guard realized he hadn't left and turned back. "What do you want?"

"It is customary for a tip..."

"Jonathan knows Senor Bustamante does not believe in tipping," he said. "Go away."

"Si Senor," Brennan replied, trying to seem disappointed and to look unimpressed.

He walked back to the elevators. Once around the corner from the hallway, he took off the white jacket, balled it up and opened the window; he placed it on the ledge, out of sight, and closed the window again.

Brennan headed down a floor. Back in his room, he waited the twenty minutes it would take for the drug to kick in. It was important to keep his mind on the task at hand; but he kept thinking about Carolyn, and how she'd almost seemed to be defending David Fenton-Wright and his decisions. Did she even realize how far out on a limb he'd be, operating in the EU without permission from the locals? Did she care?

Then he buried the idea and chastised himself; this wasn't on Carolyn; she was just trying to balance her career and her concern for her husband. After all, she was the first person to suggest he try walking away.

As the now-conscious waiter murmured and kicked against his restraints, Brennan attached the suppressor to the modified Glock barrel then slipped the gun into the back of his waistband, underneath his shirt. Then he took a wad of cotton out of his carry-on and soaked it in the same chemical he'd used in the food.

He took the stairs back to the eighth floor. It would have been easier to drug the hotel worker, too, but he preferred to avoid exposing an innocent civilian to risk, and the choke hold was unlikely to do any damage. A knockout cocktail could trigger an allergy or worse, a heart attack.

The guard at the door had seen him before, which worked to Brennan's advantage. He walked up to him smiling, a hand raised in a wave of good nature.

"Excuse me, sir," he said to the guard, "but I wanted to talk to about that tip I did not get, from about a half hour ago, when I was on shift? I do not intend to be impetuous, but I do not make much per hour, and in the present economy…"

The guard stiffened at the request and his grip tightened around the machine pistol. "Madre de… Are you stupid? Go away. The rooms on this floor are private residences and hotel staff are not welcome. And, as I said before…"

"My apologies, sir," Brennan said. He turned his body slightly to the left, as if he were about to gesture down the hallway behind him, using his left hand to slip the pistol out sight unseen. He turned quickly and pressed the suppressor against the middle of the guard's forehead. "Do not be brave, my friend. I pull this trigger and your brains will cover this door, understand?"

The guard nodded carefully and raised his hands, the pistol hanging loosely from its shoulder strap. "Turn around," Brennan ordered. The man complied. Brennan kept the gun trained on the back of the man's head, then reached around him with his right hand and held the cotton to the man's mouth and nose. He went to struggle instinctively, grabbing at Brennan's arm, but within a few seconds was slumping to sleep at the foot of the door. Brennan reached inside his coat and found his key card. He used it to flash the sensor on the handle and opened the suite.

The drug had worked as planned; all five men were face down over their meals around the dining table. It was powerful, and they would be out for at least thirty minutes and probably more, he'd calculated. There were security cameras around the suite, but if they were being live-monitored somewhere, it was with no great efficiency. Brennan had no intention of returning to the hotel once he had what he needed, and didn't worry about his face being caught on tape. The idea was to get the job done with no harm to anyone, before getting out of Barcelona for another decade or so.

He moved the food cart until it was right next to Bustamante, then rolled the man out of his chair and onto the floor; he pulled the sides of the table cloth up then moved the industrialist onto the bottom shelf of the cart, pushing his legs in so that he was curled up in a sitting position before lowering the table cloth again. He wheeled the card out of the suite, past the downed doorman and to the elevators.

Ten minutes later, Bustamante was tied securely to a chair in Brennan's room, next to the tall windows. The agent had moved the waiter, still awake and frightened, into the closet.

Brennan removed one of the last two vials from the top of the dresser and drew half into a hypodermic syringe. Then he placed a tie around Bustamante's arm until a large vein was evident, and slowly injected the mixture into his sleeping suspect.

The chemicals were a potent cocktail of sodium thiopental and scopolamine, and would be followed with a stimulant to counteract the initial knockout drops. The stimulant would keep him awake while the cocktail lowered the suspect's resistance to questions. It wasn't a 'truth serum', as no such beast exists; but Brennan had found in the past that if he had a decent factual starting point, the cocktail could shake all sorts of things loose.

He injected the stimulant, then waited five minutes, then tried to revive the gangster. Then he repeated the dose. It took another dose to stir Bustamante enough to be comprehensible, and to get him talking somewhat fluidly. His eyes flitted around in the confused manner of someone suffering a concussion, and he nodded his head slightly in all directions.

2.   114

"Tillo! Padron!" Brennan said in his best Catalan accent, standing behind the chair. "I think you drink too much old friend."

Bustamante smiled groggily. "I ... I can't see so well. Who ...?"

"It's your old friend Juan," Brennan said, banking that Bustamante knew at least one Juan. "You don't look so good, Tillo. Maybe you need another drink."

Bustamante shook his head. "No, no more. Feel so drunk in my head."

"You remember what you were saying? About Khalidi?"

He gave a half-nod, his head slumping back. "Si, si, the chairman. Bastardo! I was promised a place, you know. Then they reneged, turned against me."

"Over the shootings?" Brennan asked. "Because they think you... "

"Foolishness and nonsense. It was long before." Bustamante said, his eyes flitting closed, lids heavy. "They are all dragons, you know."

That didn't make any sense, and Brennan put it down to the chemicals. "That's funny, old friend," Brennan said with a light laugh. "Very funny. I almost thought you shot them yourself, after how they treated you."

Bustamante shook his head wildly.

"This is not so funny," the drugged man said. "Not funny so...."

"So you didn't..."

"No. Where am I?" The drugs were fully taking hold now and the industrialist had a confused, frightened look in his eyes. "Juan, I can't see you."

"I'm here old friend," Brennan said, staying behind the chair. "Do you want another drink?"

Bustamante shook his head again, "No, too much already, too much."

"So you didn't have La Pierre shot, and Lord Cumberland?"

"No, no. Not worth my time. Cut one down, another would take its place, like weeds."

"Maybe the chairman is angry with you over the bomb. Chairman Khalidi, that is."

Bustamante looked confused. "No, this is not about me. I don't understand..."

"Yes, the nuke. The South Africans lost it, right?"

"Yes, yes, the South Africans. Big money. Bigger than you know. That is on them, too. I just look, like everyone."

"Them?"

Bustamante squinted. "You know, stupid, Khalidi's group. The ACF. I ... I dream of being a boy again, Juan."

3.   115

"You are a rich man, my friend," Brennan said.

Bustamante turned his head a quarter turn and squinted at Brennan again. "Do ... do I know you?" he asked.

Brennan ignored him. He moved over to the dresser as Bustamante's head bobbed and the tycoon tried to peer around the room. The agent prepared a second chemical cocktail at the dresser then injected Bustamante again. "This will make you feel good," he said. As if on cue, a few seconds after the injection Bustamante was grinning like a junkie who'd just received the day's first fix.

"You were talking about the group, old friend, the ACF," Brennan said. "Tell me about it, about its connection to the bomb."

The Spaniard squinted his way through a few more memories before getting back on point. "It has faced much... retaliation. Bosnia, East Timor ... blood flows downhill. Abbott learned that. He knew much. And now she does, too." He giggled slightly, like an old man who'd lost his faculties in the moment of a fond memory.

"And South Africa?"

Bustamante smiled through crocodile teeth. "Si, the stupid South Africans. They lost one, lost a bomb. It was madness." His eyes began to flutter backwards. A second later, his head tipped back and Bustamante was sleeping.

Brennan felt he had all he was going to get. He started to pack up his gear. He needed to get out of the hotel – and the city – in short order. He'd try one more round with Bustamante in five minutes, after the stress to the businessman's system had subsided somewhat. He retrieved a bottle of water from the tiny refrigerator under the desk and downed it in three swallows.

The room door was flung open violently, smacking against the wall from the force of a kick. Brennan saw a chorus of shapes, men rushing in; Bustamante's men had either woken up, or others had come to spell them off duty.

And it hadn't taken them long to track down their boss.

13. /

DEC. 12, 2015, WASHINGTON, D.C.

John Younger studied his opponent's speech on his office TV.
He was looking for signs of weakness in the other man's
delivery, issues or agendas that might trip him up, anything he might be
able to use when they inevitably met in a public debate. But March was
on platform, solid.

Younger, the ranking senator from Pennsylvania, had been
sparring with Addison March for a few years. His Republican opponent
was a new face, charismatic and able to rally people to him. And in
Younger's view, March's ultra-right ideology made him a menace to
public service.

He'd been telling himself for six months that his own quest for
the presidency was as much about preventing March's ideas and
direction as promoting his own. It wasn't true, as Younger was a veteran
campaigner, and had lived off the prestige of power for five decades; he
was as morally fluid as the voter base required him to be.

But it made him feel better about the slings and arrows of the
campaign trail to tell himself that carrying on the family Democrat
tradition was about ideas and social perspective.

Each man was now the prohibitive party favorite to win the
nomination for 2016, and both had long since started campaigning
nationally for the Oval office, no longer worried about shoring up party
support.

March was scoring points on the continued absence of a
deportation-based refugee and immigrant policy, scaring his base, which
Younger believed was vehemently racist and ignorant. He continually
raised the specter of gang crime in Phoenix and San Diego, tying it to the
vast number of Mexican immigrants that both cities accepted without
ever offering statistical proof that the two were related.

His latest speech had even revived the long-dormant idea of a
wall between the two nations, an impractical and absurd concept,
Younger thought. Even March had to realize that.

Still, the man made him nervous, and Younger decided those
nerves weren't likely to be calmed until he received the President's
public endorsement.

3.

His office line buzzed. "Sir, Mark Fitzpatrick is here," his secretary intoned.

The younger man entered the office a few moments later, dressed in his customary grey suit and dark tie. "Senator," he said.

"Mark, good to see you. You said you have an update?"

"My sources at the agency say the individual discussed at the NSC session is in play, in Spain."

"They were pushing hard for Bustamante as a suspect," Younger noted. "I have to assume they're going right to the source."

"Likely surveillance to start with."

"Are we expecting news back from field level?"

"No. As discussed, this one is totally off the books."

Younger smiled. It sounded like Fitzpatrick had things well in hand. "How confident should we be with how things are going?"

"Quietly so, I'd say," Fitzpatrick offered. "You have no exposure anyway."

That much was true, and it meant that he could spend a little more time concentrating on Addison March.

He looked around at his office, its relatively small waiting area, the cheap wood paneling and small windows.

The Oval Office was much, much more appealing, Younger thought, and as much as he deserved.

AMMAN, JORDAN

A thirteen-hour flight to the east, Ahmed Khalidi was enjoying the far more opulent surroundings of his third palace. His office was the size of an aircraft hangar but, despite the ninety-five degree heat outdoors, remained at a steady seventy at all times, its marble floors cold underfoot, the whitewashed interior making it seem perpetually bright.

His mammoth desk sat halfway across the room, some forty feet from the double doors. Marble pillars adorned each corner of the room stretching up to the ceiling twenty feet above, and a pair of white tiger pelts lay in front of the large fireplace along one wall. The phone on his desk was gold, as were the door handles, lamp standards and fixtures. He had insisted on at least eighteen karats.

In truth, Khalidi spent little time there. If not for family responsibilities to his father, the Sheik, he would have remained in Europe whenever possible, enjoying his homes in Brussels, Paris, Nice and Geneva.

That, and taking care of business. He had been watching the news for an hour on the eighty-inch screen, which rose from the floor just ahead of his desk on a single button's command. There had been a brief update on the shootings of Lord Cumberland and Marie La Pierre, but no real new information was offered. As with the other five remaining ACF board members, Khalidi was nervous, worried that on any given day, he might step outside and be cut down by a sniper.

And so it fell to his long-time adviser, Faisal Mohammed, to put him at ease. It was a task the diminutive Egyptian-born aide knew would not be easy, and getting the appropriate information was costing a fortune. Fortunately, Khalidi had several to spare.

"If Arabs cannot see themselves represented among the world's leaders as equals, we will never outgrow the mistrust western culture has in us, or us in it," Khalidi was saying, finishing up a longer thought. "That, ultimately, is the entire purpose of The ACF. And if the membership be damned for profiting from that progress, then so be it. But it is essential business, nonetheless. We make decisions, develop policy and law that, whispered in the right ears, can redirect the course of history. And if I cannot even risk venturing out in public, it will become untenable."

Mohammed, a man of middling height with a young face and dark-rimmed eyeglasses, nodded and confirmed he would call their contact as they spoke and find out what the various intelligence agencies were still doing to track down the sniper. Secretly he loathed Khalidi, who for several years had openly mocked Faisal's Egyptian heritage in front of Khalidi's relatives from Yemen, Jordan and the UAE. The man was obviously unbalanced, seeing himself as the arbiter of how both the Muslim world and other faiths should proceed into the next millennium. Psychotic, perhaps.

But the man's immense wealth and power not only frightened Faisal, it also excited him, and had enabled him to do and see things that would otherwise have been out of reach.

The call was answered after three rings.

"I hear it is sunny in Pennsylvania this year," Faisal said.

"Except when it's dark and rainy," the contact replied.

"What have you got for me?" Faisal asked, once the pair had assured their identities. "We feel out of the discussion on this right now."

The contact was brusque. "There are leads being explored. An agent is in place in Europe. That's about all we know at this point."

"What leads?" Faisal asked. "What agent? We are paying you a lot of money for details, not obscure references."

"When you need to know, you will," the contact said. "In the meantime, have you tried the mistress yet? It's my feeling that if Sir Anthony were to have passed information to or through anyone, she'd be the one. He trusted her, but she was oblivious to his work."

"Efforts are being made."

"On our end as well. For reasons of potential embarrassment, POTUS is involved in this."

Faisal couldn't help but be surprised. The contact was confirming what they'd already come to suspect, that Sir Anthony had been a double agent. But now it appeared it was for the Americans, and not his homeland. A genuine surprise, Faisal thought. "Fine. But when you've got something more concrete, we want to know."

He hung up the phone. "He confirmed your suspicions," he told the chairman. "They are searching for any more intelligence that Sir Anthony might have collected. But it could be a long time."

Khalidi was worried. "Faisal, as you know, my stake in all of this is much higher than it is for others. The damage to my family's reputation…"

"I know, sir, and I will ensure there is pressure upon our man to do what he can, God willing."

"Do that, Faisal," Khalidi said. "Remember that which befalls me, befalls you also. And I think you know which one of us will come out, as the Americans say, smelling the roses."

He meant 'smelling like a rose', Faisal thought. But the idea of correcting the man did not even cross his mind. Telling him about Lord Cumberland also seemed ill-advised, Faisal decided. That nugget of information could prove useful.

Half a world away, Walter Lang hung up from the call. He felt dirty, and he wondered if there would ever come a time when he wouldn't.

He put the cell phone back into his pocket and stared silently out of the window of his D.C. walkup apartment. The room was tidy but plain, cheap old furniture, bookshelves crammed full. The lights were off, because his grim mood preferred it, although the tall windows on either side of the room let the dim light of a gray afternoon wash across the fine filaments of dust. He turned around and moved over to his favorite old armchair and sat down, one more rumpled thing in a big box full of them, the coffee table ahead of him covered with more piles of books.

If he had other options, he would have taken them. If he'd made better financial decisions, or perhaps taken a job in the private sector that paid more; if he'd have known, he wouldn't have depended upon the agency.

If, if, if.

But the treatment was going to be expensive, far beyond what his government insurance covered, comprehensive as it was. Khalidi's money might be the difference between life and death, he told himself.

The tumor had caught his doctor by surprise, a baseball-sized object lodged in his chest cavity, perilously close to his heart and lungs. Not that it would matter; if it spread to his blood through his lymph nodes, he'd been told, there would be little-to-no hope. The tumor was growing aggressively and he was going to require surgery, as well as treatments several times per week at first, along with an ongoing prescription for a highly toxic chemotherapy drug, also incredibly expensive. The treatment would have hammered at his savings, despite just a few years until retirement.

And what was he giving up? Outdated information, several days old, repeats of briefings he'd heard or given on Joe Brennan's mission. He hadn't even identified his friend by name. And Lord Cumberland was already dead. Surely that wasn't so bad, he told himself. Faisal Mohammed was no major player; he'd met him at a charity gathering a few years earlier put on by Mohammed's alma mater, Georgetown. He was a spy wannabe, a fixer for Ahmed Khalidi.

He knew, of course, that the agency would not see it as such. He suspected Khalidi was involved in the shootings, or whatever Lord Cumberland had been up to, because he'd heard Fenton-Wright slip the man's name out a half-dozen times in the days prior. But the key was that his information was already days old, unlikely to get anyone into trouble. And Khalidi was paying him more than enough to deal with his treatments and perhaps to leave his estranged wife and son something if he passed.

If caught revealing classified information, he'd be tried for espionage, probably in a closed court, and spend the rest of what little life he had left in the federal correctional facility in Butner, North Carolina. That thought did not appeal to Lang, and he prayed each night that Joe would close the file, catch the sniper before his own dual role was discovered.

It probably wouldn't end there, he knew. Once he'd taken the money, he was on the hook, beholden to his paymaster or facing the risk he'd be thrown to the wolves. It was another unsettling thought, and Walter pushed it to the back of his mind, hoping his growing anxiety would eventually recede.

3.

14./
BARCELONA

Brennan reacted instinctively as the men burst into his hotel room, ducking behind the edge of the bed and drawing the silenced pistol from his waistband in one smooth motion. The men opened fire, machine gun bullets ripping into the mattress and sending a flurry of feathers flying. Barely slowed, the slugs thumped into the wall behind him.

He'd spotted at least three men before taking cover, and when he popped up from behind the mattress he moved with machine-like precision, squeezing off three shots in quick succession, each finding its mark, two head shots and the third centre mass.

Two of the men were dead before they hit the floor, and the third lay bleeding on the carpet, twitching spasmodically. There were two more in the doorway, but they ducked back around the doorjamb.

Brennan remained crouched and moved to the corner of the mattress, looking for the slightest motion. The pair reached around the doorway in unison but stayed in cover, spraying the room wildly with fire as Brennan hit the deck. He rose out of cover again, swinging the pistol left, then right, the sequence timed perfectly as each of the two remaining guards tried to charge the room. Each went down within three steps.

Brennan looked back at Bustamante; at least two of the machine pistol bullets had hit him in the chest, and he was coughing up blood. The drugs probably weren't helping as the immobilized gangster fought for breath, and the gunfire would have alerted others. He had to move quickly.

He ripped Bustamante's shirt open, but the wounds were gaping, blood flowing freely. There was nothing he could do for him. Brennan knew he had perhaps a minute, at best, before others arrived. He retrieved the syringe from the dresser and injected the remainder of the cocktail into the dying drug dealer.

"Tillo!" Brennan smacked his face gently to rouse him. "Tillo!"

"Eh?" He was fading fast. "Feel like sleeping..." Bustamante said.

"Tillo, the bomb. Where is it now?"

"Eh? The nuke... ask the chairman. It is his mistake." He drifted out of consciousness, and Brennan slapped him twice again.

"Tillo, where is it going? You said it was being shipped?"

2.   **122**

Bustamante smiled. "Go to hell." His head bobbed twice and his heavy eyelids slammed shut.

"Tillo, it's me, it's Juan," Brennan said loudly. "Tell me where the bomb is? We need to find it."

Bustamante was nodding in and out of consciousness. Brennan knew it was futile; he had to go. He left the tycoon behind and turned to the desk. He dropped the laptop and gun into his carry-on bag and walked out of the room, heading for the stairwell, at the far right end of the corridor. The door closed slowly behind him just before the elevator slid open. A minute later, he exited a side door from the hotel to the street. He walked around the corner to the next block, dropping his gloves into a nearby garbage can as he blended into the anonymity of evening on the Barcelona street, a cacophony of police sirens growing louder.

DEC. 14, 2015, WASHINGTON, D.C.

The young man in the grey-green herringbone suit was nervous, and he paced back and forth by a window of the Capitol Club, his tension rendering him oblivious to the tasteful opulence of the place, his brown brogue dress shoes shuffling a little too much on the blue patterned carpet. He ignored the Edwardian chairs and the portraits of Republican Party greats; instead, he tried to remember the exact wording of the message Addison March's assistant had asked him to pass on.

His nerves were justified, as March was his new idol. Unsatisfied with the namby-pamby professors and community organizers adored by his college classmates, he'd looked for a leader made of sterner stuff. He found it in the smooth-talking Tennessean. The young man thought March had the charisma of Reagan and the smarts of Lincoln, combined with the aggression of his other idol, the former vice-president Dick Cheney.

In short, he believed with every fibre of his being that he was about to pass a message to the next President of the United States; and so he paced, trying to keep his hands from shaking as he gripped the message.

March kept a regular table at the Club, where he was a committee member and sponsor of an annual Wine Tasting attended by every important West Coast Republican, a significant portion of the senator's donor base. The young man expected him around by 4 p.m. but he was running late.

He paced some more.

3.   123

"Careful, son, or you'll wear a hole in this here carpet." The voice was rich and melodic, utterly friendly. He turned and found himself face-to-face with the presumed Republican nominee. March was smiling, his small teeth just visible, lips a thin line across his bony face.

"Sir, Mr. March, sir…"

"Now rest easy, son, rest easy. What can I do for you?"

"I have a message from your assistant Christopher, sir; he wanted you to know he had information on the matter you'd asked about… I mean, the EU matter…"

"I get the general gist." He took out his clip and gave the youth a twenty. "You done college, son?" he asked.

"Yes sir, Mr. March, sir."

"Then you know better than to use the same word twice in the same sentence."

The young man looked blank.

"It's a joke, son. But don't you worry about it."

The young man backed away, practically bowing. March was accustomed to adulation, and he smiled politely as the messenger withdrew. Then he made his way a dozen feet to a red sofa nearby and sat down, unfolding the copy of the Washington Times he'd had under his arm. If he knew his assistant well…

His phone rang. "Right on cue," March said as he answered. "Talk to me, Christopher. What's new?"

"Senator, I've got some feedback on that issue you'd asked about. My NSA source tells us we're pushing hard for an American-made solution to the enviro committee shootings and that Younger is one of the main advocates."

"American solution? Why on Earth…"

"No idea sir. No idea. We don't seem to have a horse in this race."

"He has the president's endorsement all but announced; maybe getting us involved was the price. POTUS always was fond of La Pierre's environmental committee."

"That's the weird part, sir. They've been talking about it for a few days, but there's been no official involvement yet and no request to join in the EU-led investigations already under way."

"What's your thinking, Christopher?"

"Maybe their 'solution' involves a diplomatic component, something other than just seconding staff to our allies across the pond. Or… maybe they have another reason for wanting control over this thing; maybe there's something about it they don't want getting out."

"Perhaps. Keep your ears open. Younger's on the stump for most of the next two months drumming up support, and that makes him vulnerable to information that breaks here first. Who knows? POTUS's anointed might just trip himself up yet."

ANNANDALE, VIRGINIA

Carolyn had slept fitfully since Joe's departure. That was nothing new; but the fact that she felt as if she'd helped to talk him into going seemed to worsen her guilt; she found herself having bad dreams, waking up several times each night, pitching and turning under the covers.

The kids had a babysitter during the week and would be back at school soon anyway; and they were accustomed to their father disappearing for a few weeks at a time on business. But her nerves hadn't settled with age and the familiarity of routine. If anything, her anxiety had heightened. Like Joe, she wondered what the real impact on them would be in the long-term.

At work, her blue suit and cream blouse felt like she couldn't get them to fit quite right, and her panty hose felt bunchy. She dropped her first coffee of the day on her laptop while near-motionless at her office desk, a supremely uncoordinated moment. Then she realized she'd missed a briefing because her phone battery had died while the laptop was down, rendering her without mail in the exact ten-minute window David had used to call everyone into his office. Then Jonah called her on her office line and said she had a half-hour to get ready for another meeting with David, and if she missed that one, refreshing her resume might be a smart idea.

She sat down behind her desk, looking at the laptop, which now bore a yellow post-it sticker with the letters "IT" in marker. Not that they were likely to grab the wrong thing. Or show up any time soon. She had twenty more minutes before going in with her boss, and the day was heading south.

Had things gone as badly as she thought with Joe? She wasn't sure. He'd been seething for the two days before leaving. But he was so non-communicative that she couldn't tell if he was mad at the agency or at her for delivering the message. That's all it was, really, she told herself. It wasn't like either of them had much of an alternative.

She made a mental note to call Callum and Ellen, to see if they wanted to come around for dinner. She needed some cheering up.

There was a knock on her office door and it swung open before she could respond. "I thought I'd come to see you, rather than making you tromp all the way over to my neck of the woods," David Fenton-Wright said.

She gestured to one of the chairs across from her desk but he shook his head quickly. "That's fine, I'll just be a moment. I wanted to piss on you again for missing the briefing, but I'm over it. What I did think you should know, however, is that we discussed Joe's mission and we agreed that we uniformly felt confident in his ability to confirm a suspect."

Jonah stood behind him, quietly taking notes. Carolyn had never liked the younger man, despite his sterling reputation. He seemed officious to an almost automaton-like degree.

And what was David up to?

"Is he okay?"

"Oh, he's fine," Fenton-Wright said, perhaps too quickly. She wondered if they had any real idea; probably not. "We believe he'll be looking into a number of new leads, however, so don't leave the porch light on." He smiled when he said it, like he thought she'd find that funny.

"David, when this is all done, will you let Joe resign? He's tired of all of this. I mean…"

Fenton-Wright turned to her glass wall and peeked through the blinds at the rest of the office. Then he turned back to her. "We'll see. You must understand, Carolyn, that his being frozen out … well, that was never my intention. We received a great deal of pressure."

"From…"

"From other agencies. Let's just leave it at that. Anyway, those relationships must endure; so it probably won't be my decision. I hope you realize that."

She nodded hesitatingly. "Of course, David."

He moved to leave, opening her door a crack before smiling at her again. "And of course, should anything untoward happen, the fact that he's been on the company payroll for so long would assure a healthy pension for you and the children."

He smiled one more time and left. Caroline sat agog at the comment, wondering if the man had Asperger's, or something. She didn't want his pension; she wanted her husband back.

DEC. 15, 2015, PARIS, FRANCE

2.

The Eiffel Tower elevator chugged north at a pace so leisurely, Brennan initially wondered if something was wrong. There were perhaps a half-dozen other people in the ancient-looking elevator cage, and a middle-aged Englishman with a round face saw his expression. "It's about a minute, maybe ninety seconds between floors," he said. "Are you afraid of heights?"

"Something like that," Brennan said. In reality, he just wanted to get to the meeting more quickly, the tension of a new, unknown source eating at him. Walter had found the contact through an old colleague, Myrna Verbish, a former agency analyst who kept up on the trade. It was the source's idea to meet at the top of the tower, as public and safe a spot as a local could imagine in the city. Brennan was holding a copy of *The Catcher in The Rye*, as requested.

"Well, most people like the view," the man said. "Just keep your eyes shut and we'll be there before you know it. The trip takes about eight minutes. The wife and I have done this before, you know."

Brennan smiled politely at the man but couldn't help rocking on his heels. The height wasn't a problem, but the confined space was adding to his impatience.

Finally, the car creaked to a halt at the observation level. Brennan climbed out, his erstwhile confidante right behind him. "You see?" the Englishman said. "It's not such a bad ride."

There were already a few dozen people on the deck. Brennan moved towards the rail. The view was spectacular, Paris sprawled out in a grand circle around them. The city had long prohibited buildings over seven stories tall, giving the central landmark a spectacular perspective; the bridge across the Seine river below was busy with seemingly tiny traffic, the Trocadero gardens running beyond it in a narrow green strip of manicured brilliance and water fountains, and past them the grand marble pillars of the enormous Palais De Chaillot, the building's two wings spread grandly, covering several hundred feet to each side.

"It's a shame, isn't it?" The Englishman from the elevator had sidled up next to him.

For a split second, Brennan didn't realize he was being addressed. "Sorry, I didn't catch that," he said.

"It's a shame," the Englishman said. He had a tan raincoat on, an umbrella folded up in one hand; he wore a flat cap and had half glasses, a large man in all respects, flecks of grey and lines suggesting he was in his early fifties. He gestured towards the palace. "It's sort of an Albert Speer-like sterile government idea of art. In fact, Hitler was said to have loved the place."

"Really?"

"Oh yes, he was quite enamoured with it, apparently. The palace they knocked down to build it was a Romanesque monstrosity in its own right, the Palais du Trocadero. But it had character, a grand blend of styles, two giant church towers, broad marble stairs. And it was built for a purpose, to celebrate a famous victory over Spain. Its unworthy replacement, on the other hand, was for an international exposition, which just adds to its sense of artifice."

Brennan raised the book slightly to see if the man was focusing on him for a reason, but the Englishman seemed uninterested. A moment later a blonde woman of similar vintage approached them; her hair was losing its artificial colour at the roots, and she had a faux fur coat over her green sweater. "Is my husband bothering you?" she said, smiling warmly. "He does go on."

"It's… fine," Brennan said. "Interesting stuff."

"You're on vacation as well, I take it?" she said, not waiting for him to answer before continuing. "We've come every year for years. Not always to Paris, of course; we also enjoy Strasbourg and Provence."

"Uh huh," Brennan said, barely paying attention. The observation deck was fairly busy and he wasn't sure if he was missing the man, who was supposed to be quite short, balding, a bookish type.

There, just exiting the elevator. The man had a grey navy pea coat on, black wool gloves to counteract the winter temperatures. Steam drifted from his mouth as he scanned the area also, a copy of the J.D. Salinger novel in one hand. He saw Brennan just a moment later and both men nodded towards the other. They met along the wall overlooking the palace.

"You've read the *Catcher in The Rye*, I see," the man said to Brennan.

"I just started it," he replied. "So don't give anything away."

Brennan looked over his shoulder. The English tourists were still close, so he gestured with his head for the contact to move a few yards away, then followed. He kept his voice low. "Do you have something for me?"

The bookish man nodded. "You have the money?"

"A thousand," Brennan said. He checked around for people paying attention once more then slipped the man an envelope.

Behind them, they heard a gasp of surprise. Brennan turned quickly, wary of any potential problems; but it was just the British woman. She'd leaned on the wide edge of the viewing area but dropped one of her white gloves; along with several other tourists, she was watching it drift slowly towards the ground.

"Oh gosh," she said as it fell almost from sight, the barest dot in the updrafts. "I really loved those gloves."

2. 128

Behind him, Brennan missed the moment when her husband casually moved behind his contact, missed the short jab with the tip of the umbrella; and he was just turning back as the Englishman strode away and towards the elevator car.

The contact was still standing there but he had a shocked look in his eyes, and they'd begun to dart around, as if he were confused; his head started to move slightly side to side, rapidly, as if he were trying to supplement poor eyesight by improving his field of vision; his lips were parted slightly as if, caught in a moment of surprise, he'd forgotten how he might look to someone else.

Brennan nodded toward him. "Are you okay? You look like you saw a ghost or some…."

The contact collapsed, his body seizing and convulsing as he went into cardiac arrest, foamy spittle dribbling out of the left corner of his mouth and onto the concrete. Brennan knew the symptoms right away, knew the man had no time. "The address," he hissed at his source, as people began to gather around. Behind the crowd, the Englishman's wife had stepped into the second car and the gate closed. "Give me the address!"

The convulsing man couldn't communicate, but his eyes flashed down quickly, towards the book in his hands. Brennan quickly exchanged copies with him, then rose, pushed his way through the crowd, saying loudly, "This man's having a heart attack! We need a doctor, now!"

Security were rushing over; there was a nurse on site, Brennan knew, but it wouldn't matter. He headed towards the elevator, cursing his own carelessness, his own casual approach. It had been the English couple; that much was obvious. The poison? Probably ricin, injected with the tip of the man's umbrella into the victim's buttocks. The toxin was deadly efficient, and the contact stood no chance.

15./

The café along Rue des Rosiers wasn't exactly Langley, but it did the trick; the street was lined with trendy shops and restaurants, the pedestrians milling amongst each other on the narrow one-way street, cars giving way by moving at a crawl.

Brennan's nerves were on edge from the incident at the tower, and he sat drinking a café au lait, going through the dog-eared copy of the *Catcher in The Rye*. It was mid-afternoon, the street outside chilly and the sky gray, but the café quiet, the only sounds the conversation between the waiter and a friend at a smaller corner table and the radio playing a scratchy old Edith Piaf song, the haunting melody drifting up from somewhere behind the main counter.

His first pass through the book hadn't spotted anything out of the ordinary, although it was only a quick scan; he'd concentrated on each line of text, looking for small pen or pencil marks, dots or lines, anything that might indicate part of a phrase pattern.

Back to the start. Brennan ignored the narrative as he turned each page; when he read it for the first time at age fourteen, he'd been fascinated by Holden Caulfield; at seventeen, he'd realized the kid's angry rebellion was just sorrow, outrage at losing his brother; at twenty, he'd read it for a third and final time, still surprised at Salinger's ability in the fifties to express how isolated youths felt when their upbringing was ruptured by loss and emotional neglect. He'd joined the navy a year later, finding a sense of community in it– and later the SEALS -- that was as strong as his own family's bonds, guidance in self and purpose that helped stave off the kind of demons that poor Holden suffered so convincingly.

Brennan shook the thought off, got back to the book. He scanned each page again line by line, not noticing anything in the text...

There, on page one hundred and five. He'd missed the marks the first time because they were beside the page number, in tiny pencil print at the upper left of the page. There was a dot, then a dash, then the number. Brennan's code-breaking training wasn't exactly extensive but it looked like a simple location key, the dot denoting a line, the dash a page. He turned to page five, then parsed down to the tenth line. The last letter of the line had been gone over in pen, just barely enhanced like a medium 'bold' of the type.

He returned to page one hundred and five; then he went forward, a page at a time, picking up each of the book locations, then building the words a letter at a time. After ten minutes, he had a string: '68 Rue du Globe, Stains'.

Stains was northeast of the city and it looked busy, middle-class, with a host of street-level shops and single-family homes behind privacy walls, along with plenty of both foot and car traffic. The taxi dropped Brennan off a block from his target address, as instructed, and he paid the cabbie with fifty euros, telling him to keep the small amount of leftover change.

He walked the block, passing a handful of small businesses: a hairdresser, a falafel café, an insurance office. His address was the first on the opposite corner, a typical three- or four-bedroom Mediterranean-style home with a red tile roof and pink stucco walls. The wall around it was about six feet high, so he couldn't make out much below the lower level windows; the back yard looked busy, though, with a few palms stretching high above, and the final few feet of the roof to a pool cabana at the end of the garden.

Brennan crossed the street and paced around the block at a slow walk using a slight head turn and his peripheral vision to check the place out, before rounding the block in left turns until he'd seen as much as he could. He looked down the street for a better vantage point; there was a five-story office block about five hundred yards away. He made his way up the street casually, then crossed over and entered through the public double doors; he ignored the front desk and walked confidently to the elevators. The first car that arrived was empty. He took it up to the fifth floor and got out, then looked for the emergency exit sign. The roof access was likely there.

The roof hatch was sloppily unlocked, but it saved him breaking through and potentially attracting attention. He climbed the short ladder attached to the wall at the end of the hallway and popped it open.

It was ideal. He crouched low and crossed over to the edge facing the villa. Brennan withdrew his small binoculars from the inside of his coat and placed the backyard into focus. It was nice, touristy, with an in-ground pool and a shaded back patio. No one was using it because of the December weather; but there was a guard outside the backdoor with a sizeable shoulder holster bulge under his suit jacket.

Okay, so probably one at the back, one at the front, a couple more inside. Best approach? Brennan considered it for a moment. *Isolate the guy at the back, use the upper balcony for ingress as it's likely where the bedrooms are, and most guards won't expect someone coming from behind them, from the inside out.*

But then there was the matter of getting Boudreau out. Walter's intel was only that Fawkes' mistress had been taken while Brennan was dealing with Bustamante in Barcelona. They didn't know who, or why. The prime suspect was that she had his intel, or at least some intel, on the ACF.

He scanned the backyard through the binoculars. *Would a few hours matter? Probably not.* Brennan always figured that when push came to shove there were two ways to do a job: the easy way and the hard way. The hard way would mean stealing a vehicle, setting it up at the front of the house then running through the place from the back, taking out the guards one by one and taking Boudreau out the front door to the car. Assuming she was even in the house.

The easy way? He scanned the street; halfway down the block a sign offered 'voitures de location', cars for hire. They'd be open in the morning, and there was a decent cheap motel down the street. No need to rush anything, maybe bring the police down on him. The extra day would give him some extra prep time, after all, and a chance to make sure Annalise Boudreau was available to be rescued in the first place.

It was early evening, the sundown, the light low. The guard at the backdoor was sloppy, straying every so often from his post and wandering forward into the garden; not far, but far enough to leave space between him and the door; far enough that the angle from the side wall entry point was behind his field of vision. The wall was about six feet high, and Brennan had waited until after dark, with little to no foot traffic about, before peeking over and looking for his opportunity.

As his surveillance had suggested, the man was inclined to walk further from the door when smoking a cigarette, maybe a subconscious hedge against annoying the non-smokers in the house. Either way, it gave Brennan time to get over the wall and drop into a shadow-covered corner.

2.

He let the man take another pass, walking towards the door and then turning on his heel before pacing back towards the garden. Brennan came up behind him quickly but quietly, staying low, catching the man unaware until the crook of his elbow was already around the man's carotid artery, cutting off oxygen. The guard slumped to the ground. Brennan scanned around the backyard to make sure they were still alone then dragged the man using his armpits until he was under the balcony that covered most of the back of the villa.

The sleeper hold was an effective technique, but its victims usually woke quickly once blood flow was restored. He retrieved a pair of plastic restraints, looping the simple plastic ties around the man's ankles and wrists before covering his mouth with several wraps of duct tape.

Brennan had been glad for the extra day; he'd kept eyes on the upper floor windows, eventually catching a glimpse of Boudreau as she was escorted from her suite to the bathroom. Then he'd rented the vehicle, banked on the house sticking to normal schedules, and waited until the light was low, shortly after eight o'clock.

He put an ear to the backdoor but couldn't hear any immediate presence. He glanced up; the upper balcony was ten feet above, a short flight of concrete steps to its right leading to the garden. Brennan took them silently, staying low to get past the first window on the floor, hugging the wall once he'd reached the balcony, sliding past the door to check around the corner of the window. It was a large bedroom, the doorway to an in-suite bathroom in one corner and a fireplace against the wall.

The master suite? He watched it for a few minutes but there was no foot traffic. He crossed in front of the door again and leaned around the corner to check the first room.

Boudreau was sitting on the end of the bed in a thigh-length red silk robe, her legs up and under her, her weight on her right hip as she flicked through the channels on a TV ahead of her, the look on her face more one of boredom than fear. The door to the room opened quickly, a man striding in. For a moment, it seemed as if he caught the slightest movement from Brennan out of the corner of his eye, as he turned that way, then quickly walked over to look outside without raising the window. Brennan scurried to one side and flattened himself against the wall as the guard peered each way through the glass; after a few agonizing seconds, he retreated into the room. The American gave it thirty seconds before slowly making his way back to the window's edge, looking around it cautiously. Inside, the guard in the dark gray suit and white dress shirt was barking some sort of instruction at Boudreau and she was arguing with him. Brennan moved back to the door, leaning against it with his weight as he listened, in case anyone tried to open it at just the wrong moment.

The hallway sounded quiet. He tried the handle, depressing it slowly, waiting for the click to see if they'd locked it or just assumed the lower guard was sufficient. The latch drew back smoothly.

Mistake number two. He opened it a crack and peered inside. The corridor ran the length of the upper floor with two rooms on each side and a 't' junction flight of stairs halfway along leading to the lower level. The corridor was carpeted, and his movements were silent.

The second door to the left swung inward; Brennan's instinct took over and he sprinted forward, catching the man walking out of the room by surprise. He was tall, in a light gray suit, and his hand flashed to his waist band, the pistol up quickly in his left hand; but Brennan was ahead of him, anticipating; he locked up the man's left wrist with his own right, twisting his own body away from the man so that they were practically back to back, wrenching backward on the gun arm and dislocating it at the shoulder, even as his trailing left elbow swung wide and backwards, driving into the back of the guard's neck. Brennan spun a quarter-turn back the other way then drove a foot downward, hard into the side of the man's knee, which buckled and tore.

He let out a shriek of pain as he went down, loud enough to be heard around the house.

Damn it. Could've done that more quietly, Brennan thought. He'd told Walter he'd avoid as much bloodshed as possible, keep anything related to Fawkes on the down-low. He strode towards the first bedroom. *Using the suppressor might have saved me some trouble...*

The first guard was waiting for him at the door, and the blade in the man's hand arced outwards in a semi-circle, Brennan dodging backwards just in time as its shiny stainless steel surface flashed past him. He drove his palm into the back of the man's shoulder, the nerve strike deadening the man's arm; the man's other arm came up instinctively to protect him even as the chair the woman was holding came crashing down on him from behind.

Annalise's eyes were wide, the broken pieces of the wooden chair in her hands.

"Merci, Madame" Brennan said.

"Uh huh."

"Are there any more?"

She nodded, her eyes drifting towards the stairs.

"Follow me," he said. "I'm going to get you out of here."

"Who are you?"

"A friend of a friend."

She looked down at the guard. "How will we get out of here?"

"Just a second," he said. Brennan ran towards the stairs, timing the overhand punch just as the first guard climbed the last step. He crashed backwards into the man behind him and both went down. They hit the landing, the first man unconscious, the second struggling to find his feet. Brennan dove down the five steps feet first, driving his heels into the man's temple as he began to rise, the bulky enforcer collapsing in a heap.

Back on the second floor, Annalise heard the crashing of bodies but stayed rooted to her spot, frozen, wondering just what the hell was going on. *If I get out of here, I swear, I'm moving in with my sister in Biarritz and never coming back to Paris...*

The stranger's head poked back around the corner of the stairs. "You okay?" he asked.

She nodded vigorously then realized she was still holding a piece of chair. She put it down carefully on the floor, like she'd offended it. "Perhaps we should leave now."

"I'd have to agree. I've got a car out front, the black Mazda." He gestured towards the stairs and she scurried over to join him. They headed downstairs cautiously, the entryway just ten feet from the last step. "I think we're good," Brennan said.

They headed outside, the muted evening street lights casting spotlight ovals on the sidewalk. The car was as advertised, parked in front of the house next door. They climbed in, Annalise taking the passenger side. "Where are we going?"

"Back into the city."

3.

"I'd really prefer not. I'd really prefer just to go to the nearest police station," she said. "The sooner I have this dealt with and I can get away from here, the better."

He started the car without responding and backed up slightly then pulled out of the curb side space. Traffic was light as he followed the streets to the main highway back into Paris. After about five minutes she said, "We're not going to the police, are we?"

Brennan shook his head. "There are some people I work with who will want to talk to you first, so I'm taking you to the American embassy."

"But… I'm a French subject."

"You're an assassination target, Madame Boudreau," he said. "The people after you believe that you have vital information about Sir Anthony…"

"They're wrong."

"Maybe so, but they'll stop at nothing to get it, and some of them are very powerful; there's no guarantee you'd be safe with the police."

He kept his eyes on the road for a few more moments before stealing a glance her way; she had one arm folded across her stomach, protective, the other elbow leaning on the arm, her fist under her chin in a pensive pose, her face morose and her pale blues eyes dim pools in the passing amber road lights. "So I don't get a choice?" she said.

"Not if you want to live," Brennan said. He felt guilty. Whatever they thought she had… "Did Lord Anthony give you anything in the last few weeks, a gift of some sort perhaps?"

Her hand instinctively went to the locket around her neck and Brennan caught the tell. She saw his look. "It's nothing, just a locket with a cameo in it, an ancestor of Anthony's."

The drive to the embassy took another half hour, Brennan occasionally stealing glances at the piece of jewelry out of his peripheral vision, knowing he'd have to tell them to take it as soon as they arrived.

He wondered if she had anything else to remember her late lover by; he hoped so. He hoped they didn't go too hard on her in trying to drag things out. It would be easier for everyone, he knew, if the locket contained some of the answers they required.

DEC. 18, 2015, WASHINGTON, D.C.

The call came through on Fenton-Wright's encrypted office line, which meant it was urgent, and probably from one of the few men in the country allowed to tell him what to do.

2.

"David Fenton-Wright," he answered.

The voice didn't identify itself. It didn't need to. "I'm back stateside," Brennan said. "We need to meet."

The deputy director dug deep to curb his temper. "You're supposed to be on leave, officially. We're not supposed to be in contact. How did you get this number, anyway?"

Walter had given it to him two years earlier but Brennan wasn't about to tell Fenton-Wright that.

"Never mind that," Brennan said. "I want to know what happened with the package in Paris."

"Safe and sound, and that's all you need to know right now," Fenton-Wright said. "The girl has been sent with some compensation to her sister's house in the south of France."

"And the locket?"

"An encoded microdot for which only we have the key. It would have been useless to any outside parties at any rate. But you did well in recovering the woman, I won't deny that. We're confident she knows nothing of real value."

"So now what?"

"Now nothing. You're to stay out of contact until we have new intel on the shootings. But for now we're confident Bustamante was our most likely suspect."

"You're kidding."

"Yes, because I'm renowned for my sense of humor," Fenton-Wright said dryly.

"But I told you he was clear on the fact that he wasn't involved, and there's all the other stuff he said, the stuff about Khalidi, the nuke...The situation has changed."

"And where should we direct you, agent Brennan?"

"That's part of the problem: I have no idea."

"You weren't supposed to interact with Bustamante. It was supposed to be surveillance."

"It was unavoidable."

"The news said one of his own guards shot him."

"It's true."

"I don't care. At any rate, I don't need operational suggestions. In fact, as I said, you weren't supposed to make contact with me, even on an encrypted line."

"So what now? My target is down."

"Head back over the pond. You're too hot, and I don't want you around here right now. Stay in Paris until I contact you. You're in D.C.?"

"Yeah."

"For now, as I said, we assume Bustamante was our man. I'll advise later on how – or if – we'll proceed."

3.

"What about the item?"

"Leave it with me; consider it off of your playing field, need-to-know. And you don't."

Fenton-Wright had a level of contempt in his voice that Brennan thought only a field agent had the right to express. He made a mental note to add it to the long list of reasons to look for payback one day as he hung up the call.

Fenton-Wright buzzed through to Jonah Tarrant. "Jonah, get me an update psych assessment on Joe Brennan. Ask them to concentrate on his issues with authority."

Tarrant didn't ask why. He knew the implication, that they might need something to hold over Brennan later. He didn't like it, but he imagined David didn't either; it was just part of the game.

Brennan met with Walter Lang at the latter's new favorite pub, which was eight blocks further west than the Czech brewpub and, as far as Walter knew, had yet to be uncovered by anyone in the media.

Walter looked sickly, Brennan thought. He'd always been a pale guy, but he was pasty, off-white, and it looked as though he hadn't been sleeping well.

"You okay?" he asked, right after sitting down across from him, back to the wall and eyes on the door.

"Sure, sure," Walter said. "You know how it is. They've got me burning the candle at both ends on this thing."

"I talked to David today," Brennan said. Walter looked surprised by that. Brennan filled him in on the conversation. "He basically told me to stand down, and to stay out of the country in the meantime."

"Have you seen Carolyn since you got back?"

Brennan looked away quickly, guilty at the thought. "No. I know I should, but I also knew David might tell me to make myself scarce. It's so close to Christmas; I didn't want to get the kids' hopes up that I'd be here on the day."

"I get that," Walter said. "Tell me again what he said about the hot item?"

Brennan recounted the conversation again, Walter looking more incredulous throughout. "So basically he suggested Bustamante was rambling incoherently."

Walter was quiet while Brennan talked. When his friend had finished, he took a swallow of his beer, then said, "I think it's true."

Brennan was shocked. "What?"

"At least, the part about the South Africans losing it. They couldn't admit it, because doing so would have meant admitting it existed in the first place. The rest of it? You got me. We'd heard rumours that it was behind the high radiation readings among the wreckage of a coastal bus crash..."

"...out of Lima, Peru, in 2009. My sources heard that, too."

"There was a known Chechen dissident onboard the bus when it went up, a man named Borz Abubakar. Security footage from the bus depot had him boarding the coach."

"So it's possible the nuke – or its payload, anyway – is on the bottom of the Pacific."

"Sure," Walter said. "It's also possible that it's not. Which, for obvious reasons, is a bigger problem."

Brennan was quiet for a moment, nursing his beer.

"What's your thinking?" Walter asked.

"Nothing. Just that it's a hell of a way to spend a Christmas, you know?"

"You don't have to. You don't have to go right away; you could go home, spend some time with Carolyn and the kids."

"You know the job comes first, bud. It's always been that way."

"Sure," Walter said. "But no one's got you on a schedule. You said it yourself, you're technically on leave. David can go fuck himself, frankly. This Khalidi thing isn't going to change the world, whatever's going on, if you take three or four days off for your family at Christmas. Maybe remember that some of us aren't so lucky, you know? You want to know what I think, Joe? I think you did what you were ordered to do; you completed your assignments. And if there's more out there? Well... there will always be more out there. The world won't end without you. Not right away, anyway."

"Maybe so," Brennan said, before taking another swallow from the beer. "Maybe so."

He stood pat on the single beer so that he could drive to the airport in safe fashion, and said goodbye to Walter after twenty minutes of conversation. He left the pub, his rental weaving its way south. The Japanese compact slipped its way onto Twenty-Fifth Street, then onto M Street, before crossing the river via Highway 29 over the Potomac River Bridge. A light turned red and he sat there staring at it for a few seconds, transfixed. He didn't have to take the parkway to Dulles. He could head in the other direction, back to Annandale. Walter was right. No one was stopping him.

The light changed. Brennan paused for a moment longer, lingering on the decision; then finally, he stepped on the gas.

3.   139

Twenty-five minutes away, Carolyn sat in the living room alone, a glass of Bailey's and ice in her left hand. She was hunched forward slightly, leaning her elbow on one arm of the chair, the drink perched with semi-permanence just a few inches from her lips. But she ignored it, staring ahead, deep in thought as the six-foot artificial Scotch pine blinked its Christmas cheer behind her, the fireplace crackling in the background.

She'd been dwelling all night on whether he'd make it home for the holiday; even if it was just for a few days, a week before the big day. There was snow outside, the kids presents were already bought and wrapped. They could find an excuse to tell them Santa had come early; she could cook them all a big bird, they could get tipsy after the kids were in bed, maybe work on another…

She shook it off and glared at the door again. She'd fixated on whether he'd make it back after finding out at work that Joe had been successful, that he'd covered Fawkes' tracks and recovered intel on the group targeted by the sniper. That meant he was done, didn't it? At least for now?

Carolyn looked down morosely at her drink. She loved him, even if she sometimes took advantage of his willingness to follow the 'happy wife, happy life' credo. She felt guilty, wondering if her career was responsible for the wedge between them of late; then she frowned and shook it off. That was bullshit, she thought. Whatever had distanced them – perhaps even just actual distance itself – was something they could work out. If only he would come home for Christmas.

She took another swallow of Bailey's, relishing the warmth from the fireplace. They'd been married eight years now, and both would have to admit the romance had died down, replaced with a comfortable familiarity – when that comfort wasn't being undermined by their often separate objectives. Maybe it was his fault; maybe realism suggested her job was the one that needed the most protection, the one that allowed her to come home to her kids each night.

The last of the Bailey's stared up enticingly at her, a thick, sweet way to get a little buzz on. The truth was, she thought, trying to blame one another wasn't going to do their relationship any good. And if there was anything to get past, it was merely the resentment that simmers when words are left unsaid.

2.

She stared at the door for another minute, but it remained sturdy and stoic, unmoved. Was it too much to ask for a break? To look up and pray to a higher power for some real help? Or was she just being selfish? There were so many people out there in the world that had it worse than their family. Maybe the thing to do, even if he didn't make it back for Christmas, would be to put on a brave face for the kids and try her darnedest to make a positive from a negative; it was the same attitude that had gotten her ahead at the agency so quickly, after all.

But it didn't stop her from feeling sad, and from missing Joe. She drained the rest of the Bailey's and sighed.

The deadbolt on the front door turned.

Carolyn drew in a quick breath and stood up, both hands on the glass as the door swung open.

Joe stepped inside.

"Hi," he said.

"Hi."

"Surprise."

She smiled and chewed nervously on her lower lip; it felt like he'd just asked her out again for the first time, and he had the same stupid look on his face as he'd had so many years before.

DEC. 24, 2015, RURAL VERMONT, NEAR THE CANADIAN BORDER

The asset was home.

But it wasn't really home. It was America, but it was a rented cabin, little more than a three-room shack on the shore of Lake Salem, just outside Newport, Vermont.

It was in the woods, deep amongst the pines, cut off from the main road and private; and it was nothing like being with the family, enjoying the holidays.

It had a rough kitchen with a farmer's sink and a big wood table, and a wood-burning stove that doubled as the cabin's heat source. The kitchen and living room were one big area, mottled in wood paneling, and the living room floor was covered with a cheap maroon-and-white carpet. A multi-colored quilt had been thrown over the couch to cover spills and stains. A cigarette-burned old coffee table against the wall held an old twenty-inch tube-style TV. Behind the big room were a bedroom and a bathroom, and that was it.

He'd stopped at the Target store in Newport and bought a bunch of supplies, basic food and some fruit, along with a bottle of scotch at the nearby liquor store that he hadn't really intended on drinking, but which he figured might come in handy if he got too bored.

The location was ideal; utterly remote, quiet, but with close proximity to the Canadian border. One of his identities was Canadian, and it was easier to fly out of Montreal with some of his wares than America. But he had no option with respect to going home; until the assignment was complete, that was out of the question now. He had weeks before his next move, and longer still before he'd complete his next job. So he had to be patient.

It was different, running solo; he felt isolated, introspective in a manner normally alien to him. But with no loved ones around to distract him from his sense of purpose, such was the nature of his duty; such was the nature of his revenge.

He changed the TV channel; Danny Kaye and Bing Crosby were on a train with Rosemary Clooney and Vera-Ellen, singing about snow. It was on every year and he didn't enjoy it anymore, not like when he was a kid. Things were more innocent then, and dumb Fifties movies with hackneyed dialogue and Technicolor were part of the holiday fun. Now, they just seemed like a lost cause, a world almost primitive, like a naïve, childish painting.

The asset hated that all of that was gone.

But that was the whole point of the assignment, wasn't it? Lost innocence and a chance to rebalance the scales for once, right? He nodded quietly to himself, resolve strengthened. He was handling things the way an American would back in the nation's glory days, he told himself, back when we still won wars and unapologetically kicked ass where necessary. He reached over from the couch to the coffee table and retrieved the bottle of whiskey. He was going to drink a toast, and then he was going to drink another, and maybe a few more after that, some scotch and ginger to help wash down those good intentions. And it wouldn't be drinking out of loneliness, no matter how much he missed his family. Instead, he decided, it would be a celebration of righteousness, the way Christmas was meant to be.

He'd checked his phone when he'd gotten in from the airport; she'd left a message, an acknowledgement that she knew he'd call back if he could, and that they'd miss him at Christmas, especially the boy. He'd saved up his allowance to get him something nice, she said.

Outside, the Vermont woods were blanketed with a coating of snow, but it was raining gently and the temperature was nearly above freezing. The sun should have been warming the horizon, going down for the evening; but the thickets of trees cut it off from view.

The asset changed the channel. Thank Christ the cabin had a decent antenna, even if the offerings were limited. The Main NBC affiliate had Meet the Press on, with clips from a news conference involving Sen. John Younger of Utah, the current Democratic golden boy. Like most former military personnel, the asset had disdain for politicians in general. Their bullshit flowed down hill onto the enlisted man, he knew. Still, it was something other than Bing and Danny; he turned it up as Younger addressed the Commerce Club of Greater Los Angeles.

"….would ask the question in return: what is Addison March doing to promote American values? He's fond of trooping the flag, but only when it's about votes, and rarely when it's about jobs. He'll close our borders; not just to illegals, but also to companies that do billions of dollars' worth of business with American firms every year. Now I ask you… is that American?"

"It is not," the asset said to the empty cabin.

"Addison March says he's for a stronger America," Younger said. "Yet he voted against a bill that would have increased drug coverage for our veterans. Is that American? Is that building a stronger America?"

The asset took a slug of whiskey. He wondered if the whole speech would be a shot at Younger's opponent. Probably. The election season was brewing. It was the only time any politician voluntarily talked about veterans' treatment, a shameful reality through multiple presidents, multiple administrations, multiple ideologies.

"My fellow Americans," Younger said, "the America in which I grew up was the greatest nation on Earth and remains so to this day." The crowd cheered madly, and the politician gave them a moment before signaling with both hands for quiet. "But we didn't have an easy road; it took guts, and bravery, and the iron will of a nation. When I was a young man, I saw our Nation's greatness corrupted in the McCarthy era, done in by scaremongers not unlike a certain breed we hear from commonly today, the people who fear and hate. I'm grateful that that era only lasted for a few years, that the forces of good triumphed, that America stood up to the black listers and fearmongers and said 'Hell no.'

"America rediscovered its direction. We did it by knowing we could always do better; we could always achieve more, always strive … for more. For a legacy we could leave our kids, and grandkids. And we won't continue to grow and thrive and develop if we allow the forces of negativity and selfishness to grow as they have in the past. We have to say 'Heck yes' to the kind of America we foresaw in the Golden days of yesteryear, the promise of JFK, Dr. King, Jimmy Carter. And yes, of our beloved president, celebrating his second term, setting the stage for the kind of positive change upon which this country has always thrived, a change drive by the heartbeat of the American people."

The crowd roared with a collective white noise that signaled Younger had hit his mark. The asset smiled for the first time all day, not a broad, toothy grin, but a satisfied wry line, content at the notion that maybe, just maybe there were reasons to be optimistic.

Of course, he knew things. He knew things the politicians didn't.

In a few more weeks, he thought, *I'll kill another one. And we'll be one step closer to a better world.*

JAN. 1, 2016, BRUSSELS, BELGIUM.

Despite the nip in the air, the tree-shrouded strolls of the Parc Royal were busy. Its broad paths – divided by a five-foot wide grass belt into two lanes – teemed with cyclists, baby strollers, joggers and power walkers rushing by the odd pedestrian commuter.

Most of the people in the park were young fitness enthusiasts. At other times of year they might have lounged in the grass, although it was too cold for that now, just below zero and jackets mandatory.

Professor Allan Ballantine looked out of place. Ballantine was approaching sixty, both broad of shoulder and large of stomach, a six-foot-something hulk with curly brown hair, a short beard, glasses. In his red corduroy shirt and brown sports jacket, he looked like the road manager for a Seventies rock band.

He had his hands shoved into his coat pockets as he strolled along the wooded path and he looked around furtively, as if trying to find a familiar landmark. Joe Brennan was seated on a bench fifty yards away and had been waiting for twenty minutes, watching the light dusting of snow fall. When it became apparent that Ballantine hadn't spotted him, he gave the older man a wave and Ballantine walked over.

"Joe Brennan?" he asked, extending a hand to shake.

Brennan got up and reciprocated. "Walter says hello."

"I hadn't heard from Walter in years before he called yesterday. I must say, it was a bit of a surprise."

"Yeah… sorry about that, professor. Please…" Brennan motioned to the bench and both men sat down.

"No, it's fine. But you know how it is when someone's been inactive for years. I had this terrifying moment where I thought they might want me to do something in the field and, as I said, it's been a very long time."

Twenty years, according to Walter Lang.

Brennan had contacted the veteran agency man after a rescue in Paris and an interrogation in Barcelona revealed a rogue nuke might soon be on the black market; both men realized he needed intel support. Lang in turn had given him Ballantine's name, because the professor was an expert in Weapons of Mass Destruction, particularly nuclear. He'd spent the prior five years working with the EU on nuclear energy policies for emerging nations, along with developing weapons inspection criteria for more traditional powers.

"Sorry I didn't just come to your office…"

3.   145

"That's all right, really," the professor said. "I imagine there's some cloak-and-dagger explanation for meeting here...?"

"It's an unofficial get together," Brennan said. "Officially, I'm not here."

"Hmmm. Sounds serious. And because you've come to me, I must assume it's nuclear."

"Something like that. Walter said you're encyclopedic with respect to the massive changes in the global arsenal over the last quarter-century."

"Well, one doesn't like to toot one's own horn," Ballantine said, "but I've kept reasonably up to date."

"What do you know about a bomb that might be available on the open market? It would have to be extremely small and lightweight, no bigger than a computer, and it has to have been around for a while."

The professor's attention was rapt. "So you're looking for a suitcase-sized nuke, something with a uranium core?"

"Something that might have involved the South Africans," Brennan said.

A knowing look crossed Ballantine's face. "Oh.... I know where this is headed, I think. The was a rumor that about twenty years ago, during its disarmament that ended its nuclear weapons program, the South Africans had lost a bomb."

"Lost?"

"Lost track of, I should say. There seems to have been a general agreement over the years to consider it merely a clerical error; that the bomb in question never existed. An urban myth, if you will."

"But you don't agree?"

"No," Ballantine said. "My conversations with a variety of their officials over the years have merely convinced me that the initial reports were correct. It's a story they don't like to talk about very much, particularly, as the missing bomb was an older weapon."

"Surely there have been international community attempts..."

"Oh, certainly, certainly. They've already investigated it several times, without luck. There are any numbers of unaccounted for weapons out there, thanks to the collapse of the Soviets. There is one train of thought..."

"What?"

"Well, there was a theory floated around that a radioactive signature spotted in the debris field of a bus explosion in South America a few years ago might have been caused by the fissionable material from the device. The source could never be determined but people were quite certain at the time that the wreckage was too contaminated to have not been in contact with some sort of core. But there's a problem with that theory."

2.   146

"How so?"

"For one, the South African low-yield weapons used a gun assembly; they would shoot one small portion of fissionable material into another, a uranium bullet, achieving a critical mass. But this form is highly unstable when introduced to water, because it produces neutron moderation, which can also cause critical mass. The bus exploded when it went off of the road and much of it ended up in the Pacific Ocean, bordering the highway it was travelling at the time. If there had been an active core aboard, it's quite possible we would have seen a devastating explosion. And for another, whoever had it would have needed to get the thing into Peru somehow."

"What happened to the bus?"

"You might remember it; there was some belief among the leftists in Peru that the government had attacked it with a rocket, which just seemed bizarre. In any rate, they never did identify a definite cause; the unofficial word was that a freelance terrorist type affiliated with the Shining Path movement blew himself up by mistake and took the rest of the bus along with him."

About thirty people had died in the crash. Brennan remembered the news stories, but few details. "Wasn't that just…"

"Six or seven years ago, yes," Ballantine said. "And the weapon went missing twenty years ago. So if there is a connection, it is a circuitous one, at best."

"What kind of damage would this device have been capable of?"

Ballantine crossed his arms. The park was quiet as they moved past the lunch hour, into the afternoon, with just the odd couple passing by. "If the rumors are true, it would be something in the twenty megaton range."

"Which means…?"

"Which means everything in a one-mile radius from the blast would be instantly vaporized. Radiation burns and fallout would kill everyone for another ten to fifteen miles beyond that in relatively short order. Beyond that? Depending on where it was set off…"

"It could kill millions of people?"

Ballantine nodded. "There's a reason countries never actually build these things anymore, you know. If someone has that weapon and intends to use it, the consequences would be utterly devastating."

They talked for a few more minutes until it became clear to Brennan that he had as much information as Ballantine could offer. But he did suggest another local research scientist might have more detail, particularly on the South African story; they were discussing the best way to get in touch with her when Brennan noticed the man in his periphery, pretending to not pay attention to them.

3.

He was sitting down the lane on a park bench, wearing sunglasses and a dark suit. He'd raised and lowered his newspaper too many times in the few minutes they'd been there. Either he was a speed reader of amazing talent, Brennan thought, or he wasn't really reading. "Where does this scientist work, exactly?" he asked the professor, keeping his eye on the man watching them.

"She's teaching and doing research at the Universite Libre de Bruxelles," the older man said. "She's very helpful; I can call ahead and we can take a cab over to meet her, if she's available."

"Sure," Brennan said. "In just a few minutes. Don't look up, but I think someone's keeping tabs on us."

"The man in the suit down the path a little way? Yes, I noticed him too. What should we do?"

"We need to find out which one of us has drawn his interest. Follow my lead."

They walked out of the park side by side, taking the nearest exit and heading down the adjacent street. After a block, Brennan checked in the rear-view mirror of a parked car as they strolled by; sure enough, the man was following at a discreet distance. "When we get to the next corner, I'm going to take a right," Brennan said. "He can't follow both of us, so this should tell us something."

"What if he follows me?" the professor hissed. "I'm not exactly in the shape I was when I was a young man."

"Don't worry, if he keeps heading straight, I'll be right behind the two of you."

"And if he doesn't?"

"If he turns to follow me, just wait on the street. I'll be along eventually."

The corner arrived and Brennan turned. There was a natural curve to the street, and he watched the window reflections as he followed the course of the block. After a hundred yards or so, he spotted the man again.

He took another quick right, into an adjacent alley, waiting until the man turned the corner; Brennan crouched quickly and swept his leg out in a semi-circle; but his pursuer was alert, anticipating a fight, and he jumped over the attempted trip, using a forward roll to put some distance between them. Both men moved into combat stances. The man was young, Asian, five-ten, in his twenties or thirties; he had a bounce in his step that suggested he knew his business. He spun a quick, whirling roundhouse kick and Brennan blocked it with a raised forearm, stepping back several paces as the pursuer smoothly transitioned from the kick motion to a blur of punches; Brennan recognized the style as Sleeping Crane Fist, the close-combat blur of blows a prescribed combination; he countered quickly and effectively, his hands, arms and feet moving with the same rapid precision as his foe, blocking each strike.

The man took a half-step back and Brennan took advantage, countering with East River Fist, throwing a pair of punches from an acute angle that he expected his pursuer to block, opening the younger man up for a reverse punch, which Brennan snapped home with the back of his fist, catching the man under his cheekbone and staggering him.

The attacker shook it off and wiped a smear of blood away from the corner of his nose, looking surprised at being caught. He charged at Brennan again, his stance shifting to accommodate Xing Yi Quan, the northern flying feet technique, a series of high-speed kicks snapping outwards as Brennan maintained his center by ducking low in horse stance, his feet wide, his body flowing with natural motion around each strike, not allowing the powerful blows near enough to cause damage. Then he moved into hanging horse, a squat, wide-footed stance that would allow him to step back quickly and avoid the full range of motion from each kick, then counter with a blow of his own.

Brennan bounced on the soles of his feet, looking for an opportunity to strike back. But the younger man was fast, faster than anyone Brennan had sparred with before. He went into a stance Brennan did not recognize initially, throwing a strike that, as Brennan moved to intercept, turned into a grabbing wrist hold -- a Chin Na Su, or locking technique. Before Brennan could react, the attacker had his thumb and wrist locked up behind him, the force feeling like it might break his arm. Brennan stamped, trying to break his assailant's toes, but the quicker man jumped backwards and fell onto one side, taking Brennan with him. On the ground, Brennan felt an arm lock around his throat, legs around his waist. The man was going to choke the life out of him, if he could. Brennan tried to force his arm up between his body and the attacker's hold, to break it up, but the pursuer was too strong. Brennan's head was getting light from the pressure to his carotid artery. He turned it as far as he could and pushed up with his feet, the man's grip slowly giving way. Brennan shoved once more, hard, until he was facing the side of the smaller man's head, then sunk his teeth into the young man's ear, tearing away a huge, bloody chunk of lobe. The man screamed and let go, grasping at the mess. Brennan rose quickly, but this time got a leg sweep in return for his troubles, and unlike his pursuer wasn't able to dodge it, going down hard.

When he looked up, the man was a block away and sprinting, one hand grasping the side of his head as the blood flowed freely. He was already too far for Brennan to try and catch up. Brennan rolled over to the alley wall and leaned, seated, against it until he'd caught his breath.

He got up and backtracked to the street. Ballantine was standing in front of a shop window a half-block away.

"What happened? Good lord, you've got blood all over your chin."

Brennan tried to wipe it away. "Not mine, fortunately."

"Who?"

"Hard to say. Could have been freelance. Very skilled."

"How did he know where we were meeting?"

"Again, hard to say. He might have been working on the assumption that I was looking for a nuke expert and then just tailed you. There are only a handful of men with your experience and knowledge; it probably wasn't hard for whoever was employing him to set up stakeouts in several locations."

"So I've got a target on my back?"

"Relax, professor; if he was after you, he'd have kept following you. No, whoever sent him was either after me or, more likely, was gathering intelligence. If he'd intended to confront us, he could have done it back at the park."

2.

"What do we do now, then?"

"Now we flag a cab down and take it to see your expert. Assuming she doesn't punch me in the face then try to choke me, she'll be an improvement."

Dr. Han Chae Young's lab was in a modern new tinted glass-and-steel addition to the venerable red-brick university. They took the elevator to the second floor and headed down a non-descript corridor to the last door on the right, simply marked C-142.

Ballantine pushed it open and leaned around the corner, not entering completely; Brennan could see the room through the narrow horizontal glass window in the door. The lab was brightly lit, a handful of tables positioned to accompany bizarre-looking interconnected contraptions, bulky chrome cylinders with octopus arms, long hoses uncoiled, connecting glass tanks to computer servers, the guts of a device suspended from a hoist, a series of brass discs turning inside it as a student tinkered with a tiny screwdriver. Brennan couldn't pretend to recognize any of it, aside from the handful of computer workstations; students in white lab coats, masks, and hairnets alternated between taking readings from the various machines and entering data at the terminals, discussing theory as they did so, going over their projects in a thoughtful manner.

Dr. Han was in her thirties, with long, dark hair that she'd swept back into a pony tail; she had thin lips and broad cheekbones, and she moved quickly when Ballantine opened the door, hustling over to join them and closing it quickly behind her.

"Protocol," she said quickly. "Some of what they're working on is sensitive." She held out a hand to Brennan and he shook. "You must be Joe. Allan said you'd probably need to speak with me."

"Dr. Han is a South Korean researcher, seconded to the school from the University of Seoul," Ballantine said.

"Allan said you're the go-to source for information on a nuke that might have disappeared from the South African disarmament, in the early nineties."

"It's my pet project." She smiled and looked slightly distant for a moment, as if caught in the thought of it. "Sort of a hobby, I guess."

"Chasing the legend of a stolen nuke?" Brennan asked. "I guess I've heard stranger ways to kill a weekend."

"But not many, right?"

"You could say that, sure." Her English was perfect, Brennan noticed. "You studied in America?"

She smiled. "University of Michigan, Ann Arbor," she said. Then she saw the puzzled look on his face. "It's got a great nuclear engineering program, basically, and I couldn't get a slot at MIT. Look, let's go get a coffee in the commissary; we can sit down and I'll fill you in."

"We're not pulling you away from work?" Ballantine asked.

She waved a hand towards the lab, shooing the idea. "It's fine. I needed a break anyway."

They took a door at the end of the hallway that fed into another non-descript passage, back into the main building. The cafeteria was just inside the main doors and nearly empty, a sea of Formica tables with a serving line fronting a kitchen at the back, along with a row of vending machines along the left wall.

"Most of the students have gone home for the Christmas break," she said. "There are a few dedicated types still kicking around, and some like myself who don't celebrate the season."

They each bought a coffee from the machine in the corner then sat down at one of the long, empty tables. "I got onto this when I was a student. My former prof at U of M was Dennis Carruthers, who did most of his work in fission. He passed away last year, unfortunately."

"My condolences," Brennan said, with Ballantine echoing the sentiment.

"It's okay," she said. "He was very old when he died; he'd been an intern on the Manhattan project, and he was well into his nineties. Anyway, twenty years ago he was advising the South Africans on how to safely disarm in the wake of its shift to a non-Apartheid democracy."

Ballantine seemed shocked. "So he knew about the weapon? But surely he passed the word on to authorities…"

"Oh most certainly," Han said. "But all he had was the vaguest story, references to something that was rumoured to have happened. He tried initially to discuss it with the South African government but was rebuffed. And he did mention that UN officials had inquired after it during the inspections that followed, again with no indication that it was actually true."

"But you think it is?" Brennan said.

She nodded. "The details at the time were interesting; there was no information about where this weapon was allegedly stolen from, or its yield, or anything like that. But there was a story that it had been smuggled out of the country by land, north along the West African coast. Problematically, Namibia is a desert and Angola was – and still is – rebuilding after decades of civil war, and that's where the trail ran cold."

"Is it possible it could have just been sitting there this entire time, without being discovered?"

2.

"In Angola?" Ballantine said. "There are parts of the country that are extraordinarily remote. If someone wanted to hide it, and the people looking for it didn't know where to start? Absolutely."

3.

17./
JAN. 17, 2016, WASHINGTON, D.C.

When Alex Malone awoke at eight o'clock, she followed her usual routine; she rose as the sun streamed through the small bedroom window, grabbed her robe from its usual spot on the floor and searched in vain for her slippers for about ten seconds before giving up and staggering, blearily, towards the kitchen.

The coffee machine was on its usual timer and a steaming cup awaited her, black as pitch. She retrieved her favorite mug from the rack by the sink, shambled over and poured a cup, then dipped her head slightly to slurp up the first inch. Her eyes rolled back in her head at the joyful flavor, the automatic bliss of knowing the caffeine would hit at any moment. "Geez, what a night," she said to the empty kitchen.

Most of the evening had been spent at a benefit staged by the Nigerian embassy. Malone had been trying to get to a particular source for a story she was working on, but it had required drinking his assistant almost under the table. Her head hurt, a throbbing reminder that she wasn't twenty-one anymore.

She took the doorway on the other side of the kitchen, to the short, twisting staircase that led to the front door of her townhouse; Malone opened the door and squinted at the glare of the sun, both thankful it was a nice day and immediately stung by it due to the hangover; she reached down to retrieve her morning copy of the *Washington Post* from the top step.

Only there were two.

At first, they appeared identical and Malone assumed the deliverer had just made a mistake. She left them both on her kitchen table while she went to get ready.

Five minutes later, she was running back to the kitchen, head and body wrapped in towels. She'd just stepped under the water when she realized why one paper looked slightly different: it didn't have her address scrawled on the front. Her carrier did it with all the papers on his route. She would have ignored it, but her reporter instinct was kicking in. So she rushed downstairs, realizing half way that she hadn't even bothered to properly dry herself first.

Sure enough, the paper on top was address-free. There was no way he'd miss one; even in the modern age of free electronic muck, the Post still printed multiple sections daily.

She picked up the copy and leafed through it, not seeing anything out of the ordinary. She went back to the beginning and started again. On the second read through, she was eighteen pages in when she noticed the blue dot, a tiny pen mark next to the second line of a story, halfway down the page. Malone went back to the beginning of the paper and started again. Sure enough, there was a series of dots. Every few pages, they'd be substituted with a short line. She collected the letters next to each of them and began rearranging them, using the lines as word divisions, until she had: Sheridan Fifth Lv 2 p lot 9 pm.

Sheridan and Fifth was the site of a popular rec centre, Malone knew. "P lot" obviously meant parking lot. At least whoever sent it had a sense of history, she thought. Meeting a source in a Washington parking lot was very Deep Throat, very Woodward and Bernstein. It also made her nervous as hell; Malone had been a good reporter for more than a decade and generally dug her own stuff up. She didn't do 'anonymous', and she certainly didn't meet people she didn't know in dark parking garages.

But… the newspaper was a tactful touch. If someone crazy wanted to take a shot at her, she reasoned, they could just have called her up about a potential story and lied. Whoever left the newspaper wanted complete privacy, but in a place public enough to allay some of their fears.

It was enough. It wasn't enough to make her feel safe; but it was enough to make her go.

Eleven nerve-clenching hours later, she was seated in her car on level two of a parking garage near the corner of Sheridan and Fifth. She waited as the clock approached nine; then she watched it go by; she gave it another ten minutes before it became apparent no one was going to make an appearance.

She switched on her headlights and started the engine. As she did, a figure stepped out from behind a nearby vehicle. Malone turned the engine off, and the lights, and then got out of the car.

The person was standing in the shadows. "You know who I am?"

She'd recognized him immediately. Malone came closer, her heels clicking slightly on the cold concrete. "Of course."

"You've been investigating David Fenton-Wright, the deputy director of the agency. The rumour is that he's next in line to become director."

"Okay," she said, offering nothing back. The less she said the more dead air was left for him to fill.

"He's just an errand boy. You need to start with the two dead diplomats, work backwards from there."

She knew he was talking about the EU sniper, a topic of discussion for months but recently quiet. "You mean Lord Cumberland and the Marie Lapierre shooting? What do they have to do with...."

"Start there. Everything else follows. The chairman has his fingers in many pies."

"I don't understand; What chairman? Her committee? Why would anyone care about an environmental committee to the point..."

"That was a great front for La Pierre, but not much more," the source said. "She was into much deeper issues. You're aware of what happened in Dar Es Salaam last year?"

"Of course; the UN did some heavy handling of a group of eco-terrorists, and in turn they killed their hostages. But I don't see...

"Be quiet, I don't have long," he said. "Compare that with other events over the last two years. Look for similarities. It's all there. Then look up a firm called AK Industrial SARL, based in Paris and Montpellier. You've heard of Ahmed Khalidi?"

"Sure, oil magnate from the Middle East."

"He is the chairman, and is based in Jordan. He has a group of insiders, political types who he meets with far more often than is healthy; its official name is the Association Commercial Franco-Arabe, or ACF. We've obtained information from a deep source, and that's all you get on that. But the names of his board members are worth looking into. Boris Miskin, former Russian cultural attaché to America. He has some sort of personal feud going on with the Khalidi right now, but we're not sure why; Fung So Dook, a state secretary for Jiangdong province in China; Yoshi Funomora, a businessman from Japan; and Hans-Karl Wilhelm, the German representative, a physician and former national politician. La Pierre was also a member and, we suspect, Sir Anthony as well."

"We? As in the..."

"The U.S. intelligence community. We've been investigating the ACF for several years, trying to tie it to operations that ultimately supported Islamist terrorist cells, among others. We believe Khalidi's true goal is destabilization and reaping the economic consequences of being able to predict it will happen in each locale, but the group also has heavy political connections, policy connections; they've used them for purposes both good and bad, sharing those connections and working as a united front."

It was a lot of information, a ton of innuendo. "What am I supposed to be looking for?" Malone asked. "I'm assuming these people have had lengthy careers already or they wouldn't have been involved with a guy like him in the first place. Why would someone shoot two of his board members?"

2.   156

"Concentrate on Khalidi," he said. "Most people in the public have never heard of him or from him, despite being the chairman of a major conglomerate. But he has some interesting history of his own."

"Interesting as in 'ha ha', or interesting as in 'blam, blam'."

"Definitely the latter," he said. "If it hadn't been for our need to pipe oil through and from the region, he might have been dealt with a long time ago. Khalidi has some interesting beliefs and even more interesting friends."

Malone wondered about the group he'd named. "Where did we get this information? Do you have someone close to…"

He cut her off again. "We did, yes. But that person is dead."

"Anyone I know? A certain French diplomat maybe?"

"Look, that's all you get for now. If you need more or get stuck on something, leave a paper out, same spot, same method."

"Can I just…"

"No, I have to go." He turned quickly and strode between the cars, disappearing into a darker area of the garage. Malone didn't try to follow; she knew who he was, knew his intel would be good. And she knew she had some work ahead of her.

JAN. 29, 2016

Boris Miskin was late for dinner, and Ivana was preparing potatoes stuffed with bacon and cheese, which meant he did not want to be late.

The driver had gotten stuck in traffic on the Beltway after Miskin's meeting with a trade delegation, but had done so on the one night when Miskin didn't want an excuse to be somewhere other than with his wife. When he climbed out of the car in front of their brownstone Georgetown home just off Thirty Fifth Street– his permanent residence when not working in Europe – the sidewalk was dusted with snow and it was already near dark.

3.

Still, better late than never, Miskin thought – before realizing how grim an idea it was in light of recent events. He'd come home for Christmas because, despite his love for his own country, he'd become accustomed to the style of living in America. On top of that he was convinced that a disgruntled individual was behind both shootings, someone aware of his collusion with the ACF. It seemed unlikely that person would follow him across the Atlantic Ocean; Miskin did not exactly advertise his U.S. residence, and a person would have had to go back several years in library newspapers to find a reference from when he was cultural attaché, which in turn had merely been a KGB cover.

He rang the doorbell and the maid, Bernice, answered the door. "Welcome home sir," she said. "May I take your bag upstairs?"

After she'd left to tend to the laundry, he took off his topcoat and hung it in the closet. Ivana had not come to the door to greet him, which was no surprise. It had been many years since his wife had been excited by the prospect of his return. He walked down the carpeted hallway to the living room entrance. She was propped up on the couch watching television, her suicide blonde hair almost in a beehive, it was stacked so high, the dry threads of it barely illuminated by the TV screen. "You keep dinner hot?" he asked.

"In the oven," she said, without turning away from her show.

He strode through the doorway at the far end of the room, which connected it to the kitchen. He kept his head down as he walked over to the stainless steel refrigerator to retrieve his chilled, pre-mixed bottle of vodka and Pepsi, then reached up to the white cupboards to get a glass.

"You should be careful, Boris Mikhailovich," a man's voice said in flawless Russian. "Too much drink has been many a man's downfall."

He turned quickly. The man sitting at the kitchen table was a stranger, dressed in black. "You know me, my friend, but I don't know you," Miskin said calmly. He slowly reached for the cell phone in his pocket.

Brennan shook his head. "Put that away, Boris. We need to talk civilly, and that is difficult to do if I'm being arrested for trespassing. Beyond that, I'm sure you're aware that the local response times are hardly those of the police in Moscow."

He withdrew his hand from his pocket. "Again, I don't know with whom I'm speaking. Please explain."

"I'm just a bird who decided your window was a good place upon which to alight," Brennan said. "Let's leave it at that. But you have a piece of information I need."

"I see. So this is… what, a kidnapping?"

"No, just a couple of quick questions."

"And if I choose to not answer these questions?"

"Well… then things do get a bit more difficult. But let's cross that bridge when we come to it."

"Okay, guy in my kitchen, tell me more. I see if I can help."

"Tell me what the connection is between Ahmed Khalidi's ACF and a missing nuclear bomb from South Africa."

If Miskin was a poker player, he was a damn good one, Brennan thought. "I don't know anything about this," the big Russian said, seemingly oblivious.

"What about the name 'Borz Abubakar'?"

Miskin looked deep in thought. "It seems familiar. Is this someone I should know?"

"Chechen dissident…"

"Oh sure! Now I get you."

"You knew him."

"I knew of him. He is the one who…"

"…blew up a bus with two dozen people aboard in Peru, back in oh-nine. Allegedly."

"Allegedly?"

"I've got a source that suggests the device may have been elsewhere at the time."

"Yeah? You want to share this source with Boris?"

"Why would it matter if it has nothing to do with Khalidi's group?"

He shrugged. "Assuming we accept your suggestion that Mr. Khalidi fronts such a group, a loose nuke is something we all should worry about. Not that it sounds likely."

"What about Khalidi? I understand you've worked together but do not think much of each other."

"This is no secret," Boris said. "But if you think he or anyone else is connected to this other matter, it is a bit foolish. We are a business networking group, nothing more. We review political policy as a hobby, recommend changes to our various contacts in government."

"Really? That's all?"

"Of course, my intrusive friend."

"Because I'd heard you were working outside that mandate a little."

Miskin's head dipped for a moment and he took on a wry smile. "This is very imaginative, yes? What did you hear?"

"Just that your group may be a little more active that is advertised. I don't know yet; but I'll be looking."

"I tell you, there is nothing that…"

Brennan cut him off. "Keep in mind, Boris Mikhailovich, that whoever shot your colleagues may yet have you in his sights. Perhaps you need outside friends more than you realize."

3.

Boris turned back to the refrigerator and put the bottle of Pepsi and vodka away. "I don't know what you think you will find, but…"

But when he turned around, the back door was open once more and the man had gone.

By the time Miskin poked his head outside to see where the intruder had vanished to, Brennan was already over the back fence and around the block. His rental was parked half a street away from the house. As he approached it, he heard voices behind him. He hugged the wall of the adjacent building to stay out of sight, then peered back around the corner, across the street to the Russian's residence.

There was a woman at the front door; she was familiar.

The bar, when he'd met Walter months earlier. She was the woman who'd walked in and made everyone nervous.

It couldn't be coincidence. He pulled out his phone and dialed Lang's number. Maybe he'd talked to her for long enough to get an ID, Brennan thought.

18/

It was late, after ten o'clock. Malone got home tired and frustrated. The tipster's information was pure dynamite, story-wise. But confirming any of it was going to be nightmarish.

She closed her townhouse door and put her keys in the top drawer of the small telephone table by the entrance. She switched off the light on the table, always left on during the day to give the place the look of someone being home, in case anyone peeked through the front window.

Then she hung up her coat in the closet behind the door before taking the stairs to the kitchen. She put her purse on the nearby kitchen table and moved to the small sideboard she used as a stand-in for a bar, grabbing a bottle of rum and heading towards the fridge for mix.

"Don't turn around," a voice said. She gasped inwardly and dropped the bottle... and it was caught, by a man's hand, from right behind her. "Don't worry, I'm not going to hurt you," said the voice. The man put the bottle down on the table, behind them.

"I have no money," she said. Years of being a reporter had steadied her nerves, and she found herself unshaken and self-controlled, even though she was frightened. "Take my purse and please leave me alone." He was probably a junkie looking for a quick fix, she reasoned. That was usually the reason for a break-in.

"I don't want your money and I'm not going to hurt you," the voice reiterated. It was strong, authoritative. It was strangely calm, as if he really meant what he was saying, and she began to turn around. But he stopped her by placing a hand on her shoulder. "Don't turn around. It's better for you if you don't know who I am." There seemed an implied threat in the comment, and she stopped the motion.

"What do you want?" she said. "How did you ..."

"You left the latch on your rear living room window undone. My apologies, but we can't have this conversation anywhere public."

Was he a source? "What do you mean?"

"Your name is Alexandra Malone, you're a writer for *News Now Magazine*, and you're working on a story about the sniper shootings. Correct?"

"Correct."

3.

"Earlier this evening, you attempted to interview Boris Miskin at his home in Georgetown. Why?"

"Like you said, I'm working on a story." If he was going to try the cloak-and-dagger routine, she was going to be obtuse as well.

"About the ACF?"

"Possibly. Why do you want to know?" There was no way Alex was giving this guy anything without some quid pro quo.

"I'm also working on something," the man said. "I think we might be looking for some of the same answers. But I'd have an easier time knowing if that's the case if you filled me in on what you know."

"That's not going to happen," she said. "I don't reveal my source information before I publish, and I don't talk to strange guys who break into my apartment."

"What you're investigating, these people... they won't put up with someone nosing around. You need to know that they're deadly serious."

"Did they send you to threaten me?" Alex said. "Because I don't scare easily."

Brennan liked her. Most people would have been terrified if they'd found him lurking in their apartment, but she was cool as a cucumber. "Nobody sent me. I just want to know what you asked Miskin, and why."

"But you won't give me anything back in return."

"I have nothing to offer," the voice said.

"We could start with who you are and go from there," she suggested. "You trust me with a face-to-face, I'll tell you what I asked Boris Miskin." Whoever he was, Alex figured, he was intimately involved. That meant he had information she needed.

Brennan thought about it. The wise thing to do would have been to listen to David, to go back to Europe and bunker in until needed. But he'd already blown that idea off. Ballantine and Han's new information had been too incendiary. "Fine," he said.

She turned around and her eyes narrowed immediately. "I know you from somewhere," she said. "We've met before. Years of writing down exact spellings have rendered me pretty damn unable to remember names, but I don't forget a face."

"I've fulfilled my portion of the deal," he said. "Tell me what you asked Miskin."

Who is he? "I have an intelligence source that claims Khalidi's ACF, is rogue; it's funding paramilitary types to clean up problems that get in the way of its commercial ambitions. He also said the chairman, Ahmed Khalidi, is mixed up in something bigger, and that he and Miskin don't like each other. I was trying, without any luck, to get Miskin to complain about the investigation."

2.

"Let me guess: he laughed off the whole thing."

"Yes. How did you know?"

"I was in the kitchen when you dropped by his house. You didn't stay long enough to get into anything with depth."

"And what did Mr. Miskin tell you… sorry, what did you say your name was?"

"I didn't," Brennan added. "He gave me the brushoff as well. But I pointed out to him that whoever came for the other committee members could go after him, too. So maybe he'll think on it, at least."

"Then what is this all about? Why the shootings, what does Khalidi have to do with it and why the level of American involvement? It's like every source I have in D.C. expects us to solve this for the EU. Why are we even over there?"

"Who said we were over there?" Brennan wasn't going to share Fawkes with a reporter, especially one fishing for confirmations on a potential ongoing crisis. "As for the rest, I don't know yet, but I suggest we stay in touch."

Whoever he is, she thought, *he's got nerve.* "Why would I trust you? You won't even tell me who you are."

"Because I broke into your apartment and didn't hurt you. If I wanted harm to come to you, it already would have." His face was deadpan; he was completely serious, and for just a moment, Malone felt a jolt of nerves. "And… because I work in intelligence." He mentioned the last factor with obvious reluctance. "And that's all you need to…"

"Walter Lang," she said, pointing at him. "That's where I know you from: you were talking to Walter Lang in a bar more than a year ago."

"And if you know Walter…"

"I know he's a good man. I know he's been honest with me at least twice since then. He hasn't given me confidential or classified information, however. And he said you were an architect."

"He's a good friend."

He could see the gears turning in her head. "You're working undercover, which means you probably work for the agency and with Walter. The last time I saw you it was the last day of the Colombia hearings. He said something about you; what was it? He said… he said you were in town for a conference."

Brennan quickly wondered what he'd gotten himself into.

She wasn't done. "A lot of people wanted to know who went into Colombia and extracted him, and there you were, obviously a covert operative of some sort, talking to him in a bar."

"Some people already know the truth about that story," he said, watching her eyes widen at the prospect of a scoop. "And they're on a need-to-know basis."

3.   163

"So what do I call you? How do I know if it's you calling me?"

"Your magazine. When I call, I'll start with the first line of the last article in the latest edition…"

"Like a code?"

"…and you respond with the last line from the same article."

"You can trust me with your identity," she said.

"I know you think that," he said, "and I know you mean it. But I also know it's not true. Whatever we're mixed up in… you have to realize, Ms. Malone, these people play awful rough. You understand that, right? Nothing inside your head is safe."

"Sure, but…"

"No buts. This is how we work it, or we don't talk at all."

"Okay," she said. "So what now?"

He couldn't gamble telling her about the nuke. If she wrote something prematurely, the ensuing panic could be catastrophic, or spook someone into arming the device. He didn't even know yet why it was in play, or if it was just a myth. "What did your source tell you about Ahmed Khalidi?"

"Very little. He just said I should check out his involvement in some trouble in Africa a few years back. I've been working on another source to get more detail."

"Africa?" He tried to keep his voice level, so that he didn't sound too enthusiastic, but she picked up on it anyway.

"Yes… why? Have you heard something that would link it back…"

"No," he lied. "But see what you can find out about it and maybe we can stitch it into the narrative as things make more sense."

She headed towards the kitchen. "Would you like something to drink, Mr…"

"I told you, my name is unimportant," he said.

"I know, but if it give me an indication of why you need …"

She'd turned back as she tried to talk him into it; but once again, Brennan had vanished.

19

Miskin acted quickly once the reporter had left. He knew there was always the potential that one of his peers might have him under surveillance. If there was a suggestion – even an inkling – that he was speaking with the media, he wouldn't survive the week.

He'd gone back to the refrigerator, taken out the Pepsi-vodka mixed and poured himself another drink. Then he headed upstairs to his study. He started his computer and opened the video conference connection. It took a few moments before his connection was accepted by each of the members.

"Russia," the chairman said. "As you are doubtless aware, it is early in the morning here...."

"I'm sorry, really, but this could not wait." Miskin and Khalidi disliked each other. But the Russian knew they'd present a united front if the ACF's work were at stake. "I had a pair of visitors today."

He told the members about Brennan and the reporter. "The unnamed man was definitely a pro, perhaps American intelligence. It would be worth checking with our own sources..."

"Done," said Khalidi. "And the reporter?"

"An Alexandra Malone. She writes for the weekly magazine *News Now*, as well as for its website. She has a reputation for tenacity that few share and has been a thorn in the side of numerous politicians in her own country over the last decade."

The Chinese delegate, Fung, broke in. "Russia, why did you not just eliminate the problem?"

"I live here," Miskin hissed. "I'm not in the habit of getting my hands dirty..."

"Evidently not," China said. "But this is untenable. We cannot track down whether Tillo Bustamante was the source of the sniper threat definitively if we must worry about scrutiny from the press."

"Agreed," said the Japanese delegate, Funomora. "Can we do this cleanly? Is there something we can float in front of the reporter that she'd prefer, a distraction?"

"I do not think so," Miskin said. "She is very persistent. She tried to get me at the Embassy, and when that didn't work she called contacts until someone was willing to give up the neighborhood in which I live. Then she literally called every neighbor for a five block radius until someone gave up my address. That's tenacious."

"This should fall to Japan," the Chinese delegate said. "The mere fact that such problems exist suggests he's not equal to his role as our head of security."

3.

Funomora stood up for himself. "Circumstances in Brussels were beyond my control. Our man got too close and initiated combat as a means of extracting himself. But he is anxious to make up for his failure. I have him here with me right now. He can eliminate the reporter. Isn't that right, Mr. Yamaguchi?"

He moved the monitor screen so that the camera was pointed at the man standing next to him. He was young, dressed in dark clothing, with sunglasses on. He nodded resolutely, a bandage still covering his missing left earlobe.

20

FEB. 12, 2016, BONN, GERMANY

Dr. Hans-Karl Wilhelm was accustomed to his life running on a schedule, and little had changed in the months since his colleagues had been shot. He was still at the mercy of the clock, so full was his day with meetings, consultations and even the odd aging patient, left over from when he still regularly practiced medicine. He continually found himself without enough hours to pursue all of his ambitions and passions.

At sixty-three, he knew he should have been slowing down. In fact, his own doctor had just told him that he risked hypertension, which in turn could lead to a heart condition, if he did not start taking his age into account.

And yet... he could not. Even at eight o'clock at night, when he should have been relaxing from the day, his wife Helga would often find him in the garage, working on one of his old cars. On this particular night, she had not even bothered to try and dissuade him, seeing the look of determination in his eye. And so he was slung underneath the 1962 Melkus, an East German sports car with an appearance somewhere between a seventies Lamborghini and a Corvette; it was a model that few in the west had ever seen.

He was concentrating on its struts; the car's wheels were removed and off to one side of the room and the vehicle's frame had been lifted with a pneumatic hoist. He lay on a mechanic's creeper, the wheels old and stiff, which he preferred for the sense of stability.

Wilhelm was trying to take his mind off of the ACF. The German delegate had felt as if he were in over his head for some time now, so grateful initially to be included in the elite group that he'd ignored his conscience, and questions about their role, on many occasions. He had justified its approach to himself many times; at his age, he had seen so many morally repugnant individuals get away with so much, it was not hard to justify working outside existing domestic laws to deal with them. And it was no longer seen as so bad to profit from the outcome, either. He had grown up in Germany after the war, feeling the pain of a nation led astray. He had grown up with his father, a staunch opponent of the Nazis who had been forced to flee his homeland, and his father had taught him the lesson of history: that if one man had acted on impulse and shot Adolf Hitler dead where he stood, early in his reign of tyranny, millions of lives might have been saved.

He recognized the irony, of course, of a non-sanctioned political body acting without the restraint of law; but he judged himself intelligent enough to help make those choices; to risk damage to the perception that political representation itself meant democracy, in exchange for the assurance that real action would be taken against those threatening freedom – and that they would be rewarded for their intervention.

Life, Dr. Wilhelm told himself, was ultimately always about leaders and followers. He had seen the mistakes a nation could make in abrogating their responsibility to occasionally take the lead, and by following blindly instead. He insisted on leading, but reassured himself nightly that it was benevolent leadership.

He turned the wrench against the nut steering bracket, trying to loosen the strut. The thing wouldn't give; he wondered if the strut and shock assembly had been changed since the car was last on the road, some twenty-five years earlier.

He was reaching up when the car dropped.

It was sudden, instant, the full weight of the vehicle pulled towards him by gravity as the pneumatic lift collapsed. Wilhelm didn't even have time to throw his arms out in front of him …

It stopped short. Somehow, the collapsing pneumatic lift had halted its descent less than an inch above him, a mere split second from crushing him like an egg. He was breathing fast and hard, terrified momentarily at what had almost happened. He tried to push off the floor with his heels, but his legs were out straight and he had no leverage.

"Frightening, isn't it, to come so close to death?"

The voice was male. The German was good, but tinged with an accent.

"Who is that?" Wilhelm asked. "Help me, please. I believe I am stuck. I do not have space to move." He managed to turn his head slightly to one side and could just make out a pair of shoes, brown, casual dress.

"Dr. Wilhelm, you have a choice to make: you may assist me in my inquiries and answer a question or two for me; or, if that is contrary to your wishes, I can remove the iron bar that is presently preventing this pneumatic spring jack from collapsing completely and that car from crushing the life out of you."

"What… what do you want?" Wilhelm asked in English.

"You came home for Christmas from Paris. What were you doing there?"

"Meetings, just … meetings. Government. Please, my friend, I am … quite frightened."

"What kind of meetings? Be specific. I'm not sure how long that bar will hold the weight."

"A group to which I belong, political advocacy. It is nothing, I assure you, just a loose association. We met."

"I know about the group. Why else would I be here, Herr Doktor? The only reason you are not dead yet is that I see something in you that I do not in your colleagues, signs of humanity."

"We... do important work." Wilhelm's mind was racing as he tried to figure out who the man could be and how much he knew.

"You sit in judgment without view to broader consequence," the man said. "I do not want to hear rationales, Herr Doktor. I merely want whatever information you have on the whereabouts over the next three months of your fellow committee members; whether they will be in Montpellier, or Paris, or Brussels – or perhaps visiting their home nations."

"I am not sure..." the doctor began to say. He heard a screeching of metal-on-metal as the bar began to slide out of its spot. "No! Wait... I ... I know some details. Plans are fluid and we are always changing...

"Just give me times, dates, places. Anything you have."

The doctor began listing off meetings he knew his fellow committee members would attend, where they would be held and, as well as he could remember, rough date ranges. "There is more, in my phone, in my pocket..."

The man crouched and reached down. Wilhelm tried to see his face, but it was cast in the shadow of the car. A hand reached roughly into his pocket to grab the phone, and Wilhelm grabbed it by the wrist, his frail, elderly hand unable to restrain the man, the grasp merely an attempt at a precious moment of human contact. "Please..."

"Thank you," the voice said as the man rose. "I realize that cannot have been easy for you."

Wilhelm had a cold, sinking feeling as he mentally connected the dots. "You ... you are the one who killed Madame La Pierre and Lord Cumberland, yes?"

"Yes."

"And you have no problem admitting this to me?"

"No," the asset said. "I don't."

He pulled the bar out quickly and the car dropped loudly to the cement floor, Wilhelm trapped between the mechanic's creeper and the undercarriage, the weight crushing his chest instantly, killing the aging doctor.

The asset had meant what he said: Wilhelm did seem like the only ACF board member with a soul. But it was compromised and valueless, the asset knew, and his death was no great loss.

FEB. 13, 2016, GERMANTOWN, PENNSYLVANIA

Sen. John Younger sat on the uncomfortable antique sofa and watched his grandchildren as they played with their new toys; he'd spent all morning with them at the store, picking out what they wanted. Little Andy in his PJs, his blonde-brown hair in a bowl cut, his attention totally focused on the giant red-plastic fire truck; his younger brother Paul just a toddler still, partly fascinated with the stuffed giraffe, partly absorbing the newness of the world around him.

His cell phone rang. He checked it, intent on letting it go to voice mail before he realized who was calling.

"Go ahead," he said. He didn't use Mark Fitzpatrick's name; he'd never trusted phone lines and he knew what his political opponents were capable of. If they knew he had such a high-ranking NSA source, he'd lose his distinct advantage very quickly. Inside the Beltway, knowledge was power.

"We have an update, Senator. The Bustamante incident was precipitated by our asset, according to my agency source. His guards were aiming at someone else."

"Unfortunate." Younger was thinking long-term; eventually, his administration might be the one having to clean up after the fact.

"Have you seen the papers today?" Fitzpatrick asked.

"Not yet."

"Then that's my other piece of news: the German board member of the ACF is dead."

"How are his people reacting?"

"Our German friends tell us they know there was definitely someone else present."

That would make people nervous, Younger thought. "When we meet with the NSC next week, it would be wise to stress that Wilhelm's death was probably a legitimate accident, unrelated to the others; let POTUS feel a little more comfortable that we're going to make our European partners look great. As long as he feels Bustamante was probably responsible and that the threat is under wraps as a result, the less involved he'll be."

"Will you be on the road next week?"

"Yes. I've got this break with the family and a local stump, and then we'll be doing the southern circuit on the bus."

"You'll be giving the happy voters a thrill over the holidays, letting them meet the next President of the United States," Fitzpatrick said.

Younger smiled at that. Fitzpatrick was proving an essential asset.

FEB. 26, 2016, WASHINGTON, D.C.

"This is blackmail. You realize that, don't you?"

The man speaking was upset, the tension accentuated to her ears by his African-accented English, even though she couldn't read his eyes behind the aviator shades. He seemed more frustrated than angry or violent; but he probably felt powerless and, as is the case for most people, it made him feel defensive.

Alex Malone felt for him, a little. The *News Now* reporter had met him in the near-empty parking lot of a restaurant in White Oak, just north of D.C., at just after seven in the morning, because he was deathly paranoid of being seen with her anywhere close to the Beltway. So they sat in his car, a dark blue sedan, parked facing the road on the dark dirt-and-gravel, maybe forty yards from the single-story white-plaster diner. They were alone in the lot aside from a pair of older model sub-compacts parked to one side of the building, in the staff slots, and Malone's car, a ten-year-old red Mazda Miata, which was in a space right by the entrance.

They sat in his car, her dressed in business clothes, fit and attractive, and him in a sweatshirt and jeans, trying to look like something other than a cultural attaché for Africa's largest nation.

But she knew what he was really like, so her sympathy only extended so far. She didn't feel guilty for trying to use him, and she certainly didn't feel guilty for using leverage to do it. In his time, Freedom Mbilo had been a politician, a war lord and a gangster; his grooming of his reputation through diplomacy had been bought and paid for, like everything important in his life, with someone else's.

"Mr. Mbilo, let's cut the shit, okay? You've fed me stories in the past because they were politically advantageous to you. All you would be doing by passing this information to me is returning the favor. I scratch your back, you scratch mine."

He lit a cigarette and Malone fought the urge to crack one of the tinted windows. He blew out a plume of smoke then said, "And yet this arrangement is not so fair that you felt I would go along with it freely."

3.

"It was a matter of necessity and I apologize. What you do in your spare time is your business," she said. "And I'm sure that as long as your wife doesn't hear about it, she won't mind either."

"Her father is a very influential man in my country."

"I know."

"He would have me killed if he discovered I had ... dalliances with others."

"Perhaps the best thing, then, is to ensure people who know about your personal habits have no reason to tell him. Or your wife, for that matter."

Malone's meeting with the mysterious agency operative had convinced her there was much more to the story of the EU sniper than had been made public. More lives were at stake, from the sniper at the least. So she'd gone to the charity event, had too much to drink with Mbilo's assistant, convinced him to tell her about his boss's mistresses as he flirted with her. Now she was twisting the knife, less than six hours after heading home in a cab, the tension underwritten by her hangover.

"And if I help you now, you will not attempt this next week on another issue?"

"No."

Mbilo sounded skeptical. "How may I believe that?"

She was tempted to remind him that he was the guy with the blood-thirsty reputation. But she let it go. "I don't care if you do or not, frankly. I have a job to do."

He reached over his shoulder to the backseat, pulling a brown envelope out of a small blue-and-silver sports bag. "This is the report of my intelligence service into activities in West Africa. You realize that this incident happened several years ago, yes?"

"I do," she said, completely unaware of any such thing.

"Then take it. It is the best I can offer. And get out of my car. I do not expect to hear from you again, Ms. Malone."

"Agreed."

"Let us best hope so. I know now what you are capable of," he said, his voice calm and focused. "I do not think you would like to find out what I am capable of."

Malone opened the door and climbed out, slamming it behind her. The man backed the car up quickly and pulled out of the lot, the tires kicking up gravel with dusty enthusiasm, leaving her behind.

She crossed the empty lot to the diner, the whoosh of traffic on the adjacent freeway already busy in the early morning. The glass door jingled as she pushed it open. Her new friend was waiting at a booth and the sound caught his attention. She took the booth seat across from him. "If we keep meeting under these circumstances, I'm going to need a name to call you by," she said as she slid onto the bench.

2.   172

"Stop fishing for who I am," the man said. "When I can tell you, I will. But anything you know now that you don't need could get you or both of us killed."

"It's contrary to my nature to stop trying," she said.

"Suck it up." he said. "Have you checked the news yet?"

"What? I caught the update on 99.1 but it was all local."

He picked up a folded newspaper lying on the bench next to him and tossed it onto the table in front of her. "Number three, Hans-Karl Wilhelm. He was crushed to death yesterday by a car at his home workshop. German authorities are ruling it accidental, a failure of the pneumatics used to lift it above the ground."

"I take it that's not what really happened," she said.

"It is what really happened; but anyone who believes it was an accident hasn't really been paying attention."

"They'll expect me to file something for the website," she said. "We have to get through this stuff quickly." She opened Mbilo's manila envelope and handed a thatch of papers to him. "Here: you go through this half, I'll do the rest."

The documents were marked classified and were in English. They were accompanied by a series of photographs. Some of them were of soldiers in battle fatigue, others of bodies – men and women, children, some killed recently, others in advanced decay. They were horrifying; flies swarmed the bodies, limbs and parts of torsos had been hacked off, piled flesh growing fetid in the jungle heat. A series of notes identified them as villagers from the Nigerian interior; it said they'd been killed in an insurrection by extremists, intent on controlling valuable oil and natural gas deposits throughout the region.

"My God," Malone said. "There must be dozens dead in these pictures."

The documents with the file included notes from investigators; a militia had swept through the village, killing men, women and children indiscriminately. It was one of several that had roamed the area for months, before government forces eventually put them down.

"They traced the money in accounts held by one of the militia leaders to a company called Novextra Energy," Alex said as she leafed through the pages. "The director of that company in Nigeria four years ago was a Slovenian national by the name of Andraz Kovacic." A picture of Kovacic was attached to the paperwork, a man with short hair, angular features. She unclipped it and handed it to Brennan.

"I recognize him," he said. "I don't know from where or why, but that's probably not a good sign."

"Because he works in intelligence?"

"Yeah. Or he's made someone's naughty list. Either way, that makes him the kind of guy you don't want to see coming your way."

3.

"How can you be sure?"

"Because I'm the kind of guy you don't want coming your way."

"Uh huh. What am I supposed to call you, anyway?"

"Over to you. Call me Joe, I guess."

"That's not your real name, is it?"

"Tough to put one by a reporter."

"Uh huh. Don't lay it on too thick, 'Joe'."

They realized they were smiling at each other. Brennan averted his glance, guilty at flirting with someone other than his wife. He went back to the file; they'd had a moment, a connection; and that was all it was going to be. He and Carolyn had troubles, there was no doubting that. But he loved her, and he loved his kids.

He shook it off and scanned each page in quick succession. "Here," he said. "There's a European company based out of the Isle of Man listed as Novextra's parent, a Kalispell Resources. The Isle of Man is notorious for having no corporate tax, making it an offshore haven for various financial instruments."

"Yeah, I saw a piece on *60 Minutes* about it a few years ago. What does that mean?" Alex said. She kept leafing through the pages. There were more investigative notes, some photocopied emails, and a copy of a business card. "Raymond Slocombe, Director of Finance, Kalispell Properties. A parent company?"

Brennan nodded. "A parent company with an address in Baltimore. Look, you should get home. I need to check this out."

Malone's eyebrows shot up faster than the price of water in a heatwave. "You're kidding, right? I'm not going anywhere except wherever you're going. I still have nothing tying Ahmed Khalidi or any of the other ACF board members to Kalispell."

"I can't be responsible for your safety. And I have no idea what we're walking into. Logistically…"

"Logistically, you can kiss my ever-widening ass if you think I'm giving up a second of this story. If I was a guy, would you presume to make a safety decision for me?"

"If you were a civilian, yes. It's not because you're a woman, it's because you're a member of the general public, unskilled in self-defense and survival and, I hate to tell you, likely to just slow me down."

"Tough. I found a source who gave us a hard tie, potentially, to the ACF and atrocities; it doesn't explain why someone's killing off its board members. But it's a hell of a story, and you know it."

Brennan gathered up the paperwork. "Then we should get going. Just remember, if things get violent, don't put me in a position where I have to choose between protecting civilians and saving you; because you're there by choice. So you're going to lose that contest every time."

2.

Malone nodded in short, rapid takes, surprised by the gravitas in his voice. She had no doubt he was serious.

They left her car at the townhouse, parked in the rear lot, and took Brennan's rented Lincoln for the ride to Baltimore. He was silent for most of the trip, keeping things impersonal, his mouth a grim line and his eyes on the road.

Malone studied him. He had an almost muscular tension, a sense that he might uncoil at any moment, as if nothing going through his mind could be allowed to be off mission or off topic. Did he even realize how surreal their lives were just then? Or was it just another day at the office for him? There had to be more to his mission than just the snipers, she thought. He'd never explained sufficiently why America would be so involved in a case that didn't involve its diplomats or jurisdiction.

How far out on a limb would he go for her? She didn't doubt for a second that her intelligence source would abandon her if he needed to. Would 'Joe' do the same? Malone wasn't inclined to consider the risks she took, or how they might affect her life and career. But leaning so heavily on others wasn't her usual M.O; she knew she should have felt a greater sense of unease, of self-preservation. Maybe spending so much time with the agent was providing a false sense of security, she thought.

Kalispell's head office was in a mid-size office tower along West Lombard Street. Through the revolving doors, a polite young woman with dark blond hair and wearing a grey suit sat behind an information desk. To one side, a security guard sat along the wall in a wooden chair, looking bored, with his arms crossed. The young woman had a wireless headset attached to her left ear.

"Kalispell Properties, one moment please," she said. "Kalispell Properties, one moment please. Kalispell properties... yes, that would be the billing department; one moment, I'll connect you. Kalispell... yes sir, we're based in the United States. Yes sir. Kalis... oh... he hung up." She tapped the earpiece. "Kalispell Properties may I help you?"

Brennan and Malone looked at her blankly. The woman's eyes flitted between the two of them. "Sir? Madam? Can I help you?"

"Sorry," Brennan said. "We're looking for Raymond Slocombe. I understand he's the director of finance?"

The woman looked puzzled. "I don't think we have anyone by that name, sir. Let me check the directory...no, no Raymond Slocombe. One moment..." She answered another three calls before getting back to them. "If you'd like I can make a quick call to human resources...?"

Brennan smiled as warmly as he could. "Thank you; that would be very helpful."

3.   175

She made the call while they surveyed the lobby. The place was underwhelming, a polished concrete floor and a series of semi-modern benches, surrounded by fake ferns. "Well," Malone whispered, "if nothing else, we know these people are guilty of lousy taste."

The receptionist cleared her throat to signal to them. "Yes... I'm sorry but this is kind of awkward. It appears Mr. Slocombe passed away a few years ago. However, if this is a financial matter, I can direct you to his successor, Mr. David Grant..."

"That would be fine," Malone said.

"No! No... that's unnecessary," Brennan interjected. "We'll come back another time. Thank you."

He directed Malone away from the desk and towards the door. "Come on," he muttered, "I'll explain outside."

On the street, Brennan looked around for somewhere convenient to keep an eye on the building and talk to Alex at the same time. He nodded across the street, halfway down the block. "That coffee shop – come on, I'll buy you one and explain."

Once they were seated at the small, round table in front of the glass windows, he pointed across the road. "What do you see?"

She looked over her shoulder, then at him. "Come on, Joe, spare me the dramatics, okay? It's still early, and I'm still hung over."

"What I see," Brennan said, "is a big building. Big enough that there might be, say, two hundred people working in it. Can you tell me how many of them are armed?"

She sighed, annoyed. "No, I can't tell you how many of them are armed."

"But you figure it's wise to just walk into the place, maybe be led up to somewhere less public than the lobby? At a company that might just have sponsored mass executions?"

"So what were you going to do if Slocombe hadn't kicked the bucket?"

"Have him meet us in the lobby, something like that."

"Fine, Mr. Security, so what are we supposed to do now?"

"Give me your phone," Brennan said.

She handed him the phone. "Don't look in my directory," she said. "I have private numbers in there."

"I just need your browser." He searched for a minute, then handed her back the phone. "That's a picture of David Grant. They may be involved in crooked business over in Africa, but they still have to maintain their image here. Corporate website."

"Okay, so we know what he looks like. So?"

"So we know that at some point, the director of finance for the home office has been responsible for sending money to Africa to fund insurgencies. Do you think they'd replace the late Mr. Slocombe with a straight shooter? I'm guessing no. Whoever took that role on has to be crooked. This is a standard rented office mini-tower with above-ground employee parking in a rear lot. At some point, Mr. Grant has to go home. Then we grab him."

"And?"

"And I convince him to talk to us."

"Convince? Is that a euphemism for some sinister agency thing?"

"Not if he talks to us, it's not. But it wouldn't hurt for him to think so, so no good cop, bad cop, okay? Just let me be bad cop for a few minutes all by my lonesome. Stay here, enjoy your latte. I'll be back with Mr. Grant in a few minutes."

"Do I have a choice?"

"No." He got up and left her with both coffees, disappearing out the front door and back down the street at pace. A minute later, Brennan was back in front of the Kalispell building. Instead of taking the broad stairs up to the front door, he followed the sidewalk another fifty yards to the parking lot side entrance, to the building's left. It led, in turn, behind the building to the large, open lot, divided into dozens of white-lined vehicle bays.

The lot was fenced, but behind the back fence was a small hill covered in pines, firs with old, dry needles. Brennan scanned the empty lot, then climbed the fence quickly and dropped over. It was a perfect vantage point, out of immediate eyesight, unlikely to draw attention.

He thought about the reporter, sitting just a block away. How would she react if she saw him working on Grant? If she actually saw how far he was willing to go to get the job done? Brennan didn't like exposing her to field work at all, but it was a necessary wrong; her source was too important for her to be on the streets without a safety net. She was probably safer with him, he reasoned, than in D.C. on her own.

Her business also meant that, best intentions notwithstanding, he couldn't trust her with all of the details yet, not until he was sure she'd keep things under wraps until any danger to the public was averted.

3.

Forty-two minutes later, the businessman walked out of the back doors of the building and headed towards his black Audi. Brennan moved quickly, scaling and hopping the fence in two motions. His pace was rapid as he intercepted Grant, just as he reached out a tan-suited arm to unlock the driver's door. Brennan flashed the pistol and said quietly, "In the car, Mr. Grant. We need a quick word, and I'll let you go back to your doubtless idyllic life." Brennan used the pistol to direct him inside. "Open the passenger door lock before you get in, or I might get nervous," Brennan added.

Inside the car, Grant kept his hands on his lap, looking frightened. "Who are you?" he said. "Look, I don't have any money on me. You can take my car…"

"Start the car, Mr. Grant."

He had a dazed look but he followed the instruction. "Where are you taking me?" Grant asked.

"That depends. You tell me what I need to know, we don't have to go anywhere. You cause me problems, I'll take you to a world of pain. Are we clear?

Grant looked sideways slowly at the gun. "We're clear. But you should know…"

"Yeah?"

"Some of the people I work for are likely to take substantial offense to intrusions into their business."

"Is that a threat, Mr. Grant?"

"No, sir…" he said haltingly. "Frankly, I'm as scared of them as you should be."

"Tell me about that, Mr. Grant. Tell me why they scare you. First of all, who are 'they'? Who owns Kalispell? I checked the EDGAR database and it's not a public company."

"The sole owner is an oil and gas conglomerate, PetroGlobal."

"Based where?"

"France. Look, I'm just a title. I move money. I don't ask questions."

"Who owns PetroGlobal?"

The man sighed deeply, nervously. "AK Industrial SARL. In turn it's controlled by the family of Ahmed Khalidi, a Jordanian national who lives in the United Arab Emirates…"

"I'm familiar with the name. Look at a picture for me." He produced the headshot from the Nigerian file of Andraz Kovacic. "You know this guy?"

Grant's eyebrows rose slightly, and his lips parted minutely. "No, I don't think so."

2.   178

"You're lying, Mr. Grant." Brennan prodded him with the gun. "From this sort of range, you don't want to know the damage a .40 caliber slug will do to someone's stomach."

"Okay! Okay, for chrissake! He's a fixer of some sort that Kalispell had on the payroll in Africa. But he left the company in 2009."

"Left the company?"

"He disappeared. Off the radar, completely. I was told to cut off transfers to him."

"How much had they sent him?"

"I couldn't say exactly; it was for the whole four years that I'd been here by that point..."

"Give me a ballpark."

"During that entire period? About six-point-two million."

Details were sliding into place, Brennan thought. Khalidi had been financing regional insurrections, probably to force local villagers off of profitable oil leases; that explained the money and the village slaughter. He certainly wasn't the first to do it. But his fixer, his money man, had disappeared. "How much of the money that you sent to him was unaccounted for when he vanished?"

Grant's head slumped. "You realize they'll kill me if any of this ever gets out."

"You knew something seriously wrong was going on, but you chose to stay."

"It's complicated," Grant said. "I had debts..."

"Don't we all."

"Who are you?"

"Do you really think it would be healthy for you to know?"

"I suppose not," Grant said. "Are you going to kill me?"

"No. But if you tell anyone about this, they will, just to be sure you aren't around to corroborate anything you told me. You know that, right?"

He nodded but said nothing.

"So how much?"

"About four million," Grant said.

"They must have torn the country apart looking for him."

"They were frantic, at the time. But in the long run, for a company the size of PetroGlobal, four million is lunch money. They got over it."

"Turn off the engine," Brennan said.

"Are you going..."

"I told you, I'm not going to kill you. But if I were you, I'd find another line of work."

Brennan got out of the car and slammed the door. The lot was still empty. He strode quickly towards the sidewalk, blending in among the pedestrians, disappearing with the crowd.

FEB. 27, 2016, WASHINGTON, D.C.

They arrived back in D.C. just after midnight, and Brennan took Malone back to her townhouse. He parked across the street. "Thank you for your help today," he said. "We made a lot of headway. Look, I know I can be a hard case, but…"

She interrupted him. "Something's wrong."

Brennan turned to look at the building. There were no cars parked on the street outside. He checked his wing mirror and saw no one on the sidewalk in either direction. "What?"

"My side table lamp."

"Eh?"

"I always leave my side table lamp on when I leave in the morning, by the front door. The telephone table. I always leave that light on…"

"Maybe the bulb burned out?"

"No, it's one of those long-life, low wattage things. I just changed it recently."

The apartment was black. "When I get out of the car," Brennan said, "I want you to slowly slide over to the driver's seat. Try and keep your shoulders level while doing it. From that distance, if anyone looking out of your apartment window has already made us, they won't realize you've changed positions. As soon as I get to the opposite sidewalk, I want you to start the car again and go. Once you're at least ten blocks away, call Walter," he said, repeating his friend's phone number twice so that she wouldn't forget it. "That's his private cell, away from even agency ears. He'll help you from there while I deal with whatever this is."

"Are you going in there?"

"I have to know what we're dealing with, whether they're trying to get to me through you, establish my possible location through a contact."

"Or?"

"Or whether they're here to kill you, Alex. Quickly… give me your keys."

She did so silently, the weight of the prospect hitting her. "I'm going to get out now," Brennan said. "Are you ready?"

Malone nodded. He opened the door quickly and climbed out. As he crossed the street, she did as he'd suggested and slid over into the driver's seat. As he reached the sidewalk, he heard the engine start; she pulled away too quickly and the tires squealed once.

And then the car was gone, and the night was as silent as it ever gets in the city, just a stiff breeze accompanied by background traffic noise from the busy road a few blocks away; somewhere, a long way off, a police siren sounded.

He'd been as honest with Alex as he thought she could take; there was no reason for anyone involved with the ACF to suspect he'd be at her townhouse. The only person anyone was looking for was the reporter. What he really wanted to know was who ordered the hit.

The fact that all of the townhouse's lights were turned off suggested someone would try to double-tap her inside her own place, maybe move her elsewhere for disposal. Brennan was expecting a single assassin; a team would be too high-profile, too visible in such a public place. The fact that the person had stashed their ride out of sight meant whoever it was had eyes on the street, which meant he was being watched for the entire time it took to cross the road and walk up the short flight of steps to the front door, separated from its neighbor by a short black railing. The light above the door gave off a feint orange glow.

He unlocked it with Malone's keys, but instead of opening the door simply left it untouched. Then he climbed over the outside rail, the angle too acute for anyone inside to see through the window, as he moved to the right of the building and down the parking lot driveway.

The assassin would have seen the lock turn; he'd know there was someone there. But when no one entered the apartment for several minutes, he would worry about an ambush of his own, Brennan thought, and begin figuring a quiet way out, probably via a side window. If Brennan was right, the would-be killer had surveyed the lay of the land and parked behind the building to avoid suspicion from being the only strange vehicle in front. That meant that, just as with David Grant, the next move would be to try and get out of there quickly.

Behind the building, he avoided going anywhere near the backdoor because of a proximity security light; instead, he followed the edge of the parking lot until he was on the other side of the property, before ensconcing himself in a shadowy corner, darkened by the presence of three-foot hedges.

It took less than thirty seconds before he heard the window slide open to Alex's apartment and the faint sound of someone dropping to the ground below. It had snowed while they were in Baltimore, and a light sprinkling covered everything. The figure emerged from the half-light on the narrow gap between the building and the property line, a man dressed all in black, scanning the lot quickly for any threats before walking briskly towards a rented black Dodge. When they were within twenty yards, Brennan strode rapidly towards the black-garbed figure, pistol out. It had worked with David Grant; he just had to avoid...

The crunch of a piece of glass under his heel may as well have been a thunder clap in the still of the evening; the assassin wheeled around in one smooth motion, a silenced pistol in extended hand, the muzzle flash dimmed by the long suppressor attached to the barrel as he squeezed off three shots. But Brennan was moving from the second he stepped on the glass, running and tucking into a forward roll, coming out of it behind the cover of a sedan as the bullets sank into its bodywork.

He peeked around the front bumper of the car and a bullet ricocheted off the metal just in front of him. The assassin had taken cover, perhaps behind his own car. Brennan looked over and across the hood; a tuft of hair emerged from behind the other car and he opened fire, his unsuppressed weapon retorting loudly, the .40 caliber slugs tearing through the body work of the other vehicle but failing to find their target.

"Cops will be here soon," Brennan yelled. "I'm guessing you don't want that."

He was right. The assassin took off at a sprinter's pace; he headed back down the side of the building, following the same driveway out that Brennan had followed in. Brennan gave chase and the assassin turned as he ran, two more shots pinging off the brick wall to the agent's right. Brennan fired on the run, his shots going wide of his target as the figure reached the street and turned left.

Brennan rounded the corner at speed... and was caught dead to rights; the man had stopped running less than twenty yards ahead and instead was waiting for him, gun extended, stable. Brennan flung himself sideways towards the ground, the two quick shots going overhead; he squeezed off two in response, prone, but the target was already moving again, heading down the block. He gave chase; the man cut down an alley to his left. This time, Brennan was more cautious, peering around the corner before pursuing. The assassin had tried the same ploy but the three shots were wasted, clipping the brickwork near Brennan's head and carving off chips and chunks.

And then there was just a clicking sound. Brennan looked around the corner. The alley was a dead end, and the assassin's clip was empty. Brennan walked around the corner, gun extended.

2.

It was the Asian agent from Brussels, he realized. Even in the dark, with his face blacked over, his build and his missing earlobe were dead giveaways. Brennan kept the pistol trained on him. "Who are you and why have you been following me?"

The man shook his head and smiled demurely.

"Why were you trying to kill Alex Malone?"

The man ignored the question. Instead, he said, "When we fought in Brussels, you showed great skill. You could not have defeated me, but you fought admirably."

His accent was Japanese, Brennan thought. "I'll ask again: Why Alex Malone? Who do you work for?"

The assassin began to walk towards him. "We both know I'm not going to tell you anything," the man said. Then he moved into a defensive stance, feet shoulder-width apart and nodded towards Brennan. "Put that toy away and let's settle this correctly."

"Hand to hand?" Brennan said.

"With honor," the assassin said.

"No," Brennan said, quickly raising the pistol and firing. He caught the assassin square in the forehead, a large red-black hole appearing immediately, blood gushing from the head wound. The man collapsed to the ground, convulsing for a few moments before breathing his last.

He could hear sirens getting closer, the police doubtless responding to a "shots fired" complaint. He looked down at the man's vacant gaze and felt a momentary pang of regret.

The man's offer had been tempting; but they weren't playing a game and there was nothing particularly honorable about any of it.

The call from Alex Malone had shocked Walter Lang initially, as there were fewer than five people on the planet with his private number. It had only taken a few moments for her to explain, however, and twenty minutes later, they were meeting at a mall parking lot in Crestwood, north of downtown.

They took Lang's car, leaving Brennan's rental in the lot.

"We're going to a friend's place. She lives in Northeast D.C.," he explained. "You can lay low there for a few days until our friend has figured out who was trying to have you killed."

"By our friend, do you mean Joe?" she asked. But Walter wasn't taking the bait.

"Is that what he's calling himself?" he replied, eyes still on the road. "Anyway, my friend is ex-agency, and she's a pro. Good soul, too. She'll be good company until then."

3.

"When is 'then'?" Malone asked. "How long is this going to take? I have a story to work on."

Lang shook his head. "You can't write it if you're dead."

It took about a quarter-hour to get to the apartment building in question, a four-story walkup. For the second time in as many days, Malone got the sense she was being taken on a guided tour designed as much to keep her away from sensitive information as to protect her.

Lang parked the car on the street out front. He got out first and scanned the area, then walked around the car and opened Malone's door for her. "Okay, let's go."

Inside the building, he rang 3C on the buzzer board.

"Yep," a woman's voice came back.

"It's us," he said simply.

The door buzzed and they entered the lobby; they took the stairs to the third floor. Malone was exhausted; but she noticed in the bright light outside the front door how pale and thin Walter looked, a shadow of the man she'd met in the pub a few years earlier – and he'd still been recovering at that point from his Colombian ordeal.

"Walter…"

"Yes, Ms. Malone."

"One, call me Alex, okay? Two, you look terrible. Have you seen a doctor or anything recently?"

Lang could only glance at her quickly, embarrassed. "I've been having some issues but they're being dealt with, thank you," he said, politely but firmly.

The woman who greeted them at the apartment door was large; not obese, but of grand proportion, standing over six feet two inches, broad-shouldered. She had a shock of lanky brown-grey hair and looked to be in her late fifties or early sixties, Malone thought.

"Alex, this is Myrna Verbish, one of my oldest friends."

Myrna extended a hand and Malone shook. "Any friend of Walter is okay with me," she said. Then she looked Walter over. "Walter, you look…"

"I know, I look terrible. I haven't been sleeping, okay? Let's just get inside and talk."

Myrna led them in and found them a place on her living room couch while she moved to the adjacent kitchen and made them tea. It was after two o'clock in the morning, but all three were wired from adrenaline. She briefly wondered why she'd said yes to Walter so easily; they were old friends, to be sure, but Myrna was divorced from the intelligence community, and with plenty of good reasons.

Malone filled them both in on her source and the African file, along with the threads that connected the atrocities in Nigeria to Khalidi's company, and Khalidi, in turn, to the shootings. Myrna looked intrigued, fascinated even, Malone thought; but Walter just kept his head down, stoic, as if his mind were somewhere else.

"So that's it," Malone summed up. "We know someone's targeting the ACF's board members, but we also know that the chairman, or one of his companies anyhow, has been involved in some dirty, dirty business."

"The assassinations could be personally motivated, then?" Myrna suggested. "Someone who lost a loved one in Africa, or at least knows about it? Probably not the former," she reasoned, "as I doubt rural villagers would have the contacts or resources."

"That leaves knowing about it," Malone said. "Joe said something, too, about information he'd received in Europe that the ACF had gone way out of bounds. He mentioned a couple of different locations: East Timor and Bosnia. Apparently they funded insurrections, to some degree."

Myrna nodded sagely then looked at her watch. "Oh."

"What?" Lang asked. He was exhausted but she looked genuinely surprised by something.

"I've just realized: it's my birthday."

All three were silent for a moment, aware of how disconnected they'd all become from the people who mattered to them. Malone's family was half a country away, in Los Angeles. None of them had anyone else in D.C.

Lang rose. "You two should get some sleep. I imagine Joe will be trying to contact me soon. I'm going to head home. Myrna, call me tomorrow with an update?"

She nodded and rose to let him out. At the door, she lowered her voice. "Walter, are you really okay? We've been friends for a long time, and ..."

He smiled at her, happy to be cared about. He put his hand on her shoulder and gave her a kiss on the cheek. "You're a wonderful woman, Myrna, you know that, right?"

"Flattery will get you everywhere," she said.

He was still smiling as he closed the door behind him.

3.

22./

FEB. 28, 2016, WASHINGTON, D.C.

Lang's phone rang at six o'clock the next morning. He'd only been home and asleep for slightly under three hours.

"Lang," he answered blearily, swinging his legs out of bed.

"This is Faisal. We have not heard from you in some time. We require a status update."

If the cancer doesn't kill me, Lang thought, *the stress will.* "There has been very little new."

"What about Wilhelm? Surely your agency does not think his death was an accident?"

"No, but we have nothing further to go on right now. I can't give you what we don't have." He had no intention of giving up their intel on Africa; he didn't want to play the two sides against each other, but holding onto two paymasters required tact.

"Then you can do something else for us," Faisal said.

"What?"

"We need a problem fixed."

"I'm not a field agent," Walter began to explain. "I haven't..."

"Irrelevant," Faisal said. "You accepted our money, Mr. Lang. Now we require something in return. There is a reporter in Washington, a woman named Alexandra Malone."

Walter got a sinking feeling in the pit of his stomach. "I know of her," he said.

"She must be eliminated immediately."

"I won't do that," Walter said. "I didn't sign up for that. You needed some intel, I provided it..."

"And we provided you with a great deal of money, money I understand you require for your medical care."

"In exchange for basic intel. I won't kill for you."

"Then you can locate her and detain her for us until someone with the stomach for the job is available," Faisal suggested. "Either way..."

"No," Walter said. "I'm sorry, but that's it."

"This is not optional, Mr. Lang. Placing yourself at odds with my employer would be most unwise. The consequences will be severe."

"I'll keep that in mind," Walter said. He hit the end button and hung up the call.

Being a field handler for twenty years hadn't killed him, nor had Colombia, nor cancer. Walter had never run from a fight; marshalling the forces to beat the disease had been behind his decision to take Faisal's money in the first place.

He decided he'd take his chances.

Brennan called Lang just before noon from a hotel by Dulles Airport. "I'm on a pair of flights, to Paris and then to Luanda," he said. "I'm leaving in two hours. What can you tell me about Angola?"

Lang was still tired, drinking coffee and reading the papers while music droned out of the radio in his kitchen. "I'm going to send you a couple of emails. One is a recent security briefing on the situation there; the other is a page from my passport, showing you what the local visa looks like. It's just a stamp, but you'll need one to get through customs. We have a papermaker in Paris who can help you with it, but it needs to be off the books, or he'll flag the agency. How long do you have there?"

Brennan checked his itinerary. "About six hours."

"That should be more than enough. Look, I'll contact him for you, have him meet you at Charles De Gaulle. Once you're in Angola, work on lining up ordinance and a guide for the area in question."

"Is Alex okay?" Brennan asked.

"She's under wraps and fine," Walter said. "Don't worry about her. I promised I'd look out for her and I will."

"I'll contact you once I'm on the ground," Brennan said. "Stay safe, okay?"

"You got it," Walter said. "Keep your head down."

"Hey," Brennan said, "they once called this place 'The Pearl of Africa'. What could go wrong?

A half-hour away, Carolyn Brennan-Boyle sat in the family living room and watched Jessie unwrap her birthday presents, relieved she seemed happy. She'd helped by giving her mother a lengthy list of suggestions. It included a kit that let her create her own perfume and makeup. Her eyes widened when she saw it under the paper and she ran over to hug her mom, who was sitting on the sofa. Then the little girl's smile faded a bit.

"Are you okay with it, sweetie? Was that the one you wanted?" Carolyn asked.

Jessie smiled and nodded, but it wasn't particularly convincing.

"You miss your father, don't you?"

Jessie nodded again. "How come daddy couldn't be here?"

"He wants to be here," she said. "You have to remember how much your father loves you. He wouldn't be away at all if it were his choice."

"Then how come…"

"The work he does is very important," Carolyn said, anticipating her child's question. "He helps keep the public safe."

She was saying the right things, but Carolyn felt a distance from her husband greater than the miles between them. Before he'd left, they'd fought often, and he'd hardly been speaking with her because of her role in getting him back into the field. At least they'd had a chance to get past that. At least he'd stopped in and seen the kids before going overseas again.

Once again, she had no idea when her husband would return. David Fenton-Wright had been deliberately vague about Joe's progress in tracking down the EU sniper. Perhaps it was just a question of "need to know," but she suspected from David's manner in the few days prior that they weren't getting far. She'd seen the story of Tillo Bustamante's death on CNN, and she knew he was considered a suspect by several agencies.

She'd always known Joe had to kill people as part of his job; or, she'd assumed it. She'd never been involved operationally with his work, but other agents had to dispatch targets with an almost routine regularity. Was that why he was so distant of late? Was it catching up to him, contributing to his self-doubt about his role?

The phone rang.

"It's me," Brennan said when she answered. "I had to call, make sure everything's okay there."

She smiled. She was glad he hadn't just let it pass. "Do you want to talk to the little beasties?"

"Yeah."

She handed the phone to Jessie first and watched her face light up as she talked to him. Then the little girl handed the phone to her brother and watched the reaction again. He smiled and laughed at something his father said. Then he came back to her with the phone. "He wants to talk to you again, mommy."

Carolyn put the phone back to her ear. "Hi."

"That was pretty awesome," he said.

"It was worth it, wasn't it?" she said. "Where are you?"

"On route to Africa, following up a lead."

David had told her he was leaving Joe in Europe for the time being. She wondered how far out of the loop she was.

"Don't ask where," he added, before she could say it. "Need to know only. Look, I have to go; my plane's boarding soon."

"Does Walter know where you are?"

"Yeah, but he's laying low for a couple of days. Don't worry about it. I'll call you in a week or so when I know what I'm doing next. Oh… they just announced my flight. I've got to go."

"Okay," she said. "I love…"

But he'd already hung up.

3.

23./

MARCH 2, 2016, LUANDA, ANGOLA

It had been seven years since he'd last set foot on African soil, but there was a familiarity to it when the doors opened and the stairs led the 747's passengers down to the tarmac at Aeroporto 4 de Fevereiro. He'd never been to Angola before; but an assignment in Gabon had offered that same humid blast of wet, hot African air when getting off the plane, temperatures in the eighties.

But it wasn't just the weather. Africa smelled different, to an outsider. The combination of local living conditions, local diet and the effect of constant heat on organic material led to a strange mixture of sweat, garbage and decay in the air. At first it was as unpleasant as it sounded. But he knew it wouldn't take long before he wasn't even noticing it. Brennan imagined New York or Washington probably smelled just as strange to someone from Africa.

The passengers filed down the stairs, the majority local but a fair smattering of foreigners among them. Angola's rich oil, gold and diamond deposits had turned it into the latest kleptocratic former communist nation, with eighty-five percent of the population in abject poverty while the remainder cut deals with multinational conglomerates to fleece the country dry. They'd even begun developing a southern satellite city to the capital, Luanda, replete with North American-style housing subdivisions, so that the foreigners could live near the nicest beaches, at Kilometre Seventeen and the Mussolo Peninsula, and not have to watch the local children and their malnourished, swollen stomachs as they starved to death.

At the bottom of the plane's stairs, a standard city transit-style bus was painted in garish, multi-shaded blue advertising colors, hocking a Portuguese soft drink with peacock subtlety. If it hadn't been daylight still, and he hadn't known better, Brennan might have been fooled into thinking Angola was stable, and normal. From overhead, looking out the tiny airplane window, he'd seen the huge Mussaque – or slum – that bordered the airport, and the many that dotted the city's landscape, wedged between blocks of old colonial homes and the friends of the government who'd commandeered them.

Across the city, corrugated tin-shack favelas told the real story; they were mostly one-room huts, with no sanitation, no running water, garbage, filth and vermin everywhere. The walls were muddled together from old packing crates, shipping containers, scrap metal, mud and wire mesh. And they were home to most of the nation's population of twenty-two million.

In 1972, Walter's briefing had noted, Angola had become known as the "Paris of Africa" or even "the Pearl of Africa", a land of abundant natural resources, beautiful weather, centuries-old Colonial architecture, astonishing beaches and African wildlife. Unfortunately, the local residents were treated like just another natural resource, and forced into indentured servitude by the Portuguese for generations. Even in the last few decades of Portuguese rule, they were prevented by law from learning skilled trades or taking jobs in those areas away from Portuguese settlers.

When the inevitable glorious people's revolution came – as it had in most of post-Colonial Africa – the Portuguese fled and left Angolans, segmented socially by tribes, fighting amongst themselves; ostensibly they each represented a modern political ideology, although in fact it continued feuds that went back five centuries, to when the Queen of one major tribe began enslaving the others and selling them to Europeans.

The civil war raged for twenty-six years, ravaging the population and leaving up to eighty percent missing at least one limb from a landmine explosion; in fact, there were estimates that landmines covered an eighth of the country, which was one of Africa's largest.

It only ended with the death of the UNITA rebel leader Jonas Savimbi in 2002. A former Pan-African Socialist, Savimbi had "transformed" into a dyed-in-the-wool capitalist conservative by the time of his death … because that was a requirement of the millions in aide he received from the U.S. His opponents, in Jose Eduardo Dos Santos' MPLA party, eventually turned to democratic reform anyway, due to the near-global collapse of Marxism… along with its money supply from the defunct Soviet Union.

The money vacuum that supplied and controlled the local power elite was filled by multinational corporations, intent on massively ramping up the country's oil production, already among the world leaders, and taking advantage of a vast mineral base. The Jesuit-trained former communist leader, Dos Santos, became a corrupt oligarch, extending his terms over and over, enriching his family and friends with hundreds of millions of dollars in patronage and business advantage. Like so many African leaders, the power he wielded within his nations border had given him a sense of superhuman ego, a complete loss of empathy, and the delusion of right-by-association. The country had a Gross Domestic Product of more than a hundred and twenty billion dollars, and yet per capita income was just shy of six thousand.

Black market dollars continued to dominate the local currency, leaving the population in poverty while their political leaders enriched themselves and built idyllic suburbs. Fourteen years after the ceasefire, as 2016 was about to begin, Luanda was the most expensive capital on the planet, due to the outrageous boom-town prices charged to foreigners to live and work there. And yet still, the locals starved. The city remained covered in the signs of utter poverty, services were near-non-existent even for the wealthy, oil-backed expats; crime was staggeringly high. A machine gun cost less than a good steak while a case of cola could set you back three hundred bucks.

To Brennan, the place reeked of the worst of human nature; power-hungry leaders, a cowed and terrified populace, foreign elements – including many American companies – more than willing to take what Angola had to offer and leave nothing behind for those who lived there. How was it allowed to go on? Even after all of his years of service, he never ceased to be struck by how people could treat one another, all in the name of personal gain.

He got on the bus to the airport terminal, which looked as though it had been upgraded from Walter's description and modernized. He muttered a quiet resolution to himself to stay on point, to follow up the story of the missing nuke and Khalidi's missing money man. He wasn't in Angola to save the local people, and he grimly reminded himself that in that part of the world, that attitude was par for the course.

2.

The trip through customs was monotonous, dull, time-consuming. Liberalization hadn't decreased the airport graft, and one of the customs workers took a bottle of whiskey from Brennan's bag – which he'd expected; he'd brought two for just such purposes. His bag search was done by hand after he'd filed around a cordon with about two hundred other tired travelers, a mix of black and white, old and young, male and female, some families with young kids, some older kids alone, some single working men. Everyone was dressed for the heat, with short sleeves, shorts, sandals.

After the search they filtered through to a row of steel-and-rubber baggage carousels then waited nearly an hour for their stuff to be unloaded. Brennan ignored the odd soldier in olive drab, the local police in two shades of blue, their white dress gloves stark against dark African skin. He walked the short distance from the carousel to the front doors and out into the city afternoon, the whirr of the cicadas a dull roar in the background and the circular road that front the terminal packed with traffic. It was hot and dusty, ninety degrees in the shade, with the stifling humidity weighing his clothing down, pinning it to his skin with damp gravity. Past the road ahead was a vast parking lot; but to his right was a taxi stand, and only one taxi. He made a beeline for it, getting there before anyone else intervened.

The driver, Rucca, was a Portuguese expat who'd married a local.

"I warn you in advance," he said. "The fares here are kind of crazy."

Brennan knew the background, the stratospheric local prices; he'd emptied his only remaining contingency account in Europe to finance the trip. "Just keep the route as short as it needs to be, okay?" he replied. "I tip better when I feel like I've been well-treated."

The driver smiled while looking back into the rearview mirror at his passenger and nodded. "Just remember that once you've been in the local traffic for a few minutes; remember that I'm on your side," he said. He chuckled slightly at the end in the knowing manner of someone who has just warned a greenhorn off of eating the hottest local peppers.

3.

The driver headed towards downtown, where old Portuguese colonial office buildings, homes and shops were slowly being dwarfed by new glass office towers, guest lodgings and condo apartments. There were plenty of signs that capitalism was beginning to lift local conditions despite all the corruption; but the poverty among those being left behind was staggering. Kids with swollen bellies walking barefoot beside his car, trying to catch up to beg for food and money; men in their thirties who looked sixty, their arms and legs thin as sinewy pipe cleaners; young teenage girls with bellies so swollen from malnourishment they could be mistaken for pregnant. They didn't dominate the sidewalks of the capital, its white plaster architecture reminiscent of Barcelona; but they could be seen amongst the crowds, down alleys, in front of shops begging for food.

The taxi cut through the downtown to the waterfront, where the newest hotels vied with the mid-sixties last generation colonial offerings. Then it followed the waterfront road, affording a view of the tankers in the bay, to the Hotel Panorama, where he booked in as Tom Smith, a geologist.

The hotel was a gem from a distance, a piece of rectangular 1960s modernist architecture with the name in giant letters across its roof, Luanda's own Hollywood sign. It sat on a peninsula called the Ilha that overlooked the water. It was built in white concrete, and the street level was open-air, with gigantic concrete columns supporting the rest of the hotel.

Up close, time and neglect told the tale. The concrete was cracking, the plastic chipped, dirty and stained. The once-red balcony railings that overlooked the water were faded to a light pink. The rooms were like something out of a youth hostel in a bad Moscow neighbourhood. The bed was hard and smelled musty, the light bulb swung free of a shade and the toilet didn't work. When he threw his bag down onto the stained, time-worn desk along one wall, a handful of cockroaches the size of his thumb scurried across the floor and under the bed.

It was a good place to keep a low profile; he knew from Walter's file that the odd expatriate event was still held in the conference room and ballroom on its main floor; but none of the moneyed and corrupt stayed at the Panorama anymore; they were at the $500-per-night Hotel Baia Luanda.

A white Citroen, bug-like and unwashed, had been behind the taxi all the way from the airport, and it was still parked outside the hotel when Brennan looked out his south-facing balcony, towards the rest of the peninsula. Angola only had about a half-dozen decent hotels, and the Panorama wasn't really one of them; it hadn't been for more than two decades. The car had local plates, too, which suggested it wasn't a tail.

2.

But he couldn't be sure. He didn't think they'd had anything close to the technology at the airport to spot his passport as fraudulent, as it was doubtless based on a real person, long dead. On a one-in-a million shot, he could have been recognized by someone in intelligence at the airport; Angola was probably still pretty busy in that regard. But he'd been a careful man his entire career and had never blown a cover, so it seemed the odds were at least that long.

The only person who knew he was in Angola was Walter, and Brennan knew he wouldn't crack for any reason.

Night was falling. Brennan opened his suitcase on the dresser, taking out his bathroom travel bag. Along the bottom of its lining, he found the tucked-in zipper and slid its bottom compartment open, revealing the two thin ceramic knives, each perfectly balanced, double-edged and razor sharp – and undetectable to an airport metal detector. He reached down and pulled up each pant-leg in turn, sliding the knives into their sheaths, out of sight. Turning back to the suitcase, he picked up a pair of thick, web-like belts, each containing a series of pockets in which to hide his cash. He hadn't bothered with the local currency, the Kwanza. Everyone in Angola would accept dollars; it was how the economy really ran. He strapped one belt on under his light shirt then placed the other inside the waterproof plastic bag he'd brought for the purpose. Then he hid it just inside the top of the toilet tank, where it was unlikely to be discovered by prying eyes or light-fingered staff.

He carried the other bottle of Cutty Sark with him as he left the room, locked the door behind him, and took stairs down four floors to the lobby. He'd made a mental note on arriving to never trust the creaking, ancient elevator.

In the lobby, a single night staff member was standing behind the chipped and aging marble-tile counter, looking bored. "Can I help you sir?" he asked Brennan in Portuguese.

"I need to find a taxi," Brennan said in English.

"It is Saturday, sir," the man answered back, also in English, his accent heavy. "There are no Taxis available in Luanda on weekends, except to and from the airport."

Perfect. "Then I need to rent a car."

"There are no car rental firms available in the evening," the man said, looking genuinely sorry. "But I can help; my brother has a car that you can hire. He is very reasonable: only five hundred dollars each day."

Brennan smiled back, just as friendly. Nothing was ever straightforward in places like Luanda. "That is a fine offer, my friend," he said, "but it is a bit too rich for me. I am just a geologist, not an engineer. Will he accept one hundred? That is truly all that I can afford."

3.   195

He looked unshaken. "I think he might consider it," he said, "if we were able to talk about a sum more in keeping with the state of the economy. Perhaps for three hundred and fifty he might be able to get away from his work and help."

Brennan had played the game before. He shook his head, looking disappointed. "No, I'm sorry. But thank you for your offer. I shall just have to make my way on foot. It's fine; it's not far. It's a shame, though. I suppose I could have gone as high as one hundred and fifty."

"For two hundred," the man said, "he would be a guide of excellence. He knows the city like the back of his hand. Anything you need – anything, if you know what I am meaning, my friend."

Brennan nodded. "Okay: two hundred a day, but he gets half up front, half when I check out in a few days. And you get a bottle of Cutty Sark." He left the bottle on the counter.

The man beamed a smile as he took it. Given the necessity of graft in the local economy, he'd probably drink the contents or share it with friends, Brennan thought, then refill the bottle with cheap whisky from Benguela or Lobito, down the coast, where they made a decent variety. Then he'd screw the cap back on so that it required real tension to open, and sell it, probably for a fair chunk of coin.

"He will be happy to help. He has a good car, a Skoda. Built in Czechoslovakia, very dependable."

"Where can I get something decent to eat around here?"

The man squinted unreadily, obviously not sure how to answer optimistically. "On the Ilha? There are some places but I am not sure you would think much of them. Perhaps you should have my brother take you to downtown, where there are some nice restaurants."

"Give him a call," Brennan said.

The man smiled and took out a cell phone. Brennan wasn't surprised; the country's landlines were undependable and likely bugged beyond belief. Now that there was a cell network, people didn't bother with the old system as much as they once had.

He ended the call. "My brother says he will be here in twenty-five minutes, and he promises you will have an unforgettable trip. His name is Cristiano."

"I'm hoping it will be unforgettably quiet and stress-free."

His smile dimmed a little. There was probably less money in "quiet." "Perhaps it would be wise to mention that to him, sir," he said. "He is very enthusiastic about offering services."

The driver's rusted, patched-together white Skoda Favorit pulled up into the Panorama's parking area exactly twenty-five minutes later, as advertised. It was old, probably from the late eighties, Brennan figured, a rectangular hunk of junk. The hatchback was missing completely and replaced with three bungee cords, strung across it to hold in anything it might be carrying. The rear body panel on the right hand side was pressed tin from some unknown source that had been crudely cut into a replacement of the original, then painted light blue, which Brennan just assumed was a natural consequence of it being in Angola, where most of the locals had little to choose from. There was light blue paint available freely because of the number of old Volkswagen Beetles of that shade imported from Brazil in years prior. The rest of the little hatchback's body was mottled with rust stains and, in a few places, actual holes going right through it.

When he saw Brennan, the driver honked the horn. It played the first eleven notes of 'Dixie', just like the General Lee from the seventies TV show the *Dukes of Hazzard*. Brennan opened the back door. "You're Cristiano?"

He nodded. "My English is not bad," he said, motioning with his hand that it wasn't particularly good. "Parlez-Vous Francais?"

"Fala Portuguese?" Brennan asked.

The driver was happy to switch to the dominant local language. "I was worried, because it can be difficult to deal with the English," he said. "It does not roll off of my tongue well. Now, where are we going tonight, my friend? And do you have my two hundred dollars?"

"I have the one hundred you get now," Brennan said, handing him a c-note. "Can you get a few things together for me? There's an extra hundred in it if everything goes smoothly."

The man's eyes brightened. "Of course, of course. What do you need?"

"I'm going to be going out into the country and I need some self-protection."

The driver sounded most pleased. "Ah! In this area I know many suppliers. We have many weapons available from the war in perfect condition. What would you like?"

Really? Brennan thought. That easily? "What are you offering?"

The man's face was a momentary mask of disappointment. "Do not worry my friend; if I was a police officer, I would have asked you for a bribe by now. But if it will ease your mind, I will tell you that the cheapest and easiest things to supply are the Makarov PM for a handgun and the AK47 for a machine gun. I will also note that the latter is the real thing, supplied by the Russians, and not the Chinese copies you find everywhere else."

3.   197

"And if someone wanted to buy a Makarov PM or two from one of your friends, how much would it be? Just out of curiosity."

"I believe they would be available for ten dollars each. A clip for each will be five dollars more. Ammunition can be had at the hundred-load for five dollars."

In a sense, Brennan thought, Angola was like Somalia, but with more buildings and overt manners. Life was still the cheapest commodity, and weaponry went for less than European cigarettes.

"And an AK?"

"Twenty dollars for the gun, ten dollars for a standard clip, fifteen for an extended. Ammunition is two hundred for five dollars. Again, there is much more of it than for the small calibre for the Makarov, which is why the former is so expensive."

Brennan nodded towards the Ilha. "I'll tell you what, my friend: how about I buy you dinner, and we talk a little more. You help me out for the next couple of days, I'll make it worth a whole lot of AKs worth of actual dollars. How does that sound?"

The man smiled broadly, leaned over his seat and slapped Brennan with a hand-clasp and shake. "Mister, I believe we are in business."

The weapons dealer was situated in an old colonial neighbourhood not far from the airport called the Alvalade. The streets were lined with villas from Portugal's heyday, Cristiano explained, plaster in shades of pastel, faded and dirt-stained from time and neglect. Most were fronted by palm trees. As with much of the city there was debris and garbage everywhere; giant dumpsters could be found every third of fourth block but were generally overflowing, the smell so bad they had to roll up their windows as they passed.

For the most expensive city on Earth, Brennan thought, it looked an awful lot like every other Third World outhouse. And for a country no longer at war with itself, there were plenty of soldiers, too. As the car navigated the pothole-ridden streets, it seemed like every tenth person was in army fatigues and carrying a weapon. The locals were a mix of obliviously happy but malnourished – generally, the kids – and worn down; the male adults wore faded dress shirts and trousers with sandals, underweight, eyes hollow and joints stiff. The local women seemed generally healthier than the men, most wrapped in colourful kangas: multi-coloured, single-sheet wrap-around dresses. Every so often, Brennan would see a pair of women walking side by side, balancing large jugs or platters of fruit on their heads.

2.

The driver pulled up outside a whitewashed concrete wall, which featured a wide, solid-metal double gate. Just beyond it, Brennan could see the second floor of a white stucco home, impressively large even by modern standards. They got out of the car. The driver pressed a buzzer button beside the gate. "Hey Francisco, it's Cristiano. I have a customer for you, a good one."

There was no reply, and they stood there for a few seconds, the driver crossing his arms and smiling sheepishly, obviously worried about whether he'd get a response. Then they heard footsteps, followed by the thick clang of a heavy bolt being drawn back. The gate swung open and a short, dark-haired man eyed them over, before nodding to go inside. Cristiano led the three across a small courtyard area, then up the concrete side steps to the expansive home's main floor. The door led directly into another small courtyard, this time inside the house proper. It was open to the night sky above, and people were lounging around on beach furniture, drinking cold beer and talking. Brennan counted nine, mostly women.

A large Latino guy in a white shirt and white cotton pants with the cuffs rolled up was entertaining two ladies at the same time from his lounger, the sun glinting off his mirrored aviators. "Hey Cristiano!" he yelled as they walked in. "Good to see you my little friend!" He said something to the two women – and kissed one woman's hand – and they both moved across the courtyard to talk to others. He got up and came over to meet his new customer; Francisco was a beefy guy with a strong hand shake and a collection of gold jewellery. "Introduce me to your guest."

The young African driver grinned widely. "This is Tom. He needs to arrange some protection, and maybe would like to shop your wares a bit, yes?"

Francisco winked at Brennan. "That can easily be arranged. Would you like a beer?" He leaned over and opened a cooler chest by a nearby director's chair. "Nice and cold."

Brennan nodded and Cristiano followed suit. Their host uncapped the two green bottles and handed them over. "Come, let me show you what we have," he said. He moved to the far side of the courtyard and slid back a glass patio-style door, leading them into a big, air-conditioned living room. At its far end, a set of stairs with glass panels under the railing led to a lower level. He flicked on a light switch as they followed him.

The basement was open concept. One entire half of the room was covered with display cases and weapons hanging from the walls. "Now what can I get for you?" Francisco asked. "Maybe an M60 copy with a handy, aftermarket flame-thrower attachment?" He walked over to the wall and took the weapon down. "This thing chews through brick walls, eh?"

Brennan shook his head. "I don't think we need to go that heavy. Is everything you have Russian?"

The arms dealer shrugged his shoulders. "It's what's out there, for the most part. I can get things in for you on special order but it would be very expensive. But then, that's why it's a buyer's market; if it wasn't, you wouldn't get past the gate, my friend."

"What I could really use is an MP-433 Grach with a suppressor, and a vest."

Francisco exhaled heavily. "The Grach? No problem. It's a new gun, so it will cost you a hundred. The vest is another matter. They are in heavy demand and short supply. Can you wait until tomorrow?"

"Possibly. I also need to round up some intel; nothing official or illegal."

The arm's dealer was nodding but he looked suspicious, which Brennan expected. "Sure, sure.... Of course if depends what kind of intel you're looking for. You want to know what movie is playing at the Miramar? I can do that. You want Dos Santos' cell number? That's punching above my weight."

"I'm looking for someone."

"Tread carefully, my friend. Cristiano, what's this about?"

"I don't know, Frankie... he didn't mention information, just weapons."

Brennan held up both palms. "Like I said, it's nothing government."

That seemed to calm the arms dealer somewhat. "Then I guess it depends what you want and how much you can spend to get it. I know some people who know some people."

Brennan handed the picture of Andraz Kovacic. "This guy may have been in and out of the country, maybe even a long time ago. I think he left something behind here and I need to find it."

Francisco's eyes widened with surprise. "You don't want much, do you? Why don't you put a bullet in my head yourself right now?"

"So you know him."

"Yeah... well, not personally. But I know people who know people, like I said. But this is interesting; I haven't seen or heard of this guy in ... maybe four years?"

"Can you find out if he's still around?"

"Sure. But expect a serious bill for this, my friend. We are talking five figures."

"For five figures, you take me to him."

"Or," Francisco said, "you can go fuck yourself with the negotiation bullshit. You have nothing here, no cards to play. I have the info and the connections. So, for ten thousand I get you a confirmation if he's alive. For another ten thousand, I get you a meeting."

It would just about drain his resources, Brennan knew. But he didn't have an option. "Half upfront, half on completion," Brennan said. "Needless to say, the people I work for will be incredibly upset if you don't produce."

"I like my head where it is, my friend," Francisco said. "I'll tell you what: the pistol is on me. The vest, you get tomorrow. The information, within the week."

24/
MARCH 3, 2016, ATLANTA, GEORGIA

Christopher Enright had been Addison March's assistant for three years. It wasn't the meteoric Washington career he'd expected out of Yale law, but he handled his tasks with efficiency and skill, and he knew March appreciated it. His boss was about to run for President; and that meant that Enright had as much riding on the next few months as the veteran politician.

So he urged caution as they took the elevator up from the parking garage to the News Network's fourteenth floor studio.

"I just think that two days after Christmas is an inopportune time to do any heavy lifting when it comes to interviews, senator," he said. "The public's collective mind is still focused on the holidays, getting visiting family out of their hair, bargain shopping... that sort of thing."

March snorted at the suggestion. "The public's collective mind could fit on the head of a pin and leave enough room for a dance number. But if it will put your mind at ease, Christopher, I will refrain from attacking POTUS and focus instead on that buffoon John Younger."

March's ego worried Enright; he expected it from any politician, in varying degrees. But in March's case, his lengthy success record both in business and politics had rendered him immune to self-criticism or introspection. The fact, for example, that John Younger had had every bit as much success both personally and professionally would seem to discount him being a buffoon. Underestimating your opponent was never good in an important race, Enright thought.

It was that kind of lack of foresight that made him think sometimes that he was backing the wrong horse. In economic policy, there was little real difference between the two de facto nominees; both were intrinsically indebted for political fundraising reasons to the financial sector. Foreign policy was where they differed, with March scoring big points among frustrated lower income voters by playing the race card, arguing that floods of Mexican and Central American migrant workers were driving down wages among the poorest. At the same time, he favored tariffs on Chinese products to help rebuild the American middle class manufacturing sector.

2.

Younger, meanwhile, was a "new age" Liberal, soft on corporate malfeasance and sheer capitalism, but demanding of social change that reflected the latest research, of programs like Success by Six to help young, poor parents cope and of improved rehabilitation programs for those convicted of crimes. His softhearted approach scared Enright half to death; the modern world was a serious place, he thought, full of seriously bad people. The John Youngers of the world didn't have the mettle for it.

So despite his reservations about March's style and his occasional hotheadedness, Enright had stuck with him. And of late, March's shots at Younger for being soft on security had been scoring with the pollsters. They were up four points from a week earlier, still trailing, but just barely.

"They're going to go hard on this suggestion from Sen. Reid that you're being hypocritical over China because of your own overseas investments," Enright reminded him. "You're good on our key messages there?"

"I know, son, I know," the Tennessee veteran said. "For the benefit of that public you're so smitten with, I will once again point out that owning chocolate farms in South America is not the same as destroying the American middle class with cheap Chinese imports." March hated this part of the campaign, the kowtowing to the least informed.

"It plays well with your base, Senator," Enright said. "Remember, without the tax revolt crowd, the old guard would still be shutting you out." The Republican old guard had made a lot of mistakes, Enright thought; but the biggest was losing sight of the average everyday voting Republican, the blue collar guy who believed in the same things they believed, even if not much of the wealth was trickling down his way. The guy with principles.

It took less than fifteen minutes to get the senator into makeup for the interview, which was being handled by Richard Glazer, a veteran anchor. March had been questioned by Glazer before and had marginally less contempt for the TV man than for most of his journalist ilk. He prided himself on the fact that he'd been successful enough for long enough in politics that he could predict most of the questions Glazer would ask.

He was right. Again. For the first five minutes of the twelve-minute segment Glazer waxed liberal about the plight of the Mexican migrant and the need for workplace equity, as well as throwing out some softball queries about life on the campaign trail.

And then with two minutes left, Glazer threw him a curve.

"Senator March, there has been a buzz for the last week in the Beltway about foreign money…"

3.   203

March cut him off. "As I've noted before, all of my investments are with U.S. companies who just happen to produce some of their components…"

Glazer interrupted him. "Senator… please… senator, that's not what I'm referring to. I'm referring of course to the buzz that when you were in private business, you had a working relationship with the Latrobe Corporation, a Texas oil concern that is in part owned by the controversial Jordanian businessman Ahmed Khalidi."

It was a gross misrepresentation, of course, the senator thought. March had been senior partner in a firm that had done some work for Latrobe, but he personally had no role in it. "Now that's just inaccurate as all get out, Richard," he said, trying to sound disappointed. "I would think a veteran journalist such as you would check his facts before making such a statement."

"Perhaps you could clarify…" Glazer began.

"I will only point out as a matter for the record that while lawyers at my firm did some work with Latrobe many years ago, I personally had no role in that work. So no, I never did work for Khalidi's company."

To the side of the set, Enright grimaced. For a veteran, March was so reliant on his charisma with the public that he was exceedingly sloppy. All he had to do was deny it; he had his version and that made it accurate, and that was all that was needed. Instead, he'd not only planted the seed of public doubt by calling it "my firm", he'd then gone on refer to Khalidi by name. It was a disaster. The communications team was going to laugh him out of the office.

He could almost feel the polls dropping.

MARCH 12, 2016, MONTPELLIER, FRANCE

In his palatial office overlooking the broad public square called Place de la Comedie, Yoshi Funomora had just finished reading the report on his agent's death. The rest of the ACF board waited on the conference call line.

"Well?" the chairman asked. "I take it your agent failed."

"He appears to have been killed professionally, chairman. Ms. Malone has friends in the intelligence community. I recommend we liaise with our security contact in the United States and determine what he thinks has taken place."

The Chinese delegate, Fung, was feeling vindicated. He had been warning his colleagues about Funomora's incompetence or months. Now, perhaps, he could see him removed and a more amiable colleague from Asia installed in his place.

"Our Japanese colleague would, of course, recommend going to another source for our information, given that his agent has failed miserably, and with fatal consequences. Typical. Perhaps, Mr. Chairman…"

"Perhaps," said Khalidi, "we could focus on the problems at hand." For once, he wanted Fung to stow his rivalry with Funomora until the larger issues had been addressed. "Japan, can we be briefed by our American contact?"

"I've arranged for it already, chairman," the stocky politician said. "He'll be on the line in just a moment."

A conference call operator said "go ahead, please."

"Is this line secure?" David Fenton-Wright asked.

He'd been briefing the ACF for nearly two years, an implied bargain in exchange for a future position among the seven. Fenton-Wright's desire to join wasn't mere vanity or self-enrichment; he knew the truth about the ACF's ambitions. Its star chamber-like power came from relationships with top security officials in every developed nation, and from its own rapid response resources. Fenton-Wright had been recruited to aide its mission representing America, and he intended one day to chair the ACF himself.

"The operator is shut out of the call and our voices are scrambled," Funomora noted. "Go ahead."

"Our asset in Europe was behind the Bustamante shooting," Fenton-Wright said. "But he is convinced that Bustamante was not, in fact, responsible for the sniper. I've told him to stay there and off the radar until we can provide further direction. As for the larger issue of the missing package, I've told him it's not his concern, so I would not anticipate any further inquiries in that vein."

"That is welcome news," the chairman said. "You do yourself credit."

"Thank you, chairman," Fenton-Wright fawned. "I can only hope to be as much help to the Association in the future."

The Chinese delegate was dissatisfied. "Perhaps our American colleague can inform us as to why there has been no progress in tracking down the sniper?"

Fenton-Wright had anticipated the question. "It is a matter of the shooter having gone to ground, vice-chairman. He stressed the word "vice" to remind Fung that he had the chairman's support. "However, we continue to follow leads and investigate probability matrices …"

3.

"Probability matrices?" Fung jeered. "Perhaps when the would-be member has decided to take this seriously…"

"I'm sure he has," Khalidi said, wary of another debate beginning. "And I'm certain our friend will prove his worth once more as the investigation continues."

"Thank you again, chairman," Fenton-Wright said. "Your support, as always, is much appreciated."

Fenton-Wright returned home after eight o'clock. He'd always been a workaholic, even in high school, which he had always assumed was the biggest reason for his success in class and his unpopularity with the other students.

It had been a similar story in his various college classes. And he'd never made many friends at the agency, either, for that matter.

And so he invariably returned home alone. He'd never really minded much, and it afforded him privacy. He closed the door to his apartment and locked it behind him, then checked his messages. Only one mattered, from an overseas number. He took out his phone and dialed it immediately.

The call was answered after a single ring. "Thank you for being so prompt," said Faisal Mohammed. "We need you to perform an additional task, one the chairman does not wish to discuss with the rest of the board."

MARCH 16, 2016, WASHINGTON, D.C.

Myrna and Alex worked in near silence, each transfixed by the content of their monitor as they sat next to each other at Myrna's twin computers, in her apartment study.

The long-time former analyst had access to a series of decent databases, including most major newspapers. They'd been going through headline after headline, cover after cover, edition after edition, searching for any sign of the ACF's unofficial activities. Bustamante had mentioned Bosnia and East Timor, and they made good starting points; they'd then expanded the hunt to include other nations in conflict over the past two decades.

She was a fascinating person, Malone thought. Her complete focus was on the task, to the point that she'd joked about having to remind herself to go to the bathroom. It was no surprise that she'd impressed Walter. Myrna struck her as having been self-sufficient in the womb.

2.

The older woman broke the silence. "It's probably what we should have expected, but even where there are battles or ambushes involving foreigners, there's not a hint to connect them to the ACF. If there are connections here, they're buried deeply beneath a surface that these stories barely scratch."

The headlines were beginning to blur together; Myrna didn't want to admit it to young Alex but she was usually in bed by nine o'clock, and it was nearly eleven. She yawned deeply, then reached for her coffee and had a big sip. The mouse wheel rolled under her finger repetitively, the screen parsing by at a rate so uniform it was probably contributing to her growing sense of fatigue.

And then she stopped abruptly. "Wait a minute now... what's this?"

Malone looked over at the screen. "It's in Chinese. You speak Chinese?"

"Mandarin and Cantonese, a couple of lesser-known dialects." Myrna kept her eyes on the screen. "This is a story from eighteen months ago in the northeastern province of Heilongjiang." She read through it quickly. "An organized crime family of some note in the city of Harbin has ended a decade-long harassment and extortion racket targeting construction companies after a deadly gun battle that left sixteen of its members dead and more wounded. The remainder of the gang, which turned itself over to police last week, was said by police to have admitted their guilt in exchange for life sentences and not the death penalty. Police said there was no truth to the wild rumours that spread after the incident, in which hardened gang members claimed they were set upon in a warehouse by foreign devils and tortured."

It could be something, Malone thought, but there was no way to know for sure. "It's not much," she said.

"Well, no – not until you consider that Harbin is also the home city of Fung So Dook, the vice-chairman of the committee."

She might have something, Malone thought. As a reporter, she'd never been a big believer in coincidences. "Let's flag it for a deeper look. Is Walter coming around tonight?" She was curious to see them together again, see how much deference the agency man showed Myrna.

"I don't think so," her host said. "He said he got called in for some work thing."

"He pushes himself too hard. Did you notice how pale and thin he's been looking?"

Myrna nodded. "I do worry about him. He's a good soul, you know, even though he's been in a dirty business for a long time. But he's always been guarded and private. There was one point at which he and I..." She let the idea hang there.

"What!" said Malone. "You and Walter, an item?"

3.

"Well, yeah... but it never went anywhere. Who knows, maybe we just weren't attracted enough to each other. Or maybe we were frightened of alienating one of the few people either of us knew at the agency who could be trusted. Still, no regrets." Myrna nodded towards Malone's cup. "Would you like some more coffee?"

"I should probably quit it for the night, if I want to sleep. But it was very nice."

"Speaking of very nice, did I get the impression correctly that you were enjoying being saved by our friend 'Joe'?"

She smiled ruefully. "You did, but Walter said he's married. So that's not going anywhere."

Malone wouldn't lie to herself; she'd considered giving him a shot anyway, secure in the knowledge she was unlikely to ever meet Mrs. Joe. But then she'd remembered how she felt when her parents briefly separated, and wondered whether Joe and his wife had kids.

"Oh, well... then I hope you have better luck in the New Year, dear," Myrna said. She went back to her screen. "It says they targeted the Fei Long shopping market on the edge of the city initially then began to demand protection money from other grocers as well. This went on and grew over the course of several years, until they were receiving proceeds from almost every Harbin construction business."

"No mention of Fung?"

"No, but I might be able to find a copy of the court proceedings on an Asian database I've used a few times before." She typed and searched for a minute more. "Yes, here it is. There's a list of the affected companies."

They searched the list of names one by one.

"Nothing," Myrna said after about ten minutes. "You?"

Malone shook no. "Company directors?"

"Why not?"

It took another hour to build a list of directors for each firm then run their names.

"Hang on," Malone said. "Here we go: the Xi Jiansung Company has a director listed as Wen Mah Ling...."

"... which also happens to be the name of Fung's wife." Myrna got up and took out her phone. "We need someone on the ground. I've got some contacts over there who owe me."

"You're quite a marvel," Malone suggested.

Myrna smiled at that. "It has been so noted."

"Myrna..."

"Hmm? Yes, dear?"

2.   208

"Do you think there's any chance still that you and Walter could end up together?" She wasn't just being nosy; Malone's career had always seemed to get in the way of her own prospects. Maybe, she thought, being Myrna's age and single made a person give up entirely, assume love was never in the cards.

Myrna smiled and thought about her friend. She'd known Walter Lang for two decades; he was so dedicated to his job, so wrapped up in agency business; she'd thought she'd lost him after the Colombia incident. But Myrna had to admit – at least to herself – that she held out hope for the two of them. She'd been alone, awash in her need for control of every second of her own life, for far too long. She needed to open up to somebody, feel that affection and familiarity.

"Maybe, dear. One never knows. Maybe."

3.

MARCH 25, 2016, CABINDA, WEST AFRICA

The flight got in early, which Brennan figured was a good thing; he needed at least a few extra hours to recover from it.

They'd taken off from a private strip just north of Luanda in what could charitably be called a plane. It was an old junker of a twin prop from the late fifties, a yellow buckboard thing. One of the cabin doors was missing and the pilots spent the first half-hour arguing about flight procedures, one eventually grabbing a manual from under his chair, in full view of the handful of passengers, and using it to demonstrate to the other pilot how to properly fly it.

Turbulence had beaten the plane around until everyone was green in the gills. Everyone except Francisco, who insisted he had an iron-clad stomach. "Wait until you taste funge with pirri pirri gindungo," he'd said, his voice raised over the roar of the props. "It's a corn paste log covered in palm oil and pirri pirri peppers that have been picked in onions and garlic, usually with whisky or brandy. It's Angola's national dish and the hottest on the planet, yet also the blandest... an amazing and diabolical contradiction."

Cabinda's airport was a lime-green concrete pillbox, its name scrawled in cartoonish paint letters, like something out of a 1960s day-care. From the air, Brennan noted, it sure looked a lot like Luanda; and it was technically Angolan territory, even though a sliver of the Democratic Republic of the Congo separated the two and a fair swath of Cabindans wanted independence, based on their cultural individuality. Their dialect of Bantu was even a different language from the tribal tongues used in the south. But their living conditions were similar, shrouded in poverty.

The town had been around in one form or another for five hundred years, but only as Cabinda from the eighteen hundreds on. Like Benguela, it was a slave port for decades until the trade's eventual demise. As was typical of the day, the king's tribe sold his rival tribe's members to the Portuguese and Belgians. A diary of one king of the Kikongo, as the land was then known, noted the sale of four thousand slaves through the area in one year.

So life there had always been difficult, while its proximity to oil and minerals made the nation valuable. Brennan was glad Francisco had come along for the first leg, at least, and brought a couple of men with him. "We'll take you as far as your man's camp and I will arrange a meet. After that you are definitely on your own," he said as they waited inside the airport for their driver, a handful of passengers and locals milling around, not moving much due to the heat. "He lives nearly eighty kilometers north of here, near the other border with the DRC."

"Why so far out of town?" Brennan asked. "You'd think his customers …

"Wouldn't mind going to him. Kovacic is not exactly a lightweight – and he's going by 'Anders Kallstrom' now, by the way. Before he starting running guns out of Cabinda, the rumour is he was fighting with a group of neo-Marxists in the Russian republics. He had a client based immediately on reputation alone."

"So his threat level…"

"… is considerable. Your guy went to impressive lengths to disappear up here and set himself up as a supplier to the Cabindan resistance movement; it's only by virtue of us doing business with the same people that I even know he exists. Come on, let's go wait outside for the car."

As remote and broken down as Cabinda was, the vehicle turned out to be a Land Rover, which made it the safest car Brennan had seen since arriving in Africa. They had minimal gear, just an overnight bag each. Francisco's plan was to set up camp in the bush near Kovacic/Kallstrom's base and be available if Brennan needed a quick escape, and he'd brought along a pair of beefy helpers, along with tents and mosquito nets. They loaded everything up. In short order, they were heading west out of town, towards a perfectly paved two-lane road that ran through the centre of the tiny province, cut from the dense jungle that surrounded it and layered in immaculate tarmac that seemed to have never been driven upon.

"Where are we going?" Brennan yelled to Francisco over the road noise.

"Your man's operations base is just south of a place called Massabi Lagoon. It's right out in the jungle in the middle of nowhere. The nearest village doesn't even have a name. They make a living by selling crocodiles caught in the lagoon and the small lakes."

Though the lagoon should have been just a half-hour from the city, the sole road ran a circular path around the Cabinda interior, through thick, dense jungle. Small shanty villages had popped up along the route every ten kilometres or so. Like Luanda, the heat wasn't blistering but the humidity made the air so wet Brennan could taste it.

3.   211

Just five kilometers from the turnoff to a second dirt road – this one just a track slashed out of the foliage by enterprising machete owners – an old colonial-style two-story building stood near the side of the road, nearly overgrown by the jungle and dilapidated, its once-salmon pink paint job almost completely worn off. Francisco nodded towards it. "We set up camp there. At one point in the nineteen thirties, someone thought it might be worth developing up here. Not sure why. The locals don't seem to have any more background on it than that."

They parked the car just off the track and got out. The building was being reclaimed by the jungle, Brennan thought, vines twisting around its porch columns, the thick grass almost up to its side windows. It probably had dry rot throughout. He tried the steps up to the porch slowly, putting weight down one foot at a time to make sure he didn't go through the wood.

It held. "I wouldn't worry so much," Francisco said from behind him. "People have been camping at this place for decades. And anyway, it's probably safer in there with a bit of rotten wood and the insects than it is out here; there are things in this jungle that would happily eat you, my friend, if you strayed out too late at night."

WASHINGTON, D.C.

Lang wondered if he could transfer.

If he beat the cancer, he thought as he followed David Fenton-Wright down the street from the restaurant, he'd put in for a move to a lower pay grade or even a different agency, maybe something in Florida helping out customs and immigration. Lying around the pool was starting to hold a certain allure, and it had everything to do with age.

Who knew, maybe Myrna would agree to go with him. He doubted it, but maybe.

Fenton-Wright had been talking about some nonsense, something about a television show he'd been watching. "… and then he just shoots her. I mean, who sees that coming? And where do they get this stuff?"

"You've got me," Lang said. "TV these days is crap."

"Incorrect, Walter," Fenton-Wright said. "There's some great stuff out there; but it's like sig ints: you have to wade through piles of crap before you get to it. Hmmm…" He pulled his buzzing phone from his pocket. "… I've got to make a stop. You know the old safe house two blocks from here?"

"Chuck Merrill's old apartment?" Lang said. "We still own that?"

"Yeah. It mostly sits vacant except for when someone in senior management needs … private time, if you get my drift."

Lobotomized monkeys could get your drift. "Sure."

"Yeah, well I left my jacket there last night. It'll only take us a second, okay?"

"Not a problem," Lang said. He'd learned that with David, the right answer was whatever David wanted to hear.

The apartment was above a Korean grocery store, a second-floor walkup. They trudged up slowly to its landing. It was the first apartment on the floor, at the very front of the building. Fenton-Wright produced a key and let them in. They walked inside, and Fenton-Wright began scanning the room. The small radio that rested on a window frame overlooking the street was on quietly, Julio Iglesias singing "La Mer," the original French version of "Somewhere Beyond the Sea," to a funkier seventies beat.

"Hmm… must've left that on," Fenton-Wright said. "Where the hell did I put it? I'll check the bedrooms. Do me a favor, look in the kitchen would you?"

Lang nodded and went into the kitchen, to their right. He took two steps in and realized he was stepping on a large sheet of plastic. He looked down at his feet. It covered the kitchen floor completely, doubled over.

Behind him, Fenton-Wright held the silenced pistol to the back of Lang's head. "I need the reporter's location, Walter," he said matter-of-factly. "Although, I'm only asking out of obligation, on behalf of our mutual friend. I know you're a better man than to actually tell me."

Walter knew what the drop sheet meant. It really didn't matter how he answered. Faisal had decided to make good on his threat. Colombia hadn't beaten him, and neither had cancer. But some streaks, Walter figured, were just bound to end eventually.

"Go fuck yourself, you officious little prick," he said.

"If it were up to me… well, let's not even go there. Sorry about this, Walter, really I am," said Fenton-Wright.

"If you knew what I thought of you, you wouldn't be," Walter said.

Walter closed his eyes. The pistol recoiled twice, the silencer reducing the end of his life to two quick decompressions of air, small bangs like firecrackers. The first one made him drop to his knees, and the second ensured that Walter pitched forward onto the plastic sheet.

3.

26/
MARCH 26, 2016, NORTHERN CABINDA

Andraz Kovacic's camp bordered the Massabi Lagoon, a sixty-mile long giant coiled snake that wound its way from fat to thin, from the interior where it resembled nothing less than an enormous lake, to the coast, where its narrow tributary rediscovered the Atlantic Ocean.

At the very edge of the body of water, a dirt road cut back into the jungle, heading east. They followed it in the rented Land Rover. The foliage on both sides of the road was dense, seemingly impenetrable to light. It reminded Brennan of parts of Sri Lanka, the sense that something dark and foreboding lay beyond the wall of leaves, branches and vines, the humidity that much heavier in the moment. The trail ended after about two miles and they came to a wire fence gate supported by two tall, thick wooden posts, the size of tree trunks. "No trespassing" signs were posted on it in four languages.

"Your guy really doesn't like company," Francisco said. "You would think just being located Hell-and-gone from anywhere would be dissuasion enough."

"Now what?" Brennan said.

"Now we ring the bell and wait for instructions." Francisco got out of the vehicle and started pulling the gate open, swinging it wide across the road as Brennan watched. "That was a joke, by the way. There's no electricity out here unless you have generators and your own power lines to transmit the stuff."

The Land Rover rolled on for another kilometre before it reached a checkpoint, where a pair of gunmen in olive soldier fatigues manned a small hut and a red-and-white barricade. One walked over to the Land Rover's driver, finger on the trigger of his AK47. He rattled off something in a language Brennan didn't recognize; Francisco's driver associate answered in kind.

"Bantu," Francisco whispered. "It's the local tribal tongue. Fewer of the residents in Cabinda speak Portuguese; in fact, for most their second language is French."

The pair chatted for a moment and the guard at the gate nodded, then took a few steps away from the car before unhooking the walkie-talkie from his belt and speaking rapid-fire. He nodded a couple of times then repeated the motion to his companion nearby, who lifted the barrier.

A minute later, the red-dirt trail emptied into a large clearing. Two long, corrugated tin bunkhouses were on its right side, perhaps a hundred yards from the banks of the lagoon. Ahead was a large two-story house built out of what looked to Brennan like the remains of shipping containers. Two Jeeps were parked in front, along with another Land Rover and a Range Rover; to the left, a massive garage or metal shop had also been thrown together out of tin. Next to it, a towering winch crane stood waiting to load or unload cargo.

They pulled up and parked next to the Range Rover. Within a minute, a short white guy with close-cropped hair exited the house and headed over to them. "Francisco?" the man asked as the foursome got out of the Land Rover. "You're Benny Goncalves' friend?"

Francisco extended a hand, and the men kissed on both cheeks as they shook. "Anders! Your reputation precedes you." The meet-and-greet was being watched over by a dozen or more armed guards and there was movement around the compound. "It looks almost like you have your own army up here."

Kovacic beamed a smile. "We are quite proud of the place, it's true. But it's not an army; just enough men to stay cautious. Besides, labor is cheap around these parts. My man Antonio tells me you want to buy some hardware?"

Francisco was earning his extra ten thousand, agreeing to use a purchase as cover while Brennan performed recon. "That's right; along with the rifles we need a few more specialized items."

Kovacic slung an arm around the man's shoulder and began walking him towards the house. "Then remote or not, you are most definitely in the right place, my friend. Come, let's go talk in the house. I have AC and cold beer."

Francisco looked at Brennan. "You," he said in French, "stay with the vehicle."

"But boss," Brennan answered in French. "He has AC…"

"Just do your job," Francisco said. "If you get bored, walk the compound a bit." He looked over at Andraz. "You mind if he looks around?"

The arms dealer shrugged. "Out here? Not much to see, but you are welcome." They strolled up towards the house together then went inside.

They'd worked out the little act before getting there; Brennan had a pocket-sized Geiger counter, along with suspicions about what Kovacic had done with Khalidi's missing millions. Given his background before Africa as a Chechen dissident and militant, there was every chance he was either the buyer or the seller of the nuke. The questions were why he was in the middle of the Cabindan jungle, and what he'd done with the weapon.

3.   215

While his guide kept the arms dealer busy, Brennan strolled by each building in turn, slipping the counter out of his pocket whenever out of direct view, to take readings. But the entire place was hot, it seemed, way too many readings from way too many sources for it to be a single device. He wondered if there was something wrong with the Geiger counter. If anything, the readings got stronger the closer he got to the main house. Under a series of suspicious glares, he strolled around the perimeter until he was almost behind it, making sure to stay in sight of Kovacic's nervous men.

Behind the house, the two sides of the perimeter fence converged at a cave mouth, at the very edge of the tree line. It was sizeable, more than just a natural cave, as if an opening had been blasted out. He kneeled for a moment and ran some topsoil through his fingers, then tied his shoelace as a pretence for the guards, before taking a small sample of the soil and pocketing it.

The Geiger counter was getting into high exposure zones. Whatever was in the cave was putting off major readings; Brennan looked at the reading and began to back away nervously.

When he was back to the main yard, he headed for the car. It was another twenty minutes before Francisco emerged from the meeting. He waved backwards towards Kovacic, who was standing in the doorway to the container house and waved back. Francisco, Brennan and their two guards got back into the Land Rover. The driver turned it around and headed back out through the main gate.

"We're going to talk more tomorrow," Francisco asked Brennan. "Did you figure out what you needed to know?"

"Not exactly. There's an old cave of some sort behind the property. The readings out of it were high. Most of the people in that camp are getting significant doses of radiation."

Francisco's eyebrows rose. "I wonder if Kovacic is aware of it, even. He did say the place was built near an aborted mining operation, so maybe…"

"Maybe they weren't mining gold," Brennan said. "You know anything about the local geology? I'm going to do a test reading when we get back to the camp. Either my Geiger counter was way off, or that camp is sitting on some kind of radioactive ore."

2.

The Geiger counter had been an afterthought on Brennan's part, and he'd been lucky Francisco's connections had come through; he'd expected to fly up to Cabinda, question Kovacic and then have a new set of leads to follow. It didn't occur to him that the bomb might be at the compound until just before leaving Luanda – after all, it had been years; whatever Kovacic's connection, it should have come and gone.

And the man still looked familiar; it was eating at Brennan, trying to figure out where he'd seen him before.

While Francisco's men got busy making a fire and cooking supper, Brennan tried to use the satellite phone, first to check in with Walter, from whom he got no answer, and second to try and get a mobile web connection, which he eventually managed. Readings suggested the soil contained Uranium, in significant concentrations. Brennan cursed himself silently for not paying more attention during his primer training.

He walked out of the abandoned old house. Francisco was drinking a beer on the front porch while the two guards cooked the chicken on an open pit out front. He tilted the bottle towards Brennan then nodded at the cooler, but Brennan declined.

"You figure out what you need to know?" Francisco asked.

"Maybe." Brennan checked his watch; it was seven-thirty, and evening was falling. It wasn't like Walter to be away from the phone when he knew someone might be checking in.

It didn't make sense. Why there? Why would an arms dealer force his customers to go out of their way so that he could set up on radioactive soil?

"How long has he been out here?" Brennan asked.

"Not sure. I'd say a year at least."

That meant there were four years unaccounted for between Kovacic disappearing from Khalidi's Nigeria operation to him showing up at the camp as "Anders Kallstrom."

"This was a hell of a long way to go for 'maybe', my friend," said Francisco. "I know you are paying me well, but so far what you've got amounts to background information, the type you could…"

"That's it," Brennan said, interrupting him. "That's the reason: it's a 'forest for the trees' gambit. There's so much background radiation …"

"Eh?" Francisco muttered. "You are losing me, my friend."

"His camp: it's been in the same location the entire time?"

Francisco yelled to one of the guards who answered in rapid-fire pigeon French. "He says the camp has grown quite a lot and moved closer to the access road. It was further in from the lagoon originally."

"And Kovacic? Does anyone know where he came from before this?"

3.

Francisco asked the driver. "He said he was operating out of a warehouse in Porte Noire." The port city in the Congo – the former Zaire – was a few hours north of the lagoon.

That fit, Brennan thought. Kovacic wasn't hiding the nuke in Cabinda; he was looking for it.

"Francisco, you up for a little recon mission tonight?"

"Hey, man, I just brought you out here. I do not get involved in other people's fights. It's bad for business."

"I don't need you to fight; just to drop me off near his base and wait."

WASHINGTON, D.C.

The call came early in the morning, just after seven o'clock, which was why Myrna Verbish knew it was something important. Few people called her anyway, which Myrna preferred. Those who did so knew her well, and knew she didn't get up that early any more.

Alex was already up and Myrna saw her tapping away at a computer keyboard, out of the corner of her eye. The call was short and to the point. "Yes?" she answered.

"Am I speaking with a Ms. Myrna Verbish?"

"You are."

"My name is Det. John Brink, Ms. Verbish, with Metro D.C. Police. Walter Lang had you listed as an emergency contact on his insurance card."

"That's correct." Myrna felt her stomach turn.

"I'm sorry to have to inform you of this ma'am, but Mr. Lang was found dead this morning in his apartment. It appears he was shot during a robbery attempt."

Myrna didn't reply. She was stunned. They'd been friends for so long, and so often coming close to more. They loved each other, she knew. And she hadn't really realized how much that meant to her until twenty seconds earlier, when she found out she'd never see Walter again.

"What happened?" she finally managed.

"It looks as though they jimmied the back window open to his living room. There was a pair of muddy boot prints right under it, although they were too smudged to be of much help. Maybe it'll be a solid lead. Ms. Verbish, we have an excellent service available to people who are feeling the way you do right now, someone you can speak with…"

Myrna didn't need a counsellor. She knew Walter hadn't been robbed, and the meticulous nature of the crime scene suggested professionals. It was agency business that had taken her best friend, the same kind of business that had prompted her to take early retirement, her nerves near shattered. Now, she just felt numb.

"Ma'am?"

She'd zoned out of the moment. "No, that's fine, detective. I'll need to contact his family and friends..."

"He has next of kin?" The detective sounded surprised.

"We worked together for the federal government," she said. "He has an ex-wife and a stepson. They were still close even after they split up." Contacting Audrey would be awkward for Myrna; she hadn't learned until near the end of Walter's marriage that their friendship had contributed to his ex-wife's ill ease.

But it had to be done.

"We can do that for you if you'd like, Ms. Verbish, so that you can have some time..."

"Thank you, detective, that would be nice." She knew she should probably make the call herself, make sure the information was sensitively and correctly conveyed; but Myrna felt disconnected, shattered in the pain of the moment, unable to take on much of anything.

After she'd hung up the phone, she sat down on the sofa, distant still. Eventually, she turned to Malone, who could see abject misery in the wrinkle of Myrna's brow and her pursed lips. "What? What is it?"

"It's Walter."

Malone knew immediately that he was dead. "How?" she said.

"The kind of burglars who leave convenient-but-useless evidence behind," Myrna said.

"You think the ACF..."

"I do," Myrna said. "If the Chinese intel comes back supporting the notion that the ACF funded multiple international incidents, we're both in over our heads, Alex," she explained. "That's why Walter's dead, and it may be why someone is going after the ACF. And whoever is behind this has major pull, with governments, with operatives, maybe even within the agency. These people are fighting to survive their own bad behavior, even as someone else tries to take them out the old-fashioned way."

"I need to write this," Malone said. "The world has to know what's going on; they need to know about Khalidi's African insurrection, and Fung using the task force to take out gangsters in Harbin. I don't doubt if we keep looking into La Pierre and Lord Cumberland, we'll find they sanctioned similar misbehavior."

Myrna had to keep her grounded, she decided. "Alex, we'll get the story, and it'll set the record. But we don't have it yet, not all of it. We still need a whole lot of answers; and whoever did this to Walter? They wouldn't think twice about killing you, hon. They may be the same people trying already."

"So what do we do now?"

"We keep digging," Myrna said. "And we hope Joe is making some kind of progress. Walter's death has to mean something."

Carolyn was having a fine day. A darn fine day, indeed, she decided. First, the director had made an appearance, had mentioned some of her analysis and had given her credit. That was a perfecto trifecta, she'd decided over her second coffee.

Then she'd realized her contract-mandated raise was kicking in that week, a little upside, to keep her mind off of Joe still being gone and the kids missing him terribly; and, to top it all off, her friend had bought her lunch again, the third time in a month. He was gay and non-threatening, and he was good company when she needed to vent and bitch.

Her instant messaging flashed a message from David Fenton-Wright. "Come see me, please, when you have a second."

They'd just met, an hour earlier. She got a nervous sensation, a tightening in her stomach. Maybe it was news about Joe. Maybe it was bad. She shook the idea off, refusing to think negatively. Maybe David had considered her request to transfer out of intelligence and into science and tech. She was convinced she could advance more quickly there, where those ahead of her were younger, less entrenched, more inclined to move into the private sector for a better deal. Her father had been an Air Force pilot, and had great respect for the science and tech division. She liked to think he would've been proud of her for making it to a leadership position on that side of the yard.

She took the elevator to his floor, her hands clasped in front of her nervously. At his office, his secretary told her to go right in. As she approached Fenton-Wright's door, she saw Jonah out of the corner of her eye, peeking around the edge of his office door from behind his desk, doubtless curious.

Carolyn knocked twice then entered.

David Fenton-Wright was behind his desk. "Ah, Carolyn, come in and have a seat if you could, I'll just be a minute."

She'd been around long enough to expect a short wait. Everyone in upper management did it; she wasn't sure if it was a ploy to unnerve or unsettle someone or if it was subconscious, a chance to exercise a little of the power that was so rarely required during the day-to-day.

After he'd finished making his point, he turned away from his computer and leaned on the desk. "Walter Lang died this morning," he said. His delivery was flat, emotionless. He stared at her for an uncomfortably long time, gauging her reaction. Carolyn's mouth had dropped open slightly and she looked shocked.

"How...?"

"Metro Police say a pair of thugs broke into his apartment and shot him when he caught them robbing the place."

"God, no... Joe's going to be crushed."

"Can you contact him?"

"No, he's off the grid. Oh God, David, this is terrible..."

"Yes," Fenton-Wright said. "It's going to be harder for Joe if he finds out far after the fact. I wonder if he's left a contact with anyone else. Maybe that reporter friend of his, Alex Malone?"

She looked genuinely oblivious, Fenton-Wright thought. *Damn. Faisal had been clear about the reporter, about dealing with her.*

"I don't know him," Carolyn said.

Still, Fenton-Wright decided, it couldn't hurt to unsettle her a bit, get her worrying about his friends. "Her. Very attractive *News Now* writer; does great pieces on international policy. I think they met in Europe, or something. That's why I was thinking she might have a contact."

"Oh." An attractive female newspaper reporter he'd met in Europe. "No. No, I don't know her."

She looked a little shocked to Fenton-Wright. Perfect, he thought. "Hmmm... Anyway, we're planning a formal agency service for Walter, likely this Saturday. Can you attend?"

"Yes," she said, her mind overwhelmed by the shock of the moment, of Walter's death, of Joe's female friend. "Yes, of course. I can get my friend Ellen to look after the kids."

"Thank you for coming in then, Carolyn. I do appreciate your time." He rose and extended a hand, her cue to exit.

She walked back to the elevators feeling numb; not because of Walter's death, which had shocked her; and not because of Alex Malone. She was shocked because Carolyn was nobody's fool: she knew right away that David was trying to drive a wedge between her and her husband; that Joe would never cheat on her, let alone risk giving information to a newspaper reporter. And that meant David Fenton-Wright was up to something devious.

That, in turn, meant Joe was in trouble.

3.

27

MARCH 27, 2016 MASSABI LAGOON, CABINDA

Francisco put the Land Rover into neutral and it rolled the last kilometer. He stopped before the last bend, unable to switch off the day running lights but wanting to avoid attention in the still of the evening. It was eleven o'clock, and once the vehicle's engine was quiet, the jungle was silent save for the camp sounds, and the surrounding hiss, chirrup, crack and cry of the jungle insects.

"This is my stop," Brennan said, his face and hands darkened with boot black, smeared in thick lines. "This might get hellish loud when it goes down, but hang tight and we'll be back in no time."

"Sure, sure," Francisco said, relighting the stub of his cigar. "But I still get the extra five thousand, right?"

In the end, it wasn't such a bad deal, Brennan thought as he climbed out of the Land Rover. The handful of small extras Francisco had coughed up was probably worth half the money.

He used the road for the first three-quarters of a kilometer, staying close enough to the edge of the overgrowth that he could duck into it if a vehicle came, but avoiding excessive noise caused by tramping over a kilometer of foliage. Once he was within site of the gates, he moved a few steps into the jungle, out of sight. He had to push forward slowly, moving brush, branches and vines aside, mindful of running into local wildlife. A snake bite would end his evening really quickly, Brennan knew.

His initial foray was a simple recon mission; he'd trace the perimeter of the compound from just inside the tree line looking for entry points, weaknesses and guard movement patterns. His mind flitted back to Colombia, more than three years earlier; he pushed the thought away. During his pass around, he'd set a charge for a distraction; he planned to enter the camp and find Kovacic, blow the charge when needed to divert attention or if cornered, and take the Chechen strongman with him. Francisco had insisted he had a safe route out through the Congo to the North and Porte Noire, if they absolutely needed it.

The jungle was almost impenetrably thick, foliage crashing into itself, branches twisted and knotted together; he got about twenty yards before pushing into a spider web so large it could have swallowed a wild pig. It was tacky like glue and strong as fishing line, ripping leaves away as he stumbled into it; Brennan had to back track a few paces to clean off – including some of the family of basically harmless Tarantulas living in the web. He reached into his kit bag and took out the half-sized machete. It was small for convenient storage but razor-sharp, with a short row of teeth halfway up the blade to rip through branches.

But it was making a lot of noise. Within a hundred yards of the camp, he stopped cutting and went back to methodically pulling the jungle aside, moving a foot every minute. The camp guards and workers had a radio on, playing a typically West African guitar and drum dance song, the ancestral roots of samba, blues and reggae all obviously there. Brennan took out his night-vision goggles and moved to the edge of the tree-line. There was a gate tower, but it appeared empty. The main gate was out of the question anyway, with two guards outside and another directly in. The perimeter of the property was surrounded by good old-fashioned barbed wire, up to about seven feet. It wouldn't prove much challenge. In the center of the yard, near where they'd parked, was a small hut with a front flap. It could have been a machine gun nest … or a bar. But Brennan didn't play odds; he just assessed where potential fire might come from, looked for the best cover to get in and out unseen and unharmed. Extractions weren't about kicking ass or being a superhuman athlete, or being able to hit guys on the run from fifty yards – which doesn't really happen in real life, except by happy accident and massive gunfire. They were about finding and maintaining good cover, avoiding being seen and, if detected, giving the enemy as little to hit as possible until out and away. Given the usually overwhelming numerical advantage to the home team, it just made sense.

The compound was poorly lit, mostly only effective against animal predators, to keep them from bumping into the barbed wire in the dark. The corners were shrouded in shadows, making easy entry points. It was a question of figuring out the angles, judging the guards and their lines of sight as they patrolled, and breaking down access. He looked at the barbed wire fence, then at the container house. The back of the top floor had a section cut away at one end, to make a balcony. It was perhaps twenty yards to cover past the fence, in potential sight of the guards. The question was whether the edge of the balcony was too high to reach. If it was anything over about ten feet, he'd have no chance of grabbing the rail above and pulling himself up.

He stooped and ran to the fence line, then crouched down on one knee to cut through the wire. Brennan entered in the shadows, nearly invisible. The back fence ran right to the cave mouth, while the container home was thirty yards ahead. He waited until the guards were turned and sprinted for the back of the house, flattening against it then checking around the corner to ensure no guards had seen him and were closing. Then he jumped for the edge of the balcony, pulling himself up onto the second level.

A screen door led inside; it was quiet and the lights were out.

The upper level had been opened up, the walls between three connected crates removed and reconfigured, to make three big rooms with a corridor just in front of them, off the balcony. Brennan checked the first and second rooms, but both were shared accommodations, with a pair of single beds, all four sound asleep.

The third room was unlocked, and Brennan swung the door in cautiously. It was more lush, well-furnished with a queen-sized bed. Kovacic was asleep in the bed in one corner. Joe crept over, leaning down to place the silenced Russian pistol against the back of the sleeping figure's head. "Andraz, wake up," he said gently.

"I'm already awake, my inquisitive friend." The voice came from behind him. Someone cocked a pistol.

Brennan raised his hands and stood up. Whoever was in the bed wasn't his target.

"Hands behind your head, please," Kovacic said. "You are in for a long night; this I can guarantee."

MARCH 28, 2016

"Wake up."

Cold water shocked Brennan back to consciousness, and he shook his head quickly to get the water out of his eyes, blinking through the haze.

They'd bound him and cuffed his hands, attached him to a chair. The room was dimly lit, maybe one of the barracks offices. Kovacic was standing ten feet ahead of him, weight on his left hip, one arm crossing his body, tucked under his other as he raised the cigarette to his lips. The interrogator standing next to him was such a cliché that Brennan started to chuckle: bald, hyper muscular, a big scar across his face, wearing a black vest and holding a pair of electrified sponge paddles.

"What's so funny, my friend?" Kovacic asked. "We have been doing this for over an hour. I would think you would have run out of reasons to laugh by now."

"Your guy here," Brennan managed, nodding towards the torturer, his breath heavy from fatigue and pain. "He needs to branch out, try other roles."

The interrogator didn't like that answer. He reached in quickly with both paddles and pressed them to Brennan's ribs, the current stunning his nervous system, a shocking pain that jolted through every bone in his body. The dose ended, and Brennan slumped in the chair again.

"Now that was not very wise, was it?" Kovacic asked.

"There's something I don't understand," Brennan said.

Kovacic looked puzzled. "Now you want to talk all of a sudden?"

"Maybe you weren't asking the right questions. But I've got one."

"Okay."

"Why no plastic surgery? You obviously had work done on the dupe who was blown up in Peru. You are Borz Abubakar, aren't you?"

His look darkened. "I suppose that answers the question of how much you know. I must assume a great deal."

"You blew up a bus full of innocent people..."

"A diversion; a ploy; a way for me to disappear for a while."

"Why the double, the misdirection?" Brennan asked. "And where was the weapon you'd purchased with the money stolen from Khalidi?"

"That was arranged by my compatriots in Europe and Chechnya, who had contacts for reasons of ideology with the Shining Path movement in Peru. The double was being sent on a circuitous route, designed to waste the time of pursuers. There was a meeting of heads of state in a Peruvian border town at the same time, a viable target. And there were...certain parties other than Khalidi who were unhappy with us."

"Certain parties?"

He shrugged and smiled. "Let's just say that not everyone involved in the deal was fairly compensated. It was unfortunate, but unavoidable. The double had been exposed to enriched uranium while staying in a "safe house" and was going to die before anyone uncovered his actual identity. Keep in mind that we compensated his family very well," Abubakar said. "By the time he was discovered, even if he hadn't died yet, the very fact that he was contaminated would convince Khalidi's many intelligence associates that he was really me."

"It worked on some people; the intelligence community thinks you're dead."

"That, in turn, would allow me the time to arrange passage of the device from West Africa to Russia."

3.   225

"Your comrades expected you to set the device off in Moscow, or St. Petersburg…"

He shook his head. "Sochi, on the Black Sea. A matter of geographical convenience. But when the bus blew up, Khalidi was unconvinced; he sent teams out to scour the globe looking for me, had them at every major airport hub. I was stuck in Pointe Noire, unable to travel safely. I had access to money and contacts, but I wasn't willing to go under the knife for plastic surgery in a small African city with poor medical facilities at best. In the meantime, the Shining Path movement took the blame for the passengers' deaths."

"Your fellow socialist freedom fighters must have really loved you for that."

Abubakar took a deep breath. "I was ostracized by the same people who had plotted with me to buy the device and use it against Russia, branded an embarrassing failure."

Brennan considered the cave mouth at the back of the camp. "You set up some side business while you bided your time. But you knew there was a chance that the device might be discovered."

He nodded. "It had been brought up by the original thieves from South Africa, through Namibia and Angola; they took a smuggler's vessel from Soyo, at the mouth of the Congo, to Cabinda, and then from land up to Pointe Noire. But they had limited resources and no contacts who would buy the thing. Within two months, the men responsible were both killed in separate criminal incidents; so it sat in storage for more than a decade with surplus farm equipment, in a corrugated tin warehouse."

Brennan was beginning to get his strength back and he used the delay to work on his bound hands, trying to pry them loose. "You had been arranging weapons purchases for Khalidi's Nigerian insurrections and heard about the bomb."

"It had been uncovered in Pointe Noire by someone who knew what it was and what it could be worth, a Russian arms dealer with wide-ranging contacts. So I had a price, I had access to Khalidi's money."

"And in Chechnya, you had a cause."

"True."

"But now you were stuck in Pointe Noire and no one back home wanted your help. So you hid it in one of the caves by the lagoon to disguise the signature of the fissionable material, but then lost track of which one?"

2.   226

He shook his head. "Nothing that foolish, I assure you. The cave suffered a collapse. They are artificial, entrances to a deeper pit designed in rudimentary fashion to prevent outside exposure to non-miners; they were designed in the nineteen thirties by a French pharmaceutical firm with a concession from the Belgians. The firm thought it had a use for Uranium in certain cancer treatments. The caves are not deep, but once our cave was cut off, it meant finding the easiest point to break through the dirt and rock from the next cave over."

"The one behind that tin shack you call a house."

"Quite accurate."

"Why try to get to it now? Why come back for it at all?"

He shrugged. "Money. First, the camp was an ideal spot to sell weapons to the new Cabindan resistance, fighting the Angolans. They have a steady flow of Euros coming in from certain supporters, and most of that now flows through me. We were not initially aware of the background radiation; it has grown as the tunnels have been opened up. Besides, I spend much of my time in Pointe Noire to avoid this place. Second, I concluded that since my brothers in arms betrayed me, and the world thought me dead, I should sell the device and reap a reward for the exile I've endured; but it took some time to find a buyer.

"And you let the locals you've hired think this place is safe, I suppose. So this is just…"

Abubakar cut him off. "No, we're not going to play that game, American. You wanted to know about the bus victims and I've made it clear that that was an unfortunate incident. We need to get back to the point of this: you telling us who you work for and what they know. I think I know the latter, but I am no longer sure of the former."

Brennan smiled. "My name is Tom Smith. I'm a geologist. I'm just here to collect samples…"

"Oh, bravo," Abubakar said, clapping slowly. "I suppose this all came to the surface because you were investigating Khalidi? Due to the recent murders of his business confederates? Why would that be an American concern? You are American, are you not, Mr. Smith?"

"I have no idea what you're talking about."

Abubakar sighed. "Don't make this more difficult than it needs to be. Hit him again, Mr. Nkube."

The interrogator stepped in and held the sponges to Brennan's side; he convulsed violently as the electric current ran through him. The big African pulled the sponges away and Brennan slumped again, barely conscious.

"People think it's the voltage that's important," Abubakar said. "But as Mr. Nkube would explain, it's actually the amperage, the resistance in the electrical current, which determines the damage. Who do you work for, Mr. Smith?"

3.

"Get… stuffed."

The interrogator didn't need to be told; he stepped in and hammered Brennan with an extended shock, the agent's torso shaking even after the sponges were removed, his muscles contorted from lactic acidosis, spit flying from his mouth.

"Enough, Mr. Nkube, enough!" Abubakar said in French. "Don't kill the man! I need information from him."

Abubakar leaned in. "How did you know we'd extracted the device? That I had a buyer?"

Brennan shook his head. "I didn't, just that it was on the move. You want truth, there's some. You were supposed to be a Slovenian arms dealer working for Kalispell ..."

"If that's true, my timing is impeccably bad, as usual," Abubakar said.

"English is impeccably good…." Brennan said.

"Thank you. I've had years to learn."

"… for a murderous scumbag."

The Chechen's face was red, flustered. "And what of my loss?!?" he yelled, slapping himself on the chest. "My country. My family. My name! I've lost everything! Once I get out of here, even my face."

"You were going to use the device on Russians civilians."

"Spare me your sanctimony!" Abubakar said. "You're an American. Your people have killed millions in wars, insurrections and revolutions around the globe, either directly like Iraq and Vietnam, or indirectly by funding dictators and murderers. You have no moral high ground, Mr. 'Smith'. I suppose your stubbornness with respect to revealing your employer means that it is government, an agency. If you were just a hired hand you would not care enough to dig in and endure this. Maybe the CIA, yes? I don't think it would be Khalidi. Does anyone else know where I am, other than Francisco?"

"You answer a question for me first."

The Chechen eyed him suspiciously. "American, you piss me off, you presume so much."

"Who'd you sell the weapon to? You wouldn't be this frantic to move it right now if you hadn't found a buyer."

Abubakar turned his head, exasperated. "You know, this was not how I wanted to spend today," he told Brennan. "Hit him again, Mr. Nkube.

The big torturer leaned in again, smiling.

2.   228

28

WASHINGTON, D.C.

Myrna leaned forward over the steering wheel and scanned the parking garage again. "Are you sure he'll be here? It's been nearly an hour, hon," she told Malone.

They'd parked at the far end of the second level, on Malone's suggestion, so that Myrna could be nearby and Malone wouldn't be potentially spotted on the street while walking in. It was unlikely her source's newspaper code had been broken, but after Walter's death, Alex wasn't taking any chances.

Instead, they waited for him to arrive. "Just remember: stay out of sight while we meet," Alex said. "I don't want him seeing you, and I have to respect his anonymity, so I don't want you seeing him. We're cool with that, right?"

Myrna gave her a sour look. "Sweetie, I was playing this game long before you were born. I think I know how to…"

"Down!" Alex snapped, as a figure appeared out of the stairwell that led up to the mall above. "I'll be back soon."

She got out of the car and closed the door, slinging her purse over her shoulder in the same motion. She walked towards the man, and they met midway across the darkened parking level, their shadows cast long by the emergency lights overhead.

"I expected to hear from you before now," the source said. "You haven't written an article in a while, either."

"You must have known it would be difficult to confirm the information you gave me," Alex said. "But we're getting there. Don't worry."

"If you need evidence, perhaps you should go back to Miskin. My sources suggest he's nervous; he suspects one of his fellow ACF board members, perhaps even the chairman, may be behind the shootings."

"Why? What…"

"Don't be naïve; there are any numbers of reasons. A power grab; to cover up bad decisions from the past; perhaps what you need to do is ask Miskin."

"When you say 'mistakes from the past', you're talking about Khalidi and Kalispell Properties; am I correct?"

"That's one interpretation. But he's not the only ACF board member who has overreached, Ms. Malone. You should know that much by now."

3.   229

"You mean the Chinese delegate…"

"I mean all of them. Like I said, don't be naïve."

"So you agree with Miskin?"

"I didn't say that. There are plenty of political forces from outside the ACF who could stand to see it exposed, to see it fail. Follow the money, Ms. Malone. Who benefits from Khalidi's group being exposed, or wiped out, or both? Where does this seem to be headed to you?"

He turned around and began to walk away.

"Wait!" she said. "I think the ACF might have had Walter killed. I think they might be trying to kill me."

"I guarantee it," he said as he walked, without turning. "But don't give up, Ms. Malone. The story is too big."

He reached the street door, opened it, and was gone.

MASSABI LAGOON, CABINDA

They'd debated shooting Brennan on the spot but in the end had decided to hold onto him as a potential bargaining chip. He hadn't revealed who he worked for, but it was probably an American agency, Abubakar had suggested, and they might be willing to pay to get him back.

So they'd housed him in a shipping container, not unlike those that made up the walls of Abubakar's house, except that it had just one small window, big enough to let some air in but not enough to do more than reach out an arm.

It was stifling in the crate, well over a hundred degrees, and dehydration had begun to set in, his eyes itching, his head hurting, breath getting shallower. Brennan went over to the window hole again and sucked in some air from outside, then scanned the environment. The guards never walked close enough to the hole to grab at keys or a weapon, so escape seemed out of the question.

If Francisco was planning any kind of rescue attempt, he was taking his sweet time, Brennan thought. Not that he suspected it to be the case; the arms dealer had almost certainly cut his losses and long since left. He wondered how often outsiders visited, whether there would be an opportunity to attract attention. He thought for a moment about Carolyn and the kids, then pushed everything personal out of his mind as unproductive, detrimental to getting the task done.

There were voices near the entrance and he craned his neck trying to see them from an acute angle through the tiny hole. The big double gates swung open and a pair of military style transport trucks slowly entered the compound, followed by a Humvee with a top-mounted machine gunner. The figures getting out of the vehicles were all in army-style fatigues, but not from any of the local militia, as far as Brennan could tell.

At the front of the convoy, one of Abubakar's lieutenants was talking to someone. It looked like… was that a woman? The body shape suggested so. Brennan couldn't see her face, but got a glimpse of aviator shades. She had long black hair under a maroon beret, and she held an M16 copy in her left hand, pointed skyward.

The discussion became animated. The lieutenant was getting angry about something, raising his voice. Brennan could see her other hand resting on the pistol butt at her hip. The lieutenant was gesticulating now, pointing towards the two barracks-style buildings, then at the truck. He took a half-step forward and she drew the pistol and fired, hitting him in the head.

One of her underlings slapped the sides of the trucks and troops began to pour out the back of each. Abubakar's men were roused from sleep, hurrying out of their barracks in a state of half-undress, guns in hand even as they buttoned up shirts and pants. The new arrivals moved methodically among them, a few steps, a volley of three shots, another one put down for good. The camp's residents were so undertrained and unprepared that the soldiers had wiped all but a few out within gunfire-filled minutes.

Brennan watched the slaughter grimly; whoever had cut a deal with Abubakar for the device appeared to have reneged. Either that, or the Angolans had discovered the camp. Neither was a positive prospect.

After a period, the gunfire slowed to a trickle, then stopped. He waited, tense. He had few options; he could hide behind one half of the container doors, hope they opened the other, try to surprise whoever was there. But that was suicide, with a guard full of armed men who actually knew what they were doing.

The decision was made for him. The giant bolts clanged back and both doors swung open simultaneously. There were a half-dozen men facing him, all with guns at the ready. But the woman standing at the front shook her head and pushed down one of their barrels, indicating to the rest that she expected them to stand down.

"Well," she said. "Fancy meeting you here, Mr. Brennan."

"Hello, Dr. Han." The military fatigues and glasses had changed her look considerably, Brennan thought, since his visit with Allan Ballantine to her lab in Brussels. "I wasn't exactly expecting to see you, either."

3.   231

She smiled. "I suppose I might have foreseen this based on your line of questioning. You've certainly forced various parties to amend their schedules, Mr. Brennan. Can I take it that it's a waste of time to ask for whom you really work?"

"You can. Same question, right back at you."

"Same answer." She tilted her head slightly, studying him with a thought to mind. "But the way you approached me in Europe, through Allan... that suggested to me that you're not exactly on official business. Am I right?" He tried to stay stoic, but she must have seen something in his gaze that she liked, Brennan figured. "Yes, I think that's it. You're working off the books, probably looking into whatever that naughty Ahmed Khalidi has been up to."

"That's one theory," he said. "What about you? I can't figure too many research professors keep SIG P226s in their nightstands, or cart them around on expeditions."

"Well..." she thought about it with mock seriousness. "Let's just say that, like you, I got in on loan and leave it at that."

"SIG P226 is standard issue for South Korean National Intelligence Service, isn't it?"

"They must get a nice discount," she said. "I'm sure the SIG Sauer company is happy to have their business."

"Now what?" Brennan said. "You snag the nuke, whisk me out of the danger zone and save the day?"

She smiled again. "Afraid not. Unfortunately, all of the excitement around here tonight is almost certainly going to bring the Angolans down on this place, probably by the morning at the latest. That means we have to get going as soon as the item is loaded. You're a time sink, Mr. Brennan, and one who might get in the way."

She barked a series of commands at the soldiers in mixed French and Portuguese. Brennan got the gist. One of the guards took Brennan's arm and pushed him back into the container, then closed the door behind him. He heard the bolt slide into place.

"You're kidding, right?" he yelled out through the small square window. "Hey... we're supposed to be on the same side!"

But if Han was listening, she didn't let him know.

29/
MARCH 29, 2016, ANNANDALE, VIRGINIA

Carolyn pushed her food around the plate. Their friends Callum and Ellen McLean had invited her over for dinner, picked up from one of several local Korean barbecue places. It wasn't dislike; she just didn't have much appetite after two weeks with no word from Joe.

The kids were with her mother for the night. She'd thought getting out of the house would take her mind off of it, but her friends had wanted to talk politics and that had turned into her thinking about the agency, which in turn was a steady reminder that the father of her children might be in harm's way.

But at least she was with friends who understood. Callum was technically retired from the SEALS, but was consulting and still away occasionally. And when he'd been serving, he was gone constantly. "You can only take it a day at a time," Ellen had told her over short ribs and bulgogi, a thin-sliced barbecued beef dish. "I know you're used to Joe telling you when he'll be back, or expect to be; but try to think about it like he's just delayed. There's no point fretting about worst-case scenarios."

She couldn't tell them why he was gone, or where, and they understood that. Carolyn also had to admit to herself that she'd become more upset after going around to their house; seeing Callum and Ellen enjoying normalcy made her yearn for it. She just wanted him home.

"We've seen him for about six hours in the last two months," she said. "Josh told me yesterday that for a few minutes, he forgot what his father looks like."

Ellen gave her an awkward look but it was obviously something she'd never encountered. "Ouch," she eventually managed. "What did you…"

"I just reminded them that their father loves them, and then we looked at the pictures I took last summer in the Napa Valley."

Callum finished his glass of water and placed his cutlery in the center of his empty plate. "I thought Joe was pretty much frozen out these days. What happened?"

3.

"Agency politics," Carolyn said. She'd had a couple of drinks and knew she shouldn't talk about the agency's business, but had lost some of her inhibition. "You know the cause of all of this was a mission a few years ago now. The guy he was helping on that case was killed a few days ago by a burglar. It all seems so pointless." Then she remembered with whom she was talking. "Sorry, Callum. You know I don't mean…"

"I know, I know," he said. "We miss him too; I have no one to shoot pool with, and when I stay home all day, Ellen and the boy have to put up with me."

"I want him home and I want the agency to accept his resignation," Carolyn said. "I'm just so tired of worrying all the time. Even a desk job…"

"Joe would shoot himself before he'd do that," Callum said. "Me too. You work in the field for long enough, the idea of pushing paper…" He shook his head. "At least he's doing what he loves, Carolyn. You can be sure he knows how to take care of himself, and how to keep himself safe."

APRIL 2, 2016, LUANDA, ANGOLA

Brennan was dreaming, a jumble of images that couldn't be reconciled, time spent in Afghanistan, trapped under fire in a trench; then just as suddenly in his backyard at home and with the kids, Carolyn arguing and laughing at him, the kids pinning him down, only to turn a moment later into an insurgent, leaning over him, blocking out the sun.

The cold water slammed into him, stinging like a nettle, the shock immediately waking him up.

He'd been chained to a wall for the first two days; they'd brought him in on a bus with blacked-out windows, but he'd caught glimpses of the prison through the front windshield, an old colonial-style concrete and plaster building on the Luanda Harbor, adjacent to an ancient Portuguese governor's mansion, still in fine condition despite two hundred years of conflict.

They'd taken his clothes, leaving only his trousers, then thrown him into a cell with a half-dozen local men; he'd managed to get some heavy shots in before they'd overwhelmed him in the tiny cell, the lack of space to operate taking away the advantage of his training; they proceeded to beat the foreigner for most of his first night, raining kicks and punches down on him, leaving Brennan curled up in a fetal position in the corner of the room, one hand above his head for protection, the other over his groin. They'd tired of it shortly before the clock, a block down the street from the prison, chimed for midnight; he'd spent the rest of the night watching the rest of the room, the low light of the moon just barely filtering through the high, barred window.

On day two, the fatigue-wearing guards came for him, picking him up under the armpits and dragging him down the corridor, first to a small medical office where a nurse patched him up and strapped his ribs; then, to a small cell in the next wing of the building, one on the first floor, the harbor seawall just below his window. The cell was filthy; the floor was smeared with dirt, his only companions a small wooden cot, devoid of mattress, blankets or pillows, and a pot in the corner for a toilet. It hadn't been emptied or cleaned in a long time, lying on one side, a small puddle of semi-damp fecal matter gathering around it.

In the afternoon, the tide had risen, and water from the harbor began to slop through the window, splashing the dirt loudly at first. Within an hour, as sunset approached, it was nearly a half foot deep, the small drain in one corner unable to keep up, the water pouring in like a faucet left open. If it kept rising, Brennan knew, he'd be in even more trouble; as it was, the water was dirty, polluted, all manner of debris floating in it. He'd huddled on the cot until it subsided, hours later, the building's overwhelmed sump pump finally drawing most of it out.

Day three had been hot; they finally brought him food, a hunk of the local bread and some plantain bananas, along with a bowl of water. But the conditions in the cell were vile; the heat began to evaporate the remaining harbor water, filling the room with a muggy humidity that topped the already damp local conditions and added in the smell factor. Brennan spent hours breathing through his mouth, trying to ignore the rank odour of dead fish and decay.

They'd come for him at ten o'clock that night; for the walk out of the block and across the courtyard, he'd been grateful. They'd led him into a near-identical four-story colonial building, then down a flight of marble stairs to its basement, where the torturer worked. Brennan wouldn't have labelled it interrogation; the methods were too crude, too designed to induce physical pain over psychological, making the subject likely to say anything he thought the torturer wanted to hear, just to stop the pain.

The subject? After the first hour, he was already thinking about himself in the third person, as if his mind was dealing with the agony as an abstraction, something happening to a different version of him. The man working on him was short, dressed in a simple button-down Oxford-style dress shirt and pants, with no pretence to military rank or social status. But despite his inoffensive appearance, he seemed to take genuine pride and enjoyment from his work, smiling gently at Brennan as if he were a small child, even as the man pulled out his fingernails one at a time.

He hadn't even started asking questions until he was through the first hand, Brennan refusing to scream, gritting his teeth and jerking spasmodically from each painful yank, each arm strapped to the chair, his ankles similarly bound.

"That must hurt," the man said quietly, his English perfect. He tilted his head slightly and studied Brennan's bleeding fingertips with clinical detachment. "What's your name?"

Brennan said nothing. The man smiled gently once more. "Well… that is fine." He reached behind him to the table that contained his tools and picked up a small, clear bottle, then unscrewed its cap. He turned back to Brennan and looked him in the eye as he poured a small amount of the liquid over his captive's raw, fingers. The isopropyl alcohol was excruciating and Brennan shuddered, feeling his stomach and bowels clench.

"I'm sorry, I didn't hear you," the man said. "What's your name?"

"Skip."

"Skip? Skip what?"

"Skip the fucking questions and send me back to my cell."

The interrogator glanced down at his own shoes again, still smiling. "That's not very polite, Mr. Smith. Your papers seem genuine but your visa stamp was a forgery, which leads us to believe you have someone in the American government facilitating your mission here, but that you came urgently. What were you doing in Cabinda?"

"Sightseeing."

The smaller man nodded then paced the room for a moment with his hands behind his back. "We have an impasse of sorts, you see, Mr. Smith: my government is presently on very good terms with your government. Much American money is finding its way into this country for investment. And so I have been informed I'm not allowed to work on you to the degree that I would prefer. A few fingernails will be forgiven. But if I were to, say, pluck out one of your eyes or cut off an ear, there might be diplomatic ramifications."

2.

He walked back to the table and picked up what looked like an old Yellow Pages phone directory. "The pages of the phone directory, however, offer me an alternative. You see, they are so thin and packed so tightly together that, when held against a human body, they make an effective protection from damage. And yet, force transferred into one side of the book via a punch still follows Newton's third law. There is an equal and opposite reaction, and the person on the other side of the book is likely to find it quite excruciating, particularly once their ribs have broken. But the skin on the outside is left unmarked. Clever, no? I believe it was invented by police in your country."

The man held the book against Brennan's ribs with his left hand then hammered a punch into it. Brennan felt it, his ribs bruising slightly. He felt it more the second time; by the third, the interrogator was stepping hard into each punch, and Brennan felt his rib crack, the sting like a gunshot. The interrogator had a wild look on his face, as if delirious from a drug. He hammered Brennan with punch after punch. "Of course," he said, breathing hard, "if you were to die from internal injuries, who could have foreseen such a thing, with you obviously having already been injured at the time of your arrest?"

He switched the book to the right-side ribs and continued hammering Brennan with bodyshot after bodyshot, another rib cracking, Brennan attempting to suppress a groan without much success.

"Is that enough, Mr. Smith?"

"You know…"

"Yes?" the man's voice was full of anticipation."

"If you stood on that phone book, people would think you were taller."

Brennan caught a flicker of genuine annoyance on the man's face before his expression once again reverted to something more serene.

"How are you enjoying our accommodations, Mr. Smith? Is your cell warm and cozy? I understand you have a sea view."

"It'll do," Brennan said.

"You may yet be there for a very long time. There has been some discussion of 'losing' your paperwork. We have had no word yet from your people, so I must assume that you are here "off the record", as they say. Do you know how many people after five years are still in here? Don't bother to answer; I can assure you, no one lasts five years. How are your ribs feeling?"

"Like it's the first day of the rest of my life."

"Good, good. Then you'd enjoy a few more?" He raised the phone book and began hammering Brennan's side with more punches. Another rib cracked, and the agent groaned loudly.

"Now, I suspect that was not a groan of pleasure, Mr. Smith," the smaller man said.

3.

Brennan was panting from the combination of stress, adrenaline and heat, the pain radiating through his side, throbbing like the world's biggest bad tooth.

"Let's begin again," the man said. "What is your name?"

Brennan was too tired to bother trying. "Fuck off," he said.

The interrogator shook his head in disappointment. "Round three, I suppose," he said. "We'll just have to have a convincing story. Let's see: perhaps you were attacked by another inmate when you took his food. Yes, that's a good rationale for losing an eye." He turned back to the table and when he faced Brennan again was holding a scalpel in his right hand. "You said something about sightseeing, Mr. Smith. Perhaps…" he leaned in close, the blade less than an inch from Brennan's eyeball, "… we can cure you of your inquisitive nature."

He used his other hand to push Brennan's head back, two fingers pulling back one of the agent's eyelids. He leaned in, his breath hot and rank, "Don't worry: soon you'll have a whole new lack of perspective on things." The blade crept forward until it was almost touching Brennan's eye.

The door to the room swung open; the interrogator took a step back. The man who entered the room was in full military dress, a colonel's bars on his shoulder. "Leave us," he said to the interrogator.

The diminutive psychopath looked disappointed and glanced once angrily at Brennan before listening to his superior and leaving the room. A male nurse was standing behind the colonel in the doorway, anxiously awaiting instruction.

"Clean him up," the colonel said.

The nurse set about binding Brennan's finger tips in gauze, alcohol-soaked cotton and bandages.

"My apologies, Mr. Smith," the colonel said. "It appears word of your captivity has somehow leaked to your fellow countrymen. Or that may be the case; I'm not certain what I'm allowed to say in this regard. However, I must apologize for my comrade's… overzealous methods of questioning."

"He broke my ribs."

"Unfortunate, as I've said. However, you are a foreign national operating illegally in our country. I must ask you to tell me who you work for and perhaps, once we have established your purpose, we can discuss the interest from your embassy in finding out whom the American is that we're holding."

"The last guy was more convincing," Brennan said. "He had that creepy movie villain vibe…"

"This is not a joking matter, Mr. Smith. If we so choose, you could be shot for espionage…"

"But you're worried that would scare of some of those Yankee dollars, right? So why should I tell you a thing?"

The colonel's face took on a stony contempt. "Perhaps another dozen hours hanging from the wall of a cell might change your mind," the military man said, walking back towards the door. "Guards, bring our guest with us. We're going back to the detention wing."

APRIL 8, 2016, LUANDA, ANGOLA

Brennan had begun to lose track of the time of day. The Angolans seemed to come and go, no one person always in charge of keeping an eye on him. They'd leave him chained up for five, six hours at a time, then let him down for one, then put him back up on the wall. Every so often, they'd wake him up with a bucket of cold water.

They didn't seem in any great hurry to make him talk; given that the rats in his cell were the size of Chihuahuas, perhaps they figured eventually his own anxiety would eat at him, and he'd say something just to be free.

Instead, he used the vermin to occupy his mind, trying to identify which rat was specifically which, and then naming them. He'd learned it as a way to pass the time from a Soviet dissident trapped in a Polish church basement for sanctuary, around the reunification in Europe. Of course, the poor Russian had been there for months and his affinity to rodents had extended to predicting which would follow him into battle, so it was possible he'd gone just a little crazy.

But it was working for Brennan – that, and the belief that once he managed to get out of there, he might be able to track Dr. Han down and thank her in person for leaving him behind in Cabinda.

The latch to his cell clicked open and the door swung wide. The same short, mustachioed colonel in dress uniform who had visited him for two weeks entered, flanked by a soldier with a machine gun. "Good Morning, Mr. Smith!" he said cheerfully in English. "And how are you feeling today?"

"I'm chained to a wall. How do you think I'm feeling?"

"More requests for your embassy for information. They're getting quite testy," the colonel said. He strode over and stood next to Brennan. "There is an easy solution to your dilemma, Mr. Smith," he said more quietly. "Simply tell us why you were at the rebel camp in Cabinda and we will let you go home."

"You were probably a colonel pretty young, eh?" Brennan said.

"Why, yes," the colonel said, smiling brightly. "How did you know?"

"Guy your size and weight is likely to have what we call 'short man syndrome', a need to overachieve."

The colonel wasn't easily shaken. He smiled, tongue between his teeth and eyes averted as he held his patience. "If we hang you from the wall for much longer, Mr. Smith, your arms are going to start stretching... instead of just your nose."

"I told you, I'm just a geologist. I was tipped that there might be an unclaimed Uranium property around Massabi Lagoon."

"Your visa to enter the country has shown to be a forgery, Mr. Smith. You have no company affiliation and your torso is covered in such an impressive array of scars and old wounds that I have trouble believing you are merely interested in radioactive rocks."

"Believe what you want."

"Explain the camp to me. Explain a dozen dead Cabindans, and an as-yet unidentified European. You're a spy, Mr. Smith."

"We've been over this... too many times." The strain of standing constantly and having his arms suspended was only half the reason for his fatigue; his ribs had yet to heal and he winced every time he moved. "They were alive when I got there. They locked me in the shipping container. A bunch of other soldiers showed up and killed them."

"And left you alive."

"And left me alive."

"How fortunate for you."

Brennan tilted his head and looked around the squalid cell. "Evidently." The truth was, he didn't know why Han had been involved or why she'd left him as a witness.

"So what are we to do with you? We could simply execute you as a clear and present danger to the national security of Angola, but we both know that would be ironic, given our existing social conditions, and quite untrue."

"Yep."

"Or we could leave you here. But in short order, that would have diplomatic ramifications also."

"I'm guessing."

The colonel's sneer was sardonic. He leaned in closely. "Were it up to me, Mr. Smith, we would work on you until you either talked, or died. Fortunately for you, my country's greatly improved relationship with America is essential to business, and I do not wish to receive, how do you say, the 'heat' from people above me."

Brennan looked him over from toes to head. "What are you, five-three? I'd say almost everyone's heat is above you."

The colonel turned away for a brief moment then wheeled around quickly, slamming a balled up fist into Brennan's stomach. Brennan grunted; he'd reflexively stiffened his stomach muscles before the blow and a fist-shaped bruise was spreading across them.

"I may not get the pleasure of having my man working the information out of you, Mr. Smith. But you are here for at least another day. It can be as unpleasant as you wish to make it."

He turned on his heel and headed for the door, followed by the soldier. Then he faced Brennan again. "An embassy official will be here to see you tomorrow," he said. "My advice would be to do whatever this person says in order to leave Angola. The next time you and I meet, I will not be so cordial."

The diminutive officer turned to leave. "Hey!" Brennan said. "Aren't you at least going to let me down?"

"You seemed uninclined to help me, Mr. Smith, and so I am uninclined to help you. But rest assured, they will have you cleaned up tomorrow before your government stops by."

True to his word, Brennan spent the rest of the night standing, sleeping by leaning against the wall when he could. The next morning, a pair of guards came for him a few hours after sunrise. They made him strip out of his filthy trousers and hosed him down in a shower room, tossing him a bar of soap halfway through. They watched him as he shaved away the two weeks of facial hair; and then they gave him back his clothing, washed and pressed.

He wondered how he'd handle the meeting with the embassy official without blowing his cover. He couldn't claim agency affiliation, but he needed some way to let the person know he needed extraction.

The problem solved itself when the man showed up, shortly after lunch. They moved Brennan to a meeting area adjacent to his cell block, a single table behind bulletproof glass, which was perforated with air holes, allowing just enough sound through for them to talk.

The official was tall, over six feet, and wearing a grey suit; he had dark grey hair and a pair of steel-rimmed glasses. And Brennan recognized him immediately. "Bill Weeks? Weeksy?"

Weeks gave him a small wave through the glass. "Good to see you too," he said loudly. "Have they charged you with anything?"

Weeks and Brennan had gone through agency training together. "No. What the hell are you doing here?"

"Consular attaché." Weeks could hardly keep a straight face when he said it. It basically meant he was the agency's point man in Angola.

"I haven't talked to you in... how long has it been?"

"About five years. When they showed me the mugshot of "Tom Smith" I almost did a spit take with my coffee. Look, if they haven't charged you, I think I can get you sprung by later today. Officially, we don't get involved in the local justice system, but unofficially these guys want us around these days. This country's a damn sight more corporate than it used to be."

"From Bolsheviks to boardrooms."

"Pretty much," Weeks said. "How're they treating you?"

"Tough. Rough joint, but not the worst I've ever been in. I feel like shit, buddy. I need to be gone."

"Well, just hang tight. Look…"

"What?" The tone suggested bad news is coming.

"Well, we've had a discussion with the guys upstairs already, and they want you out too. But DFW wants your balls in a sling; he said you were supposed to be in the EU working the sniper case. He's going to hold this against you…"

"Damn it."

"That's not all. There's some bad news, too. I've got to assume you didn't hear about Walter Lang."

Brennan felt anxiety, fear. He'd known something was wrong in the camp, when he'd been unable to reach his friend. "What? What about Walter?"

"There's no easy way to tell you this, but he's dead, Joe."

"How?"

"Double-tap. Professional job, though the official line is they were burglars."

Brennan hung his head. "Goddamn it."

"I know he was your mentor…"

"A good friend, too."

"Yeah… well, look, I'll be back to see you in the morning, okay? I'm going to make a couple of calls, but we'll get you out of here and on your way."

"I need to get home, find out what happened," Brennan said. He'd been looking forward to seeing his wife and kids more than anything. Now he had to find out about Walter.

But Weeks shook his head. "Sorry, Joe. DFW says you're going back to Europe. They've still got this shooter at the top of their minds. Miskin has a series of speeches planned during the next two months at various European locations, designed to answer questions that are being raised about his involvement with Ahmed Khalidi. It's going to put him so far out there publicly that if your guy is still active, he'll be sorely tempted to take a shot."

"Has anyone shared this with Miskin?"

"He knows the risks, although he hasn't seen our intelligence."

2.   242

"Let's not use that term too charitably," Brennan said. "And there are bigger things here that might be at play, despite what Fenton-Wright thinks."

"Yeah, DFW indicated you had a theory. He wasn't too receptive."

"Shocker. Let's hope his lack of interest doesn't kill a whole lot of people; it's not a theory anymore."

"What are we talking about here?" the field agent asked. "Or do I want to know?"

Brennan knew the limitations of having solid intel that he couldn't back up with evidence. "Not now, not yet. But maybe soon."

Weeks got up and gave Brennan thumbs up. "Hang tight, bud," he said loudly. "Before you know it, you'll be on a flight out of here. That's a start."

APRIL 23, 2016, WASHINGTON, D.C.

The President liked to stand while speaking to visitors in the Oval Office. It was probably, on some level, unbecoming of a chief executive to pace by the great windows overlooking the Rose Garden. He knew his predecessors had showed typical executive mettle by seating visitors across from them and passing on sage wisdom from on high, from behind the safety of the Resolute Desk. But he liked to stand and pace while he thought, and on those occasions when things were less officious and more cordial, to sit across from them on the plush guest sofas.

So while his potential successor sat looking uncomfortable, ahead of his desk, the President was by the windows, pacing in small circles. In the other chair, Nicholas Wilkie glanced at Younger occasionally, feeling as uncomfortable as Younger looked. He didn't like this, the mixing of agency business with presidential politics.

"Thank you for flying in to meet with us, John" he said. "I know you need to be out there campaigning, so I do appreciate it."

"Thank you, sir."

"You also know I'm a man who has a great deal of patience when it comes to getting my way. I've dealt with nothing but obstruction since getting into office, but I haven't swayed from the things I believe will keep this country great."

"Yes, Mr. President," Younger said. His shirt collar felt tight and it was warm in the Oval Office. He just wanted to make a good impression.

"Gentlemen, I wanted this Fawkes thing dealt with before Florida and the primary, so that I can begin working for John's candidacy publicly and in earnest without worrying about a major diplomatic bomb dropping," the President said. "But now we're into the full campaign swing and it's still out there."

"I realize that Mr. President, and I know you must disappointed," Wilkie said. "We're still working on it; but we have to consider the possibility that, with no more ACF board members targeted, this may blow over before Fawkes' cover is blown."

"Disappointed? That's hardly the issue. It's just a reality that my administration will look terrible if Fawkes' identity is revealed. And that means, by extension, that Senator Younger's campaign will suffer. That in turn hurts the American people."

"I understand that, Mr. President," Wilkie said.

"I want to see some real progress on this. I want you to talk to both agencies, see if we can't put a push on this."

"Yes, Mr. President. We'll redouble our efforts. There is one area of concern…"

"There are a lot more than one, Nicholas, but go ahead…"

"NSA is continuing to exhibit friction at working with the clandestine boys at Langley. There's a real fear of a leak in the agency because of the recent press attention."

"You think someone at Langley is trying to scuttle this thing?"

"I think someone's passing out information they shouldn't, yes. But I feel confident we can get ahead of it," Wilkie said. "I've got one of my best guys on it."

"Anyone I know?" the president asked.

"Yes, my deputy director, David Fenton-Wright. Perfect man for the job."

APRIL 29, 2016, PHOENIX, ARIZONA

The crowd was a chanting throng, an arena full of proud Republicans certain they were just nine months away from ending eight years in the political wilderness. Their faces were full of hope, and happiness, and a sense of security that they were about to be led back to glory by Addison March.

At the podium, he used both hands to motion for quiet, and the keeners near the front of the audience shushed everyone else. "Thank you," March said as it quieted, "Thank you. Thank you." He pointed to some supporters near the front randomly, as if singling out favorites. A group of about a dozen delegates all assumed he was pointing at them.

2.

They'd been using the applause breaks in his lengthy speech to chant "March! March! March to Washington! March! March! March to Washington!"

He motioned with his hands yet again for quiet and the throng's volume slowly dissipated. "My fellow Americans, I am humbled by the support I've seen and heard today," March said. "I am humbled by it ... and yet I am troubled also." He looked down slightly, showing the gravitas of true concern. "I am troubled that we have come to a point in the history of the greatest nation on the planet in which our values, our efforts and those of our forefathers are being constantly questioned.

"I am troubled that we live in an age where people who achieve and strive for better are cast as villains. I'm troubled that, in our America, it has become acceptable to demand – not ask for, but demand – charity from people who've worked hard to earn their living, whether that demand comes from government in the form of overtaxation, or from the Liberal left and their ongoing desire to turn our national work ethic into an easy ride. I'm troubled – but I'm not going to stand by and let it happen."

The crowd stood and roared in unison, a sheet of a hundred-and-twenty-decibel white noise. March stood smiling, nodding sagely. After a minute, he raised his hands again for more quiet.

"This country was built on the backs of the men and women who sculpted our greatness from the mud, dust and clay of the west, men and women who understood the danger of a handout, of training people to be dependent. They kept us safe from the scourge of communism – the ultimate lefty system – for five decades. They provided the nation's workers with jobs, homes and futures. They built the working capital that runs our economy and made it possible for any American, whether it's a mom running a home business while she takes care of the kids or a college student who has paid his way through school with a second and third job, to achieve greatness and pursue their dreams.

"And that's the America that I love and want to protect. That's our America. The question we are being asked in this election is whether we are ready to take it back."

The ovation was thunderous again, delegates letting March know they were. "March! March! March to Washington!" they chanted, a thousand people seemingly bouncing in place from elation.

Christopher Enright hit pause on the recording. They were watching his speech for the second time, just before midnight, in March's palatial hotel suite in Scottsdale.

3. 245

"We had a great night, senator. We straw-polled the media bus after you were finished and even the hardcore Dem outlets thought it was electric. I mean, even the guy from the *Post* was saying he had to give it to you: you were brilliant."

March would never have told his assistant but he'd dreamed of the primaries for years; dreams of grandeur and achievement and a broad social acceptance of his ideas and positions, of public demand for his leadership. "It went well," he simply said instead. "It went very well. But onward and upward, my boy. We've got Nevada in ten days."

Enright hadn't expected March's charisma and presence to be so effective at closing the gap on his competitor, John Younger. But that was exactly what the polls seemed to suggest was happening. The latest had the Republican just three points behind his opponent despite starting the campaign with a weight around his neck caused by a handful of party scandals. None had involved him, but they did involve public money and trust, and that kind of issue could undo a lot of hard political maneuvering.

Now, they were looking at double digit defeat in the rearview mirror and the real potential that the GOP candidate could score an upset.

There was a knock on the connecting door to the next room. A second later, it opened, and communications director Neal Foreman walked in. "Senator, Chris," he said.

"You're up late," March said. "We've got Tucson in the morning, and that's hostile territory these days."

"I know; my apologies. But I got hold of a first edition of tomorrow morning's *New York Times*."

"What's the gist?" March said, assuming he was talking about the primary.

"They loved the speech. But it got about three inches of space at the bottom of a story about your overseas investments."

March's head slumped for a split second, just long enough for him to be conscious of showing weakness in front of the troops. Younger and various opponents had used his former law firm's connections as fodder. Now what? "Okay, what?" He said.

"The central thesis is that you own shares in a company call TeleFonity, which is selling Voice over Internet Protocol, or VOIP software, to countries and companies in the Middle East. One of those companies is an oilfield tech services firm from Saudi named BID Ltd., or Baghribi Injection Drilling. It's already controversial for natural gas fracking and oil recovery techniques that use a lot of water in a region that sorely needs it."

"Neal, I'm tired. Can we get to the punchline, please?"

"Yes sir," Foreman said. "Well, it seems one of the principals in BID is a gentleman named Moukhtar Al-Maghrebi. Unfortunately, he's on the State Department's watch list for supplying financing and arms to Islamic militants in Libya and Algeria."

If March was shaken, his face barely betrayed a hint of it. "How involved is this guy in the company in which I'm vested?"

Neal shook his head. "It really doesn't matter, Senator. There's no win on this one. What we need you to do is divest yourself of any of that stock tomorrow morning at first light, and then we'll hold off the press for an extra hour. You can point out that the Times story is "no longer accurate" and that you in fact "had already" sold that stock in BID. If they ask you for harder timelines and pursue it, point out that this was just part of a larger investment portfolio being managed for you by an outside firm and remind them again that once you knew about the tie, you immediately sold the stock. Again, don't get into timelines, just take a couple of questions from local TV reporters for the softball nature, avoid the print guys, and move on."

"So we're going to duck and cover?" March hated trying to avoid questions and innuendo; he believed his politics and policy direction were open books, and that meant he could be as direct and strident as he liked.

"Just for a couple of days. On Saturday, Younger is attending the wedding of one of his fellow congregation members back in Germantown. What he's apparently unaware of is that back in his college days, this congregation friend – and heavy donor – ran a Campus political group called "Christ Loves Fags", with which he and supporters rallied against homosexuality and demanded people "love the sinner but hate the sin" by harassing people outside a notorious gay bar in Provo."

March smiled broadly. "So he's going to get eviscerated by his own base for saying something many of our voters would wholeheartedly agree with. There's a certain tasty irony in that, Neal."

"Like I said, senator, don't worry about tomorrow. We'll handle that, and in a few days, Younger will have made the problem disappear all by his lonesome."

3.   247

30

MAY 11, 2016, PARIS, FRANCE

Funomora was on thin ice, and he knew it. His position faced reconfirmation in less than a year; Khalidi's ground rules were made clear when he'd established and funded the ACF, a decade before.

The veteran Japanese diplomat wasn't entirely sure what he wanted; in Japan, his political currency had badly faded, leaving the committee as his one remaining keycard into the corridors of power. To rebuild his connections at home would mean spending less time in Europe; spending less time in Europe would be seen by the Jordanian as a lack of commitment to their mutual enrichment. It seemed a no-win situation, one his rivals – Fung chief among them – would doubtless attribute to his own poor decisions.

The ACF wasn't exactly a smooth ride in and of itself; decisions had unleashed the odd powder keg, from regional insurrections to civil disobedience and assassinations; things had seemed out of control for several years, and the economic consequences – often benefitting the board members to extremely generous ends – were going to eventually be brought to light. And then they would all be done for, politically, socially and economically.

Three positions remained unfilled and would remain so until the sniper was caught, the chairman had already decided. If Funomora walked away, he would be seen publicly as a coward. If he didn't, he would be embroiled in perhaps career-ending scandal. If he walked away, he would sink anonymously back into the ranks of corporate Japan. If he didn't, the notoriety that came with the position might both ruin his reputation and place him next in the sniper's sights.

And so he attended the ACF's emergency session unsure of where he stood, yet tasked with the responsibility of keeping the remaining three delegates – all of whom he had come to despise – safe for another month.

Miskin, who had been feuding with the chairman for two years, had just completed his third public engagement in as many months. There had been no hint of an incident and security had been drum tight. But Funomora could not help escape the feeling that pinning the three previous deaths on Tillo Bustamante was just too easy an answer, and that the threat was still out there. Not one of the board members really believed Wilhelm's death to be an accident.

We are all so very dirty, he thought. *We are all victims of our own selfishness.*

Khalidi cleared his throat. "Perhaps Japan can enlighten us with respect to preparations for Russia's speech later this month in Moscow."

"Of course, chairman," Funomora said. "As requested, we have liaised with the Moscow policy wonks and military intelligence. They're extremely confident that the decision to move it indoors to the auditorium will afford much stronger security and screening capabilities. They'll have the place locked down."

"They had better," Miskin said. "We have political support and relations riding on this. The reaction to the lecture series and discussion papers on the ACF has been overwhelmingly positive, and there seems to no longer be discussion among global intelligence sources about prolonged investigations."

Funomora tried to seem gracious in pointing out the obvious: "Of course, I'm sure none of us has overlooked the fact that since Tillo Bustamante's death, there have been no more shootings." He wanted to hear what they really thought, but doubted that would happen.

Fung had been quiet throughout but raised his voice. "So you think Wilhelm's death was the accident it appeared to be?"

"Officially so, vice-chairman," the Japanese delegate said. "Beyond that..."

"What about the reporter?" Khalidi asked from the chair. "Why have we not managed to deal with her?"

"She seems to have gone to ground professionally," Funomora said. "I believe she is receiving help from people in the intelligence community. Still, she has not published anything in nearly two months, and her visit to Russia's house was the last time she has been seen since our agent's death in Washington."

"Your agent," Fung corrected. "He was former Japanese secret service, was he not?"

"He was."

Fung harrumphed. "Hmmm.... I suppose we should not be surprised then that he failed. Have any of our intelligence assets offered any direction?"

"They are still hunting for her, vice-chairman," Funomora said. "But I have no doubt that they will eventually get the job done."

"Let us hope so," Khalidi said. "Your recent track record of failure does not engender confidence."

MAY 12, 2016, WASHINGTON, D.C.

3.

The phone rang at three o'clock in the morning, which for most people would probably have been an invitation to ignore it, let the machine take it, and go back to bed.

But Myrna had been waiting to hear from Brennan for more than a month. They'd made progress; that hadn't prevented Alex's frustration at being practically confined to Myrna's tiny apartment; and Myrna's online sources were giving her the impression the agency was losing interest in the sniper case, more firmly convinced the shooter had been operating under the orders of the late Tillo Bustamante.

"Hi," Brennan said.

"Where the hell have you been?" Myrna hissed. Alex was still asleep and she knew Brennan wouldn't want to stay on the line long enough to talk to both of them. Plus, if anyone was listening in, keeping her clear of details also meant keeping her safe. "We've been worried as hell."

"I got held up. Long story."

"Can you talk location?"

"No. Don't know who has ears over there. We have to keep this simple."

Myrna told him they'd been hard at work via online contacts and research. "Our group's pedigree is somewhat as advertised. And the deal for the item you've been inquiring about was brokered by a long-time competitor of another Russian friend you recently visited, initials DK."

Dmitri Konyshenko, a well-known Russian arms dealer. She'd avoided saying the name; public monitoring by the agency and NSA via co-operative telecom companies could be automatically triggered by certain keywords.

Knowing who brokered the nuke deal gave Brennan leverage to approach Miskin and bluff him, let him know the Khalidi's money was involved, that the rest of the ACF would be tarred by association and he'd be helping a rival.

"What happened to our other friend?"

He was asking about Walter. Myrna hadn't thought about her old friend in several days as her mind adjusted to the idea of living without him. "I expect we'll never know. It's entirely possible the same folks you ran into earlier were looking for him, as well. I haven't heard from the local boys in a while; I'm not sure they consider it a priority anymore."

"Well... I can't say I'm surprised." Myrna could hear the disappointment in Joe's voice. "I'm going to check in with the right people and see what they want me to do in the morning, but I'll be recommending our Russian friend for the obvious reasons."

"Keep your head down."

"I will; in the meantime, the two of you can work on tying down any more links between the group we've discussed in the past and other actions outside its mandate."

They'd managed to get everything they needed into the conversation without revealing much. Without an encrypted line, it was the best they could do, although Myrna knew there was probably nothing Joe wanted more than to have a real conversation. "You take care, okay?" she said, which was about the most she could offer.

"Yeah. Let the other half know I'm good, will you?"

"Sure."

"I'll be in touch," he said, before hanging up.

"Where the hell are you?"

David Fenton-Wright was less forgiving regarding Brennan's troubles. His private line had rung and Brennan had said "deputy director?", and DFW had bitten his head off.

"I told you to stay in Europe and the next thing I'm hearing, our embassy man in Angola is bailing you out. Angola?!? What the hell are you doing?"

For a brief moment, Brennan wished he could punch the man through an encrypted phone line. "I'm heading for Moscow. Miskin is giving a public address in a couple of days, a distinguished alumni speech at the university. He'll be a potential target and besides, I need to talk to him about a few things. I thought that was what you wanted."

"Why were you in Angola?"

"A lead, that's all," Brennan lied. If David knew he'd been pursuing Bustamante's nuclear angle, he'd have gone ballistic himself. "Nothing major."

"You were out of touch for six weeks."

"I didn't say it was an easy nothing."

"And If I didn't know better," Fenton-Wright said, "if I didn't know how aware you are of the consequences of crossing me, I'd almost think you were lying to me so you could chase after a phantom bomb."

"David, would I…"

"Don't even pretend you respect my authority, Brennan," Fenton-Wright said, more than a hint of bitterness in his voice. "You field agents are all the same, more testosterone than intelligence, and no appreciation for the hard work that goes into running this agency."

When something is threatening the very future of mankind, that's what you want to hear from your boss, Brennan thought: *a rant about how the world is out to get him.*

MAY 18, 2016, MOSCOW, RUSSIA

The early morning red-eye from Heathrow bounced once as it touched down at Domodedovo International Airport, making a few people nervous in the two-thirds full passenger cabin.

It taxied to a gate and the tired masses piled out, Brennan joining the other business travelers as they tromped down a long corridor with glass walls that gave them a view of the runway, until they reached the terminal, its broad expanses of booths, seating areas and monitors already busy at eight o'clock in the morning. The Russian airport had been refurbished since his last visit, gleaming masses of glass and steel replacing 1960s concrete bunker-style Cold War pragmatism, favored for so many decades.

Security was tight and he was patted down several times, as well as having his bags searched, a hedge against terrorism after a suicide bomb attack a few years earlier. Inside, the airport itself looked like a hundred others from the west, with no hint of its austere earlier nature, the years spent as a concrete monument to the proletariat, most of who weren't really allowed to use it. There were coffee booths, and a McDonald's, and a Starbucks with oversized muffins, and something that looked like Sunglass Hut, but in Russian.

Once through the sliding glass doors, he hailed a cab and asked the driver to take him to the Hotel Baltschug Kempinski, where he had a room reserved for Peter Taylor, a clothing company representative trying to find new markets for his company's products. He immediately regretted the choice of transportation when the cabbie informed him, politely, that traffic was so bad it would take nearly two hours to cover the forty kilometers to the hotel, and that he'd have been better off taking the train.

It was a drab and unenviable drive up until they reached their destination. The hotel was a classic building, eight stories of white plaster and a corner tower that reached above the grey slate roof, stretching into the Moscow sky like half of a child's toy rocket, its perspective idyllically trained upon the Kremlin and other iconic structures.

His room was luxurious, a far cry above most in which he'd stayed, with bright tones and light-colored wood furniture, a sitting room with a fashionably striped tan-and-green sofa set. In Russia, he was less likely to attract attention if he hung out with some of the business heavy hitters who used the Hotel Baltschug regularly, among a trio of hotels that had become hubs of the international corporate world, even at an exorbitant seven hundred dollars a night. It was also only ten minutes from the university, where Miskin would address students the following day on the need for government austerity in increasingly competitive marketplaces.

It was all a bit of a joke really, Brennan thought. He'd read Miskin's file; he was no entrepreneur, just another robber baron with the right number of soldiers and firepower at the time that the Soviet Union fell to make himself one of the top dogs. After establishing a vast petrochemical empire from communist assets bought at pennies on the dollar, he'd become ambassador to the U.S. for a decade, before fading into private life; he'd joined several large company boards, taken an official title as a cultural attaché, and spent his time looking utterly unlike the good party member he'd once been.

Brennan called down to room service for a twenty-dollar burger, before unscrewing the back of the phone and its cradle, checking inside both for listening devices. Then he went through the room one item at a time, methodically looking for more bugs. It wasn't that he necessarily expected to find them; back in the Soviet days, the unit would have been rife with fiber optic imaging and good old fashioned audio pickups. These days, Russia was supposed to be more open and respectful of its visitors. But Brennan knew their intelligence guys were just as well trained, just as good as they'd ever been. There was a chance his passport had been made as a forgery at the airport; but in Russia, that didn't mean they'd automatically arrest him. They'd be interested, instead, to find out why he was there. And if they had identified him, the room would be tapped.

He swept the room twice, checking for loose furniture buttons, under the edges of furniture, under the desk and table tops, inside the lamps and the overhead fixture. But he found nothing. That didn't mean there was nothing there, just potentially that whoever hid it did a good job. It was largely irrelevant, as he had no plans to discuss anything sensitive out loud. He didn't do that in America, and he wasn't going to start in Moscow.

The phone rang.

"Good, you're there." It was Fenton-Wright.

"As advertised."

"Yes… well, I'm calling you off. Head back to D.C."

3.   253

"What? Why? I'm already here. I just got here. What harm can there be in…"

"We'll discuss this later. Right now, I'm of the opinion that you're wasting time and resources with Miskin. There have been a dozen other opportunities in recent months for someone to take him out if they so wished, and yet nothing."

"But today is the first time he's spoken on his home turf," Brennan argued. "I thought we'd agreed these were statement killings. It's the first opportunity…"

"Look, this isn't a debate or a discussion," Fenton-Wright said. "Come home." The ACF was convinced Bustamante had been behind the attacks. The last thing Fenton-Wright needed was someone pestering Miskin on his own turf, where he had domestic political considerations to take into account. The ACF members expected him to keep that kind of heat off of their backs. "That's an order. Get out of there, now."

Click.

Brennan stared at the phone. When David hung up on someone, it meant the conversation wasn't just over, but that it was never supposed to be a discussion to begin with. Any chance Brennan had of extricating himself from the agency's blacklist would go right out of the window if he disobeyed.

He walked over to the window and looked out. He could see the university, across the adjacent river. Miskin was slated to speak in just over an hour. Brennan wasn't as worried about the sniper – who seemed to have gone to ground for months – as he was about the intended use of the South African nuclear device. And if an associate of Miskin's had brokered that deal, Brennan needed to talk to him, regardless of what David said.

Ignoring Fenton-Wright was becoming a bit of a hobby.

The auditorium was in an uncharacteristically new building, a brownstone-and-glass addition to the university's aging character. The property was littered with police and security when the asset arrived; he covered the short distance from the train station on foot, guitar case in hand, non-descript once again in dark jeans, casual dress shoes and a blue winter coat. He took the broad stone stairs up to the main doors, passing among the heavy campus foot traffic, students and professors and visitors alike. Then he stopped before entering and surveyed the area.

The asset knew where he would set up. The original speech location, outside the students' services building, had clearer lines of sight and would have made egress much easier. The auditorium only had a back balcony, above the entryway, as a possible hiding place for a shooter. He ignored it. When the time came and he squeezed the trigger, the investigation would be immediate and would start there. Instead, he'd traced the angles of the side windows to the podium then drawn an imaginary line back from them. One went directly to a two-story sciences building some two hundred yards away. The windows were open perhaps two inches, a difficult shot at the best of times, due to wind shear.

Difficult, but doable.

He crossed the two hundred yards and checked around to ensure no one was watching as he walked behind the building. On the back wall, the asset found a black metal ladder that went up to the roof. He climbed it quickly, hard-sided case in one hand, and when he reached the top he stayed low, out of sight, moving to the wall where the angle to the target intersected its ledge.

He knelt and undid the case's fasteners, then withdrew the components and assembled the weapon. He placed the sight, then used it to locate nearby trees, watching the branch movement so that he could properly gauge wind speed and direction. Then he swung the sight back to the window, through the tiny gap between it and the window frame, the crosshairs coming to rest just above the podium. Once he'd focused in, he lay the rifle down against the edge of the rooftop in the precise position. Then he backtracked across the roof, staying low. He climbed down the ladder and surveyed the area. There was a parking lot across the road that ran behind the sciences building and he crossed to it casually, hands in pockets, just another Muscovite out for a walk.

The lot was full of cars, empty of drivers; the asset moved from vehicle to vehicle. At each, he quickly knelt and looked underneath. Moscow is enshrouded in winter for seven months of the year and the asset knew from his intel that people sometimes used magnetic key boxes to store a spare under their car, in case they got locked out in dangerously cold weather. He would have simply hotwired a car, but most were new and built with engine arrest to defeat just such a theft.

It took twenty-three cars before his search bore fruit. He checked the parking slip; the person had paid for a full day and it was still morning. That meant it would still be there in two hours, more than likely, and would be his first exit choice.

He had plenty of time. An alternative would present itself, he decided, if he searched the area properly. And then he would be ready.

3.

Brennan was waiting at the auditorium when people began to arrive, getting through the doors to the free event early so that he could look them over as they entered. He was standing to one side of the stage, a policeman eyeing him suspiciously, when Miskin was ushered in by handlers. The Russian's eyes widened when he saw him. Miskin looked across the room briefly to see if anyone was paying attention as they seated him behind the front table.

When he was comfortable that his handlers had left for a few moments, he got up and walked over to Brennan's seat in the second row, taking the empty perch next to him at the end of the row.

"To say it is a surprise to see you here, my friend, would be a large understatement."

Brennan extended a hand and Miskin shook it warily. "My apologies, Boris Mikhailovich, for the nature of our last meeting. It was rude of me to drop in unannounced."

Miskin looked at his bandaged fingers. "You have accident with stove, perhaps?"

"Not my own, unfortunately."

"And today? Though my ego could use the stroking, I suspect you did not fly all the way from Washington to Moscow on a whim."

"No, no I didn't," Brennan said. "I need to talk to you about a certain missing South African package."

Miskin's face drained of color. "How do you …"

"It is a long story. But I believe that package still exists."

"Impossible. It was lost a long time ago."

"No. Those interested were duped by Borz Abubakar."

The Russian wagged a finger. "This I know is incorrect; Abubakar the Chechen died in a bus explosion in Peru…"

Brennan shook his head. "A dupe. A double."

"Polnyi Pizdets…" Miskin muttered. "You are certain?"

"I talked to him not six weeks ago, right before a South Korean agent put a bullet through his head and stole the item in question from his Angolan headquarters."

A handler came over to the stage and whispered in Miskin's ear. "We must begin soon, my American friend, but we will talk after the speech, yes? We can discuss how best to go forward from here."

Brennan kept the bluff going. "Fine, but we need to talk about your friend Dmitri Konyshenko, as well. He may have brokered a deal between Abubakar and the South Korean – I'm not sure who she represents."

Miskin looked worried. "Konyshenko… he always spells trouble for me. But we'll talk about it soon. Now, I must talk about economics, unfortunately." Miskin turned and headed back to the head table.

2.

Brennan began to walk to the back of the room. He noticed the small window in the upper balcony, doubtless where a movie projector was set up. If a sniper needed a great shot, he reasoned, that would be the spot.

But…

He looked around the room. There were only two exits: the main set of double doors and a fire exit to the left of the stage. It meant a difficult egress or evac if things went wrong. The shooter in France had been careful.

Perhaps Fenton-Wright was correct for a change; perhaps Miskin was relatively safe in the confines of the auditorium. Brennan made his way to the back of the room and found a seat on the aisle, and waited.

When the asset arrived in Russia, he knew that at some point in the following days, he might have been hunted by the authorities. And so he took a precaution: he became a local, using Russian papers to enter the country, growing a full beard, and dyeing his hair brown. With glasses added, a false paunch and a slow, wide walking gait, he looked entirely like he might be Evgeny Fyodor Anteropov, as his documents suggested.

On the following morning, he'd left his modest hotel to walk to a coffee shop near the speech, ordering a herbal tea. A man walked by his table and bent slightly at the knees as he passed, putting the long, hard-sided case down before moving on. The delivery was precise, as his associates had suggested would be the case.

Fifteen minutes before Miskin's speech was scheduled to start, the asset was climbing the ladder back up to the rooftop, the case attached to his back. This time, there were enough people within sight of the building that he had to crawl over to the rifle, or risk questions. He reached the rifle and sighted through the scope. The lectern was still empty, but people were moving about inside.

He checked his watch. It was still light, and sunset wasn't until six forty-five, another hour away. He rechecked the wind and readjusted his scope in tiny increments. He checked the room again; people had sat down, but the lectern was still…

There. A man he didn't recognize was speaking. For a moment, the asset wondered if something had gone wrong. He waited, conscious that his breath was heavy. He breathed in through his nose then out through his mouth, slowing his heart rate and calming down. He re-sighted the podium, just as the stranger finished introducing Miskin. The beefy Russian delegate placed a speech or reference sheet of some sort onto the podium, smiled and waved to the audience. The asset could hear the cheers clean through the old building's brick walls and nearly two hundred yards away, a dull roar. He sighted through the scope again, and Miskin was holding up both hands, trying to get the crowd to calm down so that he could begin.

Brennan had waited nervously for a half hour, watching the people file into the auditorium, as well as keeping an eye on Miskin's security detail to ensure they were paying attention. At the last second, just minutes before the Russian delegate's speech was slated to begin, he decided to obey his instincts and check out the movie projection room, to be sure it was empty. It was. Brennan went back to his seat to wait for the beginning of the address.

He scanned the room again; now that everyone was sitting down, it was easier to get a good look. It was always possible the shooter would try for something close range – Brennan sure as heck didn't believe that Hans-Karl Wilhelm's death had been an accident, which mean a sniper MO wasn't guaranteed.

He didn't see anyone out of the ordinary or untoward; mostly, it was college students and instructors. But he had that nervous tension again, that feeling that he was missing something vital.

Miskin was being introduced, the Dean of Political Science praising his political and commercial acumen. He made a polite joke and everyone chuckled, Miskin included. Brennan turned his head to the left slightly and saw the last light of the day cutting through the cracks in the barely open windows, thin beams of light just visible at the edge of the window frame, like a subtle glow.

The windows. He looked at the lectern, then at the windows. He got up and made his way outside quickly; he glanced back at the auditorium then followed the line of sight back across the campus. It would take a hell of a shot, but… there was a two-story building a few hundred yards away. He followed the edge of the rooftop looking for anything that broke the even line of the brick.

2.

Brennan wouldn't have seen it but for the slight recoil of the rifle as the shooter squeezed the trigger. The barrel kicked upwards slightly. A moment later, people inside the auditorium began to scream.

"No!" Brennan said. He sprinted towards the two-story building. There were people passing by on the campus paths, their heads already craning towards the auditorium because of the muffled cries from that direction. Brennan pointed towards the building across the way. "Shooter on the roof!" he yelled, pointing that way but not slowing down. "On the roof!" Caught in the adrenaline of the moment, the warning was useless: he'd yelled it in English.

He made it to the building, but the front doors were locked. He ran around to the back and saw the ladder immediately. He glanced away from the building, scanning the area for anyone moving. He spotted the sprinting figure a moment later as he entered the parking lot.

Brennan gave chase, but the man was several hundred yards ahead already. He got into a parked car and for a moment, Brennan got a slight glance: brown hair, a beard, glasses, heavyset. The car backed out of its spot in a screech of rubber, before gunning forward and out onto the street, taking a hard left and disappearing from Brennan's field of view behind taller buildings.

Brennan backtracked to the building. It was possible the shooter had left something useful behind, maybe an ejected casing or a boot print, or …

A police officer ran out from cover on the building's right side. He had his sidearm drawn and leveled at Brennan. "Get down!" he yelled in Russian. "Get down now!"

MAY 29, 2016, MOSCOW

Brennan was surprised; he'd heard horror stories from other guys in intelligence about Russian jail cells but so far, it was beating the hell out of Angola. It was clean, the cot was bug-free and he was getting two solid meals a day. He sat on the cot, stared at the bars, and waited.

On the downside, they hadn't shown any inclination after seventy-two hours to afford him his consular rights and a visit from the embassy, or legal counsel. If they were planning on letting him go any time soon, the Moscow Police weren't dropping hints. But he wondered why they were still holding him at all; if his papers hadn't held up to scrutiny, surely they'd have come down harder, he told himself.

Eventually, a guard approached his cell door. "You," he said in Russian. "Up."

3.

He went through the same routine for three straight days. He would be directed to a soundproof room, and would sit across a plain steel table from a nicely dressed detective named Victor Semenov, and a man whom nobody identified nor questioned, and who reminded Brennan vaguely of David Fenton-Wright.

"Mr. Taylor," Semenov said. He had a thin neck and bony skull, his hairline almost gone. "I trust you slept well last night."

"They left the lights on in my cell, so no," Brennan said. In fact, he'd slept just fine. He was trained to undergo far worse than a bright room. But if they hadn't cracked his phony papers, he was a clothing salesman with some sort of penchant for danger, not someone who stayed cool under pressure.

"My apologies," Semenov said. "I will speak to the warden and ensure it does not happen again tonight."

"So you're not letting me out?"

"Unfortunately, that is not up to me."

"I should be allowed to contact my embassy; I should be allowed to contact a lawyer."

"It is true, you most definitely should," Semenov said. "Should this become a formal inquiry instead of mere friendly questioning, we will ensure your representatives are contacted."

"You can't hold me indefinitely…"

"Oh, but under Russian law, when someone is suspected of being a terrorist or in league with a terrorist, we most certainly can, Mr. Taylor." In the other chair, the silent observer betrayed a hint of a smile and crossed his legs. "Now perhaps you can dissuade us of that notion," Semenov demanded, "by telling us how you knew there was a sniper on the roof of the university science building? We know you did not pull the trigger, as you were adjacent to the building when caught, and had no gloves on. Yet the rifle – American made, I might add – was free of fingerprints or identifying marks of any sort beyond the barrel rifling."

Brennan squinted at him. "The what?"

"Never mind," the inquisitor said. "It's not important. People who were in the square, they said you were yelling in English right before Miskin was shot…"

"No, that's wrong. Right after."

"Why were you even there? Surely a speech on geopolitics in Russian could be of little interest to a suit salesman from …" He checked his notes quickly, "…Akron, Ohio."

"As I told the night shift version of you, I met Mr. Miskin at a political benefit in Washington. My company donates generously to the political parties. I thought he might be able to smooth the way for me here to become an official government supplier, to the military and other functions. Russia is big business these days."

2.

"What were you yelling outside the auditorium?"

"I saw the sniper on the roof. So I yelled 'sniper'. I forgot about the language barrier in the excitement of it.

"Why did you go outside in the first place, Mr. Taylor?"

"Well... as you said, the subject matter was very dry. I knew I was going to get five minutes with Mr. Miskin after the session, and we chatted for a few minutes before..."

"Some people in the audience confirmed seeing you talk with him."

"There you go."

The questions continued for another hour. At the end, the inquisitor excused himself.

He came back about twenty minutes later. "We've contacted the American Embassy on your behalf. They will have someone around to pick you up later today or early tomorrow. While there is nothing to indicate your involvement in this matter goes beyond the cursory, Mr. Taylor, we admit to some suspicion based on your odd behavior. However, as we have no evidence in this matter to link you to Mr. Miskin's death, we are obliged to release you. My helpful advice would be to head back to Montpellier, from whence you came, or perhaps even America."

"Was that supposed to substitute for an apology for holding me for three days?"

The detective smiled. Then he walked back out of the examination room, followed closely by his silent, nameless friend.

JUNE 2, 2016, WASHINGTON, D.C.

Myrna sat quietly drinking her coffee at the dining room table and watched Alex type. Her young friend had been working on the story for three hours, occasionally pausing to look something up in her notes or online. The apartment lights were muted, just a lamp near the couch and the short bank over the kitchen breakfast bar.

"I just think it might be a mistake to tip your hand this early," Myrna said. "At least if you could wait to talk to Joe..."

Malone didn't look up. "Nope. Miskin's shooting might have been prevented if I'd have written something a month ago instead of being holed up here..."

"But who knows how much work you're jeopardizing," Myrna said. "Joe might..."

3. 261

"Joe has been gone for two months. This thing is out there, other journalists are working on it. You can be sure of that. And I have a job to do. Look, you know I appreciate everything you've done for me. But I have to tell this story now, while most of those involved are still alive."

"What are you going to say?"

"That an international industrialist is running a star chamber, acting as judge, jury and executioner, and benefiting from it personally, using political contacts from at least a half-dozen nations. That other members of his ACF aided and abetted that behavior in Bosnia, East Timor and Harbin, China. That Khalidi tried to fund insurrections in Africa."

"He'll deny everything, of course."

"Sure."

"And you're okay with hanging this stuff on your anonymous federal source? How does your magazine feel about that?"

"They trust me." Malone got the sense Myrna would keep trying to talk her out of it. "Look, at some point this stuff has to go on the record. I mean, what if the botched Africa mission was what prompted the sniper? It could be a merc or the friend of a merc who was killed there. And in the meantime, whoever doesn't want this published is trying to kill me. I think we can all pretty much figure out who that might be."

"They're going to redouble their efforts to find you, you know," Myrna said. "I just hope you realize what you're wading into."

"I do."

Myrna smiled and got up to get them each a refill of coffee. "Then publish, and damn the rest," she said. "The right people are on your side, Alex. But we do worry."

So did Malone. In fact, she wasn't likely to tell Myrna, but the entire story was scaring her witless.

JUNE 3, 2016, MONTPELLIER, FRANCE

When she published and the story broke, the reaction was predictable outrage. Khalidi expressed immediate umbrage at any suggestion he was overextending his influence and called it fiction; the EU was outraged that various European diplomats had worked with the Jordanian on allegedly dubious projects; the British government was the only party on the first day with the audacity to demand an explanation from Khalidi about his funding of African insurgents, and of Fung to explain the gang issues in Harbin.

The story even listed Kalispell as a dummy company, a fundraising front for PetroGlobal.

Khalidi scheduled a press conference in Montpellier. The chairman railed against the story, calling it a "malicious work of fiction" that was "designed to destabilize companies that employ thousands. The ongoing attacks appear personally motivated by this reporter," he said, "who I believe is an Islamophobe."

After the speech portion, reporters questioned the sheikh's son for several minutes, but he was evasive. One asked whether he had any knowledge of Kalispell funneling money to Africa, and Khalidi claimed to not know he owned the company. "I have many holdings, you must understand," he said. "This makes me vulnerable to the manipulations of the press."

But what about the allegations of involvement in domestic insurrections, a reporter asked. How did Khalidi justify such behavior?

"The reporter, Ms. Malone, has drawn very tenuous and highly imaginative links between a handful of tragedies and their proximity at the time to business holdings of some of my associates. We feel these accusations are baseless and without merit. However, we will afford Ms. Malone the same courtesy as any other member of the press and we take her concerns seriously, with respect to internal process audits of our holdings."

Did that mean there might be truth to the allegations, one reporter asked.

"No, I do not think there is any truth to them. However, when vested with significant public responsibility, we must ensure due diligence."

There were multiple questions about the shooting of Miskin. Would the members of the ACF board all go into protective custody? Would they recommend the group's dissolution?

"Absolutely not, absolutely not," Khalidi told the press. "Ladies and gentlemen, let's not conflate this story into something it is not – strongly sourced, reliable material. The ACF is merely a business lobby group, nothing more. As I've said, let's wait for the independent review, which we will establish in short order."

"But how should the international community react to such inflammatory allegations?" a reporter near the back asked.

"I would hope with measured reason," Khalidi said calmly. "There's a reason all of our members are – or were – diplomats, people entrusted to represent entire nations. And I would urge political leaders to keep this in mind."

3.

After the press conference, Khalidi returned to his suite at a local hotel. He excused all of his staff save for Faisal. "How are Fung and Funomora reacting to the increased security?" he asked, skipping any preamble and getting to business.

"They are understandably upset, sir."

"And our EU friends?"

"Also upset. The allegations regarding Africa…"

"Are true. We are both aware that some of my subsidiaries engaged in… less than ethical behavior in their quest to expand. And we are aware that when discovered, my chief executive officer had them fired."

"Of course, sir," Faisal said, finding the idea that the fastidious, paranoid Khalidi would have allowed it to take place without knowing absolutely absurd. Khalidi had asked for solutions in Africa, Faisal had offered the advice, and his employer's company had followed that advice. But now, dissonance was kicking in; with each passing day Khalidi judged himself to be less and less responsible.

"What can I do about it now?" Khalidi continued. "Our agent in Washington failed to quell this at the source. Eventually, reporters will find other evidence linking Kalispell to the African issues. And then there is…"

"I would not bring that up, sir." Although he had come to loathe Khalidi, Faisal still found himself compelled to do his well-paid job efficiently; and discussing Borz Abubakar had no upside.

"Then what?"

"Well, you have two options. You can try again to have the reporter eliminated, which may yet work. Or you can pull some strings in America and see if you can convince her publisher that the material is both defamatory and irresponsible. Even just getting him to demand to know the reporter's source might be enough. It appears much of the material has been leaked by someone with considerable state-level intelligence."

Khalidi smiled. "Faisal, you surprise me sometimes, you are so helpful."

Without me you'd probably be dead six times over, Faisal thought. "It is my pleasure to serve, sir," he said.

JUNE 3, 2016, WASHINGTON, D.C.

"PAGE SIX?!?" Alex was fuming. "Page freaking six, Ken? You must be kidding me!"

Her aging editor cowered slightly behind his old honey maple typewriter desk, which he'd carted from paper to paper for years. It had a small name plate at the front that said "Ken Davis" in fading gold gilt. Its one other notable feature was that it was almost completely covered, every square inch occupied with an assembly of pens, paper, newspapers, notebooks, coffee cups, cutlery, a tub of change, three pop cans and, perhaps surprisingly given Ken's midsection, a bottle of salad dressing.

"It's a follow, on a story nobody else is picking up much yet," he mumbled.

"Jesus H…. You remember that movie "Zoolander"? I feel like Will Farrell in that flick: I feel like I've taken crazy pills. Any reporter with half a brain should want on this."

"What did you expect?" he said. "You have a great story, but it has a lot working against it: your main source is anonymous, which means any reporter following it basically has to quote us; your overseas sources involving the Harbin incident are both nebulous and inconsistent in their accounts. You don't find the guy from Africa – you know, the arms dealer who can tie Khalidi directly to Kalispell's decisions. And that, incidentally, is the biggest reason the follow was on page six…"

"Yeah, but…"

"But nothing!" He'd been an editor a long time, and Davis only put up with so much reporter bull before moving on. "Look, I'm not going to give you a line of shit here, but the publisher hated that story. Hated it. Told me his friends in the business community – you know, our advertisers – had the same questions he did about who our main source was and what axe that person had to grind. Then there's the fact that outside of the African incident, all of the so-called "victims" of the ACF's operations were scumbags in and of themselves; plus, they were overseas scumbags, and nobody here really gives too much of a rat's ass, you know? So that's why it was on six…"

"Look, Kenny…"

"Don't Kenny me, Ms. Malone…" Then he softened for a moment. "Look, Alex, we all know how good you are. That's why we printed the first piece and gave you the cover. The follows haven't given us much more. I know if there's more solid material out there, you're the person who can dig it up. But it's like anything big: you have to follow the paper and the money. Right now, you've got the African massacre, and that's a huge piece. But the rest is mostly innuendo. You have to show intent, prove motivation, get someone to turn over on the right people. Get me something more solid that anonymous sources; get me a whistleblower on the ACF board, or in the background. Get me a line on who the hell is blowing these guys away. Get me anything! Just don't file any more of this "sources say" stuff, because I've got a good goddamn sense that if we had to take this into court, your high-level source – entirely real though I'm sure he is – would run for the hills rather than testify."

Alex sighed. She had a sense of dread, and considered for a moment that Myrna might have been right; she might have gotten ahead of her own story, ahead of the evidence – at least inasmuch as she could prove. Chances were good that her source was dead on, and that she was protected by the legal "absence of malice" clause. But it wasn't her job to just duck legal issues. She needed the whole story.

"Okay."

"Okay?" he said, having known her for years and assuming there was a catch. "Really?"

"Really," she said, pained at having to be contrite. "I'll make sure anything I give you on this from now on is ironclad. But I'm telling you, Ken – these people have already tried to kill me. There's a reason I've been laying low."

"Duly noted, princess," he said, highly doubting anyone was paying attention to who'd even written the piece. "Now get your ass out there and find us something solid."

2.   266

31

JUNE 4, 2016, MONTPELLIER, FRANCE

The conversation was succinct. Brennan's objections had been noted and discarded.

"Just don't go anywhere," David Fenton-Wright had said before he'd hung up.

Brennan wanted to tell him where to go ... but instead, he considered his eventual chances of extracting himself from the agency permanently and without fuss, and let the matter rest.

He'd tried to get an audience with the chairman about his dealings with Abubakar; he was beginning to suspect the committee might have had a role in the bus crash. But he'd been rebuffed twice.

Now David was effectively preventing him from following up the tip about Dmitri Konyshenko, who was scheduled to be at an international shipping conference in Copenhagen in a day's time. The press had almost completely lost interest in Alex's revelatory story after two days, and it almost felt as if it had had no impact at all.

He sat at his hotel room desk, checking his notes on his laptop and going over what Myrna had told him, reconciling it with what he'd learned in Angola and from Miskin.

The phone rang.

"Yeah."

"Mr. Brennan?"

He was registered under Peter Taylor. "I think you have the wrong…"

"Mr. Brennan, I know who you are. I have information for you, information I believe will be very useful in your investigation."

"Okay. Well… you know where I am..."

"Your hotel is much too public. We need to go somewhere quiet."

"We're outside of my usual stomping grounds," Brennan said. "You have something in mind? And consider that, if it's too private and I think you're setting me up, I just won't show."

"Understood. But I'm sure you will want to see this."

"Name the time and place."

"La Place Royale de Peyrou; it is a monument, the city's highest point and very public. Completely open."

Brennan had seen it mentioned in a local tour guide. "No, I don't think so. Completely open puts me potentially in someone's sights. If we meet, it's somewhere public but protected."

"Fine. There is a large aquarium in the northeast of the city…"

"I've seen the listings."

"In front of the penguin exhibit on the upper level, this afternoon at five?"

Brennan arrived early to survey the area, parking his rental in one of the handful of adjacent lots. It was as if an entire neighbourhood had been set up just to deal with parents and their kids: a giant pedestrian mall, fronted by restaurants and tourism attractions that included a skating rink, a planetarium and the aquarium itself, which was housed in a state-of-the-art facility, a grey-and-blue architectural mish-mash of circles within circles. Its front was made up of thirty feet of windows looking out onto a pedestrian concourse. Surrounding the businesses was a series of restaurants, mostly family friendly. The kids would love it, Brennan thought, and Carolyn even more for the relief factor.

He scoured the skyline, tracing over the tops of buildings, looking for easy access points for a shooter. It was probably a futile effort; if someone really wanted him dead, he knew, they'd eventually succeed so long as he was in public, in alien territory. It wouldn't necessarily be a bullet; the sniper had little access to the delegates, so a bullet from distance made sense. It might just have been the short, quick stab from the end of an umbrella, like Myrna's Paris source, or the pointy tip of a shoe, dosed in a lethal concentration of toxins. If done right, he'd hardly even notice it; and by the time he went into cardiac arrest, it would be too late.

He took the middle of several doors into the building and, almost immediately, a set of semi-spiral stairs to the upper level. It only took Brennan a minute to become anxious about the meeting location: once up the stairs, a corridor followed the contours of the building in a near-perfect oval, channeling traffic in just two directions around a central giant, multi-story tank. That limited escape routes if the meet proved to be some sort of trap.

There were multiple exhibits to the left as Brennan followed the corridor, the open tops of tanks behind iron railings. From the lower level people could see the interior of each tank through a glass wall, the entire undersea environment of artificial reefs for hundreds of fish species.

To his right, the central hub of the building contained a giant shark enclosure, though it was sensibly built right up to the ceiling, the public's view limited to a series of large round windows, like portcullises from some monstrously large vessel.

At the corridor's midway point, near the back of the building, was the penguin habitat. Rocks were carved in angular fashion into short artificial cliffs, a perfect diving off point for the penguins as they plumbed the depths of the tank. Brennan checked both directions; the place was quiet on a Monday afternoon, just a handful of tourists and some locals with their kids.

It felt wrong. It was public, but it was enclosed, boxed in. A source who wanted anonymity – would there be risk in such a place, in being seen there? Maybe not.

But it felt wrong. He was anxious, watching the people as they passed, wary of anything out of place; a young mother with a stroller, kids holding hands to avoid getting lost, a senior couple heading the other way; a single tourist, guidebook in his college-aged hand looking like he'd seen too much in one day.

The source had given him a first meeting option that was obviously out of the question; the second option had seemed more reasonable; but perhaps that had been the point.

Brennan hadn't survived in the business by ignoring his instincts. He turned back and began walking the corridor towards the stairs. The mother with the stroller tracked him, eyes flitting sideways as he passed; she seemed out of place as well, too interested in him, her expression oddly neutral; ahead, the senior couple had stopped by the fish tanks but were both looking up, as if intent on his position, his situation. He wasn't being paranoid, Brennan told himself. Each of the handful of people around him felt like they were going through motions.

It was a setup. The whole thing, the whole scene. He was sure of it.

He began to sprint, and the mother with the stroller turned quickly, her hand dipping in and out of the carriage, the machine pistol appearing in a smooth arc as she fired, rounds cutting into the walls, dust kicking up as Brennan tried to keep his head down. He ducked behind a board advertising the penguins' feeding times and drew the Glock from the back of his waistband, but before he could fire back, a chunk of the board disappeared, showering him with chips of wood. He looked back quickly; both of the seniors were twenty yards away towards the front of the building, with silenced pistols drawn, trying to catch him in a cross-fire.

A handful of other patrons screamed and ran, momentarily cutting off the older couples' view, and Brennan quickly moved to a narrow space between the two fish tanks, which offered cover on both sides as long as he could stay low. He leaned around the corner to his left; the "mom" was levelling the machine pistol in his direction but Brennan was quicker, the Glock readied and his aim true, both shots hitting her center mass; then he ducked back into cover. She tumbled to the ground after another half step, convulsing from an arterial rupture, a punctured lung filling with blood.

The 'elderly woman' tried to flank him by crossing the corridor to a small area of fake palm trees, her speed of movement betraying the grey wig, while her husband laid down suppressing fire. But Brennan had just enough angle from behind the corner of the right-hand tank to hit her before she got there. He unloaded five shots in quick succession, catching her in the legs and ankles. The woman screamed and went down, her gun sent sliding across the marble.

Brennan heard a slight shuffle of shoe on concrete from behind him and instinctively dodged sideways, the blade of a butterfly knife slashing past his face in a short, sharp arc, the tip a quarter-inch from his throat, a foot coming up quickly to kick the Glock from his hand.

He dropped into a defensive posture then jabbed upwards with an open-hand punch, blocking the attacker's arm away from him. The 'confused tourist' had almost managed to sneak up on him, but now the man's left kidney was exposed and Brennan hit it hard, with a hook, the attacker arching his back in spasmodic pain. Brennan kicked hard, sideways, the arch of his boot striking the side of the man's knee, dislocating it. The phony tourist screamed in agony and went down to one knee, but still managed to wildly swing the knife in his right hand; Brennan caught the arm and turned the man around, like dancing with a rag doll, just as the elderly assassin fired three more shots, the impromptu human shield taking each bullet in the back.

Brennan dropped him to the floor and sprinted towards the old man, who was trying frantically to get another magazine into place. As Brennan leaped into a flying sidekick, the old man dropped the weapon in favor of throwing up a cross-armed block, deflecting the kick's force. Brennan landed and rolled into a crouched position facing his adversary. The man was genuinely old, he realized absently. The old man began to go into a defensive martial arts crouch, but then staggered sideways slightly… then to his left, then backwards, as if he'd had too much to drink and could suddenly barely stand. Then he spread his feet wide, leaning back with one hand to his chin as if taking a deep drink of something.

2.

His 'Drunken Man' form was impeccable, Brennan noted, a sign of expertise in Choi Le Fut Kung Fu. The old man came out of the backward lean by lurching forward then flipping head-over-side in a cartwheel of kicks. Brennan instinctively set his feet wide and shuffled backwards out of the way. He threw a series of rapid punches, but the old man swayed backwards again, his back seemingly made of rubber as he arched it to avoid the blows. The old man did a single back flip so that he was in a balanced position again then took a quarter-turn before lurching sideways, a series of strikes catching Brennan in the side of the head and sending him reeling.

He shook off the blows, but the old man rolled sideways again and came up with the pistol. He squeezed off a shot but was a split-second too late as Brennan closed the distance and slapped the gun to one side; the elderly assassin was left open, and Brennan drove the side of his hand into the man's throat. The old man collapsed to his knees, clutching for air, and Brennan threw two more quick punches, knocking him out.

Alarms were sounding and he could hear footsteps running up stairs. He looked for a quick exit point; there was a washroom to his left, and he ran inside, the door swinging shut hard behind him. There was a window, high on the wall above the sinks and small, but big enough to get through. He clambered up onto the back of the sink; his ear was ringing from the senior assassin's punches. Brennan pushed the window open and leaned out quickly to look for foot traffic, the sound of the city instantly taking over. It led out onto the end of a metal platform that ran part of the way around the outside of the building, leading to several service entrances on the rear of the building, and then a second metal set of stairs down to ground level.

As he took the stairs two at a time, police sirens buzzed by in the street ahead, behind the walls separating the aquarium from the mall and restaurants. He found a spot where the concrete turned to a lower mesh fence and climbed it quickly, dropping to the sidewalk on the other side and walking away. A few minutes later, as police began to clean up the carnage at the aquarium, he was flagging a cab from outside a nearby hotel.

Faisal Mohammed had been behind his desk for nearly an hour, waiting for the line to blink. Finally, the call came through.

"Yes?"

"The operation was unsuccessful, sir, and the contractors have failed to complete the terms of the agreement arranged by the American."

3.

"I see."

"Would you like me to arrange other contractors…"

"No. No, that won't be necessary for now."

"Very good, sir." The line went dead.

He dialed Khalidi. "Sir?"

"What is it, Faisal?"

"The issue with the American agent, Joe Brennan, was not resolved. He is intent on getting answers with respect to the African incident…"

"I thought we had control over his movements."

"We have control of his handler, technically," Faisal said. "But he informs us that Brennan was commissioned 'below board', which is to say…"

"I know what 'below board' means, Faisal," Khalidi said, fatigued. "Can we have our contact recall him to America? If we cannot eliminate the problem, perhaps it is best to at least get him out of our hair – or, perhaps, have him stationed somewhere out of the way until things are calmer."

"I can certainly put that to our contact, sir," Faisal said. "He may not be receptive but…"

"Remind him of how much he is being paid. Remind him of our expectations, and that he can always be replaced if he does not meet them."

"Yes, your highness."

"And if he cannot manage it, remind him that we still need a solution to Mr. Brennan. Tell him to bring force to bear."

JUNE 6, 2016, WASHINGTON, D.C.

The President threw the copy of the magazine story back onto the long wooden table that sat in the middle of the National Security Council's executive meeting room. "I need answers, gentlemen," he said. "How much of this is true and how much of it is just fanciful reporter bullshit?"

They'd all read Alex Malone's work; everyone inside the Beltway had been discussing her series for more than a week. The consensus seemed to be that the ACF, at the least, was acting criminally. That meant extended opportunities to investigate, multiple opportunities for Fawkes to be uncovered.

2.

"Mr. President, if I may…" Mark Fitzpatrick said, drawing everyone's attention. "The intel on Khalidi's company funding an African insurgency is correct. The handful of other incidents to which she has referred are, as far as I can tell, also legitimate."

At the other end of the table, David Fenton-Wright kept his opinion to himself. But everyone around the table was aware of how badly the President's popularity had slid in the prior year. If he wanted to help Younger, the agency man thought, he could best do it by staying off the stump, not dragging his successor down with him. Fenton-Wright considered himself apolitical; but he reserved a special dislike for the commander-in-chief, whom he saw as weak.

"Could this get any worse?" the President asked.

"Well sir, it's already worse in that the board members appear to have used military force to settle political scores, as well," said Fitzpatrick. "The incident Ms. Malone's story mentioned in Harbin, China has been confirmed by our allies in the region."

"And how are they dealing with this?"

"They're … not, Mr. President," Fitzpatrick said hesitatingly.

"I don't follow."

"They're ignoring the story. China and Japan have often treated American domestic reporting with a large grain of salt, and Khalidi's home nation, Jordan, offers him great deference due to his lineage. Possibly, the powerful father of Fung's wife has intervened on his behalf; it's difficult to say at this point."

The President considered the implications. At least, he assumed, he would be out of office by the time the other powers began to pay attention to the ACF and, by extension, to Lord Cumberland's double life.

"There is another facet to this we need to explore," Fitzpatrick said. "It's possible that the sniper who started all of this was going after ACF board members because of its off-the-books behavior; the shooter might even have been employed by a country."

"So if we take down the sniper, it may lead us back to a diplomatic mess with… who, the Nigerians?" the defense secretary asked. "Christ, what a shitstorm…"

"Where does that investigation stand, David?" the President asked

Fenton-Wright saw his opportunity. "If we're going to distance ourselves from the ACF and Fawkes, Mr. President, I would suggest at this point that the unofficial and unsanctioned investigation into the shootings be terminated and the asset withdrawn. Really, if we don't have a horse in this race, we should get out. It's quiet right now, and the less attention we draw the better." It was exactly what Faisal wanted, and it solved the problem of Brennan's ongoing efforts to tie the missing nuke to Khalidi, Fenton-Wright thought.

The President sat quietly for a moment and thought about all of the ramifications. Fawkes had been in place long before he took office, had never become active again until the sniper. Could he use that as an excuse, in posterity, were the agent to be uncovered? Probably. Would leaving a man over there to snoop around potentially lead to more questions being posed than were answered? Also likely.

"Bring him in," he told Fenton-Wright. "Let's see if we can extricate ourselves from this mess."

32

JUNE 12, 2016, MONTPELLIER, FRANCE

The apartment was hot; it was south-facing and just three small rooms, catching the brunt of the summer afternoon sun in the Languedoc-Roussillon region, adjacent to the Mediterranean.

Brennan sat on the edge of the aging single-bed in the back room, where the shade was somewhat merciful, the thin mattress squeaking on decades-old springs whenever he got up or sat down. It was unseasonably warm out, even for the area. He had just a string undershirt and jeans on with running shoes, and the sweat beaded on his brow and jawline, as a cheap oscillating fan in the corner tried in vain to cool the surroundings.

He flicked the old twenty-inch color television from channel to channel, pausing on each just for a few seconds, just absorbing the sights with the sound muted, without conscious thought process, allowing his mind to de-stress and unwind.

Everything seemed to have gone south the moment Alex published her story, he thought. Up until that point he'd been making a plodding, dangerous sort of progress; but now Miskin was dead, Khalidi had run an effective duck-and-cover, Alex's reporting seemed to have ground to a halt ... and Brennan was on the run.

He heard footsteps on the metal stairs up to the building's second story. He got up and moved to the front window, by the door, pulling back the lacy white curtain. The first man was stocky, maybe five-eight, forty five years old, with curly black hair that was beginning to silver. His partner was younger, with a strong physique but not bulky, along with wispy brown hair and a goatee. He had a black tank top on and jeans while the older man favored a tight t-shirt and cargo shorts. The younger man was carrying a small athletic bag.

They knocked on Brennan's door and he let them in.

"You Bernie?" the old man said in French.

"Yeah."

"We're supposed to say the missus sent us."

"Okay." He closed the door behind them and they walked into the room. "You bring what was discussed?"

"Yeah. But the piece was hard to find. It's going to cost another five hundred."

3.

Brennan paused for a second as he reached for the money clip in his back pocket. Was this guy just angling for an extra buck, or was it an exploratory request, a chance to see how flush he was? He took the clip out and watched their reactions. Both sets of eyes flitted momentarily to the thick money roll but betrayed no surprise or emotion.

He peeled off three-and-a-half thousand euros in hundreds. The younger man leaned in to take the money but Brennan withdrew it quickly. 'Ah… not before I see what you've brought me," he said, nodding towards the athletic bag. The older man's eyes had stayed on the money clip, even as he leaned down to unzip the bag. They dipped south and he looked into the bag, at the same time as Brennan. The pistol he'd asked for was lying on top. The curly-haired man looked at it, then at Brennan's money, then at the gun again.

And for just a split second, no one moved a muscle.

Things had begun to unravel after the aquarium. Brennan had gone back to his hotel only to find it crawling with both police and federal agents. Disappearing into the downtown core, he'd managed to steal a cell phone from a careless tourist at a street café in order to call Myrna, from the relative quiet and security of an alleyway.

She'd in turn told him that he was a wanted man, his face all over French television stations.

"What the hell is going on?" she'd demanded. They didn't use each other's names; despite the public's general ignorance of the techniques involved, both knew that signals intelligence gatherers could flag individuals from among millions with something as simple as a name, and that a network of countries circumvented rules on monitoring their own civilians by having partner nations do it for them. "They've got security footage of you shooting a helpless John Q."

"What?!?"

"Old man, crown of white hair, brown suit, short, with a moustache."

The elderly assassin. "That was no ordinary senior," he said. "But I didn't do it. Whatever they're showing, it's doctored."

"It's a hell of a good job then. State has branded you rogue; and local yokels have been told you're armed and dangerous. And my contacts over there have gone very quiet, which they generally only do to keep me from things I shouldn't know."

"If it doesn't go without saying, I need your help."

"Of course."

2.

"Money. There's a wire office near here; there's a chance they won't have cut me off yet from everything in the system, so I'm going to this place." He gave her an address, four blocks off the actual location. "South from there, there are three more." A cue for her to look up the actual locations of the three nearest money transfer offices. "As much as you can manage." A cue to stay under the trace limit of $10,000, at which point any of the offices by law would have had to report a suspicious transaction.

"The police found the man with two to the head," she said, sounding momentarily unsure. "Are you certain..."

"Yes! He disarmed me, we fought, I won. But there were no shots fired, at least not from my end. He was damn good, too, despite his age. If someone popped him, it was after I left."

"If this was Khalidi, he has some exceptional contacts in the agency," Myrna said. "They had that bulletin out to the civil service and foreign agencies in about sixteen minutes, if the time stamp on your 'security camera' appearance is correct."

"Literally?"

"Yeah. The tape shows you shooting the guy at eleven-thirty-six in the morning. The bulletin from State went out to all embassies at... Eleven-fifty-eight. So... twenty-two minutes."

"That's still impossible. There's no way they could possibly have even ID'd me by then..."

"Which will work in your favor. Maybe you should let them take you now in one piece, instead of risking a confrontation. There's no way you lose this at a trial."

"They won't let this get to a trial. Think about it: whoever set this up is connected to people who can't be named publicly, or forced to give affidavits, or testify. I'd never make it that far."

She understood the implication. "So what are you going to do?"

Brennan had been thinking about the order of the two days prior. He'd have been gone, on his way to Copenhagen, if he hadn't been told expressly to stay. "DFW. It has to be. He set me up. He's the only one at the agency outside of Walter who has taken any leadership in this whole thing. I was below board, off the grid, heading out of the country. It had to be him."

"That means he'll have crews coming hard, professional assets, maybe even the rest of the team you faced today. You've got minutes, at best. Head to the location, I'll have the cash there for you in thirty."

He disconnected. The less time they spent talking, the better. To anyone senior at the agency, Myrna was considered off the books, long retired and uninvolved. She'd been careful when she left, letting real-life identifiers lapse, moving, changing her name and doing it properly, keeping her money in cash in a home safe. The last thing Brennan wanted was to compromise her.

It took him ten minutes to find an older-model car he could hotwire without "engine arrest" disabling the vehicle. Another fifteen minutes found him at the first wire office, careful to survey the quiet street before entering, not worrying about the security cameras inside, which wouldn't typically be networked, catching his face. Myrna had sent three payments of $9,999, one to each office. The number was probably over each company's own "suspicious transaction" threshold, but without the automatic trigger level being reached, it wouldn't report them until the next business day at the earliest.

After getting the final delivery, he'd bought a newspaper from a kiosk and checked the classifieds to figure out where the cheapest rentals in town appeared to be, then driven that area looking for the crudest, most obviously home-made "for rent" sign he could find.

The townhouse appeared to have been sweating since the 1950s, with mold spotting the upper corners of the ceiling. But it was only a hundred euros per week. It was disgusting, but there was a small convenience store at the end of the block and the section of the city was utterly anonymous. He'd ditched the car several miles away and taken a cab back to the corner store, then walked from there.

In the ninety minutes it had taken, Myrna had tapped her contacts and found someone willing to provide a driver's license and a gun. "I'm sending them over," she said. "A warning: these guys were low down on the list of suppliers. That means there are a few who said no, and if they figure you for the intended, they might try flagging it, getting in good with the agency or state. Or even taking you out themselves. And the guys coming over are straight-up dirty, so be on your toes."

"Over and out," he said.

They disconnected, and Brennan began his wait for the suppliers.

The three men stared at the gun as it lay on top of the driver's license and government benefit card. The older man looked at the gun, then Brennan. He reached into the bag and picked up the .45.

Then he handed it to Brennan. "A Glock 21, like you asked," he said in French. "Careful: there's one in the chamber."

So much for no honor among thieves, Brennan thought. "Thank you," he said. "I've had a long day and an absence of too much drama or bullshit right now is much appreciated."

The senior of the two began counting the money. "It's probably not a surprise when I tell you your picture is all over the television right now," the older man said.

"Not really."

"You should change your look."

"If I did and needed to travel, could you get me a passport?"

"The price will go up," he said. "A driver's license and social card is one thing. But if you're looking to travel, that's going to be a rich buy. Passports don't come cheap."

"Okay," Brennan said. "You're not worried about whether I did what they say?"

"Not really. Business is business."

The small chrome canister crashed through the front window and landed at the younger man's feet. He picked it up even as Brennan and the older man instinctively looked away and closed their eyes. The flash-bang grenade went off in the younger man's hands and face and he went down just as the battering ram knocked down the front door in a hail of splinters.

Brennan grabbed the bag with one hand and the older crook with the other. "My partner...!" the man yelled, but Brennan ignored him, heading for the back room, where the window sat just high enough in the wall to discourage kids from climbing out, but was still accessible. He'd left it open in case, and he jumped up and over the frame, dropping onto the dumpster below, its lid closed. Even as the older crook clanged loudly down beside him, police tactical officers were leaning out the back window. An officer had been stationed behind the building as well.

"Down!" the cop yelled. "Down on the ground, now!" He had an Ingram machine pistol, Brennan noted as he sprung outwards, kicking off the dumpster lid and flipping over the officer's head, then sweeping his leg backwards, taking the officer's legs out from under him even as the Ingram sprayed fire into the air. As the policeman's back hit the ground and the older crook jumped down to join him, Brennan hit the cop with a short, sharp jab to the center of his chin, where striking a small group of nerves can quickly knock a man unconscious if done with precision.

"Do you have a car?" Brennan asked.

"A block up and to the left. A blue-and-grey Citroen."

It was perfect, anonymous, Brennan thought. "Go! Quickly!" They sprinted to the old Citroen DS. "You have somewhere we can hole up?" Brennan asked as they flung the doors open and climbed inside.

"My cousin Gerard has a flat in Beziers," he said. "It's just down the coast..."

3.

"I know it. Let's go…"

"Wait a second," the older crook said. "They just nabbed my partner and I already helped you out. I get the whole honor among thieves thing, but…"

"I'm not a thief," Brennan said. "And those aren't regular cops chasing me. They've seen your face, which makes you a liability. You can stay in Montpellier, if you wish, but they will hunt you down and kill you. And I'm sorry to tell you, but there's a good chance your partner is dead already."

The veteran crook shrugged. "Okay." He extended a hand, and Brennan shook it. "I am Victor. Let's go."

JUNE 14, 2016, WASHINGTON, D.C.

The President sat, uncharacteristically, behind the Resolute Desk in the Oval office, the two chairs across from it both substantially lower than his to ensure that the representatives of the NSA and the CIA understood their place.

A few feet away, new NSC advisor Bill Freeman and director of intelligence Nicholas Wilkie stood waiting to be called on, if necessary. It was Freeman's first such meeting since taking over the post from Sen. Younger, who had personally recommended him.

Fitzpatrick and Fenton-Wright both looked cool and collected, which the President expected. They were trained to behave with dispassionate disconnection. He was pretty good at it himself. Most of the time.

But now, the commander-in-chief was close to losing his temper. "We agreed to bring your asset in, David, and instead he goes ballistic at a French aquarium and shoots an old man. Am I getting this right? Am I right on this? Because I recall you saying this guy wanted back in from the cold. It's not too cold out there right now, David. In fact, it's pretty goddamned hot."

Fenton-Wright kept his cool. He didn't want to antagonize the President, but he also didn't really have to worry about him, a lame duck with a minority in the house. Whether he had a future with the agency didn't really matter, either. He'd long since decided that the only person he needed to keep happy was the man paying for his eventual ascension to the ACF board.

2.

"Mr. President, as you know we immediately identified Agent Brennan to the French authorities; while the agency certainly could have done a better job of predicting how unhinged Agent Brennan had become after the Colombian affair, we had no indication that anything like this was possible. In fact, we relied on the opinion of his regular handler, the late Walter Lang..."

Mark Fitzpatrick interjected. "If I may, Mr. President... As you know, David and I don't share the most cordial working relationship. But it's clear to us at the NSA, having reviewed the video provided to the agency by its European sources, that this was an unpredictable situation."

The president leaned back in his chair and pressed the tips of his fingers together as he thought about their options. "Covering ass is all well and good, Gentlemen, but what I need to know now is where we stand, and how we proceed."

Fitzpatrick said, "We're in better shape than might appear the case. Brennan was below board, so officially he was in Europe on his own time. We'll be reiterating that position to our colleagues in the EU."

"And I've got a team helping the police over there to track him down," Fenton-Wright added. "Rest assured, Mr. President: this will be handled properly from here on in."

Malone watched Myrna prepare her equipment, slotting the lens into place on the front of the camera as she sat in the passenger seat of Malone's car.

"I don't like this," Malone said. "I really don't."

"Okay," Myrna said, "but we've been over the reality of the situation. Joe is on the run and won't be in touch at all until he's made a few more moves. And your editor is right: if your source ranks highly, he's not going to walk into court and back up what he's telling you. You need an insurance policy."

"Myrna, you've been nothing but good to me for the last two months. But revealing my source to you goes against every instinct..."

"Sweetie, you're in the deep stuff up to your neck," Myrna said. "This isn't a normal game played by normal rules. And I hesitate to point this out, but if I wasn't effectively off the grid, you'd be dead already. Walter knew that, which is why he trusted me to look after you."

"I know." She did. But it wasn't making Malone feel any more comfortable. "Okay, let's do this."

The decision to record and photograph the source had been made the night before; the situation in France, where Joe was still on the run, had only strengthened Myrna's argument: they needed an official connection, someone who couldn't deny everything down the road. It wasn't that the elderly ex-spy wanted leverage and she felt genuine distress at the idea of outing a senior source who was doing yeoman's work just by talking to the press. She didn't want to burn a whistleblower.

But they needed backup, proof. And that meant Malone wearing a mic and Myrna shooting using a low-light lens, the camera propped on the car dash for stability.

The door to the parking garage stairwell opened and her source stepped out. Malone got out of the car and closed the door gently behind her then walked over to meet him, making sure they were close enough to the overhead lights for his face to be occasionally illuminated, out of the shade for long enough that Myrna could get a shot.

"You haven't written anything since Miskin," the source said. "Why?"

"I need proof, hard evidence," Malone said. "My paper is under a lot of pressure to back up what you and others have been telling me."

"You had Kalispell. But you didn't mention the package."

She was momentarily confused. "What package?"

"Ask yourself why Khalidi's fixer disappeared with all of that money."

"Because he's greedy? It's money. What other reason…?"

"He had a purpose, a cause. He needed to fund a major purchase, a bomb smuggled out of South Africa at the end of apartheid."

Her mouth dropped open slightly. "A bomb? As in…"

"Nuclear, yes."

"Holy shit," Malone said.

"A whole lot of something, Ms. Malone, but very little holy."

"So this thing is out there somewhere, and Khalidi funded its purchase?"

"The question is what happened to the device and where it is now," the source said. "There was buzz in intelligence circles two months ago that it had reappeared on the black market, but things have gone silent ever since."

"So it could be out there somewhere, with someone who actually might use it?"

"It's possible, yes."

"Do you have any proof of this whatsoever? Because you know my magazine won't print something that inflammatory without any named sources to support it. There's no way."

2.

"Follow the money," he said. "Someone brokered the sale, a name you've already run into."

"Dmitri Konyshenko."

"If you can get anything out of him or on his company, perhaps you can figure out who purchased the weapon and where it was headed."

"So that's all you can give me? A name I already have?" Malone was beginning to wonder whether her source was willing to take the risks she needed, to give her something solid.

"You have to do some of the digging yourself," he suggested. "I can't gift wrap this for you. You know my position, how sensitive things are."

"But I need something, anything I can take back to my paper to tell them this is all real, and not just some insane conspiracy theory dreamed up because of the sniper shootings."

The source paused for a moment, as if considering the request.

"There's a firm in Las Vegas called DynaTech; ostensibly it makes the interior parts for slot machines and video lottery terminals, as well as the voting machines for some state elections. In reality it's a subsidiary of an offshore company called Dynatech Global, based in the Cayman Islands.

"A tax dodge? That's not much..."

"Not just a tax dodge; a source of funding for Konyshenko's projects over here. Not all of his money flows out of Russia."

"So I need a source at DynaTech, is what you're saying..."

"I'm not telling you how to do the job, Ms. Malone. But I would agree that that's a good place to start."

He turned on his heel and headed for the door.

"HE WHAT?!?" For the second time in recent weeks, Malone was incensed.

They'd gone back to Myrna's to look up information on Konyshenko's Vegas connection. Once Malone had gone through what she'd been told, Myrna realized she needed the whole story.

"I said Joe already knew about the nuke. That's what he was looking for in Africa." Myrna knew Alex would be upset but it couldn't be avoided. She'd known the discussion would happen, eventually. "It was a need-to-know situation, Alex. He was worried..."

"I realize that Myrna, but goddamn..." It wasn't a trust issue; Malone understood why Joe was playing things close to the vest. But that didn't make it any less irritating.

"If I'd known how good your source was earlier..."

3.   283

"But now you know who he is, you're taking me more seriously?" She had trouble hiding her annoyance. "What else don't I know?"

Myrna filled Alex in on Borz Abubakar and the theft of the bomb by the South Koreans. "Joe's feeling is that they were probably working freelance, and plan to resell the device yet again."

Alex was putting the pieces together. "But if Abubakar was on the bus that blew up, how could…"

"A double."

Alex sat and thought it through. "My God… you realize …"

"That Abubakar had nearly two dozen innocent people murdered to cover his tracks. Yes."

"And that there's a nuclear weapon out there somewhere as a consequence of Khalidi's African adventure," Alex said. "That's why he wants me dead. That's why Joe's been burned."

"Khalidi has connections at the highest levels of national security, and while I'm sure he wants the bomb recovered, he will try to ensure it's done with reputations protected. If this came out on top of what you've already reported…"

"Myrna," Alex said, looking a little distant, "I think we're in a whole lot of trouble."

33

JUNE 19, 2016, MONTPELLIER, FRANCE

They drove up from the town of Bezier to the small city as midnight neared, the darkness adding a sense of anonymity. They'd changed cars at Victor's cousin's place, and he'd taken the wheel as they followed the coastal highway, the Mediterranean to their right barely visible in the evening's dull glint, lights from villas and hotels dotting the shoreline ahead.

Behind the wheel, the Frenchman stayed silent for the first thirty minutes, giving Brennan time to consider their situation. He wondered why Victor was being so accommodating, whether there might be a bad surprise waiting for them at the other end of the trip.

But he didn't get that sense. Instead, a terse camaraderie had grown between them over the two days. Eventually, Brennan said, "So do you mind if I ask why you're helping me? You could have just stayed in Bezier, or gone south to Spain until the heat blew over."

Victor glanced at him briefly then reaffixed his eyes on the road ahead. "I don't like being treated as if I do not count," he said.

"Eh?"

"Back at the apartment, when the police came through the door… you were right, they were shooting to kill. They didn't care who I was, or who my friend Jacques was, they just wanted you dead. We were just… non-existent. People who act like that? I never liked them too much. And what can I say? You saved my ass. Victor Moutiere honors his obligations."

Brennan understood that, but he needed to be sure his new friend realized the stakes. "The guy we're going to see… if he catches us, he won't be any less likely to kill you than those cops were. There are influential people after me, people who can reach out."

"Hmmph," Victor said.

"What?"

"I've been a thief my whole life," the Frenchman said, "ever since I hit the street at age ten. Last time I checked, anyone with anything worth stealing usually took some type of steps to protect it. And I already know what the authorities think of you."

"There's no money in this."

The Frenchman gave him a quick glare, then went back to watching the road.

Clouds obscured the waning moon just after one o'clock and the alley was shrouded in darkness, its only occupants a pair of rats that had been rummaging through an overturned trash can. The cobblestone was slick from rain during the day, the barest light stolen from the tall, ornate street lamp nearby, reflected in the windows of the adjacent buildings.

The Citroen backed into the alley slowly, its headlights out.

"Are you sure this is the best approach?" Victor asked as he gazed over his shoulder and steered the vehicle carefully into the dark. Both men were dressed head-to-toe in black clothing.

"We can't be seen carrying a ladder down the street at this time of night without eliciting questions," Joe said. He'd dyed his hair jet black and touched up two days' worth of stubble. "There's no other way in."

"What about alarms? I guarantee you he's got security and a system, if this guy is as important as you say."

"Let me worry about that. Just keep the car in front of the ladder and yourself on that bus stop bench out on the street. If any police officers come along, you explain that you've broken down and are waiting for the tow but it will be up to forty-five minutes. I guarantee you he will have better things to do than to sit there and wait."

"What if they have my description out?"

"We got out quickly, and there was a lot going down. Couple that with your new glasses and haircut and my new look and we should be okay. Just be cool."

"And if something goes wrong…"

"You don't owe me anything. Take the five thousand I've already paid you and get out. Just don't shoot any cops."

"You fuck this up, maybe I stay in Beziers for a few months, eh?"

"Nice work if you can get it." Joe got out of the car. He opened the trunk and took out the collapsing ladder.

Victor followed suit. He looked at it curiously in the half-dark. "Is that high enough? He's on the third storey."

"This is only eighteen feet, but it will get me close enough to the roof to toss up a grappling hook. The edge up there is solid concrete. Then it's twelve more feet to the window ledge."

"And then?"

"And then I do what I do. Like I said, let me worry about it."

Three minutes later, he was crouched on the edge of the wide stone window sill. Victor took the ladder down, as instructed.

Brennan looked the window over. As he'd expected, it was wired to the alarm via a silver contact strip that ran unobtrusively around its outside edge. Vanity was often the enemy of decent security; he'd noted. Had the strip run across the middle of the window pane, or had he carelessly shattered it, the effort might actually have done some good. He took the small bag from over his shoulder. He removed a plastic pouch, opened it, and withdrew a golf ball-sized piece of putty, which he placed in the center of the pane. Then he took out a thin metallic object, with a ball of plastic at one end and a stylus-like blade at the other. He placed the ball of plastic in the middle of the putty and settled it until it was right on the glass but also stuck to gummy material. Then he moved the tool in a circle, rotating it from the ball in the center like a giant compass, the industrial-diamond tipped blade at the other end cutting the glass in a large circle.

He pushed inwards, gently, holding onto the metal bar of the tool. The circle of glass separated cleanly from the rest of the window, the putty keeping the pane from dropping inwards. He leaned through the hole and scanned the room, looking for any sign of pressure trigger wiring. Then Brennan dropped into the room, which appeared to be a study. He placed the piece of glass on top of the nearby desk.

Outside, Victor sat on the bus bench in front of the house, staring out at the street and keeping lookout. He tapped the cordless earpiece. "You in?"

"Yeah. Looks like his study. Doors are all magnetic strip protected but that's easy enough to get around."

"I don't understand why you don't just grab this guy and we beat it out of him, eh?"

"There's that famous French subtlety again," Brennan said. "I'm going to see what he's got in his desk and if there's a safe in here. Just be cool for a few, tell me if anyone comes in the front door of the building. I don't want any unexpected visitors waking this guy up."

Brennan checked the desk hutches and tried the drawers but they were locked. He used the letter opened from the top hutch to pry each open, easily defeating the weak locks. There was a family photo on top. The drawers contained some banking information, some personal papers and mementos, but nothing incriminating. He scanned the room, looking for the least impressive piece of art. There was a small Dutch impressionist piece of a windmill on the exterior wall. He pulled it back and found a safe. But Brennan doubted it would contain anything related to the committee: wall safes were too easily physically removed from their housing.

He looked down at the floor. If Yoshi Funomora had anything of value in his Montpellier home, it would be anchored into concrete. Brennan surveyed the room again; there was a throw rug that curiously stuck out from under each side of the desk, too narrow to suit the position but long enough to cover up something else. He walked behind the desk and moved the chair aside, then pulled back the end of the rug.

Funomora's floor safe was modern, a digital keypad set into the front next to the giant tumbler so that either or both could be used to secure it. Brennan suspected the latter, but it didn't matter. He'd been cracking tougher safes for a long time, under war zone pressure sometimes. The tumbler would be no problem; the safe was small and thin enough that, while too difficult to cut through, the sound of the tumbler discs slotting into place could be picked up with a stethoscope.

The digital lock was another matter.

He moved back to the desk. In Brennan's experience, men over fifty – particularly successful, busy ones – didn't have the hardest passwords to crack, and they often wrote down a copy in case they forgot the sequence, usually somewhere in an office. He tried the drawers again, looking to see if it had been taped to the bottom on one side or the other. He reached in behind each to make sure there was no wadded up piece of paper. He checked the underside of the desk calendar/blotter, but found nothing.

The bookshelf along the left wall was a possibility and he looked for a book that had perhaps been pulled out more recently and was sticking out further than the rest. He checked the titles for something Funomora might find sentimental or ironic.

He sensed that he'd missed something, so Brennan moved back to the desk. There was a fountain pen on top, and he opened it up to check the cartridge container, but found it empty. What was he missing. He scanned the desk again. The hutches, the pen, the family photo…

The family photo. Funomora didn't seem like the sentimental type and he spent most of the year away from his wife, who stayed in Japan. He grabbed the framed and opened it up to take out the print.

On the back, in pencil, it said "14-38-22."

WICKFORD, RHODE ISLAND

The day was beginning to drag. The Rhode Island primary was just twenty-four hours away and Sen. John Younger had shaken so many hands in the prior six hours, he was beginning to develop calluses. And yet, there he was outside a local grocery store at four in the afternoon, cutting a "grand reopening" ribbon."

He smiled for the cameras – the national press corps never took a day off during a campaign – then leaned over to whisper in an aide's ear. "I swear, if I ever have to do this again, shoot me on the spot, okay?" he said.

"It's our weakest support state for the nomination, sir," the campaign worker said. "After the showing in 2012, it's important…"

"I know, I know," Younger said, waving him off, irritated. "I've been doing this for a few years."

After the ribbon cutting had concluded, hands were shaken and backs slapped; Younger took questions from the press informally. Most were about his immigration policy or -- as Addison March had been reminding everyone -- lack thereof. The incessant focus on one aspect of his platform didn't upset Younger; he'd been around too long to expect context and depth from the daily media.

"Senator," a reporter near the front asked, "you mentioned during the event this morning that you still… and I quote… 'weren't comfortable' with Senator March's business ties. He claimed during a speech this morning that it's a drive-by slur campaign without foundation. Can you comment on that?"

Why would March have brought that issue up? Younger was surprised. They'd scored serious points over March's old legal firm and there didn't seem to be any percentage in him raising it again. What was he up to?

"While it's hardly worthy of rebuttal, I suspect Mr. March is eager to do anything he can to appear more in touch with the American people, given his numbers. My advice to him is to spend more time working with American companies and less time kowtowing to his friends in the Middle East. I think it's mind-boggling that my Republican opponent can simply push to the side the two decades his party has spent trying to destabilize that region – which just happens to have a lot of oil – for its own ends. Now, he's the great conciliator, doing business with militant Islamists and sharing lawyers with Ahmed Khalidi."

It was a gross exaggeration, but no one in the press corps was going to call him on it. The sound bites were too good, the reporters too cynical to think any of the campaign messages did much in the way of shifting the population from entrenched ideology and beliefs.

3.

"Senator, Mr. Khalidi has appealed to the international community for calm with respect to the ongoing attacks on his business associates," a reporter said. "Given the revelations of the past week, shouldn't America be examining his businesses here?"

It was the first intelligent question he'd been asked in about ten days, Younger thought. "I would say, sir, that the revelations in *News Now* at the end of March about his involvement in African atrocities, or at the very least in funding them, indicate Mr. Khalidi still has a lot of explaining to do to win back the support of the international community."

When the press conference had wrapped, he went back to his limousine with his handlers. His phone rang as soon as he'd sat down in the backseat. "Talk to me," he said.

"Senator, it's Mark Fitzpatrick. I just caught your press conference live on the news networks."

"Mark," Younger said. "Good to hear from you, as always. I assume you're calling about the handful of questions at the end?"

"I am indeed, sir. I'm already working up a background on the reporter who asked them, to see if he has a personal axe to grind."

"You heard about March's speech?"

"I think he's taking a strange approach," Fitzpatrick said. "But maybe the strategy is just working extremely well. He seems obsessed with proving he's not an Islamist sympathizer."

Younger smiled at that. "Give a true believer a shot to the core of their belief, and they'll move Heaven and Earth to prove it's sacrosanct and unvarnished. It's because they really believe it," Younger said. "He's so vehement in his belief that immigration is tarnishing this nation that he can't see the reality, which is that it contributes much more than it costs. But that will work to our advantage, Mark."

"The Latino vote is going to hate this guy."

"Happy days, Mark," Younger said. "Happy days."

MONTPELLIER, FRANCE

Brennan worked quickly. Inside the safe were bills, denominations large and small, each neatly bound in a bundle; there was also a file folder and a memory stick, and Brennan withdrew both.

2.

The lights in the room went on, the door flying open. The two security guards were both beefy, bodybuilder types, dressed sharply in a grey suit and a black one, respectively, both Japanese, their pistols extended in the expectation of immediate trouble. Brennan rolled sideways before quickly diving forward to within a few feet of them, both men unable to track the movement rapidly enough to get a shot off. They were leery, as Brennan had expected, of actually opening fire inside the apartment, and that moment of hesitation was all he needed.

He locked up the wrist and forearm of the guard to his right and swung him around so that he was between Brennan and the other guard, then slammed his elbow into the middle man's temple, the force stunning the guard and unbalancing his colleague, who stumbled sideways and dropped his gun as he attempted to use the wall for support. Brennan drove a sideways elbow into the side of the first guard's head one more time, dropping him to the ground, dazed; he kept the rotating motion going, his spinning back kick catching the second guard flush, just as he reached down to pick up his gun.

Both men were down, but the noise had been considerable. There was little to no reason, that he knew of, for Funomora to not simply call the local police, and Brennan had to act quickly. He took the suppressed Glock out of his waistband holster and moved to the door, checking the outside hallway quickly then exiting the study.

He'd taken a half-step forward when the figure emerged at the other end of the corridor, from a doorway to the right; he was a young man, lithe and smaller, dressed in black. He took a quarter-turn to his right then quickly flung both arms forward. Brennan's training kicked in before he'd even realized the throwing stars were arcing through the air towards him; he bent over backwards, arching his spine like a curved letter 'c' and dropping into a reverse crab position, the ground's impact slamming into his hands, his weight shifting back towards his shoulders so that he could push forward with all his force and kick back into an upright position as the throwing stars sank into the wooden door behind him.

And then the younger man was on him, the first blow a snapping kick that knocked his gun away, behind him; the man's style was karate, but one of the outliers, more closely related to Kung Fu than Shotokan, a hybrid of thrusts and punches from Shorin Ryu and Fujian White Crane style, his feet wide apart in Three Battles Stance, weight on his rear arch, one hand poised to strike in a coiled punch, the other extended to defend; he drove forward, a rapid series of strikes, punches flashing through the air between them; Brennan backed up at pace, frantically blocking the blows, years of training countering the motions based on an imprinted pattern, both men moving too quickly to be considering each action. The young karateka threw himself forward, a head-over-heels sideways flip, a pirouetted cartwheel in mid-air, his heel striking Brennan hard across the jaw, sending him reeling.

He sprang to his feet, shaking off the blow, wiping the blood away from the corner of his mouth. He'd misread the style, which was Five Ancestors Kung Fu, a blend of White Crane's karate-like strikes and the athletic mimicry of a monkey's leaps and kicks, the motions more fluid, controlled. The young man charged him down, a leaping sidekick intending to finish the job; Brennan ducked at the last possible second and his attacker flew overhead, rolling into a standing position and twisting as he stood so that he was facing Brennan again.

But he'd miscalculated. The first shot to Brennan's jaw had put him down, but right next to his Glock. And as the young martial artist turned around, he came face to face with the suppressor. The young man's eyes were wide as he realized Brennan had the drop on him, and his mouth dropped open in that inevitable moment of terror, when a man realizes he is about to die.

"NO!"

The bellow came from behind Brennan, at the far end of the hallway. He kept his eye on the youth and backed up a step, then snapped a quick look over his shoulder, before returning his attention to his target. It was Funomora, dressed in a bath robe.

"Please," he said in French. "I'll give you whatever you want. Please don't shoot my son."

Five minutes later, Brennan had secured all four men in the study using plastic restraint ties. He'd gagged the two security guards and the youth, and sat Funomora up in his desk chair.

"May I take it that you are Joseph Brennan, the rogue American agent?"

"You find that funny?" Brennan asked. "Your boy Fenton-Wright did an amazing job with that video at the mall."

2.   292

"He has significant resources behind him," Funomora said. "And might I ask how you knew..."

"It could only have been him," Brennan said. "And besides, it's in his character."

"Yes," Funomora said with a wry smile. "On that we would agree."

"What was his reward?"

Funomora shrugged. "You would have to ask the chairman about that."

Brennan took the memory stick out of his pocket. "Or crack this little number?"

The Japanese delegate couldn't hide his shock. "If you take that, my life may be forfeit."

"Are you asking me for compassion?"

"You spared my son. So, yes, that is what I am asking for. That memory stick contains a great many secrets that would be of no real intelligence value to the U.S., but help prevent certain associates in my home country from acting against me."

Brennan looked at the stick. "I'm going to guess Yakuza? You have dirt on them. But if they know what it is, they might be able to neutralize any attempts you make to use it against them."

"Or they may just act pre-emptively."

"What else?"

"Mr. Brennan? I'm sorry, but I don't..."

"What else is on the memory stick? There was only one, and I refuse to believe a man as careful as you hasn't kept something on each of your fellow ACF board members, ruthless as they seem to be. There's nothing useful in the paper file and nothing else in the safe except for cash, so it must be on this."

"There is nothing of the sort, I can assure you; you have been misinformed, badly, with respect..."

Brennan pointed the pistol at Funomora's son. "He's worth a lot to you, right? I notice you didn't show the same deference for the man you sent after me in Washington."

"Not you, Mr. Brennan. The reporter. Her information... it seems to be coming from the highest levels. In truth, the remaining board members, we do not even trust each other. I have suspected for some time that the sniper assassinations may be the chairman's attempt to clean up his tracks."

"For the African incidents?"

"Yes."

"For the loose nuke?"

"Yes."

Brennan studied the man's face for any hint that he was lying; but there was nothing, just fear, anxiety at the present situation. Occasionally his eyes flitted towards his son.

"What else is on the memory stick?"

"Will you return it if I tell you?"

"No. In fact I'm going to find out anyway once you give me its password. I'm just trying to speed up the process"

"I cannot do that."

Brennan turned around and looked at the son. He pointed the suppressed Glock at the young man's thigh and pulled the trigger twice, shooting him from close range. The kid screamed in agony and blood began pouring from the wounds.

"That was probably his femoral artery, and I think the second one nicked the bone. He's got about thirty minutes before he bleeds out and dies, maybe twenty if you're unlucky and don't get a tourniquet on that."

Funomora looked terrified, his eyes bulging as his son writhed in pain.

"There's a really good hospital all of five minutes from here," Brennan said "But you're not getting out of here until you give me the password to the memory stick."

"No! I mean… yes, I'll give you the password. Please, just don't let my son die. He is my world."

" The password…"

"… is 'koketsu ni irazunba koji wo ezu'"

"Thank you." Brennan withdrew the digital recorder from his other pocket. "This was a little insurance as well, and it saved me from having to take notes while you talked about my boss. What does it mean, anyway?"

Funomora looked deflated and defeated. "It is an old expression, a Japanese version of 'nothing ventured, nothing gained; it means 'if you do not enter the Tiger's cave, you will not catch its cub'."

Brennan moved around to the side of the desk and cut one of Funomora's hands loose, then took the desk phone off the cradle and handed it to him. He looked at the son, bleeding on the couch, then at his father. "Relish the irony."

He left the office quickly while Funomora dialed emergency. He took the building's stairs down three flights quickly, tapping the headset on route and informing Victor that they were leaving.

Outside, Victor pulled the car up to the front steps of the building. Brennan exited a moment later, taking the stairs two at a time and hurrying over to the passenger side. Once he'd climbed in, Victor pulled away at a normal, almost casual speed.

"You get what you need?" he asked the American.

2.

"A confession, some data. Will this get me out of hot water? Maybe. Here…" Brennan took a couple of packets of cash out of his bag. "From Funomora's personal collection. I figured I could act as your proxy, seeing as you've been helpful."

Victor looked at the cash. There had to be twenty thousand or thirty thousand euros in the bundles. "Now this right here? This is proof of why it's good to be an honourable man, and a very good thief."

"Don't spend it all in one place," Brennan said.

They set off for Bezier once more, Victor smiling most of the way. Brennan didn't tell him what he'd come to suspect, that there was still a rogue nuke on the loose, that the people he'd thought behind it seemed oblivious to its location.

And the lives of millions of people were on the line.

Across the street from Funomora's building, the asset watched events unfold through his binoculars. The figure was dressed in black when he entered through the side window, certainly not a welcome visitor. He had a friend below, in the alley, waiting with a getaway car.

Maybe someone was about to do his job for him.

He sat patiently, his rifle leaning against the edge of the wall. After about twenty minutes, the man in the alley pulled the car around out front. A few moments later, the first man exited quickly, and in the ten feet between the front door and the passenger side of the car, the asset couldn't get a good look at him.

But he knew it wasn't Funomora, which was the important point. He sighted through the side window again, into the study, the thin slice of room visible through the green-and-black night vision scope. It was the only unguarded angle to take a shot at the Japanese politician, and for the briefest moment, he saw a blur of dark robe cross in front of him. The man had moved too quickly for a clean shot or look. Another minute passed and there was more movement in the room; he caught a glimpse of one of the bodyguards who'd been in there earlier in the day. He guessed they were in the limo whenever it pulled out of the building's underground garage, its occupants protected by bulletproof glass and Kevlar body armor.

3.

He heard sirens. An ambulance pulled up in front of the building, brakes squealing from dust and pressure as it came to a halt. A pair of paramedics opened the back doors and pulled out a gurney. As they did, the front doors of the building were flung open quickly. Funomora came out with a younger man who was hobbled, something tied around his leg, trouser torn off and bloody. The younger man had his arm over Funomora's shoulder and was using him as a crutch. The two paramedics rushed over to help. Taking the weight of the injured man on each shoulder and helping him onto the stretcher, then lifting it together in practiced unison into the back of the ambulance.

It was interesting drama, the asset thought, but he had a quick decision to make. The paramedics were no real threat. *Wait until they're inside the vehicle and its moving; the target will do what concerned people always do, which is pause there for a second while it drives away.*

And Funomora did.

The bullet was a perfect shot to the apricot, exiting from the back of his neck in a fine spray of bloody mist and fleshy material. Funomora was dead before the ambulance's taillights disappeared from sight.

Just two more to go, the asset thought, *and I can go home.*

2.

34

JUNE 24, 2016, MARSEILLE, FRANCE

The port warehouse was thirty thousand square feet of emptiness, a corrugated tin giant with a dirt floor under a wood-beamed a-frame roof that towered forty feet overhead.

Joe Brennan and Victor Moutiere parked the dirt-caked Citroen outside the entrance; the building's fourteen-feet-high sliding doors were open to the elements, and an unseasonably cool drizzle of rain gently flecked its way inside; the warehouse sat at the far end of a row of similar buildings, each with an exit on one side to the loading area and another on the opposite side to the docks.

They glanced around carefully as they got out, wary of unwelcome company. The car doors thunked closed behind them; the area was quiet save for the odd cry of a seagull. It was cool in the early morning, the sun barely up.

Their steps crunched in the dirt as the two men walked over to the entrance. The site was private, as requested, and there were no other vehicles around at six in the morning; the air smelled strongly of fish and seawater.

"This is it," Victor said. The Frenchman had bags under his eyes and a gathering layer of stubble. "As I said, keep your head down and let me do the talking. They're not the types of men who follow the news, so you should be okay; and their work is first-rate."

Brennan hated taking the risk; but he had no option when it came to getting a new passport. His treacherous boss at the agency, David Fenton-Wright, had set him up for murder and now, instead of tracking a rogue nuke or figuring out who was killing diplomats, he was on the run. He needed paper to keep moving. Victor had assured him the new document could be obtained, but it was going to eat most of his remaining ten thousand. Then he planned to make his way to London by train before driving to the coast and taking the ferry to Ireland.

With some deft work by Myrna, a pilot would meet him with a Gulfstream, a jet just big enough to get them across the Atlantic without refueling. Where she planned to obtain a pilot, let alone a jet, Brennan did not know. He glanced over at Victor as the Frenchman peeked inside the building then waved for Brennan to join him.

"Looks okay," Victor said. "They'll come in from the other side, probably drive right in."

"So tactically, we're overwhelmed in this place if they bring heavy firepower."

Victor seemed pensive. "I suppose. I've known their boss a long time now, a man named Guy. He'll give you a fair shake as long as he thinks it's his best move."

"What if he thinks numerical superiority gives him the right to take what we've got?" Brennan asked.

Victor shrugged. "He's a crook, not a school teacher. The thought will probably cross his mind."

"And if it does?"

"First, we see what he does with it. Then, if things go bad, we kill him."

So, an old-fashioned sort of solution, Brennan thought wryly. "Maybe we can avoid all that," he suggested.

"Perhaps," Victor said.

Brennan had expected a flash ride, maybe an SUV like the gangsters back home. Instead, a brown Peugeot sedan pulled into the other side of the warehouse and parked. If they were planning a double-cross, he thought, they would have driven in further, given themselves a quicker escape.

A non-descript man in a white linen suit and blue shirt got out, flanked by three guards dressed casually. Their boss was middle-aged, with collar-length brown hair, slightly Gallic features. He had a briefcase in his left hand.

"That's your contact?" Brennan said under his breath.

"I know he doesn't look like much, but he's ruthless," Victor said. "Just be cool."

The four men strode over to meet them, the guards checking the perimeter but the suitcase holder seemingly disinterested in the surroundings.

"My friend," Victor said, extending a hand, which the man shook. "This is another friend of mine, Bernie. He's the guy …"

"I saw his headshots when we had the paper made," the gangster said. "He's the guy who needs the passports. So how much is he kicking back to you?"

"Just doing a favor for an old friend."

"Uh huh, for sure," Guy the Gangster said. "And I'm Charles Aznavour. This guy…." He looked at Brennan again, then opened his suitcase to take out an envelope, "…he looks familiar to me, Victor. That's never a good thing in our line of work, when you can't remember why you know someone." The gangster had that hint of concern on his face, a slight suspicion.

"But if we didn't deal with people who have a little trouble here and there, they wouldn't need your paper… or anything else you sell, my friend," Victor said.

Guy seemed to ponder the notion for a moment. "That's true. You have the money?"

"Ten thousand," Brennan said, handing his own smaller envelope over.

The man leaned in to hand Brennan the larger manila envelope... then stopped halfway, then leaned back. "That's an interesting accent. Your French is perfect, but you're not from here..."

"The paper?" Brennan said, smiling, his hand still out. His nerves were on end, alert for just such a pause.

The gangster had taken on a curious look, his eyes darting as he searched his short-term memory for something playing at his subconscious. "I think... I think I know exactly who you are now. You're the American the police in Montpellier are looking for..."

All six men stood silently, within reaching distance of one another, the moment's tension ratcheted up.

Brennan was worth a lot of money to whoever caught him.

Each looked at the other. When the bodyguard closest to Guy glanced at his boss, the smaller man nodded just slightly, almost imperceptibly. Victor saw the move, saw all three guards going for the pistols in their waist holsters at the same time. Before anyone else could react, he drew and raised the nine millimeter, took a half-step forward and rammed the barrel into Guy's mouth, while grabbing the gangster by the back of the head with his other hand.

"Nobody draws," he said. "Guns down on the ground. Now!"

Guy nodded his agreement, unable to talk. "Dngghf!" he demanded.

Brennan said, "Are you sure..."

"Yeah," Victor said. "I've played poker against this guy for fifteen years and he has a big tell. I didn't have a choice." He nodded back towards the men. "Now kick the guns across the room."

All three obliged. "What do we do with him?" Brennan said.

"We don't do anything with him," Victor said. "You're going to take that Peugeot over there and leave, because you have a trip to take. I'm going to take Guy here for a little drive and talk in my car while his men wait here."

Brennan wasn't sure what to say. In six months of almost having his head handed to him, Victor was one of the few honorable men he'd met – despite the fact that, by all social convention, he was supposed to be the worst. "You didn't have to do this," he finally said.

"It was the right thing," Victor said. "Chances are if you don't grab me in that apartment, I wind up dead. Besides, you've been paying me a lot of money. This gives me a chance to earn it."

Brennan smiled. "I thought you were primarily a thief..."

"And it's hard work, believe me," Victor said. "Now go!"

3.

"I owe you an enormous debt. I won't forget that," Brennan said.

"Yeah, yeah. Go get misty somewhere else. Leave the men to deal with things. Guy might want to kill me for a while, but you already paid him; he has no real reason to complain. And he understands that sometimes, business is business."

"Is that what this is?"

Victor smiled, a rarity. "Good luck, my friend," he said.

AMMAN, JORDAN

Ahmed Khalidi felt awkward in his own skin, fidgety. He sat on the sofa in his white linen kadura robe and keffiyeh head scarf, bored, leaning back into one corner in repose with an ice-cold glass of ginger ale in his right hand as he watched the flat-screen television on the wall.

The room, a small lounge at his father's palace, was near empty. The barest rays of light made their way through the wide, tilted window shutters. Adjacent to the sofa was a modernist armchair in steel and white leather, in which Faisal was perched, rubbing his hands nervously.

The television was on a news network, the reporters discussing Funomora's death, the EU's decision to sanction Khalidi's companies, and the isolation of the Association's remaining two members in their homeland. Facing numerous political challenges at home and a domestic scandal involving his wife, Fung was probably happy to return to Harbin, avoid Khalidi. He still had opportunities to save political face.

The Jordanian's own future was less assured. It wasn't that Khalidi had lost all of his power; he was still an influential figure in certain circles, particularly in Arab nations. But the newspaper revelations of his involvement in funding insurrections combined with the assassinations had enshrouded him in a cloud of public suspicion. And so his eighty-four-year-old father had called him home, suggesting he needed time away from the limelight, in a secure and private environment.

It felt absolutely appalling. Insulting, even. Confined.

An anchor discussed the next story. "Does the Middle East have too much influence in American politics? The surprising answers when we come back," he teased.

The image flashing on the screen as the network went to commercial was a split screen of Khalidi and Addison March, the Republican candidate.

He rolled his eyes. "I fully expect an expose by the end of the day on how I sell white women into slavery and eat their babies. How is it possible, Faisal, for me to extract myself from this situation?

Faisal had always found Khalidi to be arrogant, vain. He wanted to point out the inevitable downfall of all such men. Instead, he sighed inwardly and did his job, which was the healthy thing to do. "Lie low. Stay away from public attention for a while. Let the people who want to cluck and make noise do so, and then come back with purpose and the drive to succeed."

"It will be that easy, eh?" Khalidi said with a wry smile.

"You have alternatives that will take less time, but they are all risky and prone to making the situation even worse than it already is."

But sitting back meant handing over control to others, and Khalidi hated that. He had controlled his own destiny since childhood, the eleventh of thirteen sons and yet the most successful financially, the most prominent. No one told Ahmed Khalidi where to go, what to do, how to behave. No one except his father.

Khalidi respected and admired the sheik. But there were days when he wished the old man would make his way to paradise with a little more urgency.

"So you are saying I must sit here and wait for my future to be determined by others. Unacceptable," he said. "Have you ever known me to behave thusly?"

Faisal, who had a master's degree in economics from Cambridge, was intuitive enough to know that most of Khalidi's decisions were grounded as much in ego as logic, as much in personal gain as adhering to any larger social ethos. Unlike the Sheikh's son, Faisal had been handed very little in life, and had worked his way off of the streets of Alexandria to get to university, and to win a scholarship for his advanced degree. He was paid exceptionally well for his advice, but never once perceived Khalidi to be actually listening.

"I know that you will eventually make the wise and right decision, your highness," Faisal said.

His phone rang.

"It's David," the other party said.

"Just a moment," Faisal answered. He cupped his hand over the phone's speaker. "It's our U.S. intelligence asset," he told Khalidi.

Khalidi rolled his eyes. "Doubtless more excuses about why he has not managed to track down either his agent or the reporter. Is there anything else he can do to help us at this point?"

"Respectfully... Mr. Fenton-Wright's ongoing failures and diminishing stature with his own people suggest he is becoming more of a liability than an asset; certainly, he is of no use in the immediate."

Khalidi acknowledged the advice and made a sweep-away gesture with his hand to dismiss the caller.

Faisal went back to the phone. "Mr. Fenton-Wright, your support has been much appreciated," he said. "Thank you for calling in, but we would ask that, for the next while, you make an appointment if you wish to contact myself or Mr. Khalidi…"

"Appointment?" Fenton-Wright said, sounding irritated and surprised at the same time. "When you needed a piece of information quickly, you had no trouble calling me…"

"Thank you, Mr. Fenton-Wright. I believe I've stated our position clearly…"

"Are you actually shutting me out?!? Do you know who the fuck I am?" Fenton-Wright said, angry. "Do you realize who you're dealing with?"

"Mr. Fenton-Wright, that sort of language is not very productive or conducive to…"

"Fuck what you find conducive, you little asshole," Fenton-Wright said. "You're the man's secretary. Put me on the phone with him. I'm the deputy director of the fucking…"

"Thank you for calling. Goodbye," Faisal said, before disconnecting.

Khalidi turned his head away from the television slightly. "That sounded… uncouth."

"Nothing significant," Faisal said. "Nothing I can't handle."

LANGLEY, VIRGINIA

Fenton-Wright stood in the agency parking lot, phone in hand, contemplating how quickly things were getting out of control.

The hit team in Montpellier had missed Brennan and was frantically searching the region and contacts across Europe for any sign of him. Fenton-Wright had seen a window of opportunity in the Aquarium meet and had paid through the nose to use local undercover assets, a renowned team of close-up hitters from Paris who would ensure the job was done right.

Instead, they'd blown it. Fenton-Wright had turned it to his advantage and Brennan was a wanted man -- by the hit team, by the police, by security officials across Europe. But in the meantime, the deputy director's own value to his employer had become a question, obviously. He'd taken care of Walter Lang but failed with the reporter; it wouldn't take Brennan long to piece together why Fenton-Wright had asked him to stay in the French city, instead of pursuing leads on the so-called nuke. If Brennan ever returned safely to the U.S., Fenton-Wright would have a whole other series of questions to potentially answer.

He needed to close the intelligence loop; Walter had been a start, but someone else had to be helping the reporter, Malone. There was no way she was getting so much valuable intel without someone at the agency helping her, and since Walter was already dead, that meant another contact.

He dialed human resources. "John? David. Yeah. Yeah, I know, long time. Anyway, I'm trying to work up a profile on someone who may be tipping the press without my say so. Yeah... yeah, I know, you'd think so. Anyway, can you round me up a profile of Walter Lang's closest agency contacts? Retired and active, yeah... the top ten names."

Walter had been an agency legend, but he'd never been social or political. One of the names on the list would probably be Malone's other source. Once he'd found the source, he'd be able to find the reporter. Once both were silenced and his own exposure minimized, he would only have the problem of Joe Brennan to still handle.

On that front, he thought, he had an ace in the hole. He dialed the phone again. "Carolyn? It's David. Are you free this afternoon for a quick chat?"

Carolyn's stomach hadn't stopped churning in hours as she sat at their kitchen table and nursed a mineral water.

She'd been on a week of administrative leave, granted to her after Joe's alleged shootout in France, a story that had been molded and massaged before release to draw minimal North American press attention. But he was cut off from the agency and its resources, wanted by the police, a killer.

She didn't believe a word of it.

Carolyn had always known that covert work got dirty, even deadly on occasion. They'd married when she was just a new recruit and Joe was just out of the SEALs. Early in their relationship, they'd agreed to stop discussing the details, as much for national security as to spare her the gore; Carolyn wasn't a shrinking violet by any means.

3.

Then David had called. And now she faced a prolonged meeting about her husband, the contents of which were completely unknown to her. She'd already told herself one thing: she wouldn't be forced to choose between her husband and her job. She wouldn't let DFW put her in that position.

A day earlier, she'd talked about the call before it had even happened, while having lunch with Ellen. She'd been expecting it since the announcement that Joe was burned.

"Whatever you do, don't let him threaten your job without protecting yourself," Ellen had said. "Bureaucrats always think they can push people around as long as they do it within the rules, because they're the gatekeepers. The only way to show them they're wrong is to stand up for yourself. Make sure you have a union rep there…"

"Association," Carolyn had replied, somewhat distant and distracted at the time. "We have a staff association. Same thing, basically."

"Either way, make sure you have a rep there if they start talking about job stuff. If you protect your job, at least you can transfer to…"

"It doesn't really work like that," Carolyn had tried to explain.

Nothing at the agency worked quite the way it did at a normal workplace. There were entire areas of the building that weren't even allowed under legislation to talk to one another, where cell phones and caller ID were banned.

And Covert was in a league of its own. So much of what it did was off the books that its senior officials were left with great leeway, a flexibility to assign solutions that wouldn't even be legal in the real world, let alone leave staff properly protected.

As a senior support staffer, she was supposed to be separate from all of that – which, realistically, was as likely as suggesting someone in the communications department be apolitical and unconcerned with public relations spin. In real terms, she had the same exact problem with David as many in the agency under him did: he could do basically anything to her and get away with it, if the grounds seemed sufficient.

What would Joe expect of the meeting? She contemplated it, tried to look at it strategically. They wanted to track her husband down and he was operating off the books. So they were looking for a potential information pipeline, a hardline between their target and someone they could control. They would probably ask her to contact Joe, and when she said she couldn't, that it was up to him, they would leave her with a message designed to bring him in…

No. That was too easy and Joe would just ignore it. They would set him up; they'd be unsure of her loyalty and Joe's willingness to take her information on face value. So they'd make it something he couldn't resist, something they could dangle that she'd be sure to mention to him, something designed to catch her attention.

Thirty minutes later, she was seated across from David's desk as he reminded her of her duties to the agency and her country, the capitol laid out behind him through the large picture window. "So if at any time Joe contacts you, Carolyn, you are required as a function of your employment – whether on leave or not – to let us know about it and his whereabouts. Am I clear?"

"Yes, David," she said.

"Good." He leaned forward on his elbows casually. "Look, I know how difficult this must be for you and I want you to know that I understand what you're going through," he said. "While you have an obvious personal conflict in this matter, the agency has wonderful counselling services available if you're feeling the stress."

That was unexpected, she thought. Usually, David showed about as much concern for people's feelings as a stone. "Thanks, I might do that," she said.

"Well, all right then," he said, standing. It was her cue to leave. Carolyn was surprised. The meeting had gone surprisingly smoothly, with no attempt at leverage or bullying. She felt a little better about things.

She walked to the door. "Thank you for this, David," she said.

"Fine, fine," he said as she opened the door. "It's all a bit uncomfortable, this one, isn't it?"

"Very much so," she said.

He looked genuinely perturbed. "I know I can be a hard-case, Carolyn, but I'm not inhuman. I do see how difficult this must be for you, and I'm sorry you have to go through it."

She smiled. "Thank you. That actually means a lot."

"It'll probably all just blow over, get resolved eventually," he said. "These things turn out to be misunderstandings, difficulties in getting past the noise to the signal of what's going on overseas."

"That's been my impression in the past, yes," she said.

"Joe was just trying to do his job, I'm sure, and things perhaps got out of hand."

Perhaps? "That's a very charitable position," she said.

"Not really," David said, only vaguely paying attention to her still as she stood by the door, his focus shifting to paperwork. "He'd been looking for something for us, something hot and below board." He looked up at her again. "All this could probably have been avoided if he knew we'd already found it, but he didn't get back into contact with us when he left Moscow. If he had, as he was supposed to, he'd already know that."

"I didn't realize that," she said.

"Still…. If you hear from him, let us know? Thank you Carolyn." He lowered his head to the paperwork and she took her cue.

On the way to the elevator, she considered what David had said. Carolyn wasn't an agent, but she wasn't stupid, either. He'd gone from being DFW, noted pit bull, to David, caring boss and sympathizer, the moment she'd stepped through the door. It was a brilliant performance, Oscar worthy. She still didn't believe it for a second. And he'd waited until she was almost gone to mention, just casually, that Joe had been wasting his time, that they'd found an item he was looking for.

He'd dangled it, she decided, just as she'd expected. Now she knew exactly what she had to do: Carolyn had to get a message to Joe, to warn him; to tell him to stay the hell away from D.C.

WASHINGTON, D.C.

Malone felt like a spy in her own backyard, although she wasn't really sure what she was looking for.

It was a daily pilgrimage, one nearly two months old; she would round the block that was home to her townhouse, cruising just a little more slowly than normal in Myrna's square little Toyota sedan as she tried to spot someone out of place in the neighborhood, someone who might be there to look out for her, or for the little red convertible she would normally drive.

Then she'd pass the townhouse's steps and look for a double newspaper drop, hoping each time that her source would decide to offer up more useful information.

Instead, she'd find only a single *Washington Post* and the same sense of disappointment.

The rest of her days at Myrna's weren't that much more successful; the older former agency staffer introduced Malone to a string of new online databases and sources, but information on DynaTech – beyond the typical public filings – was difficult to come by. It wasn't that it was trying to hide its operations, it was just a great front: a firm with multiple international customers. Whatever it was up to that was illicit and that the source thought she'd find, it wasn't evident from the paperwork or news clippings.

So she cruised through her old neighborhood one more time, the mid-afternoon weather warm and pleasant but her mind on the story and whether it was unravelling.

She glanced at her doorstep almost perfunctorily, not expecting anything.

There were two newspapers.

She stepped on the brake, idling there for a moment; then she remembered Myrna's advice and slowly crept forward, scanning the street. It was nearly devoid of cars, and those she could see were empty. There could have been someone in the surrounding buildings staking the place out, she knew, but that just meant that she would have to act quickly. Malone stepped on the gas before taking the next right turn, going around the block, circling back so that she could park right in front of the building. She threw the car into park and left the engine idling, climbing quickly from the car and running to the steps, grabbing the paper and sprinting back, jumping back into the driver's seat, hitting the gas. The tires squealed with overenthusiasm but a few seconds later, she was off the block, heading downtown, occasional glances in the mirror spotting no one.

She met the source at the usual parking garage early the following morning, before most people were even at work. She had begun to wonder about his motivation, what he hoped to gain from keeping her in the loop. But Malone debated with herself whether to raise the issue, whether it might spook him when the source had already become a more infrequent presence.

He was there when she arrived, standing in the shadows by the door. "You're late."

"It's early. I don't even have my face on by now, normally."

"There have been developments," he said. "Khalidi is in hiding; but the package your friend is looking for is on route somewhere or perhaps already there."

"Tell me about Peru and the bus explosion in 2009," she said.

That caught him off guard, it seemed. He paused for a moment. "There are competing theories from multiple intelligence agencies. The official version is that a Chechen militant blew it up. Have you made any headway with the Las Vegas angle?"

"Are you kidding? DynaTech is a big, busy firm. I've only been looking for a couple of weeks and so far it's just the usual stuff. Would you be surprised to know the Chechen survived?"

He smiled. "Not really. There had to be a reason the device made it back to the open market. Again, what about DynaTech? What have you tried?"

"A wide gamut of business contacts, people in Nevada who know everybody, tech sector types, official paper, EDGAR filings. The usual."

The source sighed with mild exasperation. "I chose to talk to you because I've read your stuff and thought you could handle this. Have you even established Konyshenko's ties to DynaTech's parent?"

She was irritated by that. "Hey: you're not giving me much. I've stuck my neck out using your information up until now, caused a major international scandal and have contract killers trying to make me their next payday. A little support would be appreciated," Alex said. "At least give me an idea of what I'm looking for."

He considered that for a few seconds. "When a ship enters the country, it has to clear Customs and Immigration. It also has to register its home port and how long it intends to be docked."

"Its manifest and itinerary," Alex offered.

"Exactly. That includes all materials being shipped, for whom, and to where…"

"Are you trying to tell me that Konyshenko is smuggling the bomb into the U.S.? Is that it?"

He turned to leave. "Investigate DynaTech," he said. "And maybe you'll find what you're looking for."

PARIS, FRANCE

The drive from Marseille to Paris covers more than seven hundred kilometers on a good day if a driver can take one of the broad, smooth toll road highways that run between most cities. But Brennan was left without that option; every booth would have his photo, every one of them expected to flag police and, unless threatened, perhaps even deny him passage through the toll.

2.

Instead, he'd guided the borrowed Peugeot along every secondary road and highway he could follow, adding nearly three hours to the normally eight-hour trip. The pale blue sedan – a 1960s relic with a roof characteristically sloped from front to back – rolled by hundreds of miles of meadows, hills, vineyards, riverside towns, tiny villages and vast chateau estates, the car's chrome hubcaps and whitewall tires whirring their way north.

The traffic around and in Paris was grotesque, seemingly millions of drivers constantly jockeying for position, gridlock on every other block, speeds in crowded areas that would make a NASCAR driver blanch. Tired as he was, Brennan had to be doubly alert, and more than once found himself wondering why anyone lived there and drove, given its far-reaching transit system.

The train station was in the tenth district and traffic on the narrow roads through the city was slow; Brennan turned on the radio and scanned for a news channel. It took less than ten minutes before an update of the hunt for the Montpellier killer, and the update had changed from earlier in the day. Now the news had a description of Victor's cousin's car. Brennan took the next right and negotiated a one-way street until he was in a quieter neighborhood. He pulled the car over, grabbed his gym bag and closed the door behind him, tossing the keys onto the driver's seat. If he was lucky, someone would steal it before the police found it, and compound his pursuers' problems.

He got out and followed the sidewalk, past boutiques and restaurants, a sushi place, a travel agent, looking for a street sign to orient himself.

Rue Antin. He followed the street until he reached the broader Avenue de L'Opera, then headed northeast, keeping his head down, bag over his shoulder, just another local heading home after work. Gare du Nord was a few miles away, a brisk thirty-minute walk. All he had to do was make it unseen or, thanks to his dyed hair and moustache, unrecognized. The streets along the way were quiet, narrow, all flanked by six and seven-story concrete walkups; a truck was unloading fruit at a corner grocer; a line of motorcycles occupied the corner of the block as he headed up Rue Saint-Augustine. At its end, it merged with Rue Filles de Saint-Thomas, heading towards the Palais Brongniart, with its towering forty-foot roman pillars and wide open square.

The sidewalks were busy and Brennan blended with the tourists, young couples and students. He turned up Rue Vivienne, past the maroon awning and busy patio of Brasserie Le Vaudeville, with its view of the square in front of the palace steps.

3.

A pair of policemen patrolled the square and one of them appeared to eye him momentarily from across the street. Brennan turned his head to look at the row of motorcycles, no doubt convenient transport for the stock brokers who worked at the exchange inside the former palace. He waited nervously for the policeman to use his radio, call backup, alert someone. He kept his gaze averted for about ten paces before looking ahead but stealing a glance in the periphery.

Brennan sped up slightly, trying to clear the area before...

The policemen were moving in his direction. One keyed a microphone on his lapel and said something, then waited, then gave an affirmative back. He leaned in slightly, peering at Brennan from thirty yards away.

Brennan sped up some more so that he was walking quickly, pushing his way through the crowd on the edge of the square. The policemen behind him were frustrated by the sudden glut of pedestrians and also began to cut a path through them, moving them aside. Frustrated, one pulled his whistle and blew it hard. A path began to clear for them and Brennan heard them yelling for him to stop.

He started to run, finding his top speed quickly, pulling away from them. A block ahead on the sidewalk, a group of pedestrians stopped suddenly at a side street to allow a car past, a police cruiser barring his path. Without slowing down, Brennan changed course and headed into the nearest adjacent building; a front desk clerk yelled at him as he ran past, ignoring the elevators, searching for a back exit but finding only a glass door into the first-floor offices of a local business. Behind him, the front doors to the building swung open and police began to file in. He opened the glass door and walked in cautiously. It looked like an accountant or legal firm, with a waiting area, a pair of secretaries and a receptionist to the right of the main door. Brennan ignored her and walked the length of the office towards a red exit sign; behind him, the receptionist was yelling at him in French that it was a private business, that he needed an appointment.

He pushed open the emergency exit. Beyond it lay a long sterile corridor, with another door at the other end and a stairwell to his left. If he was lucky, Brennan thought, the door led right out...

It swung open from the outside, police officers having cordoned off the building. Two officers, both with batons drawn. The first swung high, trying to strike him in the head from the left, Brennan's left arm batting the assailant's away even as his right blocked the second officer's strike, then followed through, his elbow cracking hard into the policeman's jaw. The first officer had recovered from the change of momentum and charged in, but Brennan spun quickly on his left heel, his right foot coming around in a blurring spin kick that knocked the officer unconscious.

2.   310

Brennan sprinted up the adjacent stairs. At the second floor he checked the stairwell door, but it was locked. He didn't bother with the third or fourth, as both were too high off street level to be of any value. Instead, he continued up to the roof, taking the steps two at a time, looking for a potential route to the adjacent building. He could hear boots on the stairs, a sergeant yelling "vite, vite!", "quickly, quickly!"

At the top landing, he pushed open the roof door and ran out, the brighter light of day catching him slightly, his eyes narrowing against it. The roof was flat and wide; he crossed it quickly on foot to the edge, Paris laid out ahead of him. The gap across to the next building was too wide, perhaps fifteen feet. Even with a run it was impossible.

The door slammed open, tactical officers pouring out on the roof. "Arret!" One yelled. "Stop or we shoot! Get down on the ground!" They began to cross the roof slowly, in formation, towards him. Brennan looked at the gap then looked back at the approaching officers. One recognized what he was thinking.

"Don't do it, mister!" he said in French. "You won't make it. Come quietly and at least you can argue your case..."

They were just twenty feet away and Brennan was out of time, out of options. He knew he couldn't make the crossing. He glanced down for a moment and considered another option.

"Don't!," the officer yelled again. "Don't jump..."

Brennan dropped off the side of the roof. The officers ran over to the edge in time to see him grasp the edge of the balcony, four floors down, hanging there from one arm, the street another three stories below. Brennan tried to reach up to the fire escape with his other hand, to pull himself up. But he didn't have the strength in just one arm; the officers watched as his fingers slowly slipped off the wrought iron and he plunged.

Below the balcony, just above street level, the nearest business's awning broke the remainder of his fall, at least somewhat. He slammed into it, snapping its support poles and sending it crashing to the ground, his body hammered by the impact, the pain in his shoulder excruciating. He'd either torn something or partially dislocated it, the arm seemingly immobile from just below the shoulder. He got up slowly, the sound of the police yelling high above barely audible over the street noise; then Brennan crossed the street, disappearing into a busy pedestrian mall.

He held his damaged arm up with his other hand and made his way cautiously through the crowds of shoppers, knowing full well other officers would be on route, that the mall could be cordoned off in short order. He found a side exit onto Boulevard Montmartre, one of the city's busiest broad thoroughfares, and blended into the pedestrian traffic. After he'd gone a few blocks and was sure he'd lost the police, Brennan found a bar and used its washroom. Inside, he checked out the shoulder. It was starting to swell; he used his left hand to push it lower, so that the joint was in line again, then pushed in and up, as hard as he could, the dislocated joint popping back into place with a piercing pain that made him feel like screaming.

They had his face; they knew what area of the city he was in. Avoiding the police wasn't going to be easy. He needed an advantage. Brennan walked back out to the bar and asked the barman if there was a pharmacy nearby. The man nodded and gestured to the east. "A block or so," he said. "You can't miss it. Big sign."

At the pharmacy, he purchased hair dye, a tourist sweatshirt and a pair of oversized Ray Ban-style aviator sunglasses. He used a public washroom to apply it as cleanly as possible in the circumstance, then spent twenty minutes sitting in one of the washroom stalls, waiting for it to dry.

He continued up the street, crossing the busy boulevard, up Passage Jouffray – little more than an alley with a few businesses along it, leading into the popular tourist zone, Montmartre, and parallel to the elegant Rue de Faubourg Montmartre. Every few blocks he would see another pair of policemen, avert his glance, try and keep cool.

It took thirty-five minutes before he was within site of the train station. The Gard du Nord was grand, more grand perhaps even than the Whitehouse, Brennan thought, block after block of ornate white concrete and marble, glass, carved pillars, its name etched across the front in twenty-foot letters, the roof lined with classic statues of figures in gowns, each representing a different destination nation. Europe's busiest station, with more than a half-million visitors every single day, it was likely to be crawling with police. But the sheer amount of foot traffic gave Brennan a chance; every airport in Europe, every ferry port, would have his picture. But most weren't as busy as the Gare du Nord, nor as close to his destination. Outside the station, he used a ticket booth on the adjacent street corner to book a one-way trip on the Eurostar to London.

Paris was nothing if not predictable: inside the station, each side of the main terminal was lined with businesses, mostly cafes and magazine shops. He kept his eyes on those to his left as he took the escalator to the platform. He had a half-hour to kill before the train departed and Brennan's gaze quickly sought out the men's room. It wasn't particularly dignified, but it was less risky than sitting out in the open. Getting on board would be more difficult; they would have his picture, but the dark hair and facial growth made him look dramatically different. It would take an attentive clerk – probably earning minimum wage and therefore not inclined to pay attention – to reconcile his appearance with the shot police had sent out. Besides, it had been several days; he was no longer a lead story, just another unexercised arrest warrant among thousands.

The train trip was uneventful, with Brennan appearing to be just one more tourist among many. In London, his passport passed muster without a second glance, even though his hair was a different color. He used a prepaid Visa card to rent a car; then he began the five-hour drive to Holyhead, Wales, an unplanned tour of England's rural west, through aging stone villages and across country roads, avoiding the larger population centers. At Holyhead, he booked a ferry ticket to Dublin, leaving the rental behind and enduring the rolling, thrashing waves for two hours as the ferry crossed the Irish Sea to the port at Dún Laoghaire, an ancient harbor protected by a vast concrete sea wall. Dozens of yachts were moored to the ferry's right in a smaller marina as it cruised up to the terminal.

At the port, Brennan found a taxi and had it take him out of town, to the north, where the fields surrounding villages like Ballyboughal and Oldtown gave rise to the nickname Emerald Isle, the verdant landscape sparsely scattered with family farms and other rural fare. Just outside the coastal town of Balbriggan, the taxi dropped him off at a private airfield. Brennan paid the cabbie with his quickly dwindling cash supply.

3.

He was bone-weary from days of adrenaline, poor sleep and high-stress. As he sat on a fence outside the small private airstrip, he thought about how nice it would be to head home to Carolyn and the kids. The fatigue made the whole exercise seem futile; he was being hunted by his own government even as he tried to protect Americans from a nuclear threat; the man responsible – assuming it was Khalidi – seemed to be facing little more than public censure. He'd made no progress on the sniper or figuring out why a South Korean agent had made off with a nuke. Brennan rubbed the thickening stubble on his face. He hadn't showered in two days and smelled ripe, and he rubbed both eyes with his thumb and forefinger, attempting to get his head straight and clear the sleep out.

He took out his phone and dialed Myrna.

"Hello?"

"It's me. I'm at the pickup."

"Our lady friend knows about the package," Myrna said. "She's agreed to be delicate with it until there's hard evidence."

"Have you had a chance to tell my better half everything's cool?"

"Not yet. I'll do that this morning. You're heading slightly north of the border, I understand. The west coast is lovely at this time of year."

Canada?

"Okay. Why's that? Sudden changes in the weather?"

"Yes, or at least that's what your friend from Moscow apparently said. He's in the city and says the mountains are lovely."

"And our jet-set friend had no problem with this?" He'd asked Myrna to arrange the pickup before leaving Marseille but hadn't had a chance until then to confirm.

"He's surprisingly happy about it," she said. "Sort of digs your style."

Brennan smiled. That meant it had to be Eddie handling the pickup; they went way back. "Well okay then. What's his ETA?"

"He's solid on twenty-one-twenty GMT," she said.

That meant he'd be there in a matter of an hour, Brennan realized. "Great. One last thing: I'm sending you a file for our friend. It's audio of a conversation with an interested party from Japan. If she knows about the package, she may as well know our other old friend is involved." The more quickly he could indict David, the more quickly they'd examine his orders; the video of the aquarium shooting would be investigated properly, the timing and splice job examined, and likely his name cleared.

"Are you good for money?"

"Almost out."

"We'll figure something out," she said. "And I'll send you background on your new friend."

"Later," he said, before disconnecting. Eddie would be along soon; Myrna would get the files to Alex, who would contact her intelligent source and burn Fenton-Wright for working with Khalidi. Finally, Brennan felt like he was making some progress.

3.

35

JUNE 25, 2016, LANGLEY, VIRGINIA.

David Fenton-Wright's stomach was in knots; he paced his office with a half-cup of coffee in one hand that was quickly getting cold. He'd been waiting for some word from his European section chief on one of his local requests for an hour; he'd skipped an NSC briefing on the latest Libyan problems, risking heat from his colleagues at state and the NSA. But all of that was meaningless, he knew, if he couldn't shut down Brennan and Malone, head off their investigation before names came out.

Before his name came out.

His phone buzzed. He hit the hands-free button.

"Talk to me."

"It's Donald in Sig Int, sir. We have an interception on one of the names you forwarded. Shall I patch it through?"

He tried to go through the Sig Int roster; Donald was a strange kid with ginger hair and a red beard. He was keen for a spot as a field agent, constantly trying to curry favor. His psych profile was sketchy and Fenton-Wright wondered how he'd even gotten security clearance. His background included a propensity for violence.

But someone had obviously seen his potential uses.

"Go ahead."

"It was a phone call to Carolyn Brennan-Boyle from a D.C. number," Donald said. An address popped up automatically on Fenton-Wright's desktop. It was an apartment; the phone records went to a 'Allison Smith'.

He double-clicked the associated audio file. The caller was a woman, older, her voice husky. She sounded familiar, but Fenton-Wright couldn't place it immediately.

"Carolyn? I'm a friend of Joe's."

"Oh. Oh am I'm glad you're calling! I haven't heard a thing now in weeks…"

"He's okay. He's dealing with some big issues, as you probably know…'

"You must be Walter's friend Myrna," Carolyn said.

Myrna? David thought about it. Wasn't there a Myrna in Sig Int and Research, a dozen years ago? He remembered her vaguely; a broad-shouldered woman, efficient, a solid analyst but perennially shunted into the background. What was her name again? Verbal? Something like that. Verbish. That was it: Myrna Verbish.

"It's better if we don't use names," the caller said.

Fenton-Wright's smile was faint and self-satisfied. Brennan had tried to contact his wife; that moment of weakness and sentiment would be a fatal mistake.

WASHINGTON, D.C.

"No more stories about Ahmed Khalidi."

Kenny Davis wasn't even looking at her when he said it. The *News Now* editor had never been great at confrontation, and he figured if he avoided her gaze, Alex would cool off more quickly.

Her head dropped slightly, her mouth dropped open. "What?"

His office always smelled musty and his desk, as usual, was a pile of litter of gargantuan complexity and depth. He turned briefly and rifled through it as if needing to find something important quickly, but continued to avoid eye contact. "You have nothing hard to support any of this nuke stuff, just your anonymous sources. It's not good enough this time, Alex," he said. "This stuff is scary, scary material. Jesus, I've been a journalist thirty-two years, and even I'm tempted to call the feds and turn this over to them. We either create a panic or we slow down an investigation. But we're not indicting a man as powerful as Ahmed Khalidi on this little evidence."

Malone blew out a lungful of air. "You know, I've risked a lot just by coming in today to discuss this…"

"So you say," Kenny said. She gave him a harsh look and he backpedalled. "Don't get me wrong, okay? You're a great reporter and if you say the bad guys are gunning for you, well, you've got bigger balls than I do. But I can't be responsible for us potentially terrifying thousands of readers and getting the magazine sued out of existence."

"I spent three hours writing this…" she said. "What more…"

3.   317

"Evidence," he said preemptively. "Hard paper showing me someone in authority believes a nuke might be on its way into the country. In other words, anything you get requires official corroboration and reaction before we'll even consider another piece. You've got a lonely desk out there in the newsroom, Alex; you're already here. You might as well spend a few hours before the end of the work day making calls to your other federal sources – you know, the ones you can publicly name. See if anyone's heard this stuff. Then maybe we can move ahead."

Malone left his office feeling stung; Kenny had always backed her in the past, but increasingly he seemed more worried about his pension than her stories. Which probably made sense; the lawyers would rip any follow-up to shreds anyway. Maybe he was right; maybe she could put in a couple of hours before she headed back to Myrna's and the safety of anonymity.

She thought about the older woman and smiled. She had a good heart, and she'd understand if Alex was a few hours later for dinner.

Myrna's front door buzzer sounded, which immediately made her nervous. Her personal circle was limited and the timing was bad.

Maybe Alex had just lost her key.

She pushed the button on the ancient intercom system by her front door. It had been sloppily painted a light tan/orange, to match the walls of the entrance hallway.

"Who is it?"

"I have a package delivery here for a Myrna Verbish, ma'am." The voice was young. "Would that be you?"

"Just leave it outside the front door and I'll come down and get it. I'm not decent right now."

"Can't do that, ma'am," the young man said. "You need to sign for it."

"Who's it from? I'm not expecting anything."

A pause. "The return to sender is for a Walter Lang."

Walter? Had he sent her something before he was shot? Why delay it and then use a courier service? What would he have been playing at?

Outside the building, the young man in the brown cap and shirt with the ginger hair and red beard waited. After a few seconds had passed, the buzzer sounded.

2.

Inside the building, the delivery man took the two short flights of stairs to the third floor, second from the top, where Myrna's apartment was situated at the end of the hall, on the right hand side. He checked the hallway both ways and listened for any sounds before proceeding to the door to knock. "UPS ma'am," he said, using his free left hand to take the silenced pistol out of the back waistband of his shorts. He was nervous, on his first real assignment, a chance to impress the big boss.

There was no sound. He knocked again. "Ma'am?" He leaned in to see if she was using the spy hole to check him out. The glass exploded outward, the .22 caliber bullet passing through his left eye and lodging in his brain. He collapsed to the ground, spasmodic, the brain damage not killing him immediately but rendering him beyond repair.

Myrna opened the door slowly. The man was lying right outside it and she leaned down to see if he had any identification on him. She heard a slight noise to her left and looked up, for just long enough to see David Fenton-Wright's silenced pistol.

The two shots were quick and precise, and Myrna slumped to the floor next to the delivery man.

He'd been right to follow the young man in, he decided, and that a veteran like Myrna Verbish would see right through the delivery ruse. But she was never a field agent, not inclined to check other angles of attack, or for backup. He walked over to the bodies and took the pistol from his own gloved hand, placing it in that of the fake delivery man. Then he picked up the delivery man's own pistol and put it in his pocket. Police would be occupied for days trying to figure out who Myrna really was, or why a senior citizen would shoot it out with a man of no apparent employ, dressed in a fake delivery costume. Eventually, he might have to worry about a tie between Donald's current job and Myrna's past. But he had bigger problems to clean up in the immediate.

Myrna was still twitching, trying to overcome the inevitable, her foot shaking and her body shuddering slightly, blood entering her lungs, her breath sputtering. He stepped over her and entered the apartment quickly, looking around for her computer; it was on, her email open and unprotected. There was an audio file in the inbox from a French email address. He forwarded it to his own address, deleted the original, and flushed the computer's garbage and cache folders.

Whoever Myrna's contacts in intelligence were, Fenton-Wright decided, she wouldn't be helping Alex Malone out, or anyone else, any longer.

Malone got back to Myrna's building from the office later than she'd planned. She was still irritated by the whole argument with Kenny – and her lack of progress on named sources -- when she pulled into the parking garage. She got out of the old red Miata and crossed the parking garage to the stairwell, taking them up to the third floor.

She turned the corner and saw Myrna and another person laying in the hallway, a man. She gasped inwardly, shocked by the sight of the blood pooling around them. Before she could react, she heard a noise from the apartment, its door still wide open. She quickly turned the corner of the stairwell and moved up to the fourth floor landing, peering just over the edge of the bannister rail to watch the hallway. A moment later, a man passed by quickly, older, with sandy red hair.

She recognized him right away. She'd tried to do a profile on him once, back before it had all started.

David Fenton Wright.

And he'd just killed Myrna, which seemed certain. She waited until she heard his footsteps go down all three flights, and the front door open and close behind him. Then she rushed down and ran to Myrna. Malone turned her over. She was still breathing, clutching a hole through her neck, gurgling through the blood.

"Myrna! It's Alex, sweetie. Hold on! I'm going to call an ambulance."

She gently shook her head, smiling even as she choked slightly on blood. "No… too late."

"No! Don't you quit, goddamn you Myrna! Stay with me! Be tough for me!"

"Too late," Myrna said, her eyes wandering slightly. "My phone… call Bernie…"

Malone fumbled through Myrna's shawl pocket and found the phone. "I've got it…"

"Call Bernie…"

"No, dammit! Stay with me. I'll have an ambulance here…"

Myrna closed her eyes for a second and coughed hard. The wounds were flowing hard now, the blood gathering in a widening puddle. "Going to see Walter," she said gently.

And then she closed her eyes for the final time.

20,000 FEET ABOVE THE ATLANTIC OCEAN

2.

The cockpit door closed and Eddie Shaw entered the luxuriously appointed cabin of the Gulfstream jet. It had seating for twelve, chairs facing each other for a more social atmosphere; but the spy with the ridiculous black dye job, moustache and aviators was the only passenger.

Eddie shook his head mournfully. "You look like an extra from a Beastie Boys video."

"You're dating yourself, Ed," Brennan said. Eddie took the seat across from his.

"We have to stop meeting like this," Eddie said. "Although on the upside, no one was shooting at the plane this time. Thank bloody God; you know how much one of these things costs?"

Brennan looked around quickly. "How did you manage this anyway?"

"Pulled in a lot of markers; one of the guys I trained as a young whelp had some success in the business world, so he loaned her to me. We have to stop to refuel and clear customs in Halifax; Vancouver's another six hours beyond that."

"I'm sorry for pulling you into this," he said.

Eddie seemed nonplussed. "When I heard about Walter I knew something bad was going down; then the agency started putting out feelers to see who'd heard from you and I got real worried, bro. But you seem okay."

"It's been a hell of a few months, Ed. I haven't seen Carolyn and the kids since before Christmas, I've got a growing list of agencies that want my scalp and you know what the kicker is? Despite everything I haven't prevented a damn thing; there's a loose nuke out there..."

"Damn."

"And on top of that my boss at the agency is trying to set me up, take me out."

"You're kidding, right?"

"I wish I was."

"Joe, you know why I stayed a pilot after coming back from the Gulf? Because up here, there are just fewer problems. I don't know how you do it..."

Brennan had been running on automatic for so long, he hadn't really thought about it. "It's all just second nature now, I guess. Whenever I take my mind off the immediate and start pondering the why of it, I end up in trouble."

"Yeah? Well, the why part is easy for me, man," Eddie said. "I'm here because you asked me to come."

Brennan felt a glow of support but was embarrassed, too. "Geez, Ed, you don't have to say..."

"No," the pilot said quickly, cutting him off, "it's true. You know, when you got on board, the first thing you said before you settled back into your seat and I went into the cockpit was "thanks Ed, I guess I owe you another one. But that's the thing, Joe: you don't owe me a damn thing. Not one thing. People like Walter and me – God rest his soul – people like Walter and me, we support you because we know your character; we know you're a good man, Joe, and in your line of work, that's a difficult thing to be."

Brennan smiled a little grimly. He didn't feel good about his "line of work." Mostly, he felt dirty.

The pilot wasn't done. "So when you go get stuck in some haemorrhoid of a backwater and you need me to come get you, I don't do it so that you'll 'owe me one'. I do it because I figure whatever you're up to, it's probably the right side to be on. My old man always told me that whether we like it or not, life is about one side or the other. It's inevitable."

Brennan's phone rang. It was Myrna's number. "Talk to me," he said.

"Is this Bernie?" a familiar voice said.

"Alex?"

"Yes ... who... Joe?"

"Yeah. I'm on route to Vancouver. Where's Myrna?"

Malone gave him the news.

"We have to make that son of a bitch pay, Joe," she said. "Myrna saved my life and yours, and he killed her. He killed her, Joe. He left her bleeding in the hallway of her building."

"He'll pay, believe me," Brennan said. "I'm going to resend you the file I sent to Myrna. Chances are he's either wiped her computer already or, at the least, the recording I mailed. Take it to your intelligence contacts. They'll know what to do with it."

"But what about…"

"That's what will make it happen. There's a snippet of a conversation on there with Funomora in which he confirms DFW set me up, potentially on Khalidi's orders."

"Potentially?"

"It's enough to have him taken in, questioned. He's done, Alex. And if this doesn't get him, I promise you that I will."

Malone smiled grimly, then used her free hand to wipe away her tears. "So what now?"

"I find Konyshenko and see if I can figure out the Korean connection. I'd assumed Han was working for the Association when she stole the item in Cabinda, but that's not the case."

"I can ask my source about that, as well. Why would South Korea have any interest in a rogue nuke? It makes no sense."

2. 322

"In the meantime, you need to get to Vegas, see if you can figure out this DynaTech connection your guy mentioned."

"If you're still looking for a potential sniper motive, maybe it's Dmitri, clearing out the collective memory with respect to the device. He certainly has the contacts. He brokered the deal, allegedly, in which the Koreans double-crossed Abubakar, so he must be working with them, maybe to smuggle it into the country in the first place."

"That's one more reason to get someone inside DynaTech."

"You have any suggestions on how I can cultivate a high-level source in a matter of hours?" Malone had faith in her ability to get information out of people, but that was asking a bit much.

"You've got two options," Brennan said. "You can either find someone inside the company who's got an axe to grind..."

"Or?"

"Or someone outside the company with an even bigger one. The last time I talked to Myrna she sent me a basic agency backgrounder on Konyshenko, including his suspected criminal affiliations. That's our in. I'll send it along ... along with a little surprise for DynaTech."

LAS VEGAS, NEVADA

It was just before midnight when the charter flight got into McCarran airport, south of the city. Jefferson Kane watched dispassionately through the picture window as the cream-colored twin-prop plane landed, his hands in the pockets of his mink overcoat, which he only wore during chilly desert nights and on special occasions.

He had a richly coloured purple dress shirt underneath it, and a large platinum rope chain. Even though it was night, he still wore the same Carrera-style sunglasses, blowing the odd bubble from a wad of pink gum, a three-year-old affectation substituting for cigarettes. His hair was in narrow cornrows and he was heavy, at least three hundred pounds, which caused him to wheeze slightly when talking, a result of the hot, dusty daytime air and years of marijuana smoke.

"You want us to go out and meet the plane?" one of his underlings said. There were three of them, just hanging and waiting for him to tell them what to do. They were dressed in linen suits but without ties, perhaps in deference to the town's vacation nature.

"Nah. We'll pick her up in arrivals like normal folk. Just be cool, yo," he said. "We still got a long night ahead of us."

3.

Kane was uncommonly nervous for a man with a reputation of being stone cold when he needed to be, when business demanded it. He had no idea how the job was going to go because it wasn't like anything he'd handled before. At the same time, it was the business opportunity of a lifetime. He knew if he'd let it pass, he'd miss his shot, maybe his one shot, to become the biggest dealer in Sin City.

It had started eight hours earlier with a call from a reporter in D.C. She had information about him, she'd told him, information supplied by the kind of people who could shut him down in a minute. But instead, she needed his help, and was going to offer him a bigger chunk of his marketplace in return.

"And how, pray tell, are you going to pull that off?" he'd asked. "Who the fuck are you, anyway?"

Malone had pointed him to her recent bylines. "I think we can help each other. Meet me; you have nothing to lose."

"Except my valuable time," he'd said. "Give me one reason why …"

"Paul Parker."

Parker was Kane's main rival in the local trade. Or vice-versa, given that Parker controlled most of it. "I'm listening," Kane said.

"I'll come down tonight. There's a charter flight this evening out of Dulles."

They picked her up in arrivals, watching unsurprised as she gazed up at the giant neon "Welcome to Las Vegas!" sign, and at the slot machines in the arrival terminal, most occupied by elderly women. Malone wondered where they'd all come from or were going; or whether they were maybe locals who just liked losing their money among the relative anonymity of international travelers.

Ten minutes later, her new associates were pulling Kane's SUV out of the pay lot, on the road into the city core.

"So, you going to tell me how my name came up as the guy to talk to for this "deal" of yours?" Kane asked her.

"Let's just say there are a lot of weird people in Washington and leave it at that," Alex said. "It's one of those questions no one really wants answered." It sounded ominous enough, she supposed, without being too much of a shot at the gangster's manhood.

"So explain."

"You have one of your men break into the offices of a company called Dynatech."

"You want us to steal documents or something? Take a little 'proprietary' technology?"

"Nope. We're going to leave something behind."

2.

Dynatech's new five-story office building was in the far west of the city in a business development park; it was made of light-coloured concrete and dark tinted windows, so sterile and featureless it could have been doctors' offices, or a school, or a public library. In front, a massive parking lot held three hundred slots, all empty in the wee hours, but illuminated for safety by the dull glow of the stylized street lamps.

They pulled up alongside the curb near the glass front doors.

"Clarify," Kane said. "What, exactly, are we going to leave behind? Because if it's a horse's head or some freaky shit like that, then yo, this shit is already over."

"A piece of malware, designed to open their system up to someone outside."

"So...?"

"We can get in and take things whenever we want, including their shipping records. My sources tell me the company's owner, Mr. Konyshenko, imports a dubious amount of off-market product from the Golden Triangle and South America. Most of it winds up with your friend Mr. Parker."

Kane nodded slowly. "Uh huh." The ramifications were clearer. "And you're just going to share this information with me..."

"In exchange for you getting me access to it, yes."

"Uh huh." The rotund dealer considered the possibilities. "So if you plan on poking around somewhere down the line, I suppose you want us to figure out a quiet way to handle this, is that it?"

"Something like that."

"Okay then. Give us a few minutes to make sure everything's cool, then follow us in." He undid his seatbelt. "Shorty, Malcolm, you're with me. Malivai: stay here and take care of the lady."

Malivai was the driver. He was busy texting someone something. "What?"

"I said get your ass off your phone and pay attention, dumbass. We're going inside. Take care of the lady."

"Okay Jeff."

They got out of the car and made their way across the parking lot. The front doors were locked, and there was a manned security station just twenty yards beyond them. The gangster noticed a buzzer pad by the doors and keyed it.

Inside, the middle-aged, tall, thin security guard leaned forward nervously into a mic. "Office hours are over for the evening," he said.

"Yo, man, let us in," Kane said. "I've got to ask you something."

The guard pushed up his glasses, then shook his head then keyed his mic again. "I can't do that sir, sorry. You need a security clearance pass. You can come by in the morning after eight, however, and they can set that up for you if appropriate."

3.

Kane needed to employ some bargaining leverage. He pressed the button again. "Yo man … your employer give you good benefits for this job?"

The guard seemed a bit surprised by the question. "Not… really, I guess."

"So how much you figure they was willing to spend on the glass in these here front doors? If I take out my Glock and unload a magazine, you think this stuff is bulletproof? You think I can get in there before the police arrive to save your ass? Or, you can let us in and have a quick word. I swear man, that's all."

He held a pistol up to the glass for the guard to see, as did both of his colleagues. The security guard looked at them wide eyed, mouth slightly slack-jawed. Then he pushed the door buzzer.

Kane walked over to the desk casually. "What you make here, man?"

"Pardon?" The guard had a terrified look on his face and his hand was one inch from what looked like some sort of panic button.

"How much they pay you here, man? What's your… you know, hourly wage?"

"Nine-fifty."

Kane thought about how much he stood to make if Paul Parker's business was badly damaged. Nine-fifty? And people in Vegas called him a crook. "Yeah? Well I think anyone making nine-fifty deserves a coffee break right about now." He took out his money clip and pulled off two hundred-dollar bills. "Mr. Franklin thinks you should turn off the security system for a few minutes and take a walk."

The guard was frozen. "I…"

"Yeah?"

"I…"

Kane rolled his eyes. "Man, we ain't going to hurt you, okay?"

"But I'll lose my job if anything goes missing…"

"We ain't going to steal shit, just look around, is all." He pulled off another hundred. "This make it easier?"

"I…"

"Stop saying 'I'. Man, I'm telling you, we ain't going to disturb a goddamn thing. We'll be out before you get back in a half hour. Or…" He put the Glock down on the edge of the security desk, "… we can do this the hard way, yo."

The guard took the three hundred from his other hand. "A half hour?"

"Uh huh. You got security file access?"

"Sure."

"You wipe the last half hour, too, or we come back and find you, you dig?"

"Uh huh."

The guard got up, hastily stuffing the bills in his pocket and heading quickly for the front doors. He'd been gone about a minute when Alex came through the entrance. "What did you say to that guy? He was white as a ghost."

Kane shrugged nonchalantly. "We overcame a difference of opinion. You've got thirty minutes, sweet thing."

Alex planned on following Joe's instructions to the letter: find the largest secretarial desk on the top floor, find the computer, plug in the tiny memory stick to one of its rear slots, and get out.

She moved towards the elevator.

"Uh uh," Kane said, wagging a finger. "Those will be turned off at night. Probably need a security key or something."

She looked around. "So where...?"

He pointed to the dual exit signs in each corner of the lobby. "Those probably lead to the stairwells. People got to use the stairs during a fire. Elevator makes a pretty good oven, you think about it..."

The stairs took a few minutes, but Alex was fit and took her time. They were in no rush; it was approaching two in the morning. On the fifth floor, she pushed the door open; predictably, it opened to an elevator lobby again. She followed one of the narrow side corridors that flanked each of the elevator banks. They led directly into an executive reception area, complete with sofas and modern art, lit only by the exit signs and the moonlight that made its way through the vertical blinds covering the side windows.

She saw the glow of the flashlight, almost too late. A second later it emerged from the door on the opposite wall and the other side of the room, and Alex ducked behind the nearest desk as the arc of light swept across her surroundings.

A second security guard. She thought about the look on the other guard's face as he'd left, watching him slink away from the building. He'd probably been scared to death by Jefferson Kane; for the first time, she found herself seriously doubting Joe's judgment, getting her involved with the gigantic gangster.

The guard was taking his time sweeping the room. Had he heard something? Alex could imagine the professional humiliation of being caught in a burglary while covering a story with political overtones, like some sort of Watergate in reverse. But the issues at play were just as important, bigger than the story itself, matters of many lives and deaths.

The guard made his way between the rows of desks. Alex huddled in the foot space under one, the chair pulled in as well to make it appear an unlikely hidey hole. A set of black shoes passed briskly by and she stole a quick peek; from the back, he looked short, but also older, like his desk mate in the lobby, a thatch of grey-silver hair sticking out from beneath the back of his cap.

If he went right to the lobby, things could get messy, she thought. Hopefully he was doing a floor-by-floor check. She waited until the guard had passed down the corridor to the elevators and got out from under the desk. She crossed the room to another pair of similar parallel corridors, this time on either side of the copy room. Beyond them, another seating area was more appointed, with couches and matching short black-leather armchairs. A large teak desk sat in front of a set of glass doors.

Bingo. It had a tower on a pull-out tray below the desk, one of the possibilities Brennan had suggested. "Whatever you do," he'd told her, "don't pull the tower out." Chances were good, he'd noted that snared plugs would be pulled out of the back of the computer, increasing the risk of discovery on several fronts – in the immediate, as she struggled to plug things back in, or a day later when someone pulled the tower out again to try and figure out why their keyboard wasn't working.

Instead, she reached behind it with her left hand, feeling with her index finger, as he'd suggested, until she found what felt like a USB slot. She tried the memory stick one way, then the reverse.

It slid into place.

2.

36

JUNE 26, 2016, RICHMOND, B.C., CANADA

Brennan had been able to see the snow-capped mountains as they'd approached the city, but now it was gloomy and grey, rain coming down in firm droplets at the lower altitude as the plane descended to land.

As it touched down the urban skyline of Vancouver was barely visible through low lying fog in the early morning. Brennan didn't rush to rise, like a commercial passenger. They'd be taxing directly to a private hanger owned by Eddie's benefactor, where Ed had already arranged for a ride downtown. Neither man had said much for the rest of the flight, following the news about Myrna; Brennan felt mournful and slightly lost as he peered out the jet's small window at the quiet airstrip.

He shook it off. He didn't have time for sentiment; that could wait until later, until he was home and life seemed normal again.

Myrna's file said Konyshenko was in Vancouver to receive an award from the Russian Canadian Benevolence Association, for his financial contributions to helping orphaned children find homes in North America. They were holding the ceremony in a park on the south side of downtown, in the shadow of the Granville Bridge, the proceedings back-dropped by the city's mass of gleaming glass-and-steel towers. Brennan had the driver drop him off a few blocks away and hiked over. The ceremony wasn't for four hours, but a crew was already busy setting up a stage and seating.

He took out his phone and brought up a browser window then searched for information on Vancouver hotels. Once he had the half-dozen most expensive, he cross-referenced their locations with that of the park until he found the two closest. Konyshenko would probably move to the park as close to the event time as possible, but he would still leave thirty minutes or so for error; generous benefactor that he may have been, he was also a sociopathic arms dealer, Brennan knew, and that suggested his ego would not allow him to risk missing such a big occasion.

The two hotels were polar opposites despite similarly stratospheric price tags for a room; one was modern, tinted glass and sleek art deco décor, a high-end haven for the jet-set; the other was a grand old hotel from the railway era, concrete and gargoyles, with high tea and a formal dining room that required equally formal dress at all times.

The jet-set place might have seemed a better fit for a player like Konyshenko, Brennan thought. But he was Russian, and formal wealth, old money, held a certain allure there culturally – particularly to someone with new money. Konyshenko wouldn't want to impress spoiled rich kids and Hollywood types; he'd head to the grand old hotel, just for the extra odd whiff of power.

It was a half-dozen blocks away and Brennan walked it in the early sunshine; he stopped and got a paper and a coffee at a convenience store, eventually taking up a position across the street from the hotel, where he could watch the doors for a few minutes while he checked the news.

There was nothing of note from Europe or on the sniper investigation; Myrna's death was doubtless being treated as a local homicide, and no one in Vancouver had a reason to care. He flipped to the international page, and there was a story on the gathering race for the presidency. The Republican hopeful, Sen. Addison March, had just had his second hit speech in a row, getting high marks from pundits despite the ongoing slurs from some about his past associations with Middle Eastern money. His challenger, Sen. John Younger, had taken a rare break from campaigning on the weekend prior, and was beginning to show cracks in his cool exterior from the length of the race, the press said, with many months still to go.

Neither man struck Brennan as leader material. But it wasn't like people were taking his advice on the matter.

FAYETTEVILLE, NORTH CAROLINA

Sen. John Younger's "rest break" was a chance for him to go fishing with his eldest boy, he told the press, a weekend away from the dirty game of politics to get back to what was really important: family.

He chose a lodge in North Carolina because Fayetteville is in North Carolina, and Fayetteville – or more specifically Fort Bragg – is the largest Army community in the United States. His 'vacation' was timed to coincide with a return of several thousand troops from duty overseas and, like most moments in the scheduled life of a man running for president, was really just another photo op.

He'd spent the first day fishing with Toby, his second day making hot dogs for military families and kids alongside his son at a base event. Local TV, lacking a decent big local story, was lapping it up, and national in turn was making him look like America's best dad. He stood behind a big table with tray after tray of steamed wieners in front of him and bags of buns, using tongs to prepare the dog, then handing it, with napkin to each serviceman or his family member with his left hand, and shaking with his right. "Thank you for your service," he repeated ad nausea. "Thank you ma'am, thank you, son; thank you kindly sir, thank you." His pearly white teeth fairly glowed in the afternoon sun.

After they were done and he'd taken some softball questions from the press, his phone rang. "Senator, it's Mark."

"Mark! How's Washington, my friend?"

"Couldn't tell you, sir. I'm in your limo out in the parking lot."

Younger looked concerned. "Something big?"

"No sir, not at all; just a bunch of things upon which I can update you."

"I'll be there in a matter of moments, my boy," he said.

Fitzpatrick was sipping a whisky and ice when Younger joined him. "Good to see you're not riding on the bus," he told the candidate. "You need to relax."

"Don't believe what you hear," the veteran politician said. "There were several advantages to coming down here now, both on the fundraising and optic sides of the equation."

"I thought as much. Look, we've had a pretty huge development in the ACF matter."

"Okay."

"It looks like Fenton-Wright has stuck his foot in it. He may have been involved in some dirty business with respect to his asset, including a pair of deaths."

"You don't say…"

"I have a media contact who can apparently attest to seeing him leave the scene of a double homicide, and who has some interesting audio of him on the phone with a member of the ACF. And I've been poking around; one of the bodies appears to be a missing signals intelligence analyst who spoke with DFW a few days ago about something."

"Gracious," Younger said. "What's your handle on it, son?"

3.

Fitzpatrick looked almost wistful. He took a sip of the scotch. "Oh, he'll have to be brought in. It's a shame, really, sir; he was useful at times. But the agencies all agree, he's deep into something."

"Well, let's stay away from that 'something', at least publicly, okay my boy?"

"Yes sir. Where to next?"

"We've got Michigan in a little over a week. And so it goes…"

"Just think, senator: this time a year from now, I'll be referring to you as Mr. President."

Younger smiled at the thought. "That has a nice ring to it, Mark. Or should I say, Director Fitzpatrick."

"Now you're talking, sir. Now you're talking."

LAS VEGAS, NEVADA

Kane had been fiddling with Malone's laptop for several minutes and she was starting to get nervous.

They'd dropped her off at her hotel after their spate of industrial espionage, and she'd had a few hours of sleep before getting up at noon and booting up her computer. But she'd been unable to get the program Joe sent her running. Kane had called about an hour in to see if she'd made any progress with his information, and she'd explained her problem.

He'd arrived twenty-five minutes later with a four-man entourage, all of them reeking of weed. She wondered what they must have looked like heading through the lobby as a posse, frightening the business locals.

Then he'd set to work.

"So how come you know about computers?" she'd asked.

"Got a B.Sc from UNLV in programming," the oversized gangster said.

She couldn't help herself; it was reporter instinct to ask. "So how come…"

"How come I'm a criminal? That what you want to know, Ms. Malone?"

"Sure."

"Like they say in the movies, it's complicated. But then, I guess shit always is."

"Let me guess: your family was poor, drugs offered a way out…"

He sneered a little at that. "Man, don't treat me like some fucking cliché. I make my own fucking decisions, okay? Now let me work." He hated that she was so dead on.

He went back to tapping away at the keyboard. She paced for a few seconds, hands in pockets.

"So, you just liked the money?"

He shrugged. "Sure, I mean, I couldn't have paid for college without it. Job security's nice too, you know?"

"You think being a drug dealer is secure?"

"In this economy? Beats working. I mean, it's not like you have to sell the shit. 'Course, the insurance premiums are a little higher." He pushed the chair back slightly. "There: you're in."

She looked at the screen. "I don't see anything. It's just a desktop."

"It's the desktop of that secretary. That's what your friend's nasty-ass little piece of government software does. Lucky for him I took out the hidden toolkit that would've sent everything you gathered back to someone with an Arlington, Virginia IP."

"Thank you. That's pretty amazing." Malone felt slightly guilty at having such a typecast, stereotypical image of Kane.

Then again, he was a drug-dealing thief. "So I can just go into their system whenever I want? Won't that set off alarms?"

"Not at all. Their system just sees it as an extension of her desktop. Here's the best part: when they leave the computer in sleep mode, you can still access it. Won't turn on the monitor on the other end, won't alert anybody. We're going to have some fun tonight, girl."

VANCOUVER, CANADA

Konyshenko felt awash in power, extending his empire before the world. He strode through the expansive lobby of his two-thousand-dollar-per-night hotel in a green silk custom-tailored suit, a bodyguard on each elbow, one more walking ten feet behind them. His goatee and moustache were neatly trimmed, just dappled with grey at the top, and his eyes shone with the confidence of a man who gets what he wants.

He knew the weeks ahead might actually prove trying. He had already considered the moral implications and come to terms with his role; the end, as far as he could see, certainly justified the means. Once again, his diligence and concern from his end of the operation were bound to be appreciated by his new clients.

But it was hard for him to be humble; his rival, Miskin, was dead. That snake Abubakar had finally paid for breaking their agreement with regard to his 'device.' And now he was gaining a level of respectability in an important market.

He passed through the sliding front doors of the hotel to the car pickup area outside. The limousine pulled up and one of his men opened the door for him. He stepped inside … and before he could even close the door, the driver gunned the engine and floored the car out of the hotel driveway, leaving all three bodyguards standing on the sidewalk. The limo was cutting in and out of traffic at about fifty miles per hour, and Konyshenko reached over frantically to slam the side door shut. He hammered on the intercom. "What the hell?!? Stop this vehicle, right now! Do you know who I am? Do you know who the fuck I am?"

Brennan had kept the partition up deliberately on the stolen stretch. He keyed the intercom. "Is sir feeling comfortable back there? Would sir kindly shut the fuck up for a moment while I ask a question: where's the device?"

"So this is some sort of shakedown, is that it?" Dmitri asked, his English perfect-but-accented.

Brennan locked the rear doors. Dmitri tried them but they wouldn't budge. "Safety locks for kids," Brennan said. "We're in for a long ride if you start squirming."

"And which agency do 'we' represent?" Konyshenko asked, calming down somewhat. "Who do I mail the lawsuit?"

"Cut the shit, Dmitri," Brennan said, keeping his eyes on traffic. "You brokered the sale of a weapon a few years ago, one that has found its way into potentially unfriendly hands. My job is to find it and stop it."

"I don't know what you are talking about, my friend. Would I be right in thinking you're the 'rogue American agent' I keep hearing so much about? You are Joseph Brennan, are you not?"

"For the sake of argument…"

"Good. Then I know I am safe and do not have to tell you anything. You won't harm me."

"Tillo Bustamante thought the same," Brennan said. "Look at how that turned out."

From the backseat, Konyshenko let out a belly laugh. "This is not the cops you're talking to, Mr. Brennan. I know full well that you did not shoot Bustamante; in fact, my sources say it was his own men which, if you knew him, you would understand."

"Sure, but he talked plenty to me before they tagged him. If I could get the information out of him…"

2.   334

"You'll what? Drive me to some seedy motel room and shoot me full of sodium pentothal? Unreliable, at best. Then what? Say you get nothing? My men will be combing the city for you. Every road in and out, the airports, the train station, the ferry... No. You have no trump cards, Mr. Brennan. So I will tell you nothing and we shall see where it goes from here."

Brennan was irritated. Konyshenko had guts; he didn't doubt that. But without his information, they had no way of knowing where the nuke was headed or when it might arrive. "Look, millions of people could die..."

Konyshenko shrugged. "Millions of people die every year. What does it matter to you or me how they go about it?"

"But how well do you trust your partners, Dmitri? They seem fairly happy with the idea of getting rid of anyone standing in their way. That could include you, eventually."

"Like I said, I am a careful man. I take precautions. Those who might have a motive, they know my character and would not dare."

He had a dangerously high opinion of himself, Brennan decided. "What are you going to do when your involvement in this eventually gets out to the various intelligence agencies? Even if they can't prove it publicly, they'll demonize you privately, get your companies cut off, blacklisted."

But the Russian seemed to have become disinterested in both the conversation and the ride. "What time is it?" he said, checking his watch. He was supposed to speak in ten minutes. "If I don't arrive soon, they are going to ... how you say... round out the cavalry. I have GPS locator on my phone."

"Roll out. Or send out. But not round out."

"Your Russian any good?"

"I get by," Brennan replied in the language, perfectly.

"Good. Take me to the park, driver," Konyshenko said contemptuously. "But I wouldn't get out of the car, if I were you. My men will shoot you on sight." Konyshenko's cell phone began to buzz. "If I don't answer that, they will begin scouring the city..."

Brennan turned a corner sharply. If he couldn't get intel out of Konyshenko directly, he could leave him at his speech and perhaps get into his hotel room, tap his laptop. The park was coming up on their right, the band shell up and the seats filled. He pulled over quickly and tapped the intercom as they pulled over. "Get out."

"Perhaps you should stay for my speech, Mr. Brennan. It's very flowery and moving. Something for the little people."

"I'll pass. Get out."

Brennan's mind was ticking over, thinking of alternatives in case he couldn't get into the Russian's room. One immediately occurred: the same two bodyguards accompanied the Russian everywhere. If he wouldn't talk and wasn't frightened of the potential consequences, perhaps one of them would. It was just a matter of figuring out the right one. And if that didn't work, he decided, he would have to pay a late-night visit to Konyshenko and see just how well he stood up to the interrogation cocktail – assuming he could get to him again. He could have just taken off with the Russian, but the last thing he needed was every Canadian cop for six hundred miles on his tail.

So first things first, he thought. Once the Russian had climbed out of the limo, Brennan sped away, then left the vehicle a couple of blocks from the park and went back on foot, covering the mile quickly. Konyshenko had not seen his face, and Brennan looked nondescript. If nothing else, catching the first few minutes of his speech would let Brennan figure out the rest of his security detail, and just how many men the Russian had brought with him to Vancouver.

The park was busy, a banner near the entry declaring Russia-Canada Friendship Day; there were free hot dogs and soft drinks for kids, which had brought out families, and Brennan figured there had to be at least a hundred people in the temporary seating ahead of the stage. The deputy mayor looked sharp in a dark blue suit with a red club tie. He was talking about how important it was for businessmen like Dimtri Konyshenko to support the youth of the city, occasionally greeted with polite applause as the speech wound on. Konyshenko was seated in the first of the row of temporary chairs next to the podium, his arms folded, looking bored. One guard was seated next to him, two more were at the corners of the stage and two more were at the back of the stage, in the shadows.

That meant five, maybe six men. If he couldn't find anything in the room, he'd need to figure out which guard was most likely to talk to him, to crack under pressure. In the meantime, Brennan had about an hour at most to go back to Konyshenko's room and search it, see if he could leave ears behind.

The asset was not happy. The assignment was off plan, a wrench thrown into the works. He had no stake in the target; there was no honor in this one; he was just told it was a tactical necessity.

It wouldn't keep him from completing the mission, of course. He was a good soldier, the best. Orders that seemed vaguely motivated were nothing new to him. But he had begun to realize, with the coming of middle age, that shutting out the questions had become harder.

2.

Not that it mattered, he thought as he surveyed the target area from the apartment balcony. In the living room, the home owner was bound and gagged by the sofa. She had a wedding ring on and there were pictures around of her husband and kids, so he wasn't worried about her; she'd be discovered sometime reasonably quickly. He'd worn a mask when he forced his way into the apartment and she hadn't taken long to deal with.

Then he'd taken the rifle case out to the balcony and set up quickly. He was higher up that he'd initially liked; but his plan to shoot from the bridge had been thwarted when he realized his line of sight was cut off by the back of the tent. He knew he'd have a more difficult time adjusting for wind from on high but compared to the foothills and mountains in Afghanistan, it wasn't much of a challenge.

Soon, he was sure, he would be given the greenlight to go back overseas, to hunt down the remaining two committee members. It wasn't enough that the ACF was effectively finished, that the men involved were scurrying like rats to save their reputations. They still had to die.

For Sarah.

He hadn't thought about her in a long time, he realized. He felt a pang of guilt; was it all worth it, if he didn't keep her in his memory? She would have been thirty-one that summer, a fact his handler had reiterated back in France, weeks earlier, when he'd shown a hint of doubt. She'd wanted kids, a family of her own. Her fiancée, Mitch, had been a great guy, almost like a brother to him. They would have had great kids, been the best parents.

He swung the barrel slowly across the target zone. His target was on a slight angle to him, which was perfect, but still sitting; occasionally, the man next to him would lean forward or sway into the firing path slightly, forcing the asset to wait until the target uncrossed his arms and rose.

Showtime.

3.   337

37

It had taken Brennan less than five minutes to get to the hotel, and even fewer to steal a pass card from one of the staff. Then he'd approached the front desk, where an amiable young woman had been more than willing to help him.

"Yes, I'd like to call up to a room: 1540, for Dmitri Konyshenko."

She dialled the room and someone answered. A moment later the hotel staffer hung up the phone. "That's definitely the wrong room…"

"Oh hell," Brennan said. "Secretary must have copied it down wrong."

"What did you say the name was?"

"Konyshenko. He'll be in a suite."

She checked the registry online. "Yes, he's in…" she paused for a second, "… 1604. Your secretary wasn't even close."

"Good help is very hard to find," he said.

The receptionist rang the room. "I'm sorry, sir, but there's no answer."

Brennan took on a puzzled look. "Well I could have sworn she said… no, doesn't matter. Is there a bar here? Maybe I can wait for an hour or so. He's visiting from abroad and we haven't talked in a long time. I'd rather not miss him."

"Absolutely!" she said. "Mulligan's is just around the corner from the south of the lobby, if you take a right immediately after you come through the front doors."

"Much obliged," Brennan said, tipping an imaginary hat to her. He headed in that direction, waiting until she was busy with the next customer before turning quickly on his heel and moving for the elevators.

On the sixteenth floor he was doubly cautious, checking the entire level for guards or hindrances before using the stolen swipe card to enter. The suite was palatial – an apartment, really, with three separate bedrooms and a large sitting room, complete with one of the two wrap-around balconies that crowned the hotel.

There was a laptop on the desk in the large bedroom but he left it alone; breaking its password protection would take too long, and guys like Konyshenko always protected their technology. He considered the fixtures in the room, the lamps and the phone. But the Russian would be moving on in a few days, so that wouldn't help.

2.

He noticed the standup closet. He opened it, and a variety of Konyshenko's suits were hanging inside. Eddie had loaned Brennan a handful of small bugs, and he planted them under each lapel of the four suits, close enough for good pickup even through the cloth, but unlikely to be detected.

In all, he'd been in the hotel for less than fifteen minutes; he noticed the safe in the bottom of the closet. He probably had enough time …

Brennan headed quickly to the bathroom and retrieved a small paper cup. He went back to the miniature safe and placed the cup against the lock mechanism, then placed his ear against the cup, using it to barely amplify the sound of the tumblers clicking over as he slowly went through each number on the combination dial, looking for the slightly louder "thunk" that would accompany the lock mechanism slotting into place. The grand French doors to the balcony, combined with the altitude, rendered the room silent.

The lock 'thunked' a third time; Brennan cautiously pulled back the safe door. There were passports, airline tickets, vaccination certificate books.

And a key.

Brennan stared at it. It was for a locker, doubtless. It even looked familiar. An airport? He couldn't shake the feeling he'd seen the key before; but it was one of those vague recollections, drifting on the edge of memory.

He put the key into his pocket then closed the safe. Between it and the information he'd gather from Konyshenko over the following few days, he knew he'd have real leverage, on a source who might actually know where the nuke was.

After closing the safe, he wiped down everything he'd touched with a wet hotel towel. Through the French doors he noticed how impossibly blue the sky seemed. On a whim, he opened the door and stepped out onto the balcony.

Down below, the street scene was chaotic. People were honking horns, trying to cut in and out of lanes to the point that traffic was snarled. Brennan heard multiple sirens. A news chopper flew overhead at low altitude, heading towards the waterfront. He felt ill at ease. Something big was going on.

He quickly left the balcony and closed the door behind him, then headed back out of the room and towards the elevators.

3.

A few blocks away at George Wainborn Park, panic had set in. People were fleeing the area in the hundreds, knocking each other down even as they tried to make it to the street, scattering temporary chairs.

The initial gunshot had been the barest crack of a sound, as the asset was some four hundred yards away, as well as several stories up. The bullet had sheared off a chunk of Dmitri Konyshenko's right frontal lobe, spraying the deputy mayor with gore and blood as the instantly dead Russian's body slumped to the stage. There was a split-second pause before a woman near the front screamed and everyone began to scatter. To make matters worse, one of Konyshenko's bodyguards overreacted to movement from the corner of one eye, unloading his pistol in the fleeing crowd's direction when he thought he saw a man carrying something.

The police response was lightning quick, even by Canadian standards, a pair of cars on scene within a couple of minutes, thanks to a phone call tip from the asset's handlers, with suggestions they check both the park and hotel, and be on the lookout for a rogue American agent named Joseph Brennan.

Had Brennan known it, he might have realized that while he was taking an elevator to the lobby, a tactical assault team was taking the other car to the sixteenth floor to intercept him. The rest were stationed in the lobby, in case of just such a circumstance, and when the elevator doors dinged open, Brennan found himself immediately pinned down by officers in a crossfire position.

"Joseph Brennan, this is the Vancouver police. Lie down on the ground with your hands behind your back."

Whoever tipped the police to his presence had managed to get them there in the exact window during which he was searching the room, which meant he was either under constant surveillance – unlikely, at best – or they'd expected him to go to the room while Konyshenko was speaking.

The latter made more sense; he recalled the scene of panic on the street from the balcony, seen from above. There was no way that had anything to do with him. He thought about the Russian-Canadian Friendship ceremony, the way it was set up to have the Russian speaking at a dais. Brennan got a sinking feeling he'd been in the same position just a few weeks before, when the sniper had taken out Boris Miskin.

He'd been set up again. And this time, the police had arrived before he could flee.

He raised both hands sheepishly then said in the halting, wavering French of a frightened man: "I don't understand; could you speak slower?"

One of the officers was bilingual and repeated the order in French. Brennan approached the pair to the right of the elevator car, towards the lobby.

"Isn't this guy supposed to be American?" one said, as his partner withdrew a plastic wrist restraint tie from his pocket.

"Yeah," the other said, as he took Brennan's left arm from his head and placed it behind his back. "Fits the description though…"

He had to act quickly. Once he was in custody, the chances of getting free were slim-to-none. As the officer moved his arm behind him, Brennan kicked hard at the side of the man's knee, the joint dislocating. The second officer took a half-step forward as his colleagues screamed; Brennan shoved the first cop towards him, then as he struggled to support his colleague's weight, slid the man's pistol from its holster, moving quickly behind him, one arm around the man's throat, the gun to his head. Brennan had to take a chance that there were no snipers in the lobby, or a hostage gambit was out of the question.

"We're going to be moving with the trigger half-depressed," he said loudly. "Anyone thinks they have a shot, consider the odds of my pistol going off in the process." The lobby was deathly quiet, and a half-dozen tactical officers rose from cover positions.

He knew they'd have every exit covered and the adjacent streets blocked off; he backed towards the staff door behind the front desk, the officer walking with him.

"Just be cool, buddy," the cop said. "Nobody wants to get hurt here."

He opened the door and took them through. On the other side, a long, nondescript corridor with a dull red carpet ran past several offices, to a door with an emergency 'Exit' sign above it. "You can probably let me go now," the cop said. "I think you're clear."

"Shut the fuck up," Brennan said. He didn't like risking the man's life, but he had to bank that none of his law enforcement colleagues would be stupid enough to put a friendly in harm's way. There was no other way out. He pushed the steel door mechanism bar with his back and the emergency door opened behind them. He turned both of their bodies as they left the building, so that his hostage was facing the lot behind the hotel. There were three police cruisers, which Brennan had counted on. He only had one chance to get to one of the cars; outside, they doubtless did have sharpshooters, ready to switch him off if given an inch of leeway.

He took the hostage forward and down the steps, careful to crouch slightly behind him, to cut off any angle for a shot. He knew there could be a sniper on the hotel roof proper, which is why he had to move them quickly, the two men shuffling towards the cruiser. "Back away! Everyone back away or I'll kill him," he said.

3.

The officers around the car backed off. "Open the driver's door," Brennan told the hostage. "Carefully now."

The officer complied. Brennan turned them both so that his own back was to the car then sat down on the edge of the seat. He started the car, put it into reverse. "Now we're going to start backing up, very, very slowly, towards the end of the alley," he told the hostage. "If you don't keep up or you try to pull away from the door, I'll have to shoot you. And believe me, I'm just as good with my left as my right."

He slowly released the brake and the car began to roll backwards, door open, the hostage walking beside the door. When they were into the alley proper and two walls towered up on each side, Brennan stepped on the brake again. Once the car had stopped he gave the officer a swift push on the backside with his left foot, so that he was well away from the car, then stepped on the gas, backing out at high speed; the other officers had radioed the situation ahead, and a pair of cruisers came out of nowhere from either side of the alley, trying to block it off, shut it down like an impromptu pair of gates. The cruiser smashed against the corners of each, pushing the other cars out of the way in a shower of glass and plastic as Brennan reversed it into the street, turning in a wide arc so that he was facing the right way in traffic.

But the street was empty, save for four police cruisers a block apart, blocking each direction. They'd only just moved into position, and an officer had climbed out at either end, doubtless to deploy spike belts that would take out his tires. Instead, Brennan gunned the police motor, the four-hundred-and-forty cubic inch engine quickly pushing the car over seventy-five miles per hour; it rammed past the two cars to the north end of the street, narrowly missing the officer with the belt. Behind him, all four officers opened fire at the fleeing cruiser, but within a few seconds, it was out of range.

The cross-streets and the entire neighborhood would be locked down by cruisers, he knew. If Konyshenko had been targeted and he was being set up for it, Brennan figured, the last place they would expect him to head was back to the scene. He'd noticed the adjacent marina when he'd scouted the speech location earlier. He turned down an alley and on the adjacent street went south for a block, until the police cars at the next intersection were clearly visible. Then he pulled the cruiser over and set out on foot. If he stuck to the alleys, he reasoned, he had a chance to get to the marina. One of the power boats there could get him away from the downtown, out towards English Bay and open water, where he'd have a better chance of losing a cop boat than trying to beat multiple roadblocks. He moved quickly, trying to keep his breath steady, his adrenaline regulated as he followed the alleys between high-rises and office complexes, back towards the park.

LAS VEGAS, NEVADA

The airport was busy, packed with throngs of tourists. Kane carried the lady's bag for her; he owed her that much, and a lot more.

She bought a ticket to Seattle and checked her bag through before rejoining him and one of his men in the waiting area adjacent to passenger screening. "Look, I know we're not exactly from the same environment…" she started to say.

"You got that right."

"But I want to thank you for your help. I know you did it for the wrong reasons – so you can sell more of your product. But you need to know you may have helped save a lot of lives today."

Kane thought about that. He'd never played the hero; he gave money to the community because they were his people; but despite what she'd said, he had no inclination to become a saint any time soon. "Whatever," he said. "That list you got me turns out to be what you say it is, that's all the sweet music I need. Why Seattle?"

"The main investor in DynaTech has shipments registered as hi-tech parts coming in to both the ports of Seattle and New York. But he's closer to the former than the latter, attending an event in Vancouver today, and the ship's due in today or tomorrow. The New York shipment isn't for another three days."

"So you figure he wants to stay close to his merchandise."

"Something like that." Her phone began to buzz. "Just a second, I need to take this."

Brennan sounded winded. "It's me," he said simply.

"Where are you? You sound like you've been sprinting."

"I'm in a suburb south of Vancouver, called Richmond. Bone tired; had to take a jet ski into ocean water, then swim a distance."

"I've got the DynaTech intel. Konyshenko has a ship coming into Seattle today or tomorrow, the Liberty Lady, registered out of Liberia. He has another in three days heading into New York, the Dauntless, same company."

"Konyshenko is dead," Brennan said. He told her about the sniper and the hotel setup. "I don't have any papers anymore; left them in an airport locker. But I've got my phone, a piece and cash, albeit all incredibly damp. I'm going to make my way south; there are a few spots along the border where I should be able to get over unseen."

"My flight leaves in forty minutes," she said. "Can you get to Seattle for six o'clock? That's the earliest potential arrival time."

He checked his watch; it was almost two. There was so much they still didn't know. If Konyshenko hadn't been behind the weapon theft, but just a hired hand, that meant they still needed to find out who was responsible, as well as stopping the bomb from being used, potentially on U.S. soil. "That's pushing it, but I'll try. I have to liberate a few sets of wheels and avoid the County Mounties, but I'll get there. We have to."

Malone knew he was right. A nuclear blast in downtown Seattle would kill millions, if that was the intent. Either way, they were on their own, with Brennan wanted by the cops, a contract on Malone's head and total annihilation right around the corner.

There had to be an easier way to get a good story.

38

JUNE 26, 2016, SEATTLE, WASHINGTON

The night was stretching on, and Perry Moore was bored; the machine gun rested across his crossed arms as he strolled, the black fleece sweater keeping him warm in the growing damp chill.

He'd been walking the foredeck of the container ship Liberty Lady, his only companion the gentle lapping of the water against the hull, and the occasional check in from the other guards via walkie talkie. It was mind-numbing, spending hour after hour moving from point 'A', on the north side of the metal staircase to the bridge, to point 'B', at the other end of the ship's upper level, past row after row of twenty-foot shipping containers.

The ship was over seven hundred feet long and more than a hundred feet wide, its form not much more than the gigantic, ocean-going equivalent of a flatbed truck. There was a bridge, near the bow, a crew cabin area that extended under the stern and into the bowels of the ship, and a lift crane. Other than that, it was row after row after row of cargo containers. And over the course of the past six hours, he'd seen them all.

Liberty Lady had moored at just after five o'clock on a gloomy Seattle afternoon. Perry and his crew, who were considered notable local muscle to more than one criminal organization, had been hired to guard it. The money was good... but that didn't mean he had to enjoy it.

About seventy feet away, behind the rows of metal boxes, his friend Richie Kessler was performing the same function. His feet had probably started to hurt, too, Perry thought. But their instructions had been clear: no breaks, shift change after eight hours, three days of work.

Plus, they got guns, and maybe a chance to shoot someone. Their employers wouldn't have provided so much firepower if they weren't potentially expecting trouble.

So that had made the offer exciting to Perry and his hoodlum friends, despite the high potential for boredom.

Sixty bucks an hour was sixty bucks an hour, just to be a rent-a-threat. *On Sunday*, he figured, *I'm going to go get me an eighty-inch LED flat-screen, watch the Sounders become life-sized.*

"Cool," he said to no one. He stopped for a few seconds and listened to the water, the sounds of the harbor, the background white noise of it all combined with the drifting remnants of the city's natural din. He looked around quickly; fuck it, he thought, nobody's coming. Perry fished a small, tightly rolled joint from his top pocket and lit up, the glare from the lighter momentarily ruining his night vision, so that when the lighter went out, he could barely see around him.

The forearm circled quickly around his throat from behind, his carotid artery caught in the sharp crook of its elbow; instinctively, Perry grabbed for the arm to pull it away instead of sounding the alarm; he tried to pry his fingers under it, loosen it before ...

Brennan gently laid the unconscious guard down on the deck then slung the man's gun over his own shoulder using the thin black strap.

He'd dressed entirely in black, his face smudged over. He glanced up at the stairs to the bridge, before turning his attention back to the containers. He headed in their direction. There were four rows, each thirty containers deep; that probably meant four guards... or perhaps just three now, Brennan assumed. The one he'd laid out with a sleeper looked like a local, probably just some minor league gangster.

There were gaps every ten containers and he moved quickly to the corner of the first, listening for footfalls, getting a bearing on the guard before he could see him. He waited until the man passed, then stepped in behind him, applying the sleeper hold again, careful to catch the man's gun with his free left hand as he lowered him down.

It was too easy, he thought. If there was a nuclear weapon on board, the now-dead Russian gangster hadn't done much to protect it. The guards looked like kids; and how did the South Korean contingent figure in the whole thing? Why weren't any of its number present?

A spotlight from above the bridge swept across the deck, and straight down the second row. Brennan quickly stepped back into the gap between containers. Chances were good that no one was paying attention to the light anyway, that it was just there to dissuade would-be thieves and mischievous kids. But there was no point in being reckless.

He heard the radio chatter a second later, the guard in the next row over talking to someone; he was agitated. "What the fuck? Perry! Perry, you better not be fucking with me..." A second passed and Brennan heard him say, "Yeah... I think we got a situation."

Footsteps, multiple, inbound from all sides. There must have been more in the crew cabins, maybe another shift's worth of guards, probably two. He moved back to the corner of the containers and peered around ... then snapped his head back, the nightstick slamming into the side of the metal and just missing him as the guard rounded the corner; he had a machine pistol in his left hand, an Ingram or MAC-Ten, Brennan thought. The guard was raising it, time slowing down as Brennan's adrenaline kicked in, the pistol spitting bullets and fire at a thousand rounds a minute, even as Brennan crouched low, swinging his leg out and around in a wide sweep, taking the guard's legs out from under him, the gunfire off into the air as he left his feet, his back slamming into the deck a moment later. Brennan's palm caught him flush under the chin, and the guard was unconscious.

Sixty feet away down the row, a handful of the guard's friends were closing on him. Brennan cut back between the rows then sprinted south until he was at his full head of steam, running up the side of one cargo container and pushing off with all his strength, using the boost to catch the top edge of the box across the aisle, pulling himself up quickly so that he was ten feet above them. He waited until they rounded the corner between rows, then dropped down behind the last, dragging him back with Brennan's left hand over his mouth, his right arm choking the man out again.

The gun clattered to the ground; alerted, the guard just ahead turned around and leaped out of the container gap, spraying machine gun fire across the row. Brennan held the first guard ahead of him as a shield and grabbed for the man's sidearm as the bullets' impact drove both of them over backwards, pulling it from the holster just before they hit the deck, firing twice, the first shot missing, but the second catching the other guard in the thigh. He screamed and went down, clutching at the wound, and trying to reach for his machine gun even as his two other squad mates emerged from the next row over. Brennan moved in one smooth motion, throwing himself in their direction and landing on his knees and shins, sliding across the smooth deck to the spot between them before either could open fire, then reaching up, right hand smashing the wrist even as the left grabbed the barrel, then spinning, the butt end of the rifle catching the second guard flush, putting him out. And finally a spinning elbow strike followed by the rifle butt in the reverse direction, catching the first man in the temple and stunning him, a short front kick laying him out.

The remaining guard was crawling for his gun, his thigh wound bleeding badly, Brennan swung the machine gun around. "Uh uh." The man stopped crawling; he leaned on his right elbow and raised both hands in surrender. Brennan crouched down next to him, placing the barrel against the man's temple. He used his left hand to retrieve a black plastic wrist tie from his pocket. "Hands behind your back. Put this on," he said. The man complied, looping it over his hands. Brennan pulled it taut. "How many more?"

The man spat at him.

Brennan raised the butt end of the rifle then feinted to strike the man's head.

He cowered backwards. "No! No.... don't hit me, man! There's two more, in the cabins." Brennan pulled a gym sock and a small roll of duct tape from the little black bag. He stuffed the gym sock into the man's mouth and placed a strip of the silver tape over both.

He made his way to the cabins, his footfalls on the deck accompanied by the waves lapping against the hull. The hatch door was ajar, the lights out inside. Someone was expecting him; judging by the lack of skill on deck, they'd be nervous, trigger-happy, probably right inside the door. Brennan kicked it inward, the hinge swinging back with a squeal, the heavy door slamming into the man standing behind it. He went down hard, and Brennan could hear him scrambling to get up. The agent reached inside the room with his left hand, to where a light switch would instinctively be. A single bulb illuminated the cabin, the shadows cutting across the yellowed walls.

The man on the floor had a bloody welt on his forehead and a nine millimeter in his right hand. He reached up and Brennan jumped sideways out of the line of fire as he squeezed off two shots, the bullets ricocheting against the steel roof. The guard tried to rise but Brennan locked up the man's forearm then bent it backwards quickly at the elbow until the joint popped; the man went down, screaming, and Brennan picked up the pistol, then slammed the butt into the man's temple, driving him to the ground.

There was a second doorway at the back of the room and Brennan pirouetted around the corner, covering the room with the pistol.

2.

The knife flashed across his field of vision, cutting his hand so quickly he didn't have time to react. He dropped the pistol and caught a glimpse of the glinting blade to his left as it swung back toward him on a double slash. Brennan ducked backwards, then jumped back a foot to regain his posture. The knifeman stepped in, a blade in each hand, thrust after thrust; Brennan allowed him close so that he could parry the man at the forearms. He brought his right foot up hard, catching his assailant in the testicles. The man winced and began to double over and Brennan snapped the leg outwards, a powerful side kick catching him flush, knocking him out.

He bound and tied both men then headed back out onto the deck. If the count was right, that was everyone. Brennan took the small digital Geiger counter from his waist pouch, rented from a local outlet that afternoon, and slowly began to sweep the containers, row on row.

WASHINGTON, D.C.

In his twenty-five years in civil service, the director had maintained calm above all else. It was his trait, the gift for which others knew him, to be unruffled in any circumstance. It had brought him to the head of five different government agencies, after first exiting his military career and obtaining a law degree.

This scenario was no different; more sensational, perhaps, with more potential for public embarrassment. But a problem to be solved, just the same; and a cool head was what the agency needed to deal with its most recent crisis, he decided. Otherwise, he'd have stayed out of it all, let Jonah or one of the other senior 'decision makers' … well, make the decisions.

And so even though the news was not good, Nicholas Wilkie was smiling warmly when Carolyn and Jonah entered the office. "Have a seat, won't you both? I'm just finishing up something," he said.

He pushed the pile of papers to one side. "Right: here's the scenario. We need this disseminated to anyone inside with an interest; but for pity's sake keep it away from the general staff and the press."

"Sir?" Jonah inquired. It was obviously leading to something important.

Wilkie composed himself again. "We've had an eyewitness report that David Fenton-Wright has become embroiled in the Euro sniper affair in some manner, and has shot and killed at least one person, possibly two. One, Walter Lang, you both know well. The other was a retired analyst named Myrna Verbish.

3.

Carolyn gasped audibly.

"You knew her?" Wilkie said. "I thought Myrna was slightly before your time."

"I knew her through Joe," Carolyn said.

His eyes narrowed. "Was she in contact with him? You're aware he's been off the reservation for some weeks now."

"I know, director," she said. Carolyn had to choose her words carefully. "I haven't been in contact with him either. But I think he met Myrna through Walter; she and Walter were very close, I understand."

"Yes... well, we're sweeping her belongings looking for any signs of contact," Wilkie said. "Myrna had, by all recollection, some of the best contacts of any analyst in agency history. That would make her, even in retirement, a valuable ally for an agent on the run. But we believe it also put her in Fenton-Wright's crosshairs; the indication from our eyewitness source is that he was working for a foreign agency, supplying information on the sniper case and performing counterintelligence."

Jonah looked aghast. He was the closest DFW had had to a protégé. "I can't believe it," he said finally. "David spent a decade building the sort of power base needed to accomplish things, the sort of discipline that could have only benefited the agency."

"Or," Wilkie said, "the sort of power base that merely gave him power, to exercise positively or negatively as he saw fit. I'm sure you're aware that I'm retiring in two years, both of you; I haven't been as involved day-to-day as I should, and I'm afraid David took advantage of that, consolidating control beneath me. This was my miss, Jonah, not yours."

Jonah nodded but didn't reply. He wondered how much of it was true, and how much of it was the director protecting his own position. Did he see DFW as a threat? Was that what this was about? Surely it was some sort of setup, a way to push David out?

He had to say something. "Director, are we absolutely certain the evidence of his complicity is solid? Do we know for sure that he's guilty?"

Wilkie leaned on both elbows on the desk, looking reflective for a moment. "No. But things don't look good for him. Officially, of course, the agency is looking out for its employee and will support David in any way we can. Unfortunately, he did not show up for work yesterday, or today, and D.C. metro police are rather concerned we might be shielding one of our own. That had best not be the case; make sure that message is conveyed to the right people, as well."

"What's our next step?" Carolyn asked.

2.

"We need to find the reporter who leaked the evidence to the NSA, which of course leaked it to us. Multiple parties seem to want her head. We need to know what she's working on, what the ramifications might be to the agency's reputation, its ability to move forward proactively."

"And then what?"

"We decide once we know what's going on," he said. "If the story she's working on has security implications, we get involved. If it's merely an attempt to damage our reputation... well, there are other approaches that can be taken. Pressure can be brought to bear."

39/

Fenton-Wright had known something was wrong the moment he'd returned home, after dealing with the Verbish woman. He'd taken care of some minor housekeeping and stopped into the office for a while, then driven home to Spring Valley, a neighborhood in the west of the metro area.

When he arrived, a police officer was knocking on his front door, and he quickly pulled the car into a side street then turned around so that he could park it at an angle that let him view his home. A few moments passed and a second officer walked out from behind the house, shaking his head about something. While the two cops talked, a black sedan pulled up to the curb and parked. He recognized the men who got out, both NSA investigators, colleagues of Mark Fitzpatrick.

He was blown. Somehow, they knew about Faisal, or perhaps about Walter and Myrna.

Fenton-Wright considered his options. He needed a scapegoat, a rationale for taking Khalidi's money; he needed a way to pin the whole thing on Joe Brennan. He needed an out.

But for once, he was unprepared.

His phone buzzed. The few outside contacts he still had from his younger days had been tapped; hopefully one of them had found something. He opened the email; a former field freelancer in Canada had sent him a note that Brennan was wanted in connection with the shooting of Konyshenko, the Russian arms dealer, in Vancouver.

What the hell was he doing in Vancouver? He followed the thread of the thought back, considering Brennan's objectives up until that point. He must have pegged Konyshenko as being connected to the missing nuke, Fenton-Wright thought.

It was a puzzle, and he didn't have all of the pieces, DFW decided. But he knew who did: the reporter, Alex Malone, had been one step ahead of the agency throughout; her sources were impeccable and he was beginning to believe she might even be in contact with Brennan.

He knew where she lived, had a recent address. Eventually, she'd return home, perhaps sooner rather than later. With few other options, Fenton-Wright began to plan a stakeout.

SEATTLE, WASHINGTON

Brennan met Malone at a restaurant near the harbor, where she was busy using her tablet to try and find a source on the New York docks, someone who could keep an eye out until they could get out there.

"So?" she asked as he approached the table. She'd been sipping coffee, waiting to find out if the Liberty Lady was laden with danger. "Anything?"

He shook his head. "Plenty of guards, so there might have been some interesting product in those shipping containers. But nothing radioactive."

"I heard the sirens. Things got messy?"

"A little bit, yeah. I get the sense, though, that it was only as difficult as it needed to be."

"Huh?" What was he getting at?

"A half-dozen guys, poorly trained but heavily armed. Enough to make it seem like someone cared…"

"But not enough to actually protect something of real value?" she offered.

"Exactly."

"So this was for show?"

"Yeah, a way to delay us … but not really." He looked puzzled.

"What?"

"Well… it's like Cabinda. When I was being held by Han; if she wasn't working for the right team, she could have just shot me. Why leave me there? Why give me a chance to get back into the game? Then there's tonight. If they're expecting us to inspect the ship, why send a handful of boys to do a man's job?"

Alex considered the point; he made a lot of sense, but she had no idea what was behind the decisions. "You think we're being set up somehow, led to a conclusion?"

"It's possible, yeah. I mean, we were getting nowhere; the second I got close enough to Konyshenko to get some solid intel on what's really going on, he was iced by a sniper, probably the same shooter as in Europe."

Malone had been thinking about Brennan's African run-in with the scientist. "The question, to me, is why South Koreans are after a nuke in the first place," she said. "Maybe if we answer that, we'll have a better idea of what's going on."

The waitress came over and refilled their coffee cups. Brennan poured some cream into his decaf and waited until the woman had left. "You have any Korean sources?" he asked, "someone solid on their domestic and international policy, or in intelligence?"

"One guy," she said. "Possibly. He's a professor at George Washington. We... went out a couple of times. It was uncomfortable. He was very needy and clingy for a first and second date."

She had a look of distaste on her face and Brennan stifled a chuckle. "You want to give loverboy a call, or just pass me his number?"

Her head slumped at the thought. "I'll do it. But if you can think of anyone else who might..."

"Eddie."

"Eh?"

"My pilot friend. He's got contacts in every agency, everywhere. He must know someone over there; or maybe someone from over there who's over here."

"Okay, we try that," she said. "Otherwise, I have to call Ken Cheong and ask for a favor; and I'd rather be roasted in bulgogi sauce."

JUNE 27, 2016, HARBIN, HEILONGJIANG PROVINCE, CHINA

The dining room was elegant, a long room dominated by an eighteen-seat formal table, and accentuated by the lush, dark wood of the sideboard that ran along one wall. On each wall, gilded gold frames housed masterworks of art from more than a century earlier, imposing Dutch figures perhaps as disconnected from modern-day China as was possible.

It was near silent, save for the odd clink of cutlery and the faint strains of classical string music from the adjacent study. Fung sat at one end of the table, his wife Wen at the other, some twenty-five feet away. In the middle, and off to one side, was a waiter, keeping watch over a silver serving cart that had conveyed their roast partridge and vegetables from the kitchen next door.

He sliced a Brussel sprout into two then chewed on one half slowly, trying to keep his attention on his plate, trying not to stare at his wife. He was angry with her, and she already knew that was the case. Fung had always considered himself a master of self-control; he dabbed at his mouth absently with a white linen napkin and tried to keep his mind empty, to avoid saying something with long-term consequences. He sliced another Brussel sprout into perfect halves and ate each in turn.

At the other end of the table, Wen picked slowly at the partridge, pulling away the crispy skin and cutting off tiny portions of white meat. She ate each in laboured fashion, subconsciously looking up as she did so, tense and nervous at how he would react to her public embarrassment. She had done herself up for dinner in a traditional silk dress, her dark hair pushed up, her white powder makeup more accentuated. She wished to appear perfect and elegant, to give him an image close to the one he'd fallen in love with many years before.

He watched her through occasional glances as he leaned forward over his plate, sullen at her obvious attempt to curry favor; like so many husbands of party wives before him, he was tired of her overstepping her bounds.

The plates and cutlery clinked, the waiter nearby stoic as a statue, a veteran of the household staff, his survival instinct honed enough to know that no matter what was said between them, he heard nothing, he repeated nothing, and he knew nothing. When Fung finished his glass of wine, the waiter was at his side with the bottle as soon as his worthy leader's head began to turn to make the request.

Fung chewed on a bite of the game bird, his irritation growing, one arm leaning against the edge of the table, dinner knife in hand. She looked up and saw him watch her, and Wen forced a small, shy smile.

But his expression went cold, instantly, his gaze narrowed, his mouth contemptuous. "What are you smiling at?" he demanded. "What reason do you have to smile? Tell me that."

"I…"

"You what? You thought that while I was away, you would step into my shoes? Become Madame Fung, the Empress of Harbin? Rule over the party and the gangs alike?" He stabbed angrily at the partridge. Then he caught himself and took a deep, cleansing breath, letting the stress out. He went back to his dinner, but his mind was on the matter at hand now. How much damage had she done? Would there be an official investigation? Most certainly. But would it be serious this time, a message from the central committee that his time as the region's de facto overseer was done – and perhaps his life with it?

Corruption scandals had become all the rage. The slow shift in China to a blend of capitalism and authoritarianism had finally seemed to reach a peak point, where the excesses of one-party control were no longer any more tolerated than those of capitalism. There was a technocracy developing, a state that functioned to maintain growth, development. The committee members were increasingly leery of the old guard, increasingly willing to purge their ranks, the sheer irony of "progressives" cleaning house apparently no factor in their decision making.

Yet, despite that, she had used his extended time in Europe to flaunt his power, to demand levels of tribute from the shady operators, to exact revenge on old enemies. She had worked with Liu Bin, the wife of his business associate, to build a local powerbase through the traditional means: attacking his business enemies as "subversive and anti-state" in newspaper columns and articles, soliciting public support of those positions from his most groveling associates.

She watched him as he ate and did not reply, concerned any comment at that point might set him off again. In truth, she had simply tried to run his business for him while he was gone; perhaps she had been overzealous in a few areas; but she knew her husband, and that his own history in the city and province was hardly one of political moderation. So she remained quiet, afraid that the wrong facial expression or tone of voice might push him farther than he had gone before, to dangerous extents.

From the study, the stereo switched to Handel's *Symphony Number One in G Major*, the strings entirely too optimistic and up-tempo for the mood of the dinner. Fung briefly thought about going next door and smashing it, before once again bringing his anger under control. Perhaps if he were to beat her severely…

No. He had tried that in the past, and it had merely made her more devious. Instead, he knew, he was going to have to fix this personally, grovel before the highest-ranking committee members who would acquiesce to meet with him. He would have to bring in her powerful father and once again lose face before him, look like less of a man in front of the individual he least liked.

3.

And he would do it, because he loved her.

He hated her, too. But ultimately, Wen was as much a part of Fung's life as his own hands, central to his existence, even when he was away from her, and cursing her name. She had borne his children and stood by him in the early days, when his own family had all-but disowned him.

At the other end of the table, she watched him more attentively now, able to read his facial expressions as he worked through what he wanted to say to her. She could see his inner conflict, his anger, but also his desire to work something out, to find a solution to the very real public image problem she created.

He looked up at her again, and this time he just looked slightly sad, like a man whose job is a necessary evil, the soul taken out of him just slightly. She smiled again, because she knew what it meant, that he was going to fix everything, protect her.

"Sometimes," he said quietly, "sometimes you drive me to the point of madness."

The music switched to *Symphony Number Two in F Major*, the optimistic, bouncy fourth part, more nuanced and not as bombastic as Handel's more famous *Messiah*, but just as enthusiastic. She wasn't quite sure what to say and she watched him eat a few more bites of food before she answered. "I know," she said, smiling. "I will try harder. I promise."

He nodded gently as the strings swelled and slowed, reaching the final crescendo, before fading out.

The bullet pierced the window of the dining room that sat between two of the gold-frame portraits, piercing Fung's cheekbone in a single clean hole before passing through his neck, severing his brain from his spinal column. His head thudded to the table, his last thought that perhaps they could work everything out after all.

The asset felt ill at ease; he'd had to insist on shooting Fung, his paymasters demanding he leave it until later and instead take a role in their larger objective of preventing the ACF from ever meeting again. But that wasn't why he was there, to be some anonymous cog in a larger machine. They knew that when he took the job. They knew it was personal.

He took the rifle off of the tripod and began to disassemble it, checking the chamber first then removing the clip, then the barrel and suppressor, followed by the collapsible stock. The evening moonlight shone brightly through the stained glass in the upper part of the old synagogue's attic window. It was one of the oldest buildings in the city, a remnant of the days when Harbin was once home to an extensive Jewish population. It offered a direct line-of-sight across five hundred meters of space between the synagogue and Fung's palatial home. By the time police experts on scene had figured out angles of deflection, he'd be at the airport, on his way back to America.

It was the first time since everything had started that he felt somewhat bitter; they'd fought his decision, insisting he stay in Vancouver until further notice, his final series of tasks not far off, they promised. Ultimately, he would kill Khalidi, and exact a measure of justice for Sarah.

He kept packing his things even as he thought of his sister. She was so positive, such a happy person. She'd developed a bone condition in her teens that forced her to walk with a cane, but it hadn't even slowed her; she'd taught English to kids around the world, undertaken missionary work in other countries and even run for local office in their hometown, all before the age of thirty. When he'd been away on duty, she'd helped their mom take care of their pop, who had Alzheimer's. But more than any of that, when they'd been kids together, she'd adored him, looked up to him, never anyone other than a great sister and friend.

Fung wasn't just a necessary part of his revenge; despite what his handlers thought, the asset was convinced killing the Chinese member of the ACF would heap more suspicion upon Khalidi, who was already in isolation, facing increasing public pressure to resign, his cabal decimated by assassination, his global reputation in tatters as a result of his greed. The asset had never taken pleasure in killing, but had always derived great satisfaction from his belief that a good man with a gun could solve a lot of problems.

He placed the rifle parts in the attaché-style case and closed it, spinning the combination locks on either side of the latches then making his way out of the room towards the stairs. A moment later he was outside, heading for the busier streets a few blocks away, where a cab would take him anonymously to the airport, as the police sirens wailed in the distance.

3.

40

WASHINGTON, D.C.

Wilkie used the remote to turn off the small flat-screen television that sat in the corner of his office, on top of a side-table that his predecessor had used as a bar. The director had been watching news network coverage of the shooting in China, the scenes fairly typical of any big police investigation, reporters huddled at night behind yellow tape while officers wearing luminous yellow vests over their uniforms kept them at bay and held the peace for the investigators.

What the hell had DFW become embroiled in? The intel coming in about Fung over the month prior had been anything but complimentary, painting him as one step short of an international criminal. Coupled with the revelations about Khalidi's African dealings, it was one more sign that the ACF had run a virtual star chamber, and one without moral restraint.

And he'd missed it all; or, at least, his charges at the agency had. It had taken the late Lord Cumberland – the American agent codenamed Fawkes – to bring the ACF's work to light.

Age was a factor, the director knew; that was at least part of why he'd devolved so much control down to Fenton-Wright, the loyal deputy. But beyond that, he knew he'd been taken in. There was no doubt, based on the NSA evidence and the doctored video found on Fenton-Wright's computer, that he was guilty of treason at the least, and likely much worse. Wilkie was hurt, but ignoring his own feelings, pushing them down. He knew from other cases, other times that spotting a double was just about impossible.

The personal considerations were secondary; the director needed to set things in motion, mitigating steps that would help the agency protect its image. What would Walter have done? He wondered how things might have gone had he made different decisions a few years earlier, been less worried about whether Lang was too maverick, too set in his beliefs to compromise, promoted him instead of David. It had been such a long time…

Had he handled things correctly with Carolyn and Jonah? Both were respected in the department. Both were level-headed, calm. They lacked DFW's outward passion, but either might have been a better choice at one point that his protégé.

Wilkie picked up the phone. Carolyn couldn't become any more involved in the case than she already was, due to her obvious conflict of interest regarding her wayward husband. But Jonah? Jonah was eager to please and sharp. Perhaps he could find Fenton-Wright, get to him before he was arrested, get a feel for what had gone so terribly wrong.

JUNE 28, 2016, SEATTLE, WASHINGTON

It was a shame Eddie couldn't have arranged something formal, Brennan thought. Just getting a name out of him had taken serious negotiations, given that the South Korean contact in question was deep undercover.

In fact, the statement "are you out of your freakin' mind?!?" had been repeated during the conversation more than once.

But ultimately, Eddie had given him the name, on the promise there would be no indication of how Brennan got the information. If he was planning on outing a spy, Eddie wanted nothing to do with it. That sort of thing was bad for business.

Now the problem was how to approach Lee Kyu Sun without spooking the man. They were both seated on opposite sides of the university cafeteria, which was mostly empty, although the clatter of kitchen utensils made it seem otherwise. Brennan stared across the banks of long tables and watched his target eat alone, occasionally flicking through the pages of a folded-over magazine.

Ostensibly, Lee was a visiting professor of political science from the University of Seoul. His real job was handling western-based covert operatives for his nation's security service. Given that most of its work involved industrial espionage, and very little of it was actually in the field, he was not a busy handler, Brennan had decided.

He'd met a few of the more studious intelligence types of the years; they didn't usually like to get their hands dirty.

Brennan scoped out the cafeteria again. The place was practically empty, just an elderly lady in a pale blue cardigan eating by herself, a couple of stoners in a wall booth. He pondered confronting him at his table, to make fleeing a poorer option; the last thing Lee probably wanted was an issue with his cover job.

Instead, he waited until the professor had finished his meal then began to follow him across campus and out onto the streets of the city. If Lee was a long-time agent, he hadn't spent much actual time in the field, Brennan decided: he hadn't shoulder checked once, and he was walking too far from the adjacent store windows along the street to use them as angles of reflection, to check his six. On a hunch, Brennan checked the other side of the street; some handlers had watchers around to make their jobs easier, convenient muscle if the need arose. But he spotted no one.

Ahead, Lee turned a corner and took the narrow cross street, which was closed to road traffic. Brennan stayed with him, far back enough to not be noticed. He turned the corner... and ducked, just as the spinning round kick connected with the spot where his head had just been.

Lee was in a tae-kwon do opening stance, relaxed, weight back. "Why are you following me? If you're after money, you picked the wrong guy," he said, his accent somewhere between foreign and American.

Lee took a half-step forward before throwing out a front kick, which Brennan blocked easily.

"I'm not here to fight you," Brennan said, raising both hands. "I just need your help."

"Leave me alone, or I'll call the cops," the professor said. "I mean it."

Brennan smirked at him. "No, Mr. Lee, you won't. We both know that's the case."

Lee's face froze for a moment in a look of surprise; he'd realized it wasn't about school or a simple mugging. He turned on his heel, and ran north up the street.

For an academic, he was in good shape, Brennan thought. He wasn't going to outrun the former SEAL, however, and thirty seconds later, Brennan was closing on him. Lee turned into an alley and Brennan followed.

It was a dead end. The Korean looked around for an egress point amidst the trash and garbage dumpsters. Seeing nothing, he squared off with Brennan again in a fighting stance. "I warned you," Lee said. He sprinted at the American, dropping at the last second and sliding along the slick concrete so that he could plant a low punch into Brennan's groin, finish things early. Instead, Brennan blocked the blow, took a half-step backwards and, before Lee could rise and right himself, stepped on the man's chest, pinning him down.

For a fighter, he made a heck of a university professor. He struggled, grabbing Brennan's foot and attempting to pry himself free, like a beetle stuck under a rock.

"Just relax," Brennan said. "I just need to talk to you, for Chrissake!"

He tentatively removed his foot. Lee used both hands to push up off the ground and leaped to his feet. "You won't manage that again," he said, going back into a fighting stance.

This is getting tiresome, Brennan thought. He feinted a blow to the man's head and when Lee's right arm came up to block it, Brennan dug low, hammering the man four times with rapid, flat-palmed punches to the solar plexus. It knocked him down and knocked the wind out of him, without doing any real harm.

Brennan helped the wheezing agent off the floor. "Now, are we going to keep doing this, or are you going to talk to me?"

A few minutes later they were sitting across from one another in a nearby coffee shop. Brennan had bought them each a tea.

"Explain," Lee said when he sat down again.

"I'm aware of your employer, Mr. Lee," Brennan said. "And I have no interest in breaking your cover. At least, not now, anyway."

"I'm listening."

"My name is Joe Brennan. I work for the agency, an asset."

"Okay."

"My sources indicate that you're a handler for South Korean National Intelligence."

Lee crossed his arms. "That's creative."

"Not really. My sources know you fairly well, I'm sorry to say."

"State your piece," Lee said, without confirming anything.

"I need a piece of intel, intel you might already have."

"Again, assuming I had any idea what you're talking about..."

"I'm trying to find out why another professor from your school in South Korea, a Dr. Han Chae-Young, might be wrapped up in a smuggling operation of sorts. She's a nuclear physicist..."

"Seconded to the Universite Libre de Bruxelles," Lee said, finishing the thought.

"Exactly."

"She's dead," Lee said. "Her partially skeletal remains washed up along the shore near the start of the demilitarized zone in Korea, just under three weeks ago. They figured she'd been dead for at least six months, though the decay made it hard to be certain."

That couldn't be, Brennan thought. The timing was all wrong. "That's impossible. I spoke with her in Angola less than two months ago."

"You spoke with an imposter," Lee said. "It is the SKI's belief that Dr. Han was replaced, likely by a North Korean agent, in an effort to pass nuclear technology to her home country."

3.

That made more sense, Brennan thought; but it still didn't answer the question of why she'd left him alive. "I need to find the imposter; it's possible she has ... vital information."

"Good luck then," Lee said. "Don't you think we'd have acted by now if we knew her location?"

"Do you have a picture of the real Dr. Han?"

The professor took out his phone. After flipping through several other pictures, he held it up for Brennan to see. She looked similar to the woman he'd talked with in Brussels, but was definitely a different person. "You're right," he said. "That's not her."

Lee was staring at him as Brennan eyed the photograph. "You realize what you've done, don't you, Mr. Brennan?"

"Enlighten me."

"You've burned me. I can't go back to my superiors now and claim our operations here are uncompromised."

"Hey, I told you: my lips are sealed."

"Yes, well, that's very noble and everything, Mr. Brennan. But we both know the moment you need my help again they will become unsealed. Besides, someone else must have known to tell you, which means too many people know, which means I have to leave. Go home." He didn't look happy at the prospect.

Business was business, Brennan thought. He had no sympathy for the man. "You're lucky I don't tip the agency right now. In fact, if I hadn't promised my sources, your entire network would be down by tomorrow."

"Believe me, Mr. Brennan," he said. "You have already done enough."

"As I said, this is between us. You make your own choices. But I can tell you the sources who tipped me are solid; they'll tell me things they wouldn't tell their own mothers, let alone the agency or another operative."

"I would like to believe that, Mr. Brennan," Lee said as he rose to leave. "I really would. But the damage is done."

"This isn't a business that is high on sympathy, Mr. Lee," Brennan said. "I'd suggest that the next time you're offered a foreign posting, you tell your paymasters how much you love Seoul."

2.

41

WASHINGTON, D.C.

Dulles Airport was typically cram-packed with travellers, and Ellen McLean stood near the front of the crowd outside Callum's arrival gate, waiting to wave to him and let him know they'd come to pick him up.

Carolyn had come along, grateful for some support while Joe was away and with the kids staying at her parents' house for the rest of the weekend. But she'd started to think about what it would be like to greet him; would he even let her know somehow if he was safe, if he was out of danger?

That didn't seem likely, so a call to come out to the airport and play happy family seemed equally remote. When push came to shove, Joe was Joe: stubborn and independent, even with his loved ones.

At least Callum might still be home for him to hang around with if he did return, she reasoned. Callum's new sales job took him away just about every week, too. But he'd always fly home at the end of the trip. Carolyn had no idea where Joe even was.

"There he is!" Ellen said, waving to her husband as he stepped through the double sliding doors and jumping excitedly in place. "Hey!"

Her gesture could've been seen from the runway, and Callum smiled at the greeting before heading in their direction. When he reached them he leaned down and hugged Carolyn quickly; then he turned to Ellen, his face warm with the glorious familiarity of affection. They put their hands around each other's waists and just held each other or what seemed a full minute.

Carolyn felt creeping jealousy, but pushed it down, happy for her friend. Ellen hadn't talked about anything else all week.'

Callum looked around quickly. "No Joe?"

"He's still off the grid," Carolyn said.

"Ouch," Callum said. "I'm sorry. I know you were expecting him back before now."

"It is what it is," she said. "You know the job."

He nodded. "No movement from the agency on letting him resign?"

Carolyn knew she wasn't allowed to get into the details. "Not exactly, no. It's complicated."

"Shocker," Callum said. "Complications involving the government."

3.

"How was the new job?" Ellen asked, trying to get things back on a positive keel. "Sell any equipment?"

"We did well," he said. "New England is a good market for us. California's looking up, too."

Carolyn knew Callum's new job involved heavy travel. The rest of the details were hazy, which was fine; most people only bore their friends when they talk about their jobs, she'd long decided.

"How long are you back for?" she asked instead. "If you're taking Michael fishing, I'm sure Josh wouldn't mind tagging long."

"If we lived closer, they'd be inseparable," Ellen added. "You can handle that, right hon?"

"I've got five days until I have to go out again; if the weather holds, I'm sure we can drum something up. And if Joe gets back before then..."

Carolyn smiled bravely. She didn't know what to expect any more.

SEATTLE AIRPORT, WASHINGTON

Brennan dialed the number again, but got the same result, the call kicking over to the answering machine after three rings, Carolyn's voice telling people they weren't home just then, and to leave a message.

"Yeah... Hi babe, hi everyone!" he said trying to sound optimistic. "Just calling to let you know I'm okay and I'm trying to get home real soon. Jessie, Josh, you be good for your mom and I'll bring you each back something nice. Okay then... I love you."

He ended the call and threw the cellphone into the nearby trash can as the thousands of travelers streamed obliviously by them.

"What's with the phone?" Malone asked.

"It's hot. I had to improvise when I got out of Vancouver. It's unlikely they connected a missing phone taken from a Canadian with my whereabouts, but you never know. The agency, certainly, might assume I'd resort to theft. So it's like a homing signal, potentially."

She looked up at the departures board. "My flight leaves in twenty. I should get to my gate."

"Okay. You're sure this is the guy?"

"As best as I can tell from online sources; he's the definitive expert on keys and locks going back forty years."

"Had to be in D.C.," Brennan said ruefully. "You watch your back, Alex. You got that phone number I gave you?"

"Yeah."

"You know the drill: before you leave D.C. to meet up with me, you call that number, you tell whoever answers that "Brennan says it's New York." They'll get the context."

"Won't that put them all over your back? Who says they'll even believe it's a real threat?"

"The agency can't take the chance that I'm right. At the very least, they'll have a few small teams checking every viable target in the city."

"We could always switch places. I'll go search the New York docks for the nuke, you go talk to the egghead. I may not look like much in terms of ass-kicking, but I play a mean first-person shooter when my nephew comes over."

Brennan began to smile, thinking about how pretty Alex was when she was trying to be funny. Then he caught himself. He missed Carolyn too much to start thinking that way.

WASHINGTON, D.C.

The President smiled for the cameras, a broad, genuine grin flashing pearly whites as he shook hands with the Italian prime minister, followed by a backslap from the Italian that made even the cynical media types in the audience laugh.

While everyone else in the press room was still chuckling about the PM's joke and demonstration of affection, the President was thinking through the rest of his day, doing the math, ensuring he was still on schedule.

Ten minutes later, his aides were escorting him to the private security briefing, the half-dozen faces all familiar. "Gentlemen," he said as he entered, irritated by how long it had taken to get out of the press conference, but not showing it, doing up the second button of his dark navy suit coat even as he walked to the head of the long table. "My apologies. As you're all aware we signed a major agreement with our Italian partners today to work together on new approaches to counteracting germ warfare and protecting the public."

There was a light round of applause from around the table, an acknowledgement that even though his term was soon done, the President was still making his mark. With his potential successor, John Younger, still holding a ten-point lead over GOP challenger Addison March, his legacy was looking up.

With one exception. "So you'll forgive me," he said, his tone changing, "if I'm not a little concerned we might be taking a step backwards. I understand this is about the sniper situation."

"Yes, Mr. President," the defense secretary said, his grey hair immaculately coiffed and his red bow tie knotted perfectly, but his fidgeting fingers giving away his nerves. "It's not exactly a question of deliberately stepping back, insomuch as…"

On the other side of the table, Nicholas Wilkie recognized the potential damage to his own reputation and the agency if he let someone else own the discussion, particularly the rationales for taking further action. He interrupted. "Mr. President, as the director responsible for this fiasco up to this point, I must take full responsibility," he said. "While obviously we will have a full branch review to go over the various breakdowns in performance, I will reiterate that the current administration seems to have inherited a rather large and dirty problem from my predecessor."

"And which 'large and dirty' problem would that be, Nicholas?" the President said pointedly. "The rogue agent who French police believe murdered an elderly tourist? The deputy director who's been shipping information overseas and killing ex-spies?'

Wilkie froze for a moment. How had the President found out so much, so quickly? He maintained his stoic expression, but it was difficult, the muscles around his mouth tightening, brow fighting to prevent his eyebrows from raising.

The agency had always had leaks. Every large group does; in fact, the tighter it was perceived to clamp down on leaks, the worse they often were, Wilkie knew. But this one could cost him dearly.

Just play it cool, old man, he told himself. He leaned forward slightly on the table, trying to show confidence with his body language. "That's a colorful way of putting it, Mr. President," he said, smiling at everyone in the room, waiting as they smiled back, everyone having a slight chuckle as if it just wasn't that big a deal. "But essentially yes, that's exactly the situation I find myself having to clean up."

Fitzpatrick threw him a lifeline. "I would say it's a fair assessment, Mr. President."

"And where is the NSA's director today, pray tell?"

"The colonel's receiving treatment at Johns Hopkins, Mr. President. Today's one of his radiation therapy days."

"Ah." The Commander-in-Chief felt momentarily mortified for not making the assumption and asking more tactfully.

Wilkie said, "Mr. President, we believe the two issues are directly related, once again; the information regarding Agent Brennan's alleged malfeasance in France has been demonstrated to have been falsified by David Fenton-Wright who, as you're aware, is also being sought by every agency we can notify."

The President raised both hands in a show of momentary chagrin. "So is that good? We're only after one rogue agent, but he's responsible for both incidents?"

"It's... more easily contained," Wilkie suggested.

The defense secretary snorted. "Where have we heard this before?"

"I'm taking personal control of this, Mr. Secretary," the director said, his mouth a serious line, expression all business, no nonsense. "We will find David, and we will bring him to justice."

"What about Brennan?"

Wilkie was surprised; the President could have avoided asking. It made him wonder what he meant, exactly. "We're still unsure of his whereabouts," he said cautiously.

"But he's healthy?"

"As far as we know, he evaded police in Vancouver a few days ago in connection with the Konyshenko shooting."

"My God... I thought we'd pegged that as his competitor..."

"We've reassessed, sir," Wilkie said. "At this point we suspect he may have been embroiled in Khalidi's business and the same sniper may have once again been responsible. As for Brennan, they lost track of him just off the coast of British Columbia, but they couldn't find the personal watercraft he'd commandeered."

"Personal watercraft?" the President asked.

"A jet ski, sir," an aide said.

"So how are you going to handle this?" the President leaned back in his chair and arched his fingertips.

Wilkie knew he had to get the answer right. It was probably the closest to a final chance he'd receive. "I ... would suggest that if we can get a message through to him somehow, we should call him in. We can apologize in due time to the police agencies involved and share the information regarding David's treachery with the French."

The President knew that even a limited release of information would cause Wilkie no end of embarrassment. He admired him for being willing to take it; he was old, wealthy, powerful. He could have just resigned quietly, claimed it was a decision of age. "Fine. But gentlemen: I don't think I need to point out that we all have reputations riding on this being handled with tact. Don't disappoint me."

3.

Malone's flight got into Dulles just after two o'clock, the day sunny. She bought a hot dog from a café in the terminal before heading outside and hailing a cab, scarfing down the late lunch in a few quick bites.

Traffic was heavy and it took forty minutes to get downtown. The cab pulled up outside an older building with apartments upstairs and a small retail shop at ground level, the large window framed by wood painted a deep red. The door matched it, and a bell jingled as Malone pushed it open. There was a glass cabinet running the length of the small storefront, perhaps fifteen feet in total, with a cash register at one end. Behind the cabinet, on the wall, thousands of different keys and blanks sat on hooks, each meticulously labelled and numbered.

"Hello!" It was a man's voice, cheerful and older, slightly accented. "For keys and locks, you've tumbled into the right place!" He had grey hair and a grey-white moustache, half glasses perched on his nose. He was perhaps in his seventies or maybe even eighties, she thought. He reminded her of Geppetto, the puppet master from Pinocchio. "Sorry, I just had a little joke there. What can I do for you today, miss?"

"Mr. Yagel?"

"Theodore Jacob Yagel at your service," he said with a half-bow. He made a grimacing face as he straightened up. "Oy! The back is not what it used to be, you know, it hurts like the fershluginah unit that it is, it does…"

She smiled awkwardly at his familiarity. "I understand you have a gift for recognizing the manufacturers of keys, and I have one I'm trying to match with a lock..."

"Don't we all!" he said. "In fact, if you think about it, that's probably a pretty good metaphor for life. We're all trying to… ah, never mind. I digress. Let me see."

She took out Konyshenko's key. "I know this is asking a lot, as this might not even come from America," she said. "But if…"

He held up a hand. "Miss, this is the most common publicly shared key in the country, just about. It's an American Lockers key."

"You're sure."

"Sure as cheeseburgers ain't kosher."

"How would I find the locker?"

His eyes widened. "Okay, good I may be, but a mind reader I'm not. But you see this small number here? That's so that a replacement can be made if it's lost. It's made for them by the Master company. This your key, miss?"

"Sent to me by a friend," she lied. "He died shortly after."

"That's very unfortunate."

2.

"So…"

"So I can check their online database of key codes and contact the company; they'll know for sure."

"How long…?"

He shrugged. "Meh… they take time sometimes to call you back, but generally, they're good about things. Tomorrow… maybe Thursday?"

"Is there any way we could find out today?"

He smiled warmly at her, a gleam in his eye like a kindly grandfather. "You know what I'm going to do? I'm going to try real hard to get them to find out for me today, and I'll call you back before I close. If not, tomorrow. How's that?"

"Mr. Yagel," she said. "You're a mensch."

He waved a hand at her, embarrassed. "Ah, go on with you young people."

Brennan had warned her against visiting her neighborhood; but he was unaware of her source's communications code. She'd expected a pile of newspapers to be waiting for her; instead, either the delivery boy or another interested party was playing cleanup, and the stoop was surprisingly bare.

She walked back to her rented car. Brennan had also advised against her using her own vehicle until matters were resolved. She got in behind the wheel then sat there for a minute pondering how to handle it. She knew who the source was, where to reach him. Should she call? What if multiple messages had been swept up, or even intercepted?

She used the pay-as-you-go phone she'd picked up in Seattle to call in to work. Ken answered the assignment desk phone immediately.

"*News Now.*"

"Kenny?"

"This is… Alex? Where are you, for chrissake!? We've been trying to get hold of you for two days."

"Long story short I'm back in town," she said. "Long story long, I had to go to Vegas and the Pacific Northwest for some research."

"Christ… we're not getting the bill for that, are we? I didn't approve any off-budget travel…"

"Relax, Scrooge," she said, just a little annoyed that money was his primary concern. Annoyed but not surprised. "I'll take the tax write-off, okay?"

"Yeah, well, all hell is breaking loose down here. We got a hell of a leak on Saturday morning and we've been working on it for two straight."

"Okay." She'd been around long enough to no longer get excited every time an overenthusiastic assignment editor said he had a 'hell of a story'.

"We got a photocopy of an endorsed check written to the Addison March campaign, worth ten thousand dollars. It's from a holding company out of Chicago called 'Gayda Goodwill Industries', which purportedly raises money for medical relief charities in the Middle East."

"Let me guess…"

"Our sources at State say Gayda's on a terrorism watch list after receiving and dispersing funds to and from Islamic militants."

The implication was enormous; a presidential candidate, prospectively taking charity money from groups that funded terrorism. "This could ruin him," she said.

"I know," he said, sounding more excited than he should. "But it's your baby; so get in here, damn it."

Malone arrived at work twenty minutes later; her workspace was in its typical post-Hurricane-like state. Teddy Marsh, a photographer, was walking by as she cleared a spot for her purse. "Your desk is like a national disaster," he said. "I should take shots of it now, in case it collapses and kills a bystander." He mocked clicking a few snaps.

"You're not funny," Malone said.

Ken came over. "So what first?"

"Over to you, boss. I can hit Khalidi up for react or save that until the end, when I've got more ammo."

"What about your main source? You run any of this by him yet?"

"Or her," she added quickly.

"Or her," he said, sighing. Like most editors, Ken hated unnamed sources.

"No. The source is… out of contact right now," she said, sounding slightly unconvinced, like her own take was optimistic.

"Can you reach out?"

That wasn't the agreement, she knew. But there was also no way to be certain she hadn't missed his messages.

Besides, she thought, she'd been considering it anyway.

"I can try," Alex said.

42./

JUNE 29, 2016, MEMPHIS, TENNESSEE

Things had been going too well of late, Christopher Enright knew. His boss's campaign to lead the Republicans back into the White House had hit stumble after stumble and more roadblocks than a military base; and yet Addison March had ridden the power of his charisma past the headlines and negativity, the slur campaigns and innuendos, right into a seven-point deficit at the polls. With months still left to hit the road and press the flesh, it was achievable, they were all convinced.

And then the call had come in.

He'd heard Alex Malone's question and been paralyzed, unable to immediately answer, shocked by the content and unsure of how to act.

Instead, he stalled for a moment. "Excuse me? Sorry, that was a long question; if you could repeat it?"

"Certainly, Mr. Enright. I said 'News Now has obtained a copy of a donation receipt to Senator March's campaign from a company associated by the State department with financing terrorism. Can you comment on why the campaign accepted the donation of ten thousand dollars from Gayda Goodwill Industries, of Chicago?"

He froze again. What the Hell? Enright fell back into habit, taking a deep breath, clearing his mind of the tension of the moment, looking for the best quick answer to delay her, give him time to do research, alert the team. Tell the senator.

"As you know, Ms. Malone, we typically scrutinize every dollar coming into the campaign for moral ambiguity or such things, but as you're also aware, many a campaign in the past has had one slipped by them. I sure hope that's not the case here, but if it is, we'll certainly do the right thing and ensure the donation is returned."

Alex knew a brush-off when she heard it. She had to press the connection. "Are you aware, sir, that Gayda Goodwill in turn received a donation last year from the Latrobe Corporation, the same firm owned by Ahmed Khalidi and previously identified as having been represented by the senator's law firm? Is that a coincidence, Mr. Enright?"

Had he been able to see himself in a mirror, Enright would have been glad it was a phone conversation; his mouth had dropped open, agape and surprised, his brow furrowed. For the first time in his relatively young career, Enright felt genuine panic.

3.

"What exactly are you implying, Ms. Malone? And please be aware that the senator will protect himself from any libelous insinuation..."

"Did the senator accept a backdoor payoff from Ahmed Khalidi, Mr. Enright? People will jump to that conclusion."

He was defeated, and he knew it. But he had one last card to play, which was to put her off for a fuller comment. "I'm going to have to call you back in a few hours, Ms. Malone," he said. "Perhaps I'll have the senator for you."

"Mr. Enright..."

"Thank you, Ms. Malone, good day." He ended the call then pondered whether it was enough to slow her down, enough time to get a story in place, set the narrative, make sure the public saw it for the slur campaign it obviously was.

He hit the green button on his phone then scrolled to the senator's number. "Sir? We have a problem."

FULLERTON, CALIFORNIA

The crowd was greener than usual, college kids out to prove that the youth of America still knew what it meant to champion the little guy, Sen. John Younger figured. He needed some good news, after a week of taking shots from pro-gay rights groups for refusing to disavow a long-time friend and associate; it was a touchy subject and he hated it.

He'd spoken for twenty minutes on immigration, decrying Addison March's call for a massively increased border presence. Many of the students in the crowd were Mexican or Mexican-American, and it had gone over predictably well. But he couldn't help shake the feeling that he hadn't inspired them, particularly; they'd cheered in the appropriate doses at the appropriate junctures; but a lot of the applause was polite, deferential in the way you'd expect from a family member who has to be there.

The media scrum after the event was a snoozer, as a consequence, local yokel outlets that would get more play on the wires and national TV from his visit than they would at pretty much any other time during the next four years.

After he was done and was being led off stage, his assistant road manager took him to one side in the VIP area, roped off from the rest of the park with colorful little flags and string, a white tent in the back corner providing shade and refreshments.

"Sir, we've got a request from the West Coast Bureau of *News Now Magazine* for an exclusive sit down."

2.   372

"So? Let Stacy in communications handle it…"

"Sir, they want to do it right here and now. The writer says it's urgent."

It had to be something major. Where the hell was Stacy? He wondered if she was off charming the local print reporters again. She was a great PR flack, that kid, the best he'd had since the eighties and his time in state politics. But right at that second he needed her to screen for him.

Ah, hell… "Okay, but five minutes."

The handler smiled and gave him thumbs up. In short order, a middle-aged guy with jowls and a narrow-hipped thinness to him entered the tent, tape recorder in his left hand. He extended the right to shake. "Paul Berehowsky, *News Now*."

"Good to meet you, Paul," the senator said as genuinely as possible. "Did you drive up? I didn't see you on the bus…"

"I'm actually just the go-between, I guess," Berehowsky said, sounding unimpressed. "I'm passing you over to Alex Malone in Washington." He handed the senator his phone.

"Senator? I wasn't sure you'd agree to a quick phoner and I need to talk to you rather desperately," Malone said. "We have a developing story…" She filled him in on the details of the case. "And so it falls to you, sir, to comment on the new links between the March campaign and extremist organizations."

It was the kind of question that could excite any candidate; but with March gaining ground and the election just a few months away, it was exactly the news Younger needed to hear. "Well, Ms. Malone, I do have to say that it is shocking and deeply disturbing. I'm nearly speechless – and I'm a politician, so consider the source."

Good touch, he thought to himself. *People will like that.*

"Should your opponent resign, Senator Younger?" Malone asked pointedly.

Younger thought about that; a good political answer was about understanding the public mindset – that of the undecided, anyway. The neutral spectators, the ones unbound to an ideology, they could be dangerous. Being too aggressive made them suspicious. "Let's be clear here, Alex," he said, deliberately dropping her first name smoothly, familiarity breeding empathy. "Plenty of people in the past have been guilty of this same mistake, of accepting a donation without being careful about the source. That doesn't make Addison March a terrorist sympathizer. The man has served his country well, in the senate if not the military, and he deserves the benefit of the doubt."

"That's a surprising position," she said.

Younger smiled. She'd taken the bait and it was time to set the hook. "The man is an elected U.S. senator. He's not advising militants, he's just busy getting too little done, like the rest of us. But let's be clear: this is an egregious mistake, and I think the American people will do their usual exceptional job of reminding a candidate who makes such a mistake that they are smarter than that, that they recognize how dangerous and damaging to this great nation it could be to elect such a man president."

"So... take it into consideration at the polls?" Malone asked.

"Democracy has helped this country settle its accounts for nearly three hundred years, Alex," he said. "Back when the founding fathers were building this great enterprise, there were plenty of men they could have chosen to lead them; they chose George Washington, not Benedict Arnold."

The metaphor was muddled and ridiculous, he knew, because Arnold was never one of the choices. But no one would care; it was the kind of quote that resonated with the voter, particularly when the voter was angry.

JUNE 30, 2016, WASHINGTON, D.C.

For most of her first day back in the capitol, Malone had debated whether to call her intelligence source. But ultimately, she knew, she needed him; if she disobeyed his instructions and contacted him directly, he might stop talking to her; or worse, in deference to his rank, he might disavow having done so to begin with. The photos Myrna had taken of their earlier meeting were still somewhere in her apartment. She wondered whether her effects had been cleaned out yet, sent to family out of state.

So instead, Malone stuck to the plan and drove the rental car once more over to her townhouse, getting there just before eight in the morning, a half hour or so after the paper normally arrived.

And there were two.

She stared at them from behind the wheel, her rental parked across the street. She checked the street behind her in the side mirror, then the street ahead. It was deserted. Alex undid her belt and opened the door, getting out cautiously. She crossed her arms nervously and walked over to the stone steps.

She grabbed both papers and sat down on the step for a moment, so that she could flick through the pages. The notations were all there, and she took down the time. The place, she assumed had not changed.

Alex rolled up the papers and crossed the street again to her rental. She had a few hours before she needed to be there and there was other work to be done.

A minute later, she pulled away from the curb and headed out, not paying attention to the white compact Toyota that pulled out from further down the street a few scant moments after her, keeping a safe distance behind her car.

NEW YORK, NEW YORK

Eddie Shaw was not a happy pilot.

Brennan had burned Ed's Korean contact; then he'd shown up at Ed's Greenwich Village loft looking for a home base and asking the flyer to call the same burned agent for a follow-up.

When Eddie asked about the heat he would take for calling Professor Lee, Brennan had shrugged.

"I can't be the one to do it," Brennan said. "He already hates me. Besides, he won't have the information yet anyway. Give him another day or two and he'll probably have cooled off."

Then Brennan had spent the rest of the day at Eddie's dining room table, poring over maps, trying to figure out where, tactically, a nuclear warhead would be positioned to do the most damage. He'd decided on Manhattan, and was now using overhead online satellite photos to try and pin down a block or building that seemed an ideal location.

Eddie, eager to get the entire ordeal over with, had called Lee. After two minutes of screaming and vows to never speak with him again, Lee had told him what they needed to know.

The pilot ended the call and put his phone back in his pocket, then walked the short distance over to his apartment dining room from the kitchen and got Brennan's attention away from his laptop.

"Joe: that was our friend in Seattle. And I use the term friend loosely now, as I'm pretty sure he's never going to speak to either of us again."

"Ed..." Brennan hated upsetting his old friend, but he still had no idea what the Korean connection was, and that made him nervous.

"Look, just forget it, okay? I know how dedicated you are; I'm not happy. In fact, I guess I'm pretty pissed at you. But no one was hurt; Lee's upset but it's not like I'm short on customers. So just let it go."

"Fine."

They were silent for a moment, before Brennan said, "So... what did he..."

3.

"He said they believe the woman you dealt with in Angola is a North Korean intelligence agent named Park Jae Soo. He said they have a file on her as long as your arm, that she's quite the piece of work – and that he hopes she shoots you somewhere painful."

"Good to see I made such a positive impression."

"Don't you always?" Ed said, with a look that wasn't entirely supportive. He walked across the living room and turned on the television set.

"Thanks, Ed."

"My pleasure. So what are you going to screw up next?"

"The docks. There's a ship coming in tonight that may contain a package I've been looking for."

Ed was watching a news channel. "You catch any of this this morning?"

"What?"

"Addison March, the Republican candidate. He's doing a big mea culpa speech of some sort."

Brennan liked March. He didn't like his immigration policies as Brennan had never had anything against Mexicans or Mexican Americans; but March was a supporter of smaller government, better support for the military, things Brennan believed in. "What did he do, screw some intern?"

"Nope. Get this: he took a ten-thousand-dollar donation from an Islamic fundamentalist or something."

"Sloppy."

"But probably not fatal," Ed said. "People know these kinds of mistakes are made, particularly his base of supporters. They're not going to flee their moral tent just because there's a small leak in the roof."

Brennan realized how little he knew about his old friend, just then, discussing the banality of politics. Like most professional contacts – even friends – there was a distance when they weren't working. "You vote, Ed?"

"I spoil my ballot."

"Eh?"

"I take part. I register my opinion by spoiling my ballot."

"Why?"

The pilot walked over to the small kitchen and poured himself a cup of coffee. He motioned with the pot towards Brennan, but the agent shook it off. "It's like this," Ed said. "I'm fifty-six years old, and in my lifetime, I haven't trusted a politician. Not one. Not completely. Not in the way you'd want to trust someone who leads and directs your life."

"That simple?"

"And complicated. I've done a little reading about political ideologies and beliefs in general…"

"We've all got 'em," Brennan said.

"Yeah, and that's interesting in and of itself. We've all got beliefs, whether it's politics or faith or whatever, that we consider sacrosanct. We hold these beliefs because they help us feel secure in a fatalistic world, with only two things guaranteed: death and taxes. Most of us do so not just because we're brainwashed by our parents or something, but because these beliefs work for us. They're practical." He walked back into the living room. "But the political system? It doesn't work. Democracy is the best, most free example we've come up with. But the type practiced in our country now, and in other countries, isn't getting the job done. You look at the numbers, eighty percent of the decisions favor the people who buy off politicians, and that's on both sides of the aisle. It's just not working. The values of both parties are being betrayed, every day."

Brennan nodded. He had to admit, he felt the same way most of the time.

Ed wasn't done. "People keep saying 'we want change.' Two presidents, at least, have been elected promising it. And yet it never comes because of the way the human brain works, because we never account for the fact that sometimes, our beliefs are just wrong. On both sides of the aisle. We run a system of polarized opposites, a continual détente between people who hate each other. When we begin to fight for a system that takes individual beliefs and ideologies out of the equation, which recognizes the frail nature of human certainty, and represents everyone fairly? Then I'll stop spoiling my ballot, and go back to believing in Democracy." He turned back to the T.V., where March was finishing up his press conference. Ed slurped from his beer can. "Shit, working together was good enough for Lincoln."

Brennan wasn't sure how to answer. It was about the most personal Ed had ever been with him. He felt the same way, to a degree, but not to the extent of not taking part. But with the prospect of a night ahead searching for a missing nuke and a trail of bodies behind him prompted, in large part, by a political committee's misdeeds, he found himself wondering for the first time in many years just what he was fighting for.

LANGLEY, VIRGINIA

The overhead neon tube lights had been extinguished through most of the floor, but in Jonah's office, a small lamp illuminated his desk top and the series of small headshot photographs of his colleagues, which he'd arranged in a hierarchal tree, beginning with the director alone at the top.

3.

He refused to believe David was acting alone. He'd been Jonah's mentor for four years, and if he'd turned or betrayed the agency, it could only be because he was being coerced. But the volume of information that had leaked out of the agency about the task force and the missing South African device suggested someone was definitely passing secrets. He wasn't ruling David out completely, because Jonah knew you could never truly trust anyone in intelligence work. But if he was right, and David was being manipulated, that meant someone else was the leak, someone still on the inside.

He looked down the pyramid again; the director was a possible, if only because he had complete insulation, when required, from any scrutiny. Underneath him were David Fenton-Wright and the clandestine service's director, Adam Tyler. Beneath them were their four principal assistants, including Carolyn and Jonah. Beneath them was another row of four, the regional section chiefs, including the late Walter Lang. The pyramid contained another eighteen senior officials and a handful of assistants.

To its right on the table he'd laid out what he knew of the staff structure at the NSA, beginning with the colonel and then directly below him, Mark Fitzpatrick. A handful of the spots in the smaller pyramid were filled by Post-in notes with question marks on them.

He'd been working on it as a puzzle ever since being called in by the director. Jonah wasn't just looking after his own interests; he knew David had a genuine love for his country, that it was his dream to run the agency eventually. He couldn't believe he'd have gambled it away, or that it was all a lie.

What about Carolyn? He picked up her picture; she was an assistant, but she had access to all of the information that was leaked; her husband was looking less like a disgrace every day, but that didn't mean he wasn't tipping the media, or that she wasn't tipping him. She was certainly quiet enough to be ruthless; she'd been promoted multiple times in the decade prior, but still had among the lowest profiles in the office. Was that by design, to give her the sort of unnoticed access someone would need to betray their own?

His cell phone buzzed. Jonah was single and spent most of his spare time reading or doing research, so he wasn't expecting it. The number was unfamiliar.

"Jonah Tarrant."

"Jonah? It's me."

"David?!? Jesus Christ, David… Where are you? Why haven't you come in?"

"I've been set up. Look, I know what they must be telling you…"

"You got that right."

2.   378

"But you know me, Jonah; you know I wouldn't shoot an old hand like Myrna in cold blood."

David had always been a pragmatist, Jonah thought, but never as ruthless as that. "What the hell is going on, then?"

"It's complicated. Look, I have a meeting with a source in about an hour. Can you meet me there?"

Jonah nodded to no one in particular then switched to a note app on his phone. "Where am I headed?"

"It's a parking garage, at a fitness centre downtown. I'll give you the address."

43/

WASHINGTON, D.C.

Malone felt uneasy, which would have been natural in the circumstance, except that she felt it more than usual, a creeping tension that had her checking the shadows in the parking garage, looking behind her occasionally as she made her way to the stairwell in the back corner, a palpable fear. She looked down from the top, between the railings, the stairs descending in a cement semi-circle. Then she made her way down to the third level, her flats echoing off the concrete steps.

The meeting area was near the back corner, among the square concrete pillars and the shadows. Her source was waiting for her, hands in the pockets of his brown wool overcoat.

"You didn't answer my earlier contacts," he said. "I left papers…"

"They must have been taken up by the paperboy when I was out of town. I'm sorry. I thought about calling you…"

"No, that would have been a mistake. I'd have assumed you were burned at that point, that you'd already given me up."

"Everyone in the city is trying to track you down, you realize that? No one out there is making any assumptions about who my source is but they all want a piece of you. Anyway…" She removed the memory stick from her purse and handed it to him. "Here. This has everything I've told you so far about David Fenton-Wright's involvement in Ahmed Khalidi's business."

The source's eyebrows shot up. "Hard evidence?"

"A recording, a confirmation."

"Astounding."

"You'd know better than I," Malone said. "Tell me something…"

"Go on."

"Tell me why you don't just lay it all out for me: who started this with the shootings, who stole the nuke, how Khalidi connects the two?" It had been nagging at her for weeks.

"Just like that?"

"Just like that. Seriously: what the hell is going on? The ship in Seattle was another dead-end but that's no more than we expected by now…"

"You do recognize how sensitive my sourcing is, right? That some of the stuff I'm giving you could only have come through a handful of very senior people, and that as a consequence, it could be tracked back to me?"

"I know, I get that…" Alex was beginning to feel exasperated. "It's just… I feel like the clock is running down on us, counting down too quickly for us to catch up."

"Don't give up," he said. "You've come too far to back out now. And you know the potential consequences."

She didn't need to picture a mushroom cloud over New York. The notion was ever-present. "I'm not giving up. But we're running short on leads."

"Where's Brennan?"

She hesitated. He'd never been that direct about her associate before. "In New York, trying to track down the device."

"Good. As long as he keeps his priorities straight, we still have a shot at this thing."

They turned quickly, surprised by the sound of squeaking hinges. Thirty yards away, the door to the north-side stairwell swung open.

BROOKLYN, NEW YORK

Through high-powered binoculars, Brennan watched the dozen men working. He was perched on the guardrail by an upper roadway, overlooking and leading down to a long, wide customs-and-excise freight yard, the shipping containers row on row, the area brightly lit by tall floodlights.

It was a huge open yard surrounded by twelve-foot mesh fences topped with razor wire; no one else was working in the late evening, and without his binoculars, his surveillance targets looked like toy soldiers.

He raised the glasses again and focused in. The crew wore black. They'd been removing crated items from a container and loading them into the open back of a transport trailer. The effort suggested they had to be heavy components.

Brennan had gotten to the docks right around the time the ship made port, waited for hours and identified who was in charge, then followed the process of customs taking the containers and moving them to the supposedly secure yard for inspection before their eventual release. But someone at the yard had been paid off, the gate security defeated.

He watched through the binoculars as a pair of men took the first of two long wooden crates and slowly picked it up, bending at the knees. Their care was evident as they maneuvered it towards the back of the truck. He panned forward, to just ahead of the truck where three men were talking, illuminated by the headlights. Identifying the leader and going after him would cut to the chase, keep his men from getting trigger-happy. These looked like military, serious players. Taking them out one at a time wasn't a realistic option.

He knew he had a short ops window. The second container had just been opened and it had only taken them fifteen minutes to empty the first – save, he assumed, from whatever they'd left behind for customs. At the other end of the yard, a fenced gate slowly slid back. A dark-colored sedan pulled in, then made its way across the short open parking area, and down along the central row, towards the truck. It pulled to a halt, its red brake lights glowing. The two front doors open and Brennan watched the passenger get out, a man in a suit. He turned, and Brennan saw his face.

He nearly dropped the binoculars.

It couldn't be, he thought. *Could it?*

He raised the binoculars again, using the autofocus button to keep the image sharp.

Terrence Corcoran.

It had been fourteen years, but he knew the cold eyes, the square jaw line, the puffed-out chest. The older ex-SEAL's hair had turned white, but was still in a neat brush cut, as if he was still in the service. And he was still running the show.

He was talking to a younger man, also in a suit, but with a Mac-Ten machine pistol slung over his shoulder. At the end of the conversation, the younger man moved to salute but Corcoran stopped him, looking around self-consciously for a moment.

Both ex-military? It made a perverted sort of sense, Brennan thought. The best way to handle something like the Cabinda extraction or this op was to use mercs, guys who'd been in a unit, knew how to work together without thought to outside distractions.

Terrence Corcoran. His mind went back to Iraq, to Bobby; the emotions came flooding in, and Brennan felt his anger build. He took deep breaths, watching the men talk, allowing his pulse to slow. Whatever his involvement was, their past dealings made it a sure bet it wasn't good.

Brennan began to make his way down to the yard, hugging the shadows, trying to keep his mind in the present.

David Fenton-Wright's pistol was already out and extended as he came through the parking garage door; it was pointed directly at Malone.

Her source had reacted quickly, withdrawing his own gun from the inside of his raincoat pocket, levelling it right back at the man.

They stood there in the wide circle of light cast by the harsh neon tube overhead, the two men frozen in place.

"Put it down, David," Mark Fitzpatrick said.

"You!" Fenton-Wright said. "Fitzpatrick! You fucking traitor! You're *News Now*'s source. I should have seen it..."

"You can get off the high horse, David," Fitzpatrick said. "Everyone knows the dirty business you've been up to."

Malone was frozen in place, not wanting to even breathe too hard, worried she might prompt Fenton-Wright to shoot her, or that Fitzpatrick might do it for her, by threatening the agency man with a pistol.

"Don't you know what you've done?" Fenton-Wright told the NSA man. "You've undermined years of work, compromised everything I've built. And for what? Are you sleeping with this dumb bitch, is that it?" He gambled, swinging the pistol quickly over so it was pointed at Fitzpatrick, the two men in a standoff. Fenton-Wright needed the girl alive; he needed to know where Brennan was.

"Be smart, David," Fitzpatrick said. "Give up now, let me take you in, get your side on the record. This doesn't have to go down like this..."

"Shut the fuck up!" Fenton-Wright said. He was trying to control his anger; Fitzpatrick had been a thorn in his side for years, and here he was, the likely architect of all of the deputy director's problems. He nodded towards Malone. "You, empty your purse out onto the floor. Do it!"

Malone was still numb, not sure what to do; she'd seen Myrna die, seen the evidence of what Fenton-Wright was capable of; but she fought through her fright, crouching slightly at the knees, unclasping the purse and emptying it onto the cold cement.

Fenton-Wright nodded at the small red light emanating from the jumble of contents. "See? She's recording you, you idiot!"

Fitzpatrick shrugged. "So? She's a reporter. You don't think I expected that? You see, that's the thing about doing what you really believe in, David. You don't have to second-guess yourself."

"I ought to just shoot you and take my chances..."

"Good thinking, genius," Fitzpatrick said. "You're a wanted man, David. I shoot you, I'm a hero. You shoot me, you're just some nut job rogue intelligence officer who took another victim."

Fenton-Wright had already thought it through, already knew the truth of what the NSA man was saying. But he still had one more card to play.

Behind them, the southside door swung open.

BROOKLYN, NEW YORK

There were many business lessons to be taken from military life, Terrence Corcoran had long before decided, many ways in which the corporate world could adapt and adopt the control an NCO had over a unit, mold it to their particular ends.

He liked the idea. He hated the Navy, and had done so even while serving; but for a man as wretchedly crooked to the core as the former chief petty officer, it had been a smorgasbord of opportunity, to kill and to loot. And he knew when he got out that a lot of his former "comrades" in arms were down on their luck, eager for almost any work he gave them, and any pay that actually made its way down to them.

Mercs offered a convenient show of strength whenever required, broad shoulders for lifting, and not too many questions. So he sat in the rear passenger seat of the sedan, smoking a cigarette and watching them move crated merchandise from a shipping container into a truck.

His driver had offered to get them each a coffee from the old café across from the main entrance, and he was waiting for him to return, nonchalant, aware that they'd be done in a half-hour and that his payday wasn't far off.

The side door across from him opened and he looked over perfunctorily, expecting the driver and his beverage. Instead, he found himself starting down the barrel of Brennan's suppressed pistol. "Good evening, Chief," he said. "Or is it just Terry to your friends now?"

Corcoran's eyes narrowed and it took a perceptible second before he made the connection. "Well now who do we have here? It's young Mr. Brennan. SWO First Class when you discharged, wasn't it?"

"I'm sure you'd know."

Corcoran stared at the barrel. "You're not going to shoot me, Joe."

"Oh please, please, give me a reason to shoot you, Terry. You so deserve it."

"Huh. Yeah, I heard about Bobby. Tough break."

"I should shoot you for his sake alone."

The older man had to grin at that. He always liked Joe. He had a set. "You here sightseeing, or is there a particular reason for threatening me at gunpoint?"

"These crates haven't been inspected by customs yet."

"So what, you're a customs agent now or something?"

"As far as you're concerned, Terry," Brennan said, "I'm the guy with the gun who hates you."

"Okay."

"So what's in the container?"

"Car parts."

"Bullshit. And keep in mind that if I have to go through some of your guys to get a look, I'm going to shoot you first. Several times."

"Components. Some computers. Seriously…"

Brennan cocked the pistol. "Goodbye, Terry…"

"Okay! Okay! Just… don't, okay? There's a casing assembly, looks like it's for a bomb of some sort."

"And…"

"Timer, some switches… look, I'm just doing a job."

Brennan snorted at that. "You never did a day of the real work in your life. How you managed to bribe or blackmail your way into the SEALs is beyond me."

"Lots of things were."

Brennan gritted his teeth and held his temper. He didn't have time for things to get personal. "Where are you taking this stuff?"

Corcoran shook his head. "We weren't given a final destination, just a handover spot. We drive there; we turn everything over to a new crew."

"You're lying."

"Why would I bother? Like you said, I'm just a hired hand on this, and you're the guy with the gun."

"So when…"

"In two hours. We're supposed to take this stuff just out of the city, up north of Yonkers to a truck stop called the Double J."

"And then?"

"Then we wait for it to be picked up, I guess. Look, Brennan, I don't know who you're working for these days, but I've got good paying openings for…"

Brennan smacked him in the nose with the butt end of the pistol. Corcoran yelped and grabbed at it, bloodied. "Fucker!" he said.

"Don't ever insult me like that again, Terry, or I'll forget why I decided not to kill you in the first place. What's the meet code?"

Corcoran pinched at the cut on his nose and tried in vain to stop the blood flow. "You fucking prick…"

3.

Brennan smacked him again, this time with the flat of the gun to the temple. The older man recoiled in his seat and clutched with both hands at the impact point, moaning slightly.

"The next time I have to do that, I'm either going to break something or you're going to get a nasty concussion, or both. What's the meet code?"

"A phrase," Corcoran said, wiping more blood from his nose. "Doesn't matter, though."

"Eh?"

"There's a code red number; you leave here, I dial it, the meet's off. Brennan, these people are real pros. You think they don't have contingencies? More than one delivery coming in to more than one location? You really haven't learned shit since Al Basra, have you? There's always another angle, Brennan. You're just too stupid to figure that out."

"Who hired you?"

"A wire from a bank account in the Bahamas." Even with the blood running down his face and the banged up head, Corcoran was smiling; he knew Brennan wouldn't shoot him without necessity or without being ordered, and he knew he had no helpful information. "You can beat me senseless, but you're not getting shit."

He hated admitting it to himself, but as with Konyshenko, Brennan had no leverage. He couldn't call in the cops over the customs breach without staying as a material witness, and he was wanted himself. All that would spur would be a bloody shootout, anyway, knowing Corcoran.

"I can't deal with you right now, Terry, but remember our little conversation tonight; because at some point, I'm going to find the bomb you were helping someone build, and I'm going to take them down. And then you're going away for a very, very long time."

Corcoran smiled again, smugly. "Well, you just give it your best shot, there, young Joey. You just give it your best shot."

"Oh, I will," Brennan said. Then he hit Corcoran hard, on the point of the chin, with the butt end of the pistol, knocking him cold. The old man slumped back into the seat, unconscious. "Don't you worry about that."

Brennan rifled through Corcoran's pocket and found his phone. He dialed 911 and told the police they'd find a body in the backseat of a car at the customs lot. It wasn't entirely untrue. He tossed the phone down next to him and left as quietly as he'd arrived.

2.

WASHINGTON, D.C.

The parking garage had been empty when Jonah arrived, but he'd heard voices, pegged them as coming from a lower level. When he reached the third floor, he'd heard David's voice and been sure he'd found the right place.

His boss's requests had been simple: give me the benefit of the doubt, and bring a gun.

Jonah hardly ever took his pistol out of its lockbox. Like a lot of guys, he'd aspired to be a field agent at some point but had long ago decided his future lay in management. But he'd had it at the range just a week earlier, requalifying. He knew how to shoot, if he had to.

The door swung open.

There were three people, perhaps twenty-five yards away. He recognized David and Mark Fitzpatrick immediately. It took him a second or two to realize the woman was the reporter, Alexandra Malone; they'd mentioned during a briefing on Brennan that she might be working with the rogue agent. Was he somewhere around, too? David had a gun pointed at Fitzpatrick and vice-versa.

Too many thoughts to process at once, Jonah thought.

"Jonah!" David said. "Am I glad to see you! Fitzpatrick is the leak! He's a fucking traitor, Jonah…"

David had been his mentor for years. Jonah raised his pistol and sighted down the barrel at the NSA agent.

"Don't listen to him!" Fitzpatrick said. "Jonah, he killed Walter. He killed Myrna Verbish and he's going to kill all three of us if you help him!"

He didn't know who to trust. The woman looked frightened but she was standing closer to Fitzpatrick. Was she just siding with her source, or was David really going to shoot her? Jonah swung his pistol over to David and chambered a shell. "David…

"Jonah, son…you've known me for nearly a decade. You know deep down I'm being set up, that I would never do any of those terrible things. For God's sake, son…"

Jonah turned the gun back to Fitzpatrick. "Mr. Fitzpatrick, I'm sorry…" he began to say.

Malone got the sense everything was about to go horribly wrong. She had to interject. "Jonah, I know you don't know me…"

"You're the reporter."

"Yes… think about that, Jonah. I'm not an agent; I'm just a journalist talking to a source about a rogue agency boss. You know what David did…"

"I know what you say he did…"

"Don't listen to her, Jonah," David said. "Listen to me, son. She gets inside people's heads. That's what she does for a living. Don't trust her. You know for a fact you can trust me. Go with the team that got you here."

He swung the pistol back towards Fitzpatrick. "Have you been leaking agency secrets to this woman?"

"We've been working together to uncover David's treachery," the NSA man said. "Ask yourself how much Ms. Malone had to gain personally from all of this. She was just doing her job, and so was I."

"Shoot him, Jonah," David said, "or we'll never make it out of here, son."

Jonah had been at the agency for a relatively long time now. He knew how to make his own decisions, how to evaluate things with cold analysis, how to rationalize the difficult choices. He'd seen David do it week in and out. And just then, he realized something: "You know what," he said, swinging the cocked pistol back towards his boss, "in all our time working together – in all the time that I've worked for you – I don't think you've ever called me 'son' before. And you sure as hell haven't done it three or four times within a few minutes. Sometimes, David, you try too hard."

Fitzpatrick smiled. "Kid's got your number."

Fenton-Wright had to think. The numbers were against him but there were always other options. He shifted his aim slightly to the left, training the gun on Alex Malone. "Okay, really quickly and gently, you're both going to put your pieces down on the ground, or the civilian dies first."

Jonah felt a wash of disappointment. "Oh... David..." He shook his head.

"We don't have time for this shit," Fenton-Wright said. "Guns down, now!"

Malone reacted without thinking, darting sideways as quickly as she could, trying to get behind Fitzpatrick. It had occurred to her in an instant that Fenton-Wright's aim would track that way.

All three men fired, the gunshots cracking through the sharp echoes of the long, empty parking garage. Fitzpatrick took a sharp breath inwards, expecting the sharp stab ... then exhaling when he didn't feel it.

Fenton-Wright felt the hot, piercing pain of a bullet, then looked down, seeing the blood and instantly weak, falling to one knee, confused. He patted at the matte of blood forming through his dress shirt, pouring from the wound to his chest. He looked over at Jonah, who was still standing with the nine millimeter raised, his face frozen and aghast. "Shit," Fenton-Wright said, his knee buckling as he collapsed sideways to the ground, his body stiffening slightly as his heart tried to keep up with the arterial flow then seizing, arresting, ending his life on the cold slab of concrete.

Jonah and the NSA agent both rushed to Fenton-Wright's side. Jonah turned him over, but his eyes were already glassy, his functions gone. "I think he's dead," Jonah said. He felt a sudden rise of nausea and turned around to quickly vomit on the pavement behind them. Fitzpatrick checked Fenton-Wright's pulse.

"And the knowledge of who paid him off, unfortunately." Fitzpatrick took out his phone. He called in to the duty officer, explained what had happened. "Yeah, yeah…make it ten." He ended the call. "We'll have a team here in ten minutes," he told Jonah. "Look, you only did what you…"

Then he stopped. He'd lost track of Alex Malone. He looked around them, but the rest of the lot was already empty.

44

As soon as they'd gone to check David Fenton-Wright's vitals, Alex had beaten a retreat. Somehow, their meeting place had been blown, and that meant that for the immediate, she couldn't trust Fitzpatrick. Either he'd told someone or…

Had she been followed? It hadn't occurred to her until just then. She sat behind the wheel of her car, two blocks away, waiting for the light to change. Maybe. She thought she'd been careful, but she wasn't a pro. Maybe he'd staked her house out, broken the newspaper code.

She was tired and frustrated, running on adrenaline. Her source was compromised, Fenton-Wright had died without naming anyone, and they were still no closer to finding the bomb Brennan claimed was out there, somewhere. Khalidi was still both a suspect and a target.

Alex needed something resembling good news and she needed it quickly. The light changed and she nudged the car ahead, driving a few blocks before she realized that she didn't know where she was going. She had to tell someone what she'd just witnessed, get a story going. She checked her phone; it was nearly eleven o'clock, and there was little to no chance anyone would still be at the office. She couldn't call Ken at home, put him at risk. She needed a place to go for the night; as she drove up 18th Street, she saw a familiar building, the YWCA. Alex smiled; it beat sleeping in the car, she thought.

JULY 1, 2016, NEW YORK, NEW YORK

Brennan woke late, the sun already high over the city and his phone buzzing.

He got it on the fourth ring.

"Yeah."

"You sound like crap," Malone said.

"I was out until the wee hours scouring Yonkers for a potential target."

"Yonkers?"

"Long story. What time is it?"

"Time for you to get up. It's ten-forty-five and I'm heading your way."

"Eh?"

"I got a hit."

2.

"You've lost me," Brennan said. "Seriously, I'm half-awake here."

"The key," she said. "My expert got a call back on the key. It's to a locker at a gym in Queens. We've got a lot of work to do."

"You got that right." He'd spent the night in Yonkers pondering how Corcoran had come to be involved; it couldn't be a coincidence, someone so prominently tied to his past. Once again, Brennan felt like he was being manipulated. "I have some questions for that source of yours, too, though."

"Not an issue anymore, unfortunately," she said. "Things went kind of haywire last night. My source is no longer secure and Fenton-Wright is dead."

"How?" He was all business, she noticed, no hint of satisfaction.

"He found out where I was meeting my source. His assistant, Jonah, showed up. It got out of hand quickly."

"Are you going to tell me now..."

"No. That's not how it works. I can't contact him or vice-versa, but I'm still not going to break his confidence."

"So where were you in all this?"

"I ran as soon as the shooting started."

"Smart."

"Let's not stretch things," she said. "Anyway, I've got a flight out in forty minutes to La Guardia."

He promised to meet her there, then hung up, shaking off the worst of the fog as he headed for the washroom. Maybe they still had a shot at this thing; maybe Fenton-Wright's downfall would give Brennan an avenue back in with the agency, support to go after Corcoran, track his paymaster.

Or maybe whatever was in that locker would give them the answers they needed, the road map to stopping a nuclear catastrophe.

MEMPHIS, TENNESSEE

It had occurred to Christopher Enright early in the unfolding hours of his political boss's latest problem that there were better ways to handle it. For one, he was convinced there was more to the donation than a face-value mistake.

3.

For another, as he'd discovered a day earlier, there was an irregularity. The campaign worker who'd raised it was a volunteer and older, no one with any pull. But she was sure she'd specifically turned down a request from the same Gayda Goodwill Industries less than a year earlier, and made it clear that the campaign didn't want its money. After all, Gayda was on a list she'd been given of companies in the Chicagoland area to avoid. She was absolutely sure of it, she'd said when she called in, because the name reminded her of the term 'gaydar'.

Curious, Enright had asked the fundraising branch to get a copy of the check receipt out of records, so that he could take a look of it. But there was no copy; they had copies of every other receipt out there, but not the Gayda donation. The record of the deposit was there; so they'd taken the money. But there was no copy of the receipt.

That had sent him after a calendar of who'd handled deposits out of the Midwest in that period, which had led him back to a now-departed campaign volunteer named Aaron Nacostic ... of whom he could find no other record. The address they'd been given more than a year earlier when he'd signed up proved to be a dead end, as did his number.

It was all too convenient, Enright thought. He'd been trying to tell the candidate that something was wrong for several days, but had had trouble getting hold of him. Addison March's "March to Washington" was busy at a pitstop in South Dakota; then Wisconsin; then south to Kansas and New Mexico. It had been a full day since he'd left his messages.

He stood in the hotel lobby and tried the senator's personal line again. Maybe it was too late, Enright thought; maybe March had fallen so far behind – eighteen points in the latest poll – that he should just pull the plug.

The politician answered. "Christopher. I thought we were routing all calls through the communications folks..."

"Yes, sir, my apologies; it's just that we might have a situation developing with respect to the Gayda Goodwill story."

March sighed audibly. "You can stop trying to make me feel better, Christopher; I'm quite aware that that particular millstone is responsible for our existing predicament."

"But I think perhaps there's more to it," Enright said. "The paperwork doesn't lineup properly for one. Then there's..."

"Christopher..." March sounded tired. "You're a good man; but I've got investigators working on this. You don't need to get involved."

"Senator, I'm certain that if I just had a few days..."

"No can do, son; we need you working on the undecideds, shoring up the delegates..."

"Sir, the party is still completely behind you; the delegate count..."

2.   392

"…Is an important historical marker, Christopher. Posterity must be considered. Besides, these are well-trained men. If there's any discrepancy, I'm sure they'll catch it in time for us to use it in the campaign."

"Senator, I can't stress enough how I feel…"

"Enough," March said. "Now I know how you feel, my boy, and I will give it some thought. But leave this with me. You have more important work ahead."

He hung up, and Enright stood for a moment in the mid-level din of the lobby, staring at his phone. Was March really that naïve? Did he really believe it was beyond his opponent to try and set them up in some manner, to engineer an embarrassment? Enright felt disappointed with his mentor, even a little hurt that his concern was being downplayed.

He checked his watch then called for a cab. He had work to do at the Memphis office; maybe, he thought, it would help take his mind off the matter.

NEW YORK, NEW YORK

It was early evening by the time they got there. The gym in question didn't look like the kind of place that would be popular with wealthy Russian gun runners; in fact, the prevailing script on the front of the small pink stucco boxing club in Queens was graffiti, and a hole in one of the front windows had been patched over with tape and old fight flyers. The neighborhood was solid middle-class, rough but not tough; Brennan and Malone stood in front of the gym, each looking as puzzled as the other.

"You figure Konyshenko for a fight fan?" Malone asked.

"Not the fair type. Plus, this isn't exactly the big time. Place looks like it used to be a bodega or something."

Malone gestured towards the twin glass doors, also covered in old flyers. "Well?"

"After you, madam."

The inside was slightly more impressive, Malone thought, thanks to the old black and white photos that lined the walls, memories of better years.

But only very slightly. A bored-looking middle aged guy in grey sweats and a Radar O'Reilly-style jeep hat was behind the front counter, reading a copy of Ring magazine. He raised an eyebrow when he saw Malone. "How you doin'?" he asked with a greasy wink.

Then he saw Brennan. "Oh. Hey. What can I do you two for?"

Alex held up the key. "Friend of ours asked us to get something from his locker."

3.

He looked disappointed by the mundane request. "Round the corner at the end of the room. Gents only in the guys' locker room."

The corridor in question led to the main sparring area, where two rings were set up along with a series of heavy bags hanging from the rafters, and speed bags screwed to the wall. The place was fairly busy, a young guy skipping rope in one corner, sparring in both rings. Malone nodded toward the bench seating by the wall. "I'll wait here."

Ten yards away, a boxer who was stretching saw her watching and smiled at her.

"Enjoy the view," Brennan said.

"I've seen worse," she said, smiling back at the younger man, all the while being careful that she didn't miss the bench and fall on her backside.

Brennan found the locker quickly. Inside was a large manila envelope. He retrieved it, ignored by the three men changing and drying off from showering.

In the main room, Malone was watching the sparring. She rose as Brennan approached, spotting the envelope immediately. "Curiouser and Curiouser," she said.

"Alex in Wonderland?" he said.

"Something like that. Come on, let's hit the coffee shop down the street and open this puppy."

MEMPHIS, TENNESSEE

Enright's day had gone from bad to worse. His Chicago source was now hesitant about repeating her story, and word had already filtered down from the road crew that the senator was unhappy with him, which made the local staff just as hesitant to do their jobs with him in the room.

After five hours of phone calls, haltering performances from the local yokels and a lot of half-glances tossed his way, he'd called it quits for the day and gone back to the hotel. Not a heavy drinker, it had nonetheless occurred to Enright that the bar in the lobby held a particular appeal after such a rotten turn of events.

So he sat at the faux-marble bar and drank a couple of scotches, downing the first quickly and taking his time with the second. The place was a prototypical fern bar, with the plants in question filling two corners – or silken replicas, anyway. The rest of the place was filled with square bar tables made to accommodate travelling groups that usually didn't exceed four – or two and two dates. The bar itself fronted a dozen stools and ran perhaps twenty-five feet in length, backed by an obligatory Jack Daniels mirror and an always-lit faux neon sign advertising Cerveza Corona.

2.

He sipped the scotch. What was March thinking? In his few brief years with the senator, Enright had come to respect his boss's coldly efficient mindset, his ability to push aside the distractions. But this wasn't a distraction; this was something much more. He wondered if someone had gotten to the lady in Chicago, scared her out of talking. Her hesitancy also seemed like something more; a day earlier, she'd been practically bubbling at the prospect of helping her political hero. Now she was hanging up the phone and saying 'please don't call here'.

Enright considered his options; the associations with Khalidi and now Islamic militants would sink the candidate in November. It wasn't that he doubted March's ability to mount a comeback, as he'd seen the senator do it in other races. But the presidency would be won on the fine margins that lie between the ranks of the politically committed, a few states swinging one way or the other. Maybe it was time to cut his losses, Enright thought, and to step away before his name became associated with March's inevitable defeat. It seemed impossible that March could still have an ace up his sleeve big enough to turn things around.

Or...

There was another option. The election commission was making a major show these days of cracking down on fraud; a case involving the presidential race would make its day. At the very least, it would probably call in the cops. They might even dig around John Younger's campaign looking for a motive, if they thought the Chicago volunteer was credible and could get her to talk.

His eyes narrowed as he finished the rest of the scotch. It was time to act, and to take the candidate's faltering presence out of the equation.

Enright looked around the bar; it was nearly midnight. The place was almost empty, just a handful of dubiously aged young ladies in one corner, giggling and drinking colorful martinis. At the far end of the bar was another woman; he hadn't noticed her come in. She was lean, curvy, and her black cocktail dress hugged her figure as she leaned forward on the bar. She smiled at him before looking down at her drink, her eyes flitting demurely back in his direction.

Enright got up and walked over, drink in hand. "Hi, I'm Chris," he said, flashing his pearly whites. "Do you mind if I join you?"

She smiled back. She was beautiful, he thought, way out of his usual league. "I'm Annie." She extended a hand and they shook gently, and she held his hand for just a split second longer than he expected.

Wow, she's really into me, Enright thought. He smiled again, some of the pressure of the day lifting away. He'd never dated an Asian woman before. He wondered what her background was; Chinese, he thought... or maybe Korean.

3.

45

NEW YORK, NEW YORK

They sat in quiet reflection, the coffee shop empty besides the two of them and the thin, pasty white waiter/cook, on the late shift, looking about as disinterested as could be. Outside, the restaurant's neon orange-and-blue 'open' sign reflected off the large window pane next to their booth. It was raining lightly.

Malone wanted a cigarette. She hadn't smoked in eleven years, since a year after getting out of college. But she could practically smell it now, and that nicotine yearning was there, as if it had only been a day since she quit. She pushed it away.

Brennan sipped his coffee. They'd both read the file; it was brief, after all, just a few pages of notes and a handful of memory sticks. But it was shocking, outlining Borz Abubakar's deception, the destruction of the bus in Peru; from there, it took a turn, outlining how evidence of Konyshenko's past arms deals had been used by representatives of a shadowy European cabal to blackmail him into shipping weapons' grade Uranium and bomb parts into the United States. Though he admitted to great profit from the shipments, he also stated his guilt in the letter, an admission that he knew he what could happen as a result, along with a request that whomever found the letter might pray for his soul.

"Nearly thirty people dead, millions of others threatened," Alex said with an edge of despair. "And for what? An arms deal gone wrong?"

His only identifiable contact with the cabal had been Terence Corcoran, though Corcoran had mentioned a 'Faisal' as being in charge.

It contained nothing else.

"No location. No indication of a motive. No clue who hired Corcoran to blackmail him. And it had to be him? Someone from my past?"

"Khalidi." she suggested. "His fingerprints have been all over this from the start."

"I don't know… someone has been pushing us towards him. He's just too easy, too convenient a boogieman. And if he were planning something like this, why get us onto him in the first place by assassinating his fellow ACF board members?"

She shrugged. "Maybe they knew too much about his funding of the nuke purchase in the first place; maybe he'd tired of them or no longer needed them and was simply cleaning up."

"No, that's not it," Brennan said. "Those assassinations were the loudest possible show of force. He could have had been much more subtle. Those shootings were about making a statement. This whole thing couldn't have been more designed to guarantee outside interest in Khalidi's activities. In fact, once the second shooting happened, it was almost guaranteed his African activities would come up at some point. Any man as powerful and ruthless as him has enemies."

They were silent again. If Khalidi wasn't responsible, then who? It made so little sense; a conspiracy to bring a nuclear bomb into the U.S., but one in which intelligence agencies were being strung along for a ride. *Why give them a chance to prevent it?* Brennan wondered. What did someone have to gain from concocting a terrifying conspiracy but then helping them to stop it?

"I feel like we're being played, still," he said. "But even that we can't be sure of. We still have no idea where the device is."

"There must be something we've missed," Malone said. "Some piece of evidence that points us in the right direction."

They went over everything, going all the way back to the shooting in Montpellier, followed by the assassination of Lord Cumberland. They covered everything Brennan learned from Bustamante and in Cabinda, the information Malone gleaned from her federal source and the African file.

But there was nothing.

"Maybe your magazine will get another tip…" Brennan began to say, before Malone raised a hand and cut him off.

"Just a second… let me think for a second. You said the guy you knew from years back… what's his name?"

"Terrence Corcoran."

"Terrence Corcoran. You said he had a meet set up in Yonkers. So they were heading north."

"Sure, but like I said, I spent hours touring the area looking for any sign or any potential target. And it doesn't matter anyway."

"Why?"

"Well, because every simulation or projection ever run on this sort of scenario says the bad guys go for the maximum population hit; in this case, that's downtown."

"But he said they had a contingency, right?"

"Sure."

Malone thought about it some more. Then she said, "Give me your phone."

"This is a preloaded, picked up by Eddie."

"Doesn't matter. I just need maps."

She brought up an image of the state. "Let's go against the prevailing theory. It hadn't helped us so far, right? So let's look north."

Brennan chafed internally at the idea. It wasn't his style to ignore sensible intel. "You know, they don't just make those projections up. They're based on…"

"I know, I know," she said. "I'm not criticizing the military. Jeez, Brennan…"

"Okay, okay: explain."

"So maybe they're going against the grain on this. Whoever set this up has managed to implicate Khalidi, bring down Fenton-Wright, and destroy the ACF. That kind of thinking just seems a little more devious and a little less obvious than your typical meat-headed fanatic."

"Absolutely."

"Let's assume they had New York as a potential target, but Corcoran's shipment was needed for that, and you brought the cops in."

"Okay."

"Plus, the city's covered in agents looking for them. So they go to 'Option B', by landing something out of town, up river at a secondary target."

He peered at her critically. "Alex… you're stretching."

"Humor me."

They both examined the small screen as she scrolled to Yonkers then kept going north from the city, away from the densest populations. A series of suburbs scrolled by, including New City, West Haverstraw, Croton-on-Hudson.

"Nothing," Brennan said. "Unless you want to kill a whole lot of upper-middle-class boomers."

"Be patient," she said. She scrolled further, the map following the contours of the Hudson River.

She stopped scrolling. "Bingo," Alex said. "I think you owe me a beer for that."

"I'll pay you later," Brennan said. He put his jacket on as he climbed out of the booth, taking a twenty from his wallet to leave with the bill. "We better get going."

JULY 2, 2016, AMMAN, JORDAN

Ahmed Khalidi paced the white-and-grey marble floor of his palace's sitting room, hands behind his back, his body language tense and troubled.

Increasingly, he awoke each morning feeling more insecure than the last, and there seemed to be little possibility of the situation improving in the immediate future. He had come to rely on Faisal for all of his information, but his assistant had less and less to tell him as the days went by. The EU had moved to freeze his assets and he continued to be guarded around the clock by a corps of security personally picked by Faisal.

The situation was beneath him; it angered him that he had to rely on a servant, that his family's name and his fearsome reputation were no longer enough to guarantee his intentions were fulfilled. His colleagues had been systematically cut down like lambs to the slaughter – although in some cases he conceded it nothing short of just – and the influential contacts he had maintained within U.S. intelligence had been eliminated.

And so he paced the room, unsure of how to direct his energies, tempted to insult both the Prophet and his God by having several stiff drinks, keenly aware that he already had ample reason to pray for guidance.

There was a knock on the door.

"Come."

It opened and Faisal entered the room, typically dapper in a light grey suit. "Your highness," he said with a short bow. He made a sweeping motion with his arm, and a young soldier in tan-colored army garb followed him into the room. He was perhaps eighteen, with a narrow face and a wispy moustache. "This is Private Aboud."

"What is this, Faisal," Khalidi asked wearily. "You had best have some information…"

"Be quiet," Faisal said. "Old fool." He reached inside his suit jacket and removed a nine millimetre; he took a small suppressor out of his side pocket and screwed it onto the barrel.

Khalidi was flabbergasted. His face turned red with embarrassment. "Faisal! How dare you speak to me thusly! I shall have you flogged, you Egyptian dog…wait…what are you doing?"

"Private Aboud is a simple boy, recruited for this task specifically from an institution in Aqaba, where he was committed for being unable to care for himself," Faisal said. As if to confirm the statement, the private said nothing, staring ahead wide-eyed and glassy, oblivious to what was going on around him.

"I don't understand…" Khalidi managed to say, before Faisal held the barrel up to the boy's forehead, and pulled the trigger, killing him instantly.

3.

Faisal walked towards his shocked employer. "Initially, the news reports sent out by the state press agency will merely confirm you were killed by an assassin but that you heroically took his life in the process," he said. "It will not be until later that they find the evidence among his belongings, implicating you in the explosion that reigned Hell upon America, that they realize young Private Aboud died a hero, trying to prevent a tragedy."

The wealthy Jordanian's mouth dropped open. "My God, Faisal…" he said. "You cannot mean this. What have you done?"

"Me?" Faisal said. "Don't worry about me, sir." He raised the gun and shot Khalidi through the mouth. The chairman dropped to his knees, eyes instantly distant and confused. Faisal walked over and kicked him over. "I'm nobody."

He took his phone from his pocket and dialed a number.

"Yes?" A man's voice replied.

"It's done. The official statement will go out in two days. You have until then. The remainder will be dealt with after everything has been taken care of on your end."

"Your task is complete," the voice said. "The money will be wired by noon."

"I hope never to hear from you again," Faisal said.

"You won't."

The line went dead.

Faisal looked down at Khalidi's prone body. Ultimately, he knew, people would suspect his involvement; he had rarely left Khalidi's side in a decade. But memories are short, Faisal knew, and the money would last a very long time.

JULY 3, 2016, WASHINGTON, D.C.

The President wanted it to be over.

On one level, anyway. Really, he wanted another four years, another eight, another twelve; whatever it took to help build a stronger country. He had at least that much faith in himself.

But facing a grave national security threat, declining popularity numbers and a lame duck administration, paused in time by the inertia of career fear? He just wanted it to be over.

Four more months, he told himself as he twiddled his ballpoint pen, sitting behind the Resolute Desk while some of his top advisors sat in front of it and fidgeted, each trying to look less guilty than the next.

"Would perhaps one of you gentlemen like to explain to me how deputy director Fenton-Wright managed to so thoroughly evade our internal screening and policies? Our own security? Anyone?"

Fitzpatrick was there as a courtesy; the NSA had a direct interest, and he had a personal one, even though forensics had shown it was Jonah Tarrant's shot that had killed the rogue spy. But Wilkie, the Colonel and the Defense Secretary knew they were all seen as complicit, given that they'd all promoted and supported Fenton-Wright's role on the National Security Council. They'd treated him like the golden boy for the president's entire final term.

Eventually, though, the director knew it fell to him. Wilkie cleared his throat then said, "I will, of course, offer my resignation…"

The president rolled his eyes. "Give it a rest, Nick, okay? I've known you for twenty years. I don't want your resignation. I want a genuine answer. Do we even know who was paying him?"

"We suspect the Russians, Mr. President," the defense secretary interjected.

"We've just gotten a lead to trace on that today sir," Wilkie said. "When he died, Fenton-Wright had an unlisted cell phone on him. We've run back several of the calls made from it in the months prior, and he took part in some telebanking with an outfit in Switzerland. Now, as you know, the Swiss are much more amenable these days to working with us…"

"Bottom line it, please," the President said.

"Money was transferred into accounts held by Fenton-Wright in Zurich. Given the routing, they suspect the transaction originated in the Middle East. But by tomorrow we'll have a definitive answer."

That was one issue potentially resolved, the president thought. "What about your other rogue agent, the asset in Europe?"

"Agent Brennan is still out of touch, unfortunately sir," Wilkie said. "But we're taking steps to track him down and assure him that he is very much back in the fold. It's our understanding sir, per our briefing note to you, that he is at this present time working on a case of grave urgency involving a potential weapon of mass destruction."

"Weapons of… English, please, Nicholas."

"Mr. President, there's a stray nuclear warhead out there somewhere. But as you know, that's nothing new; in the wake of the Soviet empire crumbling, all sorts of things went unaccounted for. This one, by contrast, originated in South Africa, built before the fall of Apartheid. But the truth of the matter, sir, is that we need to know why this one is being discussed in vague intelligence whispers everywhere, why it just hit the open market and, according to our intelligence, may be in play somewhere right now."

The president got up and stood in front of the window, looking out at the drizzle that covered the Rose garden. *Four more months of this lunacy,* he told himself. *Then I can take a break, do some writing. Watch the kids grow up. Maybe do some lecturing on public policy.* He turned back to the room. "Well, gentlemen, I don't envy him. Wherever your agent is, let's all wish him luck."

46

PEEKSKILL, NEW YORK

Malone sat on the edge of the motel double bed and watched Brennan going through the small collection of weapons and useful items he'd borrowed from Ed. He had a grapple and rope, wire cutters, plastic explosive, a pistol, wrist ties and more.

The television on the bureau was turned to a national newscast, Washington figures reacting to the apparent suicide in Memphis of Addison March's press agent, Christopher Enright. It was sad, Alex thought; she'd barely known him, even though she'd spent several long, heated discussions on the phone with him. The story about the donation might even have pushed him over the edge, she thought. It had definitely shaken him.

She pushed the idea away. "You look like you're loading up for trouble. I have to ask you again: can't we just go in, at this point? We know what the target is…"

"We think we know," he said. "We have no evidence of anything. No bomb, no confirmation – and no guarantee after Europe that I won't be shot on sight if I let them know where I am."

"So we…"

"We do nothing. I'm going to do some recon around the facility while you lay low."

"Oh come on…"

"If you have to go out, grab us a couple of days' worth of supplies and two new prepaid phones. If -- or when -- I confirm anything is up, we call in the cavalry."

"Fair enough. If I go with you," Alex said, "chances are I'll just get shot at again."

The asset had picked up the small convoy just outside the city, trailing it in a black Range Rover he'd rented for the occasion.

It wasn't just a flight of fancy; his employer wanted him to test the situational awareness of his hired guns, see if they stopped to find out who was so interested. Sure enough, he'd been on them for maybe twenty minutes when the line of three trucks and a car pulled over and waited for him to pass. Once he'd done so, he gave them a wave to let them know he was the friendly they'd expected then dropped back in behind them, watching the scenery slip into the blackness of the night and the road pass under the car's headlights.

3.

It only took an hour to reach the small town. At night, it looked like every other small town he'd been to, a handful of houses and stores, a handful of small streets, nothing over three stories tall. And like the others, it seemed to just be a place where people could hang their hats, a town without a purpose…

And then he noticed it, a glow through the tree line as if something large were being illuminated by the moon. They passed a mesh-fenced main gate, where twin sentry boxes and razor wire kept the right people in and out. Opposite it, a cemetery on a hillside cast an appropriately grim pall over the place.

It was huge, and even hidden by the trees and a line of local homes, the glow continued for close to a mile before the road slipped back into the dimness of the hour and the occasional streetlight.

The final stage of his mission made the asset nervous, because he didn't understand it. Taking out the ACF members had been a simple act of humanity, given how much suffering they'd caused, and had fulfilled his personal objectives. But babysitting a group of engineers felt like a waste of his time.

Plus, there was the general lack of detail, aside from his final assignment. He'd been treated as a valued asset to that point, given his targets and allowed to operate with a free hand. But this was guard duty, about as thrilling as washing dishes on KP. There were some specific instructions about where to set up and who to keep his eye on, but for the most part it would be hours lying in wait, then one kill, easy as fish in a barrel.

It wasn't the asset's style.

They'd told him about Khalidi during his flight in; that he'd already been taken care of. The asset felt empty about it, as if something had been taken away from him. The chairman was the last link between the ACF and Sarah's death. Avenging her had been his real mission; working with his handlers had just been a means to an end. But his sense of duty wouldn't allow him to just walk.

In the end, he'd agreed to a few more days on the road, away from his family, away from happier times and places. The asset was tired of it all, shaken sometimes by the sense that, no matter how unfair Sarah's lot had been, he would never be able to bring her real peace.

Maybe it was because he knew she would have disapproved; but then, that was part of what made her a wonderful sister. She held fast to her principles, including her belief in the sanctity of life.

And they killed her anyway, the asset thought. He gripped the wheel more tightly, staying focused on the road. A few days in a small town wouldn't change that.

But the job wasn't done yet.

2.

The tree line ended, but the series of low-level industrial buildings behind barbed wire continued, the roadside lit bright without the trees to interfere. *A few more hours*, the asset told himself. *A few more hours, and I can go home.*

Brennan sat on the hill across the road from the Indian Point Energy Center, watching it through Ed's thermographic goggles. There were two guards at the front gate, but also what appeared to be regular patrols along the razor wire fence that ran for more than a mile in each direction. Within a few dozen yards of entering, there was a parking area and the faint outline of a pair of buildings and, even at night, the area was heavy with foot traffic.

Indian Point was euphemistically named for a three-unit nuclear power plant. It was one of the oldest still operating in the world, only surviving because of a pair of extensions to its operating license, approved until local grid contributors introduced new sources to replace its two thousand megawatts of daily electricity production

The tree line kept most motorists from seeing it unless they were on the opposite bank of the Hudson River. But they weren't missing much: a pair of long red brick buildings containing the generators, a pair of cooling towers that looked like grain silos cut down to half-size and made of concrete, a giant red-and-white banded smoke stack. Indian Point was a relic; one of its three reactors had been shut down for years but never decommissioned and the other two had long histories of safety violations. Locals supported it for its employment and reviled it for its dangers. But after a half century, it was still operating, feeding the growing need for power among the connected generation.

It had been studied as a potential terrorist attack site for years, Brennan knew. But the six-foot thick reactor containment walls and forty-foot deep spent fuel pools, it was believed, could withstand even an airliner crashing into them.

They'd been thinking too small, he knew. A nuclear blast in the plant's proximity? That would make it the ultimate secondary target, taking even the smallest dirty bomb and turn it into a contamination nightmare, spreading decades' worth of stored radioactive material through the environment. The initial heat and shockwave at ground zero might kill a few hundred thousand but the heat and force would easily breach the power plant's containment areas; the magnified contamination and proximity to the Hudson River would pollute water along the eastern seaboard for generations, and the airborne toxic ash would spread the radioactive devastation to neighboring states.

3.

He raised the goggles. Talk about overkill, Brennan thought wryly. For most in the state, it would be worse than if they'd been quickly and mercifully evaporated at ground zero. A bomb planted directly in New York might have wiped out a few million more, and much more quickly; but the half-century of stored contaminants at Indian Point could render much of the Eastern U.S. uninhabitable for decades.

There was an army base nearby, and West Point Military Academy was just up the road. Both would be next-to-useless once a device was set up somewhere within the community; the troops would be vaporized along with everyone else in the twin towns of Buchanan and Peekskill. He put the goggles back on and scanned the area, changing settings and magnification until he was familiar with the outline of the plant property.

The South African device was supposed to be small, less than five kilotons. To ensure its blast radius destroyed the storage pools and vaporized the reinforced brick structures, it would have to be set off less than a mile from the plant.

That limited their options. Brennan took out his phone and looked at the area on the map again. There was a public park adjacent to the property, just up the road. But it would have eyes all over it, he thought. There was a dead-end road just south of there, off of Bleakley Avenue. He pulled up an overhead photo on the satellite app. What was that, a school? No, a warehouse of some kind.

He turned his head and magnified the goggles, scanning the horizon, slowly panning back towards the property. The distances looked right.

Brennan took the goggles off and stored them in their case, which he then slung over his shoulder using a thin leather strap, before setting off on foot. His car was already parked past the potential target site, at a fast-food restaurant parking lot in the adjacent neighborhood. No sense ignoring the opportunity to take a look, he thought.

WASHINGTON, D.C.

Carolyn was so nervous her knees felt weak. She'd worn a dark blue power suit for the day and was trying to muster up as much courage as possible; but she hadn't heard from Joe in so long, and every time the phone rang she thought it might be terrible news.

When the director called her in for the second time in a week, her stomach did a back flip. She sat in the waiting room for what seemed like ages but amounted to ten minutes, before Jonah left his office and joined her, sitting quietly across from her, fingers pursed together, leaning forward. Another couple of minutes went by with the secretary's tapping at her keyboard the only background noise.

What would she tell the kids? They'd discussed it, briefly, when they were a young couple and felt so impervious to the whims of the future. If he went missing, they'd joked, they could tell the kids he'd taken on the challenge of being the next great astronaut, and was somewhere up in space, getting the lay of the universe. They'd wait until the kids were old enough to tell them the truth: that they'd lost their father in the line of duty.

The secretary picked up her phone. "Yes sir," she said. She hung up. "You can both go in now."

The director sat rigidly behind his desk and waited until they'd taken the seats across from him. "Thank you, both, for coming in. I wanted to update you both on the situation with respect to Deputy Director Fenton-Wright and Agent Brennan. Carolyn, we need to track Joe down; he's been completely exonerated by the evidence found in David's apartment, and we need to know the status of his current mission. Can you find him?"

Carolyn was relieved it wasn't bad news. "Sir, I'm not sure how you want me to help. I imagine Joe's changed phones and identities a half-dozen times by now. The one thing I could suggest..."

"Yes?"

"Well, before he was... before the incident, David mentioned that he'd been working with Alex Malone, the *News Now* reporter who broke the Khalidi arms scandal story. I'm sure she has people she contacts; an editor, perhaps?"

"Go on."

"We appeal to the magazine's greater sense of national security. If the briefing notes are correct and he's pursuing a weapon of mass destruction, they'll get a message through to her, and consequently to him."

Wilkie smiled. "It's hardly ideal, but it's a start. Jonah... I wanted to talk to you about the shooting. I know you're taking the mandatory assessments and counselling, of course, but I wanted you to know, in the meantime, that the agency appreciates your bravery in the face of such a difficult situation."

Jonah hadn't looked well since the day Fenton-Wright had died, Carolyn thought. He looked like he wasn't sleeping. He smiled thinly at the comment for a brief moment, then returned to his stoic gaze.

3.

"When you get back from your leave, I'd like to talk to you about taking on David's role, at least until a full-time appointment is made," Wilkie said. "You've done stellar work over the last few years."

Jonah frowned. "Thank you, sir," he said, his face a mask of self-doubt. "I'll work hard to keep your trust."

"Well, we have one other positive to report out of all of this, which is that an anonymous tip in New York led us to a shipment of parts that may have been required for the weapon in question to function, and a handful of arrests," the director said. "Here's hoping we've already locked this one down tight."

"Yes sir," Jonah said.

"And Carolyn..."

"Yes sir?"

"If Joe does contact you, convey my sincere apologies for his treatment to this point. We will make things right."

She smiled and nodded as she rose. But Carolyn's faith in her employer wasn't what it had once been.

PEEKSKILL, NEW YORK

Malone stared at the three new phones that lay on the motel bed and debated whether or not to call her editor.

It wasn't that she was confused about her role, she kept telling herself; she was a human being first, a journalist second; and she'd promised Joe that she wouldn't write anything else about the case until they could be sure the bomb was under wraps.

But it was a great story, if he was right. The phones weren't traceable to them; what would it hurt if she called in quickly just to fill Ken in on the story? They could get a team ready to join her, including the best photographer on staff.

And it was just in her nature, she had to admit. She loved breaking news.

She picked one of the phones up and turned it on. She tapped the phone app button and a keypad came up. Malone took a deep breath. It was such a good story. But she'd promised him...

She was torn.

The motel room door handle began to turn and she reacted with a start, tossing the phone down. Brennan entered carrying a brown paper bag, which he tossed onto the end of a twin bed. "Sandwiches," he said. "There's not much available after six in this town that isn't fried."

Malone hoped he hadn't seen her with the phone. "Thanks," she said. "How did your recon go?"

"There are a few possible scenarios, but they all would involve a detonation close to the facility, within about a mile. I took a drive by a warehouse within that area; it's on a dead-end road, with neighbors that use trucking."

"So lots of vehicles in and out."

"Uh huh; along with the waste trucks going to a nearby business, I counted eight in less than ninety minutes. And nobody's going to suspect it as ground zero for a bomb; not with the city only an hour or so away. The troops on site won't be able to help; the ones barracked nearby won't be of any use."

"Any signs of use?"

"Yeah, couple of heavies with walkie talkies. No visible sidearms but you can bet they're there."

"Sounds like the kind of place where an extra set of hands could come in…"

"No. Absolutely not. I need you here to call in the cavalry. If the device is there, we're going to need help dealing with it."

Malone looked incredulous. "You don't really think I'm staying here, do you? Look, Joe, whatever else you think of me, I do my job well. This is the story of the year, maybe the decade, and I'm not sitting in a motel room while it goes down."

"I said no, and I meant it. Alex, these people …"

"Alex, these people are dangerous. Yeah… getting a little tired of that one, Joe. I knew the risks when I got involved. You know what? I don't work for you. I've helped you, you've helped me. We make a pretty good team, I think. But I'm not sitting on my butt while you go running off to catch the bad guy."

Brennan's head hurt but he had to think around her; he couldn't have Alex in the middle of a potential firefight if things went wrong. But that didn't mean she couldn't be useful. "Fine. But you stay with the vehicle and the phone. You get a signal from me to confirm the device is present then you call the numbers I've given you. That's how this goes down."

"What part of 'you're not my boss' didn't you…"

"What part of 'bound, gagged and tied to a motel chair don't you understand?" Brennan retorted. "Because so help me, Alex, I'll do it. This is bigger than a news story and …."

"And it isn't a game. I know."

He paused for a second. "I was going to say 'and I'd like to see my kids get older'."

Malone felt awkward and foolish. "Oh," she muttered, flustered. "I'm sorry. I didn't think…"

3.   409

"It's okay. Like I said, just stay in the car. I'll get a signal to you either by a call or some other obvious cue, like every light in the place coming on."

"Or someone throwing you through a window."

"Probably, yes."

She smiled. He was handsome, in a rough sort of way. But more than that, he seemed utterly committed to what he thought was right.

"When…"

"Tonight. We can't wait, for obvious reasons."

"Obvious?" She'd been travelling, off and on, for weeks; she'd been shot at, seen Myrna killed, lost Walter. Malone was as tired as she'd ever been. "Sorry, but I'm not that well attuned to the obvious right now…"

"Look at the date. Tomorrow's the Fourth of July."

47

WASHINGTON, D.C.

The New York arrests left the director with an immediate problem: he now had no doubt that Joe Brennan was right, and that someone was trying to assemble a nuclear weapon; that left the question of whether the attempt had been foiled, or whether there was a contingency. Terrence Corcoran, the ex-SEAL arrested at the scene, had openly bragged of one; and he'd been just as happy to inform their agents that he knew nothing. The computer guys were working on his mail and phone contacts going back a year, trying to run traces on payments and to lock down commonalities between meeting places.

But it wasn't amounting to much.

The National Security Council meeting had a grave feeling to it, a sense that for the first time in a long time, the discussion was about something tangible and real.

"We've locked down New York," Wilkie told the assembly. At the end of the long conference table, the president leaned on the arm of his chair, propping his chin up with the same hand, looking uncomfortable. "The agency and the NSA are working hand-in-hand to conduct a borough-by-borough search, and we have analysts working around the clock to narrow down potential targets throughout the city."

The president leaned forward on the table. He'd been listening to Wilkie explain the mission for several minutes and recognized the immediate priorities of the situation. But he was curious about the circumstances. "Nicholas, how is it that it took us so long to cotton on to this? Surely there must have been rumblings in intelligence circles…"

"No, sir, unfortunately not. Our knowledge of this ongoing attempt has come purely as a byproduct of Agent Brennan's investigation into the sniper shootings and is, in some manner, tied to the same clandestine business association we'd been working to infiltrate for several years."

The NSA's Fitzpatrick chimed in, "We know there's a definite tie between the attempt to secure the weapon and the shootings, because of the evidence uncovered by the reporter, Alex Malone, about Khalidi's involvement in Africa. But if we could figure out that tie specifically, it would go a long way to pinning down a final target."

Halfway down one side of the table, the secretary of defense had been quiet, leaning back in his chair with his hands clasped on his ample stomach. "Are we sure this is a genuine threat, Mr. President? It seems like these boys don't have a whole lot to go on, other than the word of some dead Spanish arms dealer and a whole lot of hunches."

"I'm sure," Wilkie said. "Brennan could have turned himself in any number of times and taken on Fenton-Wright's frame-up. But he chose to stay in the line of fire because his objective was too important to give up."

Jonah was sitting to Wilkie's right. "Coupled with that," he interjected, "there's the fact that the reporter, Alex Malone, has been in heavy contact with him, and we've seen some of the leaked material that she has managed to get her hands on. She might be comfortable chasing ghosts, but I doubt her magazine would be, unless they had faith she was onto something big."

"So we're taking our cues from the media now?" the defense secretary asked. "Mr. President, what the NSA and CIA are asking – what they're already doing – has potentially terrifying ramifications. If word gets out in the city that there's a nuke on the loose, the stampede out of town could hurt a lot of people. The bridges and roads will be jammed. The loss of life from car accidents alone would be high, let alone the panic that can set in during a major episode."

That prompted a silent pause around the table as people weighed his concern. Jonah couldn't believe it. He had to say something. He leaned forward on the table. "Mr. President..."

"Yes, Mr. Tarrant?"

"While I understand and commend the defense secretary for his diligence in thinking this through, I think it's important to consider the alternatives to getting involved. Let's say the secretary of defense is correct, and there is no nuke. Well, we've spent a lot of money on an operation and perhaps made some people nervous. Press might even have a field day with it, if they get it."

"Okay..."

"But let's say it's genuine and we don't do anything about it. If a weapon went off in the city, it could kill close to ten million people. How would it appear to the world if it knew we had advance knowledge of the threat, but did nothing to stop it?"

Optics aside, the president knew, it was a decision no one could live with; the memory of the twin towers was still fresh for the nation. The trauma of another attack would send a shockwave rippling across America. It would lead to a new era of fear, one that would be easily exploited by his political rivals, to the detriment of his party and the public.

2.   412

But as ever, his advisors were being more tactful than necessary. "Mark, what's your take?" he asked Fitzpatrick.

"The defense secretary is correct, sir, in that we don't have a whole lot to go on," he said. "The weapon has been missing from the South Africans' old pre-freedom stockpile for some time, and there have been any number of opportunities before now for someone to use it."

The defense secretary looked pleased. Then Fitzpatrick added, "Having said that, it's clear from Fenton-Wright's betrayal that the covert operation involving Agent Brennan was being influenced by outside players; the very intent could have been to keep us away from this much larger scenario."

It wasn't clear what he was recommending, the president thought. Typical of Fitzpatrick to hold as much middle ground as possible.

"So what then, Mark? Keep the New York operation up and running? If so, for how long?"

"I would suggest until it finds something, sir, or we get word from Agent Brennan that there's nothing to find."

"Have we had any progress in getting hold of him?" the president asked.

"No sir," Wilkie admitted. "But we do have a lead on his reporter friend; if we can get through to her, she knows how to reach him."

"Couldn't we just broadcast something, some kind of all clear…"

"No sir," Wilkie said. "Unfortunately, we don't know where or what situation Brennan is in; broadcasting his picture or a contact request could blow cover, or simply alert whoever he's tracking that he's on their trail. It's a risk we can't take right now."

The president sighed. *Just a few more months*, he thought. "Then let's hope this reporter is still with him and checking in at work. Unbelievable. The most powerful nation on the planet and we have to rely on a member of the press to get anything done."

BUCHANAN, NEW YORK

The warehouse at the end of the dead end road was the size of a small aircraft hangar, a tin-siding-covered orange building with a corrugated roof and glass windows at the front that made it look like a former showroom, maybe for off-road vehicles and other big toys.

3. 413

Brennan sat across the large parking lot from it, a hundred yards away. He huddled in the tree line and surveyed the area through Ed's night vision goggles. There were a half-dozen cars parked outside and two large trucks, similar to those he'd seen at the customs yard.

They'd parked by an adjacent business on the other side of the lot, in a spot away from the handful of streetlights, where Malone could clearly see the front and left-side doors of the building. She'd been nervous about his intentions, wanting something more specific than just "I'll give you a signal". But Brennan had insisted they needed to play it by ear, improvise a warning. "If worst comes to worst, I'll let you know somehow," he'd said.

He refocused the goggles. There were two guards outside, one by the front door, another to the side. He swept the edge of the property but saw no one. Something seemed off; if this was a military-grade op, they would have had guards walking the perimeter, probably with sentry dogs. But there were just the two, both smoking cigarettes, guns slung over their shoulders and not even looking remotely prepared for trouble.

It reminded him of the customs yard and the ship in Seattle; both had seemed like large-scale smuggling operations; neither had been well-protected. Was it just arrogance, a resolute certainty on the part of whoever had planned this? He wasn't sure, but Brennan was never much of a believer in good fortune. If they were this sloppy, he reasoned, they were foolish enough to actually set the device off. Maybe they weren't so much sloppy as fanatical and overconfident.

He followed the edge of the lot until he was at the right front corner of the building. There were no signs of alarms, either, which was doubly foolish. A military op would have booby-trapped the perimeter, setting off alarms as soon as someone tripped them. He pressed himself flat to the right-side wall of the building and followed it until he found a window and peeked through.

The place was bigger than a football field, and there were several vehicles parked inside near the front, followed by a series of shipping containers and crates that effectively split up the room. Behind them, towards the back, white tables had been set up so that technicians could work on assembling various components. Just beyond them, another wall of crates cut off Brennan's view to the back of the room.

He needed a way in. He ducked under the window sill and followed the wall to the rear of the building. There were voices coming from behind, where a loading dock or back door would be, Brennan thought. He listened for a minute as the men talked, trying to get a sense of how many were there.

"What time we supposed to be gone?" one said. His accent was American.

"Figure by noon tomorrow."

2.

"Noon? We're gonna get stuck in holiday traffic, just watch."

"Quit your bitching. Jesus, you complain a lot."

"You worried about what all of these Chinks are doing with this shit?'

"Hell no. I don't get paid to worry about that."

"No?"

"Hell no. I just get paid to shoot any asshole that tries to bother them."

"Hey Donny! Donny, you got another cigarette I can borrow off you?"

A new voice said, "Borrow? Like you're going to fucking return it?"

"Then give me one, if it makes you feel any better."

"Fuck you; support your own habit, motherfucker."

Ex-army guys probably, Brennan figured, same as at the customs yard. Better to avoid them for now. No percentage in starting a fight with who-knew-how-many others nearby.

He crept back around the building and found a gap in the adjacent tree line, to his right. His shoes had soft soles but even so, he trod carefully, wary of attracting the guards' attention. It took a good five minutes to silently make his way behind the trees to the opposite side of the building, where another guard stood alone on sentry duty outside the side door. It would have been easy to take him out with a quick choke hold, Brennan figured; the man wasn't paying attention to his surroundings, instead wandering around in circles aimlessly, bored out of his mind after a few hours of duty.

But they were doubtless checking in on radio every so often. If he was going to use one of the existing entries, he was going to have to wait until right after a radio check before taking them down.

Then there was the window, where he'd started. He quietly made his way back; the view through to the room inside was cut off by the crates, but if he could find cover quickly, Brennan thought, he could worry about moving around inside after. He checked the window lightly to see if it was locked, pushing up against the top outside frame. It slid up six inches, but then locked into place.

Have to find the latch, he thought, reaching around the corner of the window with his right arm.

He heard voices. Brennan snatched his arm back. A few more seconds passed and they got closer. They passed by, and Brennan heard a snippet of another language. Korean? He wasn't sure. He moved to the corner of the window and slowly peeked over. One of the two men had continued on and was just rounding the corner, where the crates separated the front and back of the warehouse. The other had stationed himself directly in front of the window.

3.

So much for the easy route.

Need a diversion, Brennan thought, *something conclusive enough to ensure they'll move away from my entry points.*

He used the cover of the trees to move south, until he was adjacent to the edge of the lot and the handful of parked vehicles. Lighting one on fire wouldn't do it; unlike the movies, cars don't blow up when lit, Brennan knew. The tires might pop, but mostly it would just be a bonfire as the gas evaporated. If there was anyone intelligent inside the warehouse, they'd send a couple of guys to deal with it before anyone local was alerted.

No, he needed something more significant.

One of the cars was a late nineties model, and Brennan used the shadows to make his way over to the older green sedan. Its parking stall was pointed directly at the building. The timing would have to be perfect, he knew. There was a good chance the one guard in front of the building would scurry out of the way, which would give Brennan time to get back into cover.

He searched the tree line until he found the object he needed, a heavy rock with one flat side. He crept around the car until he reached the drivers' side and tried the handle. It was unlocked, which saved a few seconds. Once in the driver's seat, he took the sling bag from over his shoulder and opened it, taking out his multi-tool to crack the plastic open on the bottom of the steering column and accessed the ignition. He'd needed an older car; anything newer would have engine arrest protection in case someone tried to hotwire it.

Brennan started the car, the day running lights immediately flaring, the guard in front of the building suddenly alert, gun coming off of his shoulder. He peered toward the car when it suddenly started revving its engine, like someone was flooring the pedal in neutral. Then it shot forward towards the startled man, his eyes wide as the car's headlights race towards him. He dove out of the way as the car smashed through the front windows of the building, a terrific crunch of glass and wood.

At the edge of the parking lot, Brennan was too busy moving quickly to watch the wreckage, although the car had continued on into the building for a good twenty yards before slamming into a heavy container, the rock becoming dislodged from the gas pedal. As he'd expected, the devastation had sent the rest of the dozen or so hired hands running in that direction. Brennan made it to the window; he slipped inside quickly, guessing correctly that its guard would have been one of the first to run to the front.

He dropped to the floor inside, crouched. The crates to his left were stacked twenty feet high and cut off the view of the front of the warehouse. Those to his right cut off the back; at the end of both rows was a small gap, just big enough for a forklift to turn around and to use as a corridor through the building. There was a set of stairs on the opposite wall, running above the side exit to a metal runway that circled the building, just below roof height, and allowed access to a truncated second floor, which only covered half of the building's length but doubtless contained the office area. It was a good vantage point. He crossed quickly to the other side of the warehouse and made it up the stairs before any of the guards returned; then he began to look for an overview position that might tell him what they were actually dealing with.

WASHINGTON, D.C.

Carolyn was exhausted, tempted to put her head down on her office desk and get some sleep, even though it was just barely nine o'clock at night.

Ellen was looking after the kids. Carolyn had worked for two days to find someone, anyone, who might be able to get in touch with Joe; she'd gone through every scrap he'd ever kept from his SEAL days, every memento, contact, note or commendation. She'd parsed every computer file, rung up every old friend.

She hadn't really expected to find anything, because she knew how careful he was. He kept his work and home lives separate, and it was evident. So she'd gone in to work and asked for every record involving her husband that she was allowed to access, every mission debriefing, every training notation, every folder.

Her office phone buzzed, which was odd given the hour.

"Carolyn Brennan-Boyle."

"Carolyn? Hi, it's Terry Menzies... from research?"

She hardly knew him, but Terry had a good rep. "What's up Terry?"

"Well... yeah. I have this request here that we've been working on for a while. Only thing is, it was put in by Walter Lang, and as you're no doubt aware..."

"Of course," she said.

"Anyway, Walter had us putting together a list of potential shooters, anyone with a sharpshooter rating from the Forces who might be working freelance now. I'd almost finished it when he died, so I figured I'd hang back tonight and take a crack at it."

"Okay."

"It was mighty long, we're talking more than three dozen individuals."

"Not much of a shortlist."

"Yeah, well, that's what I thought; but Walter was looking for anyone with a tie to the deadly bus blast in Peru a few years back, so I took it on as a little project and I came up with a name. You want me to email all of this over to you?"

Really, she knew, it should have gone to Jonah or the director first. "Sure," she said, for once ignoring the little voice that told her to play it safe, by the books. "Sure, I'll take a look."

"Okay, sending it over now. Give me a ring back if you don't get it; I'll be in the office for another twenty minutes, at least."

"Back tomorrow?"

"Absolutely."

He hung up and she waited a few minutes, checking the news headlines online before going into her mail and retrieving the file. It was extensive, with personality profiles and backgrounds, military psych assessments, past test scores.

None of that mattered. What mattered was the name, staring out of her screen at her like an accusation. Carolyn's mouth dropped open.

"Oh my God," she said.

48

BUCHANAN, NEW YORK

Malone had been expecting something dramatic, and the car that had just shot across the parking lot and crashed through the front of the warehouse certainly qualified; that had to be Joe's signal.

She dialed the number he'd given her.

It only rang once and was answered. "Wilkie."

She recognized the name right away. "Is this Nicholas Wilkie? Sir, this is Alex Malone, with *News Now*."

"How did you get this number?"

"That's not important sir. I'm in New York State, with Joe Brennan."

"Where are you?" his voice sounded grave.

"We're in a small town called Buchanan, about a mile from the Indian Head nuclear plant. There's a warehouse at the end of a local avenue." She began to give him directions but he cut her off.

"We'll have a team there within an hour. Don't move from where you are, Ms. Malone; I can't stress enough how dangerous this situation is, and we won't have time to look out for civilians on scene."

"Okay." That didn't sound good, Malone thought.

"If you have a safe location now, stay in it. Don't move a muscle. As I said, we'll be there within the hour."

He hung up.

Malone lowered the phone and looked at the building. Now what? Brennan had been clear that he wanted her to stay away from any action. But Malone knew she wasn't going to get the best out of the story by staying in a car a quarter-mile away.

She checked her purse and took out her digital camera and her tape recorder. At the very least, she reasoned, she was going to get as close to the action as possible without getting in the way. In her experience, that was pretty close.

Alex slipped out of her car and quietly made her way to the middle of the lot, crouching behind a car for cover. She used the camera's optical zoom to get a tightly-cropped view of the action in front of the building, where men in bulletproof vests were pushing the car back out of the building, extricating it from mangled wood framing at the same time.

Then she noticed the dim light coming from the building's west side. A doorway? If nothing else, she thought, it might be a good vantage point to scope out the interior, see what was going on inside. She started a wide half-circle of the property, looking for an approach that wouldn't be easily seen and eventually finding one in the shadows of the adjacent building. Only a short mesh fence separated the two properties and she climbed over, dropping into the long grass and brush on the other side.

The door was unguarded; he'd probably run up front with everyone else, she reasoned. It was just fifteen feet away, and despite Joe's demand for her to stay on the periphery, much too tempting. Alex took a furtive glance around, then made her way to the door and pushed her way inside.

WASHINGTON, D.C.

The jet out of Dulles was just about to take off, taxiing its way to the beginning of its runway. Jonah and the director had seats opposite each other, so that they could compare notes on route to New York State.

They were landing at Stewart International, an air strip just southeast of Peekskill that served both the military and private planes. The agreement was that nobody federal was to contact anyone local; the chance of a County Mountie tipping the target was too great.

Before they'd left, he'd met briefly with the NSA's Fitzpatrick; despite his own misgivings about whether he was ready, Jonah had found himself cast completely in David Fenton-Wright's former role as deputy director and Wilkie's right-hand man. That meant liaising frequently with other agencies, the NSA foremost among them. Fitzpatrick had agreed immediately with his assessment that both agencies were needed at ground zero, and that the risk of losing senior staff was far outweighed by the need for leadership on scene.

Where they'd disagreed was on the tangential issue of operational security; Jonah was convinced Fenton-Wright hadn't been the only leak in the agency and had suggested as much to Fitzpatrick, who'd answered defensively, arguing that the NSA was as tight as a drum.

Outside of the fact that, in reality, no agency could claim to be impervious, it was a rash statement, Jonah thought, particularly when he'd just seen Fitzpatrick, a week earlier, talking to the reporter Alex Malone.

The NSA man had justified it by pointing out that she'd tipped him to a meeting with Fenton-Wright, and without her help they wouldn't have taken the rogue deputy director down. But Jonah suspected Fitzpatrick may have been talking to her long before then; someone had been leaking Malone details of the sniper investigation for months. It could have been David, he thought; he'd utterly misjudged his former mentor's intentions, after all. But Fitzpatrick's reluctance to discuss the issue made him suspicious.

The NSA man was at the other end of the private jet's passenger cabin reading a magazine; he noticed Jonah watching him and gave him a quick smile, which Jonah returned, before casting his eyes down to the report on the table in front of him. Jonah looked up again and Fitzpatrick was watching him right back.

"How are you, my boy?" Wilkie said, breaking the silence. "A hell of a first week at the new job, I must say."

"Yes sir," Jonah said. "Just keeping a focus on what we know."

"Something's bothering you."

Understatement of the century, Jonah thought. "Several issues, sir."

"You don't believe David was the sole leak, do you?"

"No sir." Jonah was surprised by the question. "Do you mind if I ask why…"

"Because I'd reached the same conclusion," Wilkie said. "The variety of information, the impact… it's been too far-reaching for one man and one agenda."

"I was thinking…"

"You were thinking that perhaps our friend Mr. Fitzpatrick likes talking to the press."

"He's one of the few people who had access to everything Alex Malone reported," Jonah said. "They were together at the parking garage; she's been right all the way down the line, which is rare for any reporter these days."

"If you're correct," Wilkie said, "the question will be what we do with it. There is the rather important fact that everything she reported has been of vital national interest. The stories spurred action and led us to where we are now."

"We can't just let it go," Jonah warned.

"We won't. But there may be some tact required in dealing with Mr. Fitzpatrick. It could be quite valuable to leverage an NSA ally."

BUCHANAN, NEW YORK

The asset had been reading when the car crashed through the front of the warehouse. His perch in the upper rafters of the building, just above the front entrance, gave him a perfect overview not only of the warehouse, but in particular of the accident.

Or distraction. That seemed more likely, he thought as he watched the hired guns surround the car, weapons at the ready. Something weighing the gas pedal down would do the trick. He'd been expecting something, anyway; he'd been told there would be some sort of attempt to shut the operation down.

Not that any of it mattered to the asset; his orders consisted of a short instruction list, with just one task: eliminate a single final target.

He picked up his rifle and braced it on the tripod, then used the power scope to survey the enormous building. After a few seconds of seeing nothing, he clicked the small switch on the side of the scope mount and turned on thermal imaging.

There. While the men below him were conveniently occupied with the car, there was a target sneaking in from the east, through the window. He followed the body heat signature as its man-like shape moved up the staircase to the second level. Then he switched off the thermal and tried to get a closer look.

No dice. The man was sixty yards away and had his head turned, facing towards the warehouse's back end, probably trying to figure out what the crew of Koreans was up to. It was possible the intruder might be a mission impediment; but it didn't seem likely. He wondered briefly if he was the same operative he'd spotted sneaking out of Funomora's building in Montpellier.

It didn't matter. The asset had one task that night, one shot to take. And then it would all be over.

Then Sarah could finally rest.

The upper floor of the warehouse was little more than a short steel grate floor and some desks. Brennan followed the catwalk around the perimeter of the building and looked the area over before he was certain he was alone. Then he took up a vantage point where the gaps in the grate were large enough to see into the back area of the lower level.

He counted eight lab-coated technicians. There was someone in uniform barking orders at them, a woman; again, it sounded like Korean. He couldn't make her out right away, but the voice was already familiar.

Park Jae Soo, the North Korean operative.

2.

He could just barely make out what they were doing, which seemed to involve placing the device in a final casing. It looked like an oversized bullet that had been stretched on a rack, the chrome gleaming slightly under the harsh overhead lights. The men moved carefully with the internal workings, a mish-mash of wires on a circuit board, a large cylinder of material in yellow packaging – an explosive perhaps? There was a long metal tube leading from the packaging towards the front of the device, a delivery barrel or pipe of some sort. It led into a larger chamber that filled up the nosecone.

It suddenly occurred to Brennan that, for all of his work in the months prior, he hadn't taken the time to actually learn the inner workings of such a device. He'd gotten a general outline from Ballantine in Brussels; but if push came to shove, he realized, he had no idea how to defuse one safely. He'd just have to rip the wiring out, and pray like hell.

He craned his neck slightly to get a steeper viewing angle into the room, trying to figure out security. He knew the three men stationed at the rear of the warehouse would have an open entry point, which meant he'd have to deal with them, at the least. The scientists were probably specialists, and unlikely to engage. Park was a different matter; she was probably highly trained, his most obvious obstacle.

Ed had left him with a few tricks. A flashbang would take everyone in the room out for a minute or so, long enough to get in and destroy the device's wiring. But that didn't help him with the three-on-one guard situation outside the back door.

Park had stopped giving orders to the technicians and taken out her phone. She made a quick call.

"It's ready," she said simply. Then she nodded a few affirmatives. "A call from your phone will trigger it, and as you requested, we have a backup from my phone." She offered a few more affirmatives. "Yes sir, I realize that. Thank you sir; it's my honor and duty."

That didn't sound good, Brennan thought. If Park was the backup plan, that meant she was willing to die for the operation.

Malone crept furtively along the western wall of the warehouse, sticking to the shadows near the stairs. She'd seen a few guards but had managed to stay out of sight herself. She needed to find Brennan, Malone figured; wherever he went, her story tended to follow. There was an area past the last line of packing crates; judging by the space to the wall, it was at least six hundred square feet. She moved to the edge of the crates and peered around the corner.

3.

A handful of men were working at tables, while two were crouched in front of a long bomb-like cylinder, minus the tail fins. A Korean woman barked instructions at people for several minutes before taking a phone call. She nodded several times and the call took about a minute. Then she put the phone away and went back to goading her workers. She was tough, not letting up on them an inch, and even though Malone couldn't understand the words, it was obvious she was trying to keep them to some sort of timetable.

She needed to get closer; a picture of them actually working on the device could be Pulitzer material, Malone knew. She slipped the digital camera out of her coat pocket and leaned around the corner. It was a risk to move into their line of sight, she knew, but the workers had their heads down, and the woman wasn't looking her way. She lined up a picture, a close-cropped shot of a technician with a screwdriver; he was bull-necked, with a pencil-thin moustache, and he was working meticulously on a peripheral device attached to a circuit board.

She pushed the button and in the viewfinder a small warning light blinked for a moment; *what did that... Oh Hell*, she thought.

The flash.

It popped just as the thought entered her head, too late to do anything about it. Alex had never been much of a shooter, but in an age of free news and drastic cost cutting, everyone was expected to contribute. She'd always had the camera on auto, always let it make the decisions about whether she had enough light.

The flash was bright, more than enough to swivel every head in the room.

Alex turned and ran, not bothering to stay and try to talk her way out of it. She headed directly for the side entrance. She could hear the footsteps behind her, the frantic voices, the woman screaming in Korean. Her heel clacked on the polished concrete floor and her breath was short, the door just twenty yards away...

The guard stepped out of nowhere, the butt of the rifle catching her flush in the forehead. He turned into a soft blur as Alex fell hard, the world out of focus, sideways, as she plummeted into unconsciousness.

2.

49/

The asset watched it all play out with a sense of ambivalence. None of it meant anything to him anymore. He just wanted to go home, and he leaned against the rafter beam, looking down at the expanse of the warehouse, tired after so many weeks on the road.

He didn't bother to raise his rifle for a closer look. He could tell generally what was going on, even though it was nearly eighty yards away and dimly lit; it was irrelevant to his final task, which was on the clock. First, the woman had pulled out a camera with a flash on it, which would have almost been comedic if the circumstances hadn't seemed so serious. Second, the group of scientists working on the device had started running around like chickens with their heads cut off, unsure of whether they were in trouble with American authorities.

Then the guard had struck the woman, knocking her cold, which stirred his anger. He raised the rifle and sighted the guard's head through the scope, then thought better of it and lowered his weapon. A moment later, another figure stepped out of the shadows of the adjacent staircase to the offices and threw a vicious elbow that knocked the guard equally unconscious. Then the man turned, his back to the asset, and picked the woman up, tossing her over his shoulder in a fireman's lift. He began to run towards the side door.

Now that was interesting. He raised the rifle again and tracked the scope smoothly over to their position, following their movements and keeping the crosshairs on them. Before the asset could get a good look at who it was, the man turned again, his path cut off by guards with Chinese AK47 knockoffs. He had the same build as the man in Montpellier, that was for sure, and he moved with the assurance and sense of self-preservation that comes from having been under fire. Ex-Marine, maybe even a SEAL, the asset thought.

The man was laboring now under the extra weight, turning the corner between the row of containers to try for the side window. But the guard had returned to his post after the earlier distraction. The angle from the rafters down to the action was too tight for the asset to see the pair anymore; but he could still see the guard by the window, raising his rifle, screaming at them to back off. A foot flashed across the front of the man, kicking the rifle away and prompting the startled guard to back down himself. Whoever he was, the asset thought, he wasn't going down without a fight.

Or perhaps he was. The rest of the guards had caught up to them, rushing down the wide corridor between stacks of crates, surrounding the couple, guns high. A moment later they were being cuffed.

The asset had been told to expect disturbances. It was all just part of the procedure, as far as he was concerned. He reached into his upper pocket and took out the already unwrapped fruit protein bar, taking a fair-sized bite before returning it to the pocket. It was getting late, and he needed to keep his energy up for show time.

DES MOINES, IOWA

The campaign staff were staying up, enjoying the fact that they were getting a half-day off for the Fourth of July, just a few hours away.

Officially, of course, none of them were working, including the candidate. Officially, their day out in Des Moines pressing the flesh and eating barbecue would be completely unofficial.

Addison March was next door, listening to them through the thin hotel suite wall. He smiled to himself. It was going to be an important day, the Fourth. He had an appropriately weighty speech memorized, a damn impressive eight minutes of solid reflection on America and national security. He had a great place to deliver it, with families thronging to the state fairgrounds; and by memorizing it, doing it off the cuff and not at a podium, he was going to make it look like one of the most impressive conversational ad-libs in campaign history.

Everything could turn on how he handled the Fourth, he thought, as he listened to them laugh and joke, the music louder than it should have been. Most of them were young; they didn't really understand, not yet. They were overcome by their zeal for campaigning, their ideological need to proselytize. He knew the stakes were much, much higher.

March had prepared for the speech his entire life, really. He'd been using his flair for oratory and drama to advance his political perspectives since long before his days in office. As a businessman and lawyer, he'd once been a powerful fundraiser and PAC chairman for the Republicans. Before that, he'd been a Young Republican, and before, a high school student council president. It was in his nature, and he knew he would seize the moment yet again.

2.

He glanced absently at the newspaper on his nightstand. There was a campaign story on the front page, an assertion that he remained nine points behind, a woeful figure in the modern age of a split electorate. Given everything he'd been accused of in the month prior, he was wryly surprised the party hadn't asked him to step aside at the last moment; at one point, a week earlier, he'd been down eighteen, wondering if everything he'd worked towards had been torn from him.

But he'd never quit before in politics, and he'd maintained appropriate results. He'd never given up until the war was won.

NEW WINDSOR, NEW YORK

The director was down the steps from the plane to the tarmac almost as quickly as they were lowered, moving spryly for a man in his late sixties. Jonah rushed behind him to keep up. A series of cars waited nearby, a rolling operations center for the forty minutes it would take to get to the target location.

Representatives from the SEAL counter-terrorism unit DEVGRU and the Army counterpart Delta Force were waiting by the cars, a pair of sharply dressed officers; their expressions were stone slabs of serious intent.

The director shook each's hand in turn. "Colonel Ellis. Lt. Commander Hirsh. This is my assistant, Jonah Tarrant; he'll be in on all of the decisions today. Are we ready to roll?"

"Yes sir," the Navy man Hirsh said. "We've got eyes on target and are establishing recon, including locking down body numbers with thermal and establishing our best entry and exit points."

"Good. And the reporter, Alex Malone?"

"She doesn't seem to be on scene, sir. And her phone has been turned off."

That wasn't so good, Wilkie thought. "Any word from Agent Brennan yet?"

"No sir. But there are signs of a disturbance at the location. There's a guard posted in front of the target location, several more behind, and there's significant damage to the front of the building, along with a damaged vehicle in the lot that looks like it might have been the cause."

"Jonah?" the director asked.

"One of Brennan's operational MOs has been to neutralize the opposition's numerical advantage via significant distraction; he might have been improvising."

3.   427

The director turned back to the military men. "Technical support?"

"We've got two leading weapons experts on scene as well as a former member of Team Six who has since taken a degree in nuclear engineering. We're in a position to disarm as soon as we control the building. But there's an issue."

"Yes?"

Jonah interrupted. "They can't tell what the status of the device is, or whether the people who brought it here are fanatical enough to actually detonate it. They may have some sort of failsafe switch or quick trigger..."

The director understood the ramifications. "So any attempt to go in hot and they might blow the thing?"

"Yes sir," the young lieutenant commander said. "That's pretty much the sum of it."

"Then we need to know what's going on inside that warehouse, gentlemen." the director said, heading for the cars. "We need eyes on that device. Let's get going."

Brennan awoke to a sudden, sharp pain. He glanced down to his left hand, which was tied to the arm of the wooden desk chair with a plastic restraint. His right hand was similarly immobilized, but it was his left that hurt, because the Korean agent had just run the razor-sharp blade of a knife over it. A thin incision was beginning to bleed badly, droplets running down the side of his hand and wrist.

The place sounded quiet, near empty.

"Oh good, you're awake," Park said. She had a strange look on her face, he thought, like an excited child. "We haven't much time and I debated just shooting you both, but I need to know if I can expect any more company."

He blinked, his head still ringing from a rifle butt blow, and looked around the area. The technicians were all gone, save two men working on the final portion of the casing. Alex was sitting a few feet away, also tied to a chair, still unconscious. His first thought was that she might be seriously hurt; his second was that he wanted to let her know just what he thought of her decision to go walkabout.

"This is the part where I tell you it's insane to set off a nuclear weapon..."

"... And I tell you that the west is decadent, and corrupt, and needs to be purged of its arrogance once and for all."

"Yeah... that part," Brennan said. "Park, you know they'll make sure you go up with this place..."

"I'm aware of my fate," she said.

2.   428

"This place is quiet. At least you let the workers go," he said, trying to gauge their numbers.

"We only need a handful here to ensure everything goes as planned. There was no reason to keep them."

"How big of you."

"I've prepared for today for a long time, we all have. This is an opportunity to assail evil, Mr. Brennan, to leave my mark on the world as someone who was willing to die for what she believed in. How do you suppose you'll convince me otherwise?"

"Leave your mark? For every nut job who agrees with you, a thousand normal people will remember you as a homicidal maniac."

"A thousand fools, a thousand dead souls on the American treadmill of productivity over purpose, of self over community and family and tradition, of profit over honor."

"That's the narrative they've taught you, sure," he said. "Want to hear the one they've taught us about you? How North Koreans are all mindless zombies, soulless robots who do the bidding of a tyrannical, psychotic narcissist?"

She smiled smugly. "Your attempt at psychological influence is amusing, Mr. Brennan. Are you so far gone yourself, so subservient to the agency that you don't consider your own fate, or that of your colleague? I'm ready to die for what I believe in, Mr. Brennan. Are you?"

"I guess we're going to find out," he said. "Because I'm not telling you shit." If he was lucky, Brennan thought, the commotion involving the car had been enough of a surprise to prompt Alex to make the call. If he was unlucky, they were both dead anyway. Either way, he had no immediate option but to stall.

"Why here? Why not in another major center, where the death toll would be even higher? Why not L.A. or Dallas, or D.C?"

She had a look of rapturous fanaticism when she spoke. "New York is the heart of the American financial empire, the belly of the beast. Had our associates not failed in their earlier task and assembled the device yesterday, it would have been midtown Manhattan. But killing millions of your fellow vermin and making New York uninhabitable for a few decades will have to do. It will also send a message to the rest of the world that North Korea is a nuclear power, and not afraid to defend its values."

"Values?" She was completely insane, he thought. "Is that why Khalidi hired you?"

She smiled at that, not biting at the attempt to identify her employer. "You're joking, surely?"

3.

A few feet away, Alex began to stir. "Your friend is going to wake up in a few minutes. Or… is she?" Park asked. She walked over to Alex then took the pistol out of her belt holster. "Let's say you aren't afraid of death, Mr. Brennan. I'm sure you'd rather I didn't kill your lovely friend. So why don't you tell me what we can expect between now and a half-hour from now?"

She pointed the .45 at Alex's head.

Brennan said, "So? If you're really planning on setting off that thing, neither of us has much time left anyway." He was pulling his wrists away from the chair arms, trying to work the restraints loose. But they were designed to be unbreakable and he wasn't making any progress.

"No? Okay, I'll just shoot her…" She placed the barrel against Alex's temple.

"No...! Look, it's not going to make a difference what I tell you. I was listening to your conversation. There's no way they'll arrive before your handlers can make that phone call and trigger it. There's no reason to do that."

Park appeared to be weighing her options when a guard ran up to her. "Sir, you need to see this. We've got a situation outside. It looks like we might have some sort of law enforcement around the perimeter of the property."

She smiled at Brennan. "Hours, eh Mr. Brennan? Don't go anywhere until I get back," she said, before following the guard toward the front of the building.

Brennan knew he only had seconds. He couldn't break the restraints, but that didn't mean the chair was equally tough. He leaned forward and stood up, the chair suspended from his arms. Then he pushed off the ground as hard as he could, jumping up and backwards, so that his full weight came down on the chair's frame. The hard edges banged into him like a battering ram, but the chair shattered as they hit the floor, pieces flying in multiple directions. He ignored the pain in his back; it felt like he'd rebroken a rib, but Brennan didn't have time to complain. He shook off the loose wood from the chair arms then headed quickly over towards Alex.

He was about to try and untie her when he saw movement out of the corner of his eye, the flash of chrome from a muzzle being raised. Instead, he pushed Alex's chair over, banking that she'd be safer from gunfire lying on her side; then he rolled out of the way even as Park and the guard opened fire, the bullets pinging off of the walls and concrete, one even ricocheting off the bomb casing. Before they could fully round the corner he was to his feet, balanced and ready. The guard rushed into the area, rifle out in front of him. Brennan grabbed the barrel, shoving it at first down and then, once the gun butt was squarely under the man's chin, back up towards him, taking the man out with one hard thrust.

He stepped sideways quickly as Park fired two more shots, both missing, then spun into a low leg sweep, taking her feet out from under her, the pistol flying into the corner of the workspace.

Park sprung to her feet from her back almost as soon as she hit the ground, at the ready. She crouched low, feet slightly at each side, knees apart, one fist splayed across her torso, the other held high to block or offer an open palm technique.

Brennan took a deep, cleansing breath. "Chen style? I hate Chen style."

"Most people do," she said, as they circled each other. "It's hard to hit what you can't touch."

He struck quickly, lunging in with a front kick, trying to use his size and speed advantage to close the gap between them before she could react. But instead of moving, Park twisted at the waist with the speed and dexterity of a diver, making herself small, his foot brushing by her. She shifted her weight to her inside foot and kept the rotation going but pulled it in tight, so that she was spinning around his torso in the same motion, her foot pirouetting three hundred and sixty degrees, the torque at her waist snapping it around like a whip, catching Brennan flush in the right hip, striking a nerve and instantly numbing it.

He stumbled sideways as she readjusted her stance, ready for a rapid rebuttal. Brennan shook the blow off. "And that's why I hate Chen style," he muttered. "It's like getting your ass kicked by a ballerina."

She said nothing, turning her torso away from him to the left as she stepped in, then to the right, his concentration fixed on her body movements and losing track of her hands. A flurry of punches followed, part of a prescribed pattern, Brennan able to block more than a dozen blows in quick succession before, inevitably, one broke through his defense, the open palm catching him in the solar plexus. He turned slightly just at the point of contact, absorbing some of the blow's strength and avoiding having his wind knocked out, settling instead with half-losing his balance, stumbling backwards. She followed up smoothly with a solid kick to the side of his knee, which he felt give slightly, an instant sprain that send a shock of pain through the nerve.

3.

Brennan backed away, half-limping, creating as much distance as she'd immediately allow. Her technique was near-perfect, he thought. It made it difficult to go on the offensive; Chen style allowed an expert practitioner to use his or her opponent's weight against them, using locking holds to throw them off balance followed by rapid strikes derived from Chinese boxing.

So he motioned for her to advance, cupping his hand upside down, fingers beckoning her forward. "If that's the best you've got," Brennan said, "this isn't going to last long."

That annoyed Park, and she charged in again, shifting her focus at the last second to his midsection, a flurry of open palm blows designed to weaken his legs via nerve and gut strikes. On the last flurry, as he backed away blocking, Brennan turned sideways, allowing the punch to drift past him, using its momentum to take her by the wrist, turning his hips quickly to toss her half way across the room.

Park absorbed the throw expertly, landing hard but recovering quickly, rolling back to her feet. "Judo? Against a Korean? That's a little on-the-nose isn't it, Mr. Brennan?"

"I'll take whatever you give me," he said. The truth was, Brennan was an expert; but Park was a master. Her movements looked silken, they were so smooth.

Out of the corner of his eye, he could see Alex stirring, trying to fight her bonds. If he was lucky, Brennan thought, she'd manage to get free on her own then get the hell out of there.

The distraction nearly cost him, Park reaching in a smooth motion for her ankle, a throwing knife tossed backhanded as he looked away, the blade skimming by his chin before it lodged in the crate behind him. He pulled it out of the wood and tossed it aside in a show of mock contempt, making sure it landed near Alex. "Time for us to stop playing around, Park," he said. "Let's see what you're made of."

It was time to go on the offensive; counterattacking hadn't been working, Brennan reasoned.

He took a half-step forward then heard the sound just behind and to his left, ducking at the last second as the guard behind him opened fire, the bullets tearing through the nearby table tops. Brennan pushed off the floor, sliding backwards along the polished concrete so that he was beneath the man, facing up. He slammed a pair of fists into the man's groin, and the guard went down in a weeping mess, clutching his bruised privates.

The man's rifle clattered to the ground beside him, and Brennan quickly grabbed it. He turned, saying, "Got any more help around…"

It was as far as he'd get; Park pistol-whipped him from behind, sending Brennan back into dreamland.

2.   432

50

"What's the situation, colonel?"

The director was fatigued and had been working since six that morning; but he had no intention of showing it. They'd set up a command post across the parking lot in a tent. The building was surrounded and a pair of Delta Force operatives had gone in for a closer look.

The colonel pointed to the building as he talked. "A truck pulled out about an hour ago with nearly two dozen mercs inside and a bunch of eggheads, maybe Chinese. We waited until they reached the avenue before taking them in. They're being gone over now by an interrogation unit to see what we can get out of them quickly. We've got two guards remaining, at least, there and there, front and side. We've got a third in the rafters who will be tough to neutralize; the position is well guarded, above a steel eye-beam. In the back we've got four heat signatures, but three of them are on the ground and perhaps unconscious."

"Eyes on any of our people?"

"Negative, sir. The interior is arranged to make surveillance extremely difficult. With your permission, we'd like to drill a hole for a fiber optic line near the back of the warehouse, so that we can get a proper look."

"What kind of exposure would that create?"

"Some noise, but minimal. We use a special drill, extremely slow and quiet."

"How long?"

"Perhaps ten minutes."

The director checked his watch. It was ten minutes before twelve. "Jonah?" he asked.

"They could be looking at midnight as a target time," Jonah said. "Or they could wait until the Fourth is in full swing tomorrow, get the maximum psychological effect."

The director reserved his impatience. "That's two options. What do you think they're most likely…"

"I think they could do it at any moment," Jonah said. "And if they're professionals, they'll be aware by now that we're out here. So time is against us."

The colonel could tell where the conversation was headed. "I don't want to send eyes in there blind, sir," he said. "We've had too many past instances where…"

3.   433

The director held up both hands. "Peace, colonel, peace. Jonah's not trying to override your idea; we're just considering the timing. Ten minutes may be five minutes more than we've got."

"We have an alternative," the colonel said. "We can send in a robot. If we've got eyes on us already, the worst that happens is we lose the unit. Best case, it gets to the back of the building and gives us a good look."

"Do it quickly, colonel," the director said. "And have your teams ready to go in five."

Malone woke in stuttering fashion, her eyes barely able to open; her head pounded from the force of the rifle blow and her right shoulder felt numb from the weight of leaning on the nerve for too long.

She was on her side, she realized. Her hands were still bound to the chair; she pivoted her head around and could just see enough to know Joe was unconscious on the floor nearby. There was someone else there, too; a guard, maybe? She tried to shift her position slowly, pulling the chair along with her, doing it gently to avoid making noise. She managed to turn it forty-five degrees, enough to see the Korean woman working on the device.

Park took a key out of her pocket. Then she opened a small, square panel towards the tail end of the cylinder and slotted the key into a lock; a quarter turn switched on a small green light. The woman turned away from the bomb, walking towards the adjacent table. A series of candles had been set up on its surface, like a small shrine. Several photos were leaning against the candlesticks. She started to light the candles.

The scene reminded Malone of an old war movie, the part in which the Japanese kamikaze pilot prepared himself for death. She looked around, frantically, for something to pry her wrist ties loose.

The throwing knife was nearly flat and she almost didn't see it, lying in the shadows of the table to her right, just visible out of the corner of her eye. She looked back at Park for a moment, just to make sure she wasn't paying attention; then Malone began to slowly drag the chair that way, trying to make as little noise as possible.

Park took out a phone and placed it on the table beside the makeshift shrine. Then she took a small square pillow from the tabletop and placed it in front of the shrine. The pillow's position on the table had obscured a digital clock from view; it read eleven-fifty-seven. Park kneeled on the pillow then leaned forward to light incense that sat in jars next to the pictures. Park raised both hands in front of her in a sign of prayer and closed her eyes.

2.

The knife was almost within her grasp; Malone shuffled the chair a few more inches, before checking on her captor again. Park was immersed in her prayers, having a conversation in Korean with someone. Her God? Her ancestors? Malone didn't care. She had to reach that knife. It was just six inches from her right hand; her elbow was bruised and hurt like hell from the initial fall and from her attempts to cross the room; Joe was still unconscious. Malone held off a wave of anxiety and hopelessness. She wondered what time it was and how many minutes she had left; she slid the chair another six inches, the wood squeaking loudly enough on the concrete floor to make her wince, but again not drawing Park away from her ceremony. The blade was near her fingertips, as if she could almost brush the handle.

She needed to manoeuvre herself around, swivel the chair so that her immobilized hand could grasp the end of the knife between her fingers, lift it off the floor enough to turn it, slide the blade under the plastic restraint.

The digital clock read eleven-fifty-eight.

The Delta Force commander hurried back to the command post, a dark-colored eighteen-wheel truck-and-trailer that was parked on the far side of the warehouse parking lot. The door hissed open for him and he jogged up the three stairs.

Inside, the director and his aides were gathered around a makeshift tactical map of the property.

"Sir," he said.

"Colonel," said Wilkie. "What have we got?"

"The robot confirms our initial assessment. The two guards at the front are no problem."

"But?"

"But the one in the rafters is positioned over a steel girder, more than thirty feet up, and the one in the back is with the device. We have two unconscious prisoners, it appears, including one matching the description of your man Brennan and another of the reporter, Alex Malone. There's also a guard."

"Recommendation?"

"Go in hard and fast from three points," the colonel said, pointing to the map, "here, here and here."

"Time?"

"Twenty seconds from breach to control, maybe thirty. Might take longer to flush the guard out of the rafters but we'll have the device by then."

"Time to disarm?"

3.

"The expert says it can be done quickly, in a matter of a minute, maybe two."

"Then we go in one minute," Wilkie said, looking at his watch. "It's two minutes to midnight, gentlemen. We may be cutting this extremely close."

Joe was beginning to stir, his body shifting slightly on the floor.

Come on, Malone thought, *if ever I needed your help it's now, dammit.*

She pushed the chair a little further using her feet, wincing again as the wood squeaked its way across the polished concrete.

Then she felt it, the slightest of raised edges brushing the fingertips of her right hand. Something metal.

The knife. She grasped frantically for it, only able to use three fingers and a thumb, pincer like. Malone managed to raise its pommel just above the ground... then dropped it, the knife clattering loudly enough to draw Park's attention. But instead of trying to stop her, the North Korean agent ignored her, turning her head back to the shrine, tears rolling down her cheeks as she submitted to the inevitable.

The clock ticked over to eleven-fifty-nine.

Malone stretched her hand as far as she could in the same vague direction, hitting the thin edge of the knife blade again. She tried to grasp it between her thumb and forefinger. The blade rose shakily off the concrete... before the weight of it made her finger shake slightly, the blade clattering back to the concrete again.

"No goddamn it!" Malone said. "Just a little closer."

From the front of the building, she heard the sound of glass shattering, voices. Then there was a bang from the direction of the side door, commands being shouted as a tactical team breached the building. A brief burst of gun fire followed, then another.

Malone glanced back to the makeshift shrine. Park had picked up her cell phone and was dialing.

"They're too late," Park said quietly. "In thirty seconds, my employer will detonate the device. And if that is unsuccessful, I need only to hit 'send' and this forsaken nation will burn in nuclear fire."

Joe groaned a few feet away. "What...."

"Joe, wake up!" Malone said. "Dammit, please Joe!" She tried to pick the knife up again and managed to grasp it, before turning it so that the handle was in her palm, the blade under the wrist tie. She tried frantically to saw it back and forward, but the knife's edges weren't sharp enough and she wasn't getting enough leverage.

2.

The clock ticked over to midnight.

Park held her arms to either side and looked up, but with her eyes closed, a look of serenity on her face. "It's time," she said.

She stood silently. Malone was frozen, her eyes flitting between the clock and Park, expecting a momentary flash, a blinding heat, anything. From thirty yards away she could hear footsteps, boots on the ground, pounding their way towards the back of the building.

Park glanced down at the bomb, its gleaming chrome sullied only by the small square opening where she'd removed the switch panel.

Footsteps echoed along the corridor approaching them, soldiers' boots. Park looked down at the clock again, then at the device. She looked anxious, obviously worried that the bomb hadn't been triggered already.

She unlocked her phone with a finger swipe.

"No!" Malone yelled. "Please… please, I have a family, friends…"

"It's better this way," Park said. "It will all be over very, very quickly. You won't feel anything."

The tactical team reached the corner of the work space, the lead poking his head and muzzle around the corner. "This is the government of the United States. Everyone here is under arrest. Get down on the ground, with your hands on your head."

"Goodbye, Ms. Malone," Park said with a half smile, her face slightly sad.

She pushed the 'send' button.

3.

51

In Malone's mind's eye, she'd always had an idea of what it might be like to see a nuclear explosion; the mushroom cloud, the shock of heat, vision seared blood-red, the chromatic scale all out of whack as the blast vaporized her and everything else within range, the horrifying reality reduced to a split-second.

She pulled at her wrist restraints; she couldn't even cover her face in reflex when Park hit the green send button. She closed her eyes tight and prayed quietly, thinking about her parents and her little brother, and all of the people she loved but would never see again.

But nothing happened.

A second or two went by, and Malone opened one eye, then the other. A few feet away, Brennan leaned up on his elbow, shaking off the pistol-whipping. Park was looking at the phone, bewildered. The tactical team rushed into the room, weapons high.

"Down on the ground!" the commander yelled at Park. "Down on the ground, now!" They were about twenty yards from her, but Park didn't drop as requested, instead standing there confused; she craned her head around, trying to figure out what had gone wrong, vaguely aware that somewhere in the warehouse, another phone was ringing.

"Down now!" the tactical team leader screamed again.

At the other end of the warehouse, the asset's phone had begun to ring. That was his cue. He leaned back against the beam, using his knee to brace the rifle, and looked down through the scope. As soon as the crosshairs were centered, he squeezed the trigger, two decades of training and instinct taking over in a smooth motion, with no second-guessing the recoil.

The .50 caliber slug covered the sixty yards in well under a second, most of Park's skull exploding on impact, spraying the area in gore. Alex's mouth dropped open before her stomach caught up with what she was seeing. She turned to her left and vomited heavily, even as the near-headless North Korean's torso collapsed to its knees, then to the ground. "Jesus Christ!" the tactical team leader said, wincing at the sight. He turned around quickly. "Who fired that? Which sonovabitch fired that shot?"

Brennan had only just made it to his feet, and had caught the slightest muzzle flash out of the corner of his eye. He tapped the team leader on the shoulder patch with the back of his hand. "Up in the rafters."

2.

"The fourth guard?"

Brennan picked Park's pistol up off of the floor and headed for the front of the building. A pair of soldiers were standing near the west wall, guarding a rope that trailed down from the rafters high above. "There's a fourth guard in the rafters," the colonel said as they approached the pair. "We've got him pinned up there..."

"No, you don't," Brennan said pointing up and in the other direction. "There's a skylight halfway down the side beam along the other wall."

Sure enough, enough moonlight made its way through the upper opening to show that it had been left unsecured.

"Damn it!" the colonel said.

"Give me that!" Brennan said, grabbing the M16 from a confused corporal. He sprinted for the gaping hole where the front doors had once been, out into the dimly lit parking lot, his eyes scanning the area as completely and quickly as he could.

There.

In the woods, the gaps of light between the trees were being intermittently broken by the shadow of someone quickly fleeing the scene. Brennan gave chase, ignoring the broken rib and the throb in his head, willing himself on. He crashed into the tree line, pushing aside sharp branches, stumbling through roots and shrubs until he emerge on the other side.

The asset was fifty yards ahead already, going towards a Jeep parked beside the road. Brennan stopped abruptly, raised the rifle to his shoulder and sighted the fleeing shooter. Then he squeezed the trigger.

The man went down hard, face first into the grass and mud on the roadside. Brennan sprinted after him. Behind him, he could hear a police siren closing. He reached the man and rolled him over.

"Oh Jesus," he said.

"You've ... got to be kidding," the wounded man sputtered.

Brennan's mouth was wide open. He shook his head slightly in shock, eyes wide and disbelieving.

"Callum?! Christ... Callum?! You're the sniper?"

"You shot me. Goddamn, Joe, you shot me..."

"That was you in Moscow? And Montpellier?"

Blood was beginning to soak through his friend's shirt. The shot had gone through his vest somehow, or hit an open gap, Brennan thought.

"Feel faint..." Callum said. "Think this might be it, bud..."

Brennan felt panic. It was alien, unfamiliar territory for so many years. Behind him, a vehicle's tires bit into the gravel as it ground to a halt. "Callum... I don't understand..."

3.

"For Sarah, my sister," he said. He was panting, barely holding consciousness. "They killed her, Joe. Khalidi and his greed, Borz Abubakar…"

His sister; he'd said she'd died in an auto accident. Brennan never made the connection, the timing. A car door slammed. Two more police cars ground to a halt a few feet away.

"Hang on, Callum," Brennan said. "Please… Dear God, please hang on…" He cradled his dying friend in his arms. "For the love of God, someone… get a doctor. We need a doctor."

The officers converged as Brennan held his brother in arms, barely lit by the overhead street lamp in the earliest hours.

At the command post, the last of the guards was being booked and loaded into a detention van. The director and Jonah were standing by the trailer, being briefed by the colonel, as a group of local and state police cordoned off the road and kept both the public and media away.

It hadn't taken long for word to get around the small town, then out via its local newspaper reporter to the wire and the city papers, and within an hour, the place was crawling with press. Malone watched it all seated on the side steps up to the trailer, a blanket around her shoulders and a cup of hot herbal tea in hand, courtesy of a federal victims' services worker. She was told to wait until they were ready to debrief her but the truth was, she wasn't ready to go anywhere yet. She knew she had to file; she had to call Ken and tell him she had the story of the century, and art to go with it. But instead, she sat there, her face, hands and arms still featuring the odd little spatter of Park's blood that the aid worker had missed in the near-dark of the parking lot.

The woman's death had been surreal and had rocked Malone, as had the final few moments. She wondered why they'd been spared, what had happened to make the fates decree that the device wouldn't go off when Park made the call. And she felt a little empty and numb for the experience being over.

Jonah saw her from the corner of his eye and walked over. "Ms. Malone?"

"Mr. Tarrant."

"In a parking lot again, no less. We have to stop meeting like this," he said.

She gave him a thin smile. "Thanks for trying. I think I might be in shock, a little."

"That's understandable."

"Where's Joe? Have you seen him?"

"Not in the last twenty minutes, but I'm sure he's here somewhere. Look, we'd like to offer you a flight back to D.C. with us on the director's plane. We'd have a chance to debrief you at length and you could get away from…" he pointed around at the near-chaos around them, "… all of this for an hour or two."

Her first instinct, her gut feeling, had been to shrink away, to assume she couldn't trust them. People had been hunting the two of them for months; their friends were dead, and a few enemies, too. But Tarrant had a warmth about his approach, a sense for the first time in longer than she could remember that the other person didn't have the most vested of interests in helping her.

"Okay," she said. "Okay, I'd like that. Thank you."

He began to walk back to the director's side.

"Wait!" she said. "What about Joe?"

"I imagine we can make room," he said. "Assuming he takes us up on the invitation. He's turned us down before, you know." He smiled when he said it, and for a second, Alex felt like things were a little bit normal again.

52/

JULY 5, 2016, WASHINGTON, D.C.

By the time Malone got home to her townhouse it was just past dawn.

They'd been back since before three in the morning, and she'd promised Jonah to not only continue her debriefing with them on the following Monday, but to get some sleep and take some time off to recover.

So of course, she'd immediately called Kenny and gone in to work. Newsman that he was, he understood why, and they began working on the story and special edition while most of the nation slept.

The headline and second deck when she left the office had been unequivocal, a damning condemnation and, doubtless, the start of a long national headache: Nuclear Attack Foiled, with the subhead "Attack financier tied to presidential candidate". The story outlined everything: the Association Commercial Franco-Arabe's attempts to cover its tracks, to Borz Abubakar's use of Khalidi's oil insurrection money to buy the nuke in the first place, to the resulting fatal consequences to a bus-load of tourists and locals in rural Peru.

It outlined Callum's role in the sniper attacks, and his motive, along with the fact that he was being manipulated by an American paymaster, someone other than the duplicitous David Fenton-Wright. While it didn't state implicitly that Addison March was that paymaster, it did note his ties to Khalidi, and Enright's suicide two nights before the nuclear plot was exposed, along with Khalidi's assassination by a vengeful Jordanian soldier. People, she knew, would draw their own conclusions. March might never be directly tied in, she knew, but he would be investigated, scrutinized, and his chance at the White House was gone.

She opened the door to the townhouse. The telephone table answering machine was blinking furiously, but Malone ignored it. She hung her coat up, but left her overnight bag in the hallway. She kicked off her boots and headed for the bedroom to collapse for a well-earned twelve or so hours of sleep.

Malone flung herself onto the mattress. It felt good; a little soft compared to the motel, but good.

But something was wrong.

She wasn't sure what it was at first, but it was familiar; she'd run into it before as a reporter, just not on such an important story.

Doubt.

It was itching away at her, ever present.

There were too many questions unanswered, things that didn't add up. Like how two of Brennan's former colleagues wound up involved, when Addison March couldn't possibly have influenced the agent's involvement. Or why the North Korean agent had let Joe live in Angola. Or why Callum had taken Park out. Or why the device didn't go off.

And that was just scraping the surface.

She sighed a little, both tired and dismayed. Malone knew what she had to do. She got up and found her phone on the nightstand; then she dialed Kenny.

"Hey boss … yeah… yeah, I know, me too…but we have to kill it. We have to kill the story, just go with the basic wire piece for now, on the site. Something's up. Look… yeah… I know, but look, just trust me on this. We can't get this wrong. The stakes are too high. Besides, everybody else is going to draw the wrong conclusions. Think how good we'll look when we get it right."

She'd barely gotten off the line when her phone rang. "Yeah?"

"It's Brennan."

"Joe! Where the hell are you? You didn't make the flight back…"

"I had something to take care of and some things to check out. So you're in D.C.?"

"Yeah. What's going on?"

"Checking into some loose ends," he said. "You file a story yet?"

"Yeah..."

"Kill it. Like I said, loose ends."

The tone was decisive. Tired as she was, Malone's reporter instincts kicked in. "You know, don't you? You know what's actually going on."

"Yeah. And I'm so goddamned tired of running, Alex. Get your tape recorder out. There are a few things you need to know."

In the end, Malone wasn't surprised that her part in the whole thing came down to meeting with her same secret source, away from prying eyes and the Capitol Hill crowd.

Only this time, it was at a small pub about twenty blocks away, a favorite of an old friend of Joe Brennan's. Walter would have wanted to be there, Malone thought as she walked into the bar with Ken Davis at her side. Myrna, too.

The place was busy, lots of young college types hanging around drinking the cheap eight-ounce glasses of draft. Fitzpatrick was at the back of the bar, in a booth by himself. He had a glass of water in front of him but looked otherwise unfazed by the events of the days prior.

"Ms. Malone, Mr. Davis," he said, raising the glass. "To a job well done. Please, join me." He motioned to the bench seat across the table.

Alex was composed. She'd had a few hours' sleep, finally. "Well, that's a tempting offer, Mark," she said. "But I thought you'd like to see the headline we put together for a special edition of the magazine."

She tossed the mockup onto the table. Addison March's face grinned back, almost taking up the whole page. The headline indicted him thoroughly.

Fitzpatrick grinned, a rare show of emotion. "Spectacular," he said. "Absolutely perfect." He picked it up and nodded approvingly. "I especially love the picture you used. He looks like such a stereotypical evil Republican robber baron type. Just perfect."

"I guess you'll be disappointed, then, because it's never going to run," Davis said. The editor picked up the cover mockup and folded it into two, then in half again. "In fact, for posterity's sake, I'm just going to hang onto this." He put it into his coat pocket.

Malone peered at him. "You have weird priorities sometimes, boss."

"What the hell are you talking about?" Fitzpatrick asked. "Alex, what is this…?"

"You can stow the act," Malone said. "We know you hired Callum McLean and Terrence Corcoran – your old CO back in the day, right, Paddy?"

Fitzpatrick's face was cold, impenetrable. "That's pretty clever, Ms. Malone. Mr. Brennan, I presume?"

"Once I told him you were my source, he looked you up. As cover agent, he'd had virtually zero dealings with the NSA, so he didn't make the connection until he saw your photo."

Fitzpatrick leaned back against the rear corner of the booth, relaxed and confident, beer in hand. "It's a shame that connection will do you no good. Corcoran is unlikely to testify on anyone's behalf, as you're well aware, and Callum McLean was so unfortunately shot by his old Navy buddy, Joe Brennan."

She could have sworn the corners of his mouth twitched slightly, as if he was suppressing a gleeful smile. He was pure poison, Malone thought, and he had to go down. "Yeah, about that…" she said.

She looked back towards the door. Callum and Nicholas Wilkie entered together, alone with a pair of police officers. Callum walked slowly over to the table. He was still recovering from the bullet wound to his shoulder, with one arm in a sling.

"Paddy," Callum said, nodding towards him.

"Well," Fitzpatrick said. "Well, well. It seems news of your demise was greatly exaggerated."

"Oh yeah, no doubt. You underestimated Joe; not that he'd take the shot even if he knew it was me. He would have, in the circumstances. Joe's nothing if not about doing his duty, so you were right about that. I see him, I pause because of who it is, he takes me out. He closes the information loop for you. But you severely underestimated how good a shot he is from fifty yards, on the run. We didn't even get a good look at each other before he put me down."

"What have you told them, Callum? I'm sure he's come up with all sorts of stories to try and account for his complicity in this," Fitzpatrick said.

"I told them what you offered me: a chance to get revenge against the men who got away with my sister's murder."

"This is all complete nonsense, of course," Fitzpatrick said. "Some vague association we had twenty years ago, a conspiracy theory."

"I have evidence; wire transfers to my account, recordings of your voice claiming this was an off-the-books mission, making it sound official."

The NSA man had a shocked look, and it immediately struck Malone for its naïveté.

"And I have pictures of our meetings in the parking lot," Alex said. "Then there were the tips you offered, each designed to get us closer to the target, but each a little off, or coming up empty like in Seattle; everything pushing us closer to Khalidi, then the ties between Khalidi and Addison March. The donation that you check washed and redirected via a plant in the March campaign – which is what Christopher Enright figured out. There's a hotel security camera that has footage of him meeting Agent Park in the hotel bar, by the way."

"Well…" Fitzpatrick said.

"Well indeed. You led us on a chase, Mark," Alex said. "You used Callum's grief, and Corcoran's greed. But the techs have examined the weapon. It would never have gone off. That was why you had to kill Konyshenko and Park, close the information loop. This was never about an attack. It was about winning a campaign, ruining a candidate's reputation. Joe Brennan was supposed to see Callum and take him down, his sense of duty giving him the drop on Callum's remorse. You probably had Khalidi's murder arranged, as well. And the public is left believing that a man running for president almost financed a nuclear terrorist."

The NSA man had a look of futility. "I want my lawyer," Fitzpatrick said. "And then I want to cut a deal."

JULY 8, 2016

MEMPHIS, TENNESSEE, 10:26 P.M.

Four days later, the attempted terrorist attack continued to dominate the television news, and like the faithful braying sheep they were, the broadcast journalists spent hour after hour outlining the story that had been leaked on the day: that Ahmed Khalidi's money purchased a dirty bomb, that his radical associates tried to blow up New York … and that Republican presidential candidate Addison March was a supporter.

Sen. John Younger had been following the coverage religiously, watching his opponent's reputation disintegrate before his very eyes. He sat alone in his hotel room, smiling, his tie undone and a scotch and ice in one hand. He was, he had already decided, having the single finest week of his life.

March had held several press conferences to angrily deny the associations, but the paper trail made it impossible. Every day of that week there had been calls – demands, even – for his resignation not only from the presidential race, in which he was now thirty points behind and dropping quickly, but from his House seat as well.

Younger took a fat cigar from his pocket, a King Edward Invincible corona, thick and musky. He bit one end off, then spit the tobacco into his hand and put it in the ashtray on the table. Then he took out his lighter and proceeded to puff, glad that he could have a smoke away from the glare of the campaign spotlight.

The lighter flame flickered heavily, then blew out. Younger turned his head to follow the source of the gust. The tall, sealed hotel window had been forced open, and a man had just finished climbing through it, dressed all in black.

2.

He had a silenced pistol in one hand.

"Senator," Brennan said.

Younger looked at the gun. "Are you going to shoot me?"

"This is the part where I'm supposed to tell you that you won't get away with it. That we know Mark Fitzpatrick was working on your behalf when he planned and executed everything."

"And I suppose I'm supposed to cower in fear and repent my sins? Is that it, Mr....?"

"You can call me whatever you want," Brennan said. "It doesn't really matter. Fitzpatrick told us everything: how you planned the sniper shootings to draw America into this, knowing of Lord Cumberland's role as an undercover agent and Khalidi's tie to the weapon. One investigation would meld perfectly into the other. You led me on a hell of a chase."

The senator slowly swallowed the rest of the glass of scotch. "Not that anyone would believe any of this nonsense," he said. "I assume you must be here to arrest me, if Mark had some sort of evidence to support this flight of fancy."

"He doesn't," Brennan said. "He tried to cut a deal, give you up in exchange for a lighter sentence. But he had nothing really to give, except claiming a series of meetings, instructions from you."

"Ah," Younger said. Then his face soured as he realized the alternative. "That would explain the entrance through the window, then. So you're here with a silenced gun, but you're not here to arrest me."

"No senator."

"It doesn't occur to you that Fitzpatrick is trying to save his own skin? I mean, certainly, he offered guidance and advice to me when I sat on the NSC, and he was a loyal supporter..."

"He took a polygraph, senator. And he passed."

The color had begun to drain from Younger's face. "A polygraph wouldn't be admissible evidence in court," he said haltingly.

"I'm not here to arrest you, like I said," Brennan reminded him. "But sometimes we have to work around the law. We have no evidence with which to prosecute you, Senator Younger, nothing to prevent you from continuing on in your presidential campaign, which you would doubtless win. And I'm not your judge and jury."

"Then..."

"I'm just the executioner," Brennan said. He raised the pistol and fired.

EPILOGUE/

JULY 9, 2016, WASHINGTON, D.C.,

For the first time in her career, Malone put a story to bed knowing part of it was a lie.

When the public read that week's edition of *News Now*, they would learn that Mark Fitzpatrick had arranged the sniper attacks and the failed nuclear threat, all under the guidance of presidential candidate Sen. John Younger, with the fallout designed to engulf Khalidi – a known Muslim radical – and Republic candidate Addison March. Upon learning his role would come out publicly, Younger had committed suicide via a single gunshot to the head.

Of course, the last part wasn't true. She'd heard all of Fitzpatrick's interrogation statements, given access as part of her deal with the agency, a deal which would see the deceased Younger rightly take the blame in her exclusive, while Malone ignored the fact that Fitzpatrick's statements had contained not one shred of hard evidence against the late politician.

She sat at her desk reading the edition, just delivered from the printing plant. So much else had been excluded from the piece; there was no mention of Joe Brennan, or Walter Lang, or the agent known as Fawkes. But the story was solid, a labyrinthine tale of crooked companies, smuggling and spies.

"You look happy." She looked over the top of the magazine. Ken Davis had taken the seat across from her.

"Yeah. Yeah, I guess I am," she said.

"I know you don't like cutting deals…"

"But this was different, I know."

"Look…" He paused for a moment.

"Yeah?"

"I just want to apologize for making this harder on you than it had to be. I should have trusted you more."

"You were just doing your job."

He nodded. "Sure. But you were going above and beyond that, Alex. A lot of people… they probably won't remember the byline tomorrow. But they'll remember the story, even if they don't know you helped save a lot of lives."

She blushed, embarrassed. "I'm not sure what I'm supposed to say to that."

"Say you'll be back at work next week. We need you."

She smiled. "I'll be back at work next week."

"Well good," he said, rising. "But if I were you I'd cool it on hanging out with spies for a while."

She thought about Joe, about how he'd told her just a night earlier how much he wanted to get home. "I don't think that will be a problem," she said. "I think, for now, everything is good."

Carolyn sat at the kitchen island and sipped on her coffee. Ellen McLean had visited earlier in the evening, driving back home after a get-together that had been nothing short of miserable. They'd told her that her husband had been duped, tricked into serving what he thought was a government paymaster. But it didn't matter; he'd admitted he knew it was wrong anyway, technically unsanctioned, that he'd done it to avenge his sister.

And so he was still going to jail. The only question was for how long.

It was just after ten; the kids had just gone to bed, and she waited for the phone to ring. Despite everything that had gone down in the few prior days, she still hadn't heard from Joe. He had to be hurting, tired, not just from what she'd gathered from the news reports, but for what had happened to his best friend. How would he deal with it? And did it mean more time away from them, away from his family, more of his fear that he might expose them to his other life?

The front door lock turned. It opened slowly, a figure stepping into the house quietly, trying not to wake anyone.

"Joe?" she said.

He stepped out of the hallway and into the living room, a suitcase in one hand, a gym bag in the other. He looked tired, thinner. Older.

"Hi," he said.

"Hi back," she said. She went to him, put her arms around his neck and he leaned in, kissing his wife gently on the lips.

"I missed you," he said. "I missed you and the kids so much…"

"I know," she said. Before the assignment had begun, six months earlier, they'd been fighting, stressed, frustrated and tired of one another. Now, in the dark and quiet of the evening, they stared into each other's eyes and forgot all about that. They remembered that they lived for each other, for their family.

Brennan smiled and kissed her again. It made it all worth it, he knew, to be with his family; to see those he loved, safe and sound.

THE END

ABOUT THE AUTHOR

Ian Loome is a former Canadian journalist. He grew up in Africa in a communist dictatorship, where a weekend tennis match was often against a member of the KGB or East German Stasi. He has lived around the world and covered stories ranging from executions and homicides to fun features.

As an author, he wrote Shadow Agenda in 2015. The global spy thriller garnered impressive reviews and is available through Amazon Kindle Unlimited.

His second novel, the Mafia action-drama **Old Wounds**, was released in August 2018.

His third novel and second Joe Brennan story, The Ghosts of Mao, was released in November 2019. He continued Joe's story with "Master of the Reich" in 2021.

Ian can be contacted at sampowersthrillers.com or at lhtbook@gmail.com